VM FROST

Front Stack

Table of Contents

Acknowledgements

While Front Stack is a work of fiction, I would like to thank all of those real life characters that have been the unwitting inspiration for the creation of their fictional counterparts. My particular thanks must go to: Adam M, Frank H, Craig S, Victoria LB, Steve M, Mark W, Andrew H, Mark WJ, Chris D, William K, and Neil A.

My special thanks go to Bruce Fisher of *Tour Design*; who after over countless glasses of red wine and a little too much pestering designed a great book cover, and Neil Algate, who did me the honour of proof reading the manuscript.

Last and most definitely *least*, my thanks must go to the over-zealous fuckwit who led Operation Apple on my old patch. Listening in to my radio transmissions, said fuckwit, berated me for not making an arrest. My misdemeanour? Not arresting a homeless kid with special needs who had shoplifted a mini-pork pie because he was hungry. The shop manager - recognising that a prosecution wasn't in the public interest - was satisfied with my solution of banning the kid from the store. When I was called before fuckwit, and explained the expense that would have ensued had I arrested the kid - appropriate adult, solicitor, court costs etc - and all for a pie costing forty copper pennies; the detection obsessed woman literally screamed: 'And your point is?'

So, yes, thank you Ma'am. Thank you for being the prime cause of my switching to the Met, as without having done so, I would never have got to meet the characters in this book...

*Upon his beat at midnight hour, marauders armed he
found
He baulked their plans, but in the fight they felled him to
the ground
And when the clang of bells proclaimed our Saviour's
natal day
His bones lay frozen in his gore, his soul had flown away.
No soldier laid on battlefield, nor Jack-a-tar at sea,
Can gain more noble epitaph or die more brave than he.
They have their comrades' voice to cheer and succour when
they fall
But he had fought for right, alone, and died at duty's call.*

Extract from "*The Uniform*" by Police Constable William
Emsden Christmas1893

For the girls and boys in high vis - you know who you are...
Thanks for the laughs - and keep ticking the boxes.

Owing to the rigid design, speed cuffs can be applied in one of four different positions. In British police training, these positions are termed 'front stack', 'palm to palm', 'rear stack', and 'back to back'. Many forces teach two positions to their officers, but some teach all four. The 'stacked' positions are those where, once applied (assuming a standing prisoner), the handcuffs are vertical and the wrists pass through the cuffs in opposite directions, resulting in one hand on each side of the handcuffs.

Borough
noun /ˈbʌr.ə/ /ˈbɝ:.oʊ/
A town, or a division of a large town.

Task Force
noun [usually singular]
A group of people who are brought together to do a particular job, or a large military group who have a military aim to achieve.

Also by VM Frost

By Conscience Bound

The Boy In Wellington Boots

Dead Or Alive In Purgatory

The players in order of appearance:

PC Vinny "Jax" Jackson
PS Neil Pugsley
PC Bill Franklyn
PC Paul Goode
PC Chloe Kilburn
PC Simon "Lurch" Coverdale
Inspector John "The Man" Williams
PS Ian Jarvis
PC Adrian "The Cat" Black
PC Craig "Dynamo" Johnson
PC Graham "Intel" Clarke
PC Emma "Babes" Cash
Balvinder Kapoor
PC Billy "Kenyan Cowboy" Kimathi
Angie Brown
Calvin "Spoons" Anderson
"Whispering" Jill Lomax
Doctor James Pigeon
PC Tam "Porridge Face" Morris
Nadine Cousins
PC Ollie "Bullseye" Knight
Aleksis Viksna
DS Jim Dempsey

Prologue

"Why is it us? Why us?"
"Because we're here lad. Nobody else. Just us..."
(From the film Zulu)

The unmistakable sound of pounding hooves to Jax's rear, announced the welcome arrival of the Met's mounted branch. Above the tumult of the riot, he heard the PSU guvnor's hoarsely shouted command of: "Split!"

Skippers echoed the order, relaying it to the shield serials under their command. The cops repeated the command, yelling through their balaclavas to make sure everyone along the line had got it.

Hours of public order training drills kicked in. Jax heard the shout ripple along the line and although distorted and muffled from inside helmets, the word was instantly familiar. Jax yelled: 'Split!' as though his very life depended on it. His gloved hand tightened around the shield's metal handle and he prepared to move.

Along with his weary comrades; his shield held up to protect his body from a mob hell bent on ripping him apart, Jax shuffled out of the front line in the way he'd been drilled at the POTC centre at Gravesend, before wheeling left and forming up in single file on the pavement. The short shield serial to his right did the same, followed by the long shields. With the cordon now collapsed and formed up on either side of the road, the way was now clear for the mounted officers to deploy.

Seconds later, several tons of sweating horseflesh

1

thundered gloriously past and joined the fray. The sight reminded him of a troop of rescuing cavalry in the old cowboy and Indian films he'd watched in days of innocence. At the POTC, the horses had faced nothing more harmful than tennis balls thrown by cops acting as rioters; but tonight, in the fiery cauldron that was the Tottenham High Road, the mounted cops had everything but the kitchen sink hurled at them.

For Jax, the long day had been a baptism of fire, but for others - the old sweats - it was a replay of riots past. The only difference being, was that they were now equipped with proper protective kit instead of outdated tunics and improvised shields of dustbin lids, with which to ward off bricks. The appearance of the snarling mob that faced them today was unchanged: their aim to injure or kill the hated pigs still prevailed.

Replacing injured officers from the TSG, he, along with a handful of cops more used to dealing with drug dealers, teenage yobs and domestic incidents; were made to feel welcome by the TSG cops, to whom public order situations were bread and butter. All the peacetime rivalries and sense of elitism from the riot cops were set aside for the duration, and Jax and the other casualty replacements were welcomed into the anonymous fraternity of black flame retardant overalls and blue riot helmets.

The flames from the fiercely burning buildings reflected off their misted up visors while the acrid smoke billowing from smashed windows and careering wheelie bins threatened to choke them from behind their sweat-soaked balaclavas; but as there was simply no one else to stem the tide of crazed rioters, they held the line; folding back into a cordon once the horses had charged through them.

Just as they did at Gravesend, the cops felt a moment of respite as mounted branch pushed the mob back. But unlike Gravesend: where the rioters played the game and dispersed; here at Tottenham, they simply retreated a few yards and waited. Once the horses had wheeled and withdrawn back behind the dismounted serials, they charged the hurriedly reformed shield line, their hands filled with fresh missiles with which to attack the cops. Seconds after Jax had taken his place back in the cordon, a full beer bottle smashed against his shield, showering him and his comrades with broken glass and sticky alcoholic foam.

As a former soldier in riot-torn Northern Ireland, he was no stranger to the hatred shown to those who choose to wear the Queen's uniform - but at least there - he'd had the comforting weight of a rifle in his hands. Bone-weary, he reflected that this, was another ball game altogether...

Chapter One

Saturday the 6th of August 2011
'The Famous Five'

Metropolitan Police Constable Vinny "Jax" Jackson jockeyed his way impatiently through the mess that was the Kilburn High Road. Long since overwhelmed by countless buses, trucks and delivery vans, the High Road, designed for more genteel times was now all but un-navigable.

The wrong side of forty, Jax had left school at sixteen with no qualifications. He'd gone on to work as a baker; then short order cook, before enlisting in the British army, where he rose to the rank of sergeant. Leaving the army at around the time of the first Gulf War, Jax had undertaken all manner of employment - a bit of security work, assistant to a vehicle examiner and even moonlighted for a shady character in Manchester who had won a contract to paint the exteriors of a string of funeral parlours. He'd never been particularly drawn to becoming a police officer, but on whim, while working as a social worker in a residential kid's home for troubled adolescents; he'd filled out an application form for the police and after a long wait, been accepted.

Standing at five foot eight inches tall, he'd never have made the regulation height had he applied a few years earlier, but equal opportunities had prevailed, and it had been decided that in order to attract recruits from more diverse backgrounds such as those races who are naturally shorter than their European counterparts; the height limit would be abolished. In the event, this only served to attract a new wave of short British recruits - including Jax!

Athletically built, he'd never quite escaped the military fitness regime, that had been imposed upon him from an early age and if pushed he could still do an eight-minute mile. His close-cropped red hair had started to go grey at the temples and with this, the fiery nature of redheads began to abate, leaving a fairly mellow character who through life's experiences, had learnt to keep his temper and impetuosity at bay.

That said however, it was still liable to manifest itself when he was subjected to extreme provocation! Controlled aggression, he'd found, was a valuable asset when facing threats of violence out on the street. His philosophy - drawn from a life of varied employment and contact with people from all walks of life, was that he'd happily chat to anyone on the street regardless of their criminal past, so long as they showed him respect - but take the piss and young red-haired Jax would make a sudden guest appearance!

Some bright spark at the Yard - possibly in a cost cutting attempt by way of disbanding the costly and unpopular Territorial Support Group - had come up with the promotion inducing idea of creating area task forces. These newly formed units were to be drawn from boroughs Met-wide, and their members would be used in a kind of TSG role. The idea had been to encourage boroughs to bid for the task force teams to deal with whatever the pressing problem of the day was.

Since the borough commanders were, to not only release valuable resources from their area, but also donate money to the central pot to cover overtime payments, a sweetener would have to be found. The idea had been sold to reluctant senior leadership teams, that here at their beck and call, were three teams of officers who could

5

descend on their trouble spots and stop and search anything that moved.

Applications were invited from team officers but unsurprisingly, the prospect of working seven shifts in a row with one weekend a month off - and in many cases up to two hours travelling time from home bases - hadn't impressed anyone. It had been expected that there would be little, if any applicants. When the deadline for setting up the new teams came and went with no more than a handful of volunteers, the grown-ups at headquarters threw their toys out of their prams and demanded that willing or not, officers had to be found. Eventually two or three pressed officers had their fortunes told and were packed off to Kilburn. It hadn't been too long though, before it became apparent that none of these officers were carrier drivers. The grown-ups had stipulated that at least one officer had to be a carrier driver and they were, by now, jumping up and down!

Casting around for manpower, Jax's borough commander at Houndshale had decided to utilise officers from non-core duties and his beady eye had settled on Jax's unit. Grandly called the Borough Task Force, the unit was responsible for proactively patrolling the borough's burglary, robbery and drug dealing hotspots. They weren't slaves to the radio and were given free reign. The BTF had been a good number, and being made up exclusively of level two public order officers, they were generally the first to be used to quell protests in town and keep warring football yobs apart at matches.

Each team had at least one carrier driver, and when rumours began to abound, each one of these officers moved heaven and earth not to be the one sent to Kilburn: where a God-awful shift pattern awaited. Pre-emptive strikes came thick and fast with so-called welfare issues at the forefront - too far to travel, childcare issues, dog care issues - the list had been imaginative!

Eventually, all avenues of protest exhausted, Jax -

who was the longest serving member of the unit, had been summoned to the inspector's office and told the good news - he'd be going to Kilburn for six months and there was nothing more to be said! Nothing that is, apart from the words of reassurance that: "Six months would pass before he knew it!" Jax doubted this very much, but powerless to prevent this forced posting, he'd packed up his kit and transferred it to his new locker at Kilburn.

Arriving at the nick, he'd climbed the stairs to the canteen, where he'd joined the assembled "volunteers" from the rest of the northwest cluster boroughs. Sitting among the glum faces in that age-old atmosphere of the first day at school, he'd listened to the forced optimism doled out by the inspector, and prepared for six months of seven- day weeks.

Jax had been relieved to find that generally, the team to which he'd been seconded had not only been a decent enough bunch, but being forcibly bound together by the same fate; they'd shared a common bond - that of unwilling volunteer! Actually, he'd quite enjoyed the change of scenery that working pan-London was now providing. There had been exceptions however, and working on the borough of Brent, had been one of them.

Brent, along with other boroughs has gang problems. Shootings and stabbings are commonplace. Among other things, the purpose of the newly formed task force had been to relieve beleaguered team officers through the stopping and searching of gang members and known robbers. Consequently, resentment among the local "slag" was never far from the surface, and every stop was resented and resisted. Added to this was the tendency - unique in Brent as far as Jax could see - for middle aged, middle class, white people to involve themselves in the stops. Sometimes they would stand there, quietly observing and filming the stops, and other times, attempt to obstruct and frustrate the officers. It has to be said, that nine out of ten people stopped, already had convictions for robbery, drug supply etc, and it wasn't uncommon to stop and speak to a fourteen-year old kid who barely reached the officers belt buckle, only to find that he already had a string of previous convictions!

A week of patrolling the hostile streets of somewhere like Harlesden without a day off, took it's toll, and had Jax and his new team mates counting the days until they could go back to their home boroughs. Two months had passed since his forced attachment to Kilburn, and he and his team mates had settled into the routine, found common ground and begun to exchange crude banter and enjoy each other's company.

The second carrier driver on the team was Bill Franklyn. A chain-smoking, bearded hulk of a man with jet-black hair and a penchant for thrash metal, he'd been a nightclub doorman in a previous life. While possessing a heart of gold, it wasn't wise to fuck with him. Paul Goode was a wiry boxer of Anglo-Irish descent who spoke in cockney rhyming slang. His favourite word was: "Toby." In rhyming slang, "Toby," is the first part of "Toby Jug," which, rhyming with "mug," meant just that. Paul never used this as a term of endearment either!

A bundle of energy stuffed with one-line put-you-downs, his blazing blue eyes shot a blend of sarcasm and humour from beneath his unruly mop of blonde hair. Paul was a handy guy to have around when the shit hit the fan.

The only female member of the team was Chloe Kilburn. Daughter to a Falklands War submariner, she was bright as a button, attractive, and sharp as a razor. She possessed the innate ability to cause all males who met her to do her bidding with the minimum amount of coaxing. When the male banter got a bit too much and bordered on bullying, Chloe was adept at using her intelligence and education to issue withering put-downs. Despite her obvious good upbringing, should the carrier conversation get too filthy; rather than become embarrassed, she'd more than match the guy's explicit gutter language. Chloe could get down and dirty with the best of them.

The team was skippered by Neil Pugsley, an intelligent, softly spoken graduate who was a capable sergeant, calm under pressure, and had the ability to deal with the disparate and sometimes difficult bunch of officers assigned to him.

Saturday the 6th of August 2011, had felt the same as any other day - Groundhog Day. Finally reaching the nick at Kilburn, Jax climbed wearily out of his car, stretched, and made his way inside to make his ritual cup of tea, which he'd take out into the back yard and drink with a cigarette.

An informal briefing revealed that they were to spend the shift patrolling Kensington and Chelsea. The male members of the team had especially welcomed this news: Saturday in this area would be knee deep in scenery of the posh and scantily clad female variety! They'd been told that there were a couple of hours of overtime available. Not being something that was offered routinely, the fact that the extra time was to be spent among the rich and beautiful of Kensington, had met with universal approval. Of course, it wouldn't all be pleasant: there were areas of Notting Hill that were home to enough unpleasant youth to keep them all busy. Then, an hour into their period of overtime, it all kicked off...

Hearing on the grapevine that some kind of serious disorder was going down, the skipper tuned his radio to Tottenham's channel. The duty officer's voice, frantic with a mixture of fear and desperation, screamed over and over for reinforcements. He sounded like a drowning man: a man out of his depth, and knee deep in the brown and sticky stuff. Whatever his past, he'd long since been promoted away from the sharp end, moved up a floor and been consigned to community issues.

The killing of a local man by armed officers had

opened Pandora's box and the dead man's family wanted answers. Besieging the police station, they demanded an audience with someone in charge. With the borough commander away on leave, it had fallen to the hapless duty officer to try and placate them, but his efforts were in vain, and before long, the family of the shot man were joined by ever swelling numbers of angry locals - some genuinely feeling aggrieved - but many more intent on forcing there way into the building and ransacking it. Tottenham police station was starting to resemble the movie set of Fort Apache The Bronx. Officers outside the station came under attack, police patrol cars were trashed and set on fire and mob rule began to take over. Once the mob had run out of police cars to wreck, they turned their attention to buses and local businesses, and before long, Tottenham High Road was ablaze.

Out of Jax's team of seven, one was on leave, with another not being riot trained. Jax, Neil, Chloe, Bill and Paul, had been trained to deal with such situations: earning this right through voluntary attendance at the Metropolitan Police Public Order Training Centre at Gravesend in Kent. To maintain the status of a level two officer; at least one annual period of training had to be undertaken over two days. Actually, Chloe had only attended Gravesend once a few weeks before, and had yet to be deployed in the role.

The training was good and as realistic as it could be, but trained officers normally wouldn't have to deal with real life situations beyond policing football matches and the odd protest in town. Tottenham, it seemed, was shaping up to be something different entirely, and the screams of the duty officer at Tottenham that day, left the five Task Force officers with no illusions as to that fact.

Jax steered a course back to Kilburn nick; the mood became subdued and sombre. A few minutes before, the carrier had been alive with banter and posh Chelsea girl-spotting; eliciting comments like: "Look at the tits on

10

that!" and, "she can keep those boots on!" All talk of shagging posh birds evaporated as they listened in silence to the desperate pleas of the duty officer at Tottenham.

Listening in remotely to the tragedy unfolding over the radio, Jax was transported back to March 1999 and the year that he'd joined. During a classroom exercise, the instructor had adopted a bizarre method of bringing the wide-eyed and boisterous recruits down to earth. Getting them to arrange two lines of chairs one in front of the other, she'd told them to imagine that they were seated in a police carrier. Her bemused charges had obliged, while laughing and joking, and when the chairs were in place, she'd told them to find a seat and sit down. Asking for silence, she'd inserted a tape into the classroom machine and pressed play.

A crackling, noise, conveying chaos and despair filled the classroom. A plaintive plea, not unlike that of the present day duty officer filled the room before fading and being replaced with static. '*That*,' the instructor informed the group, 'is the sound of PC Keith Blakelock, just before he was hacked to death on the Broadwater Farm estate in Tottenham.'

Twenty-six years and two months later, the five level-two trained officers of the North-West Task Force, tumbled out of a real carrier in Kilburn, and wrapped in their own private thoughts, prepared themselves to relive the horror of a quarter of a century before.

Having assumed that he'd have no need of his level-two equipment, during what he'd anticipated would be an uneventful attachment; Jax had left it all at home. They'd all been told that as part of the new team, with separate financing from the rest of the Met, they were to be ring fenced, and as such, not part of the pool of level two officers. Now, in the harsh reality of the wheels well and truly coming off - money - it appeared, was no object.

While the other four struggled into the ballistic plastic assortment of protective guards for shoulders, arms, lower legs, thigh and groin, he went in search of a set of un-needed kit in the locker room.

Finding the other team sergeant's kit bag, he joined the others in the yard and began to strap on the off duty sergeant's body armour. In the past, when deployed to so-called public order situations, Jax and his mates tended to skimp on the armour: wearing only the basics, such as leg and arm guards. Policing a football match, or some demonstration by the loony left, didn't normally warrant wearing the full kit. The groin guard was the main bug bear - putting it mildly - if you needed a piss, finding your cock from deep within a boiler suit-type overall and fishing it from deep inside a groin guard, was a pain in the arse. Consequently, level two officers tended to risk assess the situation and level of anticipated violence, before getting dressed in what was about as practical as a medieval knight's armour.

Not so this day though. After strapping on every inch of ballistic plastic available to him, Jax donned his stab vest, before getting a helping hand to shrug into his one-piece flame retardant overalls. He was now ready to go, but the fact that he had filched a sergeant's kit, meant that the accompanying NATO riot helmet, was adorned with the three high visibility stripes denoting the rank of a sergeant.

Along with the insignia of rank, NATOs depict the originating force and borough of the wearer in abbreviated letter form. 01FQ would denote Metropolitan Police, Houndshale. Now, Jax may have been a sergeant back in his army days, but to wear the insignia of a supervisor in a riot situation, risked attracting a whole lot more shit than a lowly constable! Not only would he be expected to lead the troops in the confusion of a riot, but he would have more than likely attracted the increased attention of the mob!

In the end, the situation was resolved when the skipper swapped his, as yet chevron-unadorned helmet

12

with Jax. This meant that Neil now wore the helmet of a sergeant from Houndshale borough and Jax wore the helmet of a constable - albeit from Kensington and Chelsea! The skipper's helmet had seen better days, and apart from the visor being scratched and difficult to see through, the mechanism that allowed it to be lifted when not in use, was broken. This meant that the visor could only be in the down position, and all attempts to raise it resulted in the visor flopping straight back down again. This would later cause Jax much frustration.

Much huffing, puffing and swearing later, the five were ready to go, and while the boys loaded their kit bags on to the carrier, Chloe walked over to Jax. Her normally mischievous eyes suddenly serious, she asked in a small voice:

'You will look after me won't you?'

He'd reminded himself that she'd only been to the public order training centre once, and hadn't ever been deployed as a level two officer - not so much as a football match. Tottenham was as in at the deep end as she could ever be! Putting an arm around her, he'd gruffly replied that of course he would, but that she'd be fine. A spark of reassurance glimmered briefly in Chloe's doe eyes and she clambered onto the carrier.

Jax double-checked they were carrying six long riot shields, eight round, short shields, fire extinguishers, and a first aid kit. Walking back around to the front of the carrier, he checked the mechanism locking the windscreen mesh shield. He'd never had to deploy the shield in anger, only ever having driven with it down during a carrier course at Gravesend.

Grabbing a quick cigarette, he sucked the life out of it before heaving himself into the driving seat like some heavily armoured knight climbing onto his steed. Firing up the powerful diesel engine, he made one final check of his kit, tucked his fire retardant balaclava under his belt, and waited for the skipper to get directions over his radio.

By now, the besieged officers on the Tottenham High Road had been bolstered by a PSU - one inspector, three sergeants and twenty-one officers - from the TSG, who now formed a very thin blue line holding back ever-increasing numbers of rioters. The immediate area surrounding Tottenham police station was filling with more and more hostile locals. In an attempt to restore some organisation, the grown-ups had worked out, and transmitted a "safe" route, along which reinforcements could travel in order to avoid roaming bands of yobs. Perhaps realising that there was no such thing as a safe route, the instruction to come directly to the police station was quickly superseded by the order that all police units were to travel to a safer rendezvous outside the immediate area of conflagration.

With the pleas for assistance from Tottenham still coming thick and fast, the skipper took the bold and correct decision to ignore the RV instructions and head straight for Tottenham. By now, the mood on the carrier was one of: "Let's get there and sort these fuckers out," and with that, they plotted a course for Fort Apache The Bronx.

Jax had a bit of local knowledge, and as such could get the carrier to Tottenham, but once they reached the outskirts of the besieged town, he would rely on Bill - sitting up front - to take over the navigation and direct them via the previously transmitted safe route. With map books a thing of the past, Bill punched the details into his iphone. Streaking along the horribly congested North Circular Road, like some giant turbo jam sandwich, the carrier with blue lights flashing and sirens wailing, bullied its way through the evening traffic. Once on the outskirts, Jax handed over to Bill, who directed him along ever narrowing streets towards the police station.

As they neared the seat of disorder, it soon became clear that the route previously declared safe was no longer so, and threading his way through streets choked with

14

parked cars and teeming with glassy-eyed people, their faces fixed in anger, Jax felt panic gnawing at his gut. He could almost taste the atmosphere. The hatred in the air was reminiscent of his time as an internal security soldier in 1980's Northern Ireland; when as a driver on mobile patrol, he'd tipped his vehicle onto its side. Within minutes, a baying mob had surrounded his stricken Land Rover and its trapped occupants. As he drove along one particular narrow street which led to the High Road, animal instinct told him to turn around and get the fuck out of there.

Reversing back down the street, he managed to manoeuvre the unwieldy carrier into an adjoining street without hitting any parked cars, and turn around before the locals realised what an easy target had fallen into their laps.

By now, scarcely a word was spoken on the carrier; the gung ho attitude of "let's get among the bastards," was evaporating with every futile turn Jax made to extricate them from the hell of the side roads. Quietly, but urgently, Jax urged Bill to plot them a route the hell out of there. Hunched over the small screen of his phone, beads of sweat gathering on his furrowed brow, the big doorman: all thoughts of thrash metal expunged from his mind, tried to get a grip on his bearings. Somehow, more by luck than judgement, the five reinforcements finally broke through the tangle of angry streets and found themselves at a junction that led directly to their beleaguered buddies at the nick. The surreal scene that confronted them resembled Dante's Inferno.

By now, the mob had moved on from the police station, which had allowed a scant sterile ring to be thrown around the nick. Failing to breach the building, the mob, by now numbering several hundred, had made their destructive way along the High Road leaving burning police cars and torched buses in their wake. The street was literally ankle-deep in bricks, masonry and assorted debris, all previously hurled at the police, and now forming a treacherous carpet beneath the feet of fire crews and newly arriving officers. The thin blue line had managed to push the yobs a couple of hundred yards back down the road, and now held them in check just short of the Aldi supermarket on the right hand side of the road.

Abandoning the carrier outside the nick, the five hurried inside where they were briefed by an inspector. Welcoming the fact that they had ignored instructions to go to the RV, he thanked them, before directing them to the front line, where they were to bolster the TSG.

Grabbing short shields, pulling on balaclavas, and drawing batons, the five ran past burning buildings and vehicles to the front of the line. There, TSG officers; under the steadfast leadership of a lone inspector, had been holding back the mob for several hours. Equipped with only four long shields and with officers going down with injuries in front of the new arrival's very eyes, they were doing their level best to hold the ragged line. Supplemented by evidence gatherering officers equipped with video cameras, the line had been ragged indeed, and scarcely spanned the width of the street. Plugging the gaps on the left flank, Jax and the new arrivals prepared to do battle.

Within seconds, Jax's NATO fogged up. This always happened at Gravesend. There, the instructors recommended wiping the inside of the visor with soap, but this did little more than delay the onset of fog for a few minutes more. Once that balaclava was on and hot breath exacerbated by exertion and the heat from petrol bombs entered the NATO, blindness would ensue. It wasn't safe to lift the visor in training situations, let alone on that night in Tottenham - but at least at Gravesend, you could get away with sneakily lifting it halfway on occasion, thus allowing it to clear.

Unable to see Jack shit, but needing to watch for

16

danger, Jax tried in vain to peek out from underneath the fucked visor. In the end, he took to holding it open with one hand, while dangling the shield from his forearm and holding onto his baton with the other. Several near misses from full beer bottles later, however, he managed to tear a strip of cardboard from a vegetable box outside a looted shop, and with a bit of glove-fumbled help from Bill, managed to wedge it into the hinge of the skipper's helmet. Unbelievably, this Heath Robinson method acted as a friction hinge and was to endure the Tottenham riots!

By the time Jax and the other four joined the fray, the front line was around fifty yards from the supermarket. Literally, as they joined the TSG officers, the supermarket began to smoulder, before it too burst into vivid orange flame and quickly began to burn. The mob was formed of around twenty hard-core yobs with a couple of hundred others to their rear. Of the twenty, there were half a dozen brazen enough to persistently probe the police lines, trying to break down the cordon. They did this by hurling bottles, full beer cans, bricks, lumps of masonry, fire extinguishers from looted shops, and lengths of scaffold pole.

Dragging industrial-sized wheelie bins, set on fire, this bolder element teamed up and pushed them towards the police line. Several yobs tried and failed to ignite petrol bombs, but threw them at the cops nonetheless, spattering them in petrol. From time to time, an officer, distracted by hours of fatigue, would drop his guard and fall victim to a direct hit from a missile, causing him to fall to one knee. This delighted the baying crowd.

Among the cacophony of chaos, word was passed along the police line that some of the yobs; having looted a butcher's shop, had now armed themselves with knives. This was confirmed when Jax saw two masked men gripping fierce-looking boning knives, and doing their best to get around the sides of the long shields to stab the officers behind. Witnessing this act of attempted murder,

17

the officers on the short shields decided there and then that all bets were off. There would be no text book strikes to legs and arms as taught at police training college - if any of these animals came close enough, their hate-filled heads were the *only* targets in play.

There had been much made by armchair critics with regard to police tactics during the riots. Why had the police stood by while buildings were set on fire, businesses looted, and all manner of criminal acts perpetrated? What these morons didn't know - or bother to enlighten themselves with - was the fact, that in order for the fire brigade to be able to battle the multiple fires - and save the lives of those trapped within - they had to do it in a safe environment. When it came to targeting the authorities, a yellow fire helmet was no different to a blue police helmet. Consequently, the tactic during those first desperate hours, had been to make ground, hold that ground, and allow the fire fighters a sterile area in which to work.

Creating this sterile environment fell to those brave officers armed only with plastic batons and short shields, and in the safe confines of the training centre at Gravesend, this is how the tactic was taught:

Six officers are equipped with long shields (only four in Tottenham.) They take the middle of the street and spread across it from kerb to kerb. Two sections of short shield officers stand behind them and are used to make frequent pushes towards the crowd. Once they have gained ground by pushing a hostile crowd back, they retreat back behind the safety of the long shields, and then move as one into the space cleared by the short shields. The officers playing rioters generally retreat obligingly, allowing the officers to move towards their objective.

Now, this works fine at Gravesend, and although it isn't made easy through the use of other officers hurling wooden bricks, milk bottles and petrol bombs, the centre

18

isn't in the business of injuring officers. In the event that this should happen - and it often does - a nice man in an orange safety bib blows a whistle and suspends the exercise while the wounded are tended to. The officers training at Gravesend also have the luxury of a sergeant to the rear who kindly uses his fire extinguisher to put out burning policemen! This isn't to say that training at Gravesend isn't realistic, but all exercises come to an end, and are repeated until the troops get it right. Following a debrief, they can then go off to get showered, and if lucky, go to the bar for a few beers before bed.

At Tottenham, there were no wooden bricks and no trainer to halt the proceedings with his whistle. More importantly, short pushes forward with the short shields carried by Jax and his fellow officers, only seemed effective for seconds, after which, the crowd would come right back and fill the space just battled for by the short shields. In fact, rather un-sportingly, the yobs at Tottenham didn't even have the courtesy to allow the retreating officers to get back behind the scant protection of the long shields before attacking them anew!

Yobs wearing jeans, tee shirts and training shoes, hadn't found it too difficult to outrun the riot officers. Weighed down by body armour, they'd done their best to not only drive them back, but also inflict some damage. Having seen the earlier attacks by knife men and endured hours of attack, Jax yearned for some pay back. His shield, when presented edge forward and thrust into flesh was capable - if aimed correctly - of inflicting the kind of injury to someone's face, known in the trade for obvious reasons, as a "wide mouthed frog."

He'd also forsaken his level two baton, favouring instead his day-to-day Asp. This expandable baton made from metal, lacked the reach of the longer plastic baton, but in Jax's opinion: what it lacked in reach, it more than made up for in striking power. He'd only used the plastic one once - against a pissed up football fan, who'd forced his way into the rival fan area of the new Wembley stadium, where he'd run amok with his thuggish mates and attacked rival supporters. Jax had swung his plastic baton against the thug's leg, but it had done little more than tickle the bastard. He'd stuck it at the bottom of his kit bag and never used it again.

The short shield pushes had presented some opportunities, in the form of those yobs foolish enough to try and hide in the alleyways along the route of the push. Separated from their cohorts, they'd suffered the wrath of the officers that had noticed them hiding there. Actually, so scarce were the opportunities to get at the yobs, that when a moronic alley-hider was found, the officers practically fell over one another to rain down as many baton strikes as they could, before the idiot was able to flee.

In the event, Jax hadn't got to create a wide-mouthed frog, but had managed to liberally deploy the hard, cold steel of his Asp. Its only disadvantage had proved to be its tendency to collapse after every second strike! It was during these forays into enemy territory, that Jax: resuming his position in the embattled line, fell victim to multiple lumps of debris, not unlike the deadly showers of concentrated arrows launched by English bowmen during battles of old.

A full beer bottle was thrown with such ferocious venom, that it shattered on impact with the armour covering his shoulders, showering him with cheap, foamy lager. Another unidentified object crashed into the radio clipped to his chest, cracking the screen. A brick caught him on the unprotected area of his foot, and he'd had to dodge a two-foot tall fire extinguisher, swung by its hose and launched at his legs.

Hour after hour of unrelenting short shield pushes began to take their toll on the men and women. Their faces covered by sweat-soaked balaclavas, they strained their eyes, in an attempt to focus through misted over, and completely opaque helmet visors. In the man-made furnace that was the burning High Road, dehydration began to set in. At some point, an unknown officer to his rear tapped Jax on the shoulder, and raising his visor, pulled away his soggy balaclava to pour delicious cold water down his parched throat.

Bill had taken it upon himself to pull some of the larger pieces of debris to the rear so as to prevent further injury. Looking to his right, Jax saw the big ex-doorman like some latter day Hercules, dragging an eight-foot section of metal *Heras* fencing thrown by the mob. To Jax's left a lone protester was attempting to bully his way past an officer. He was launching into the: "It's a free country and you can't stop me" routine and: "just because I'm black" etc etc... A typical provocateur, he was pulling out all the stops in an attempt to get the officers to use force to prevent him pushing past, all the while, belligerently repeating: "Go on then, arrest me!" This was a distraction that the put-upon officers just couldn't afford at that moment, but fortunately, after a frustrating thirty minutes, common sense on behalf of his female partner prevailed. After she'd called him an idiot, he finally backed down, retreating to an area, from where he could safely witness the hated white policemen coming under attack.

In the space of around two hours, the best that Jax and his exhausted fellow officers could manage, had been to retake no more than twenty yards of rubble-strewn road. Jax sensed rather than heard the next players to enter stage right. Glancing over his shoulder, he saw a welcome sight - that of half a dozen giant police horses picking their way through the debris and forming up behind him. Yes! he thought - Some heavy-duty reinforcements at last!

Jax hadn't been alone in noticing the new arrivals, and after setting fire to what seemed to Jax, every other building to his front; the mob surged forward again

21

before banding together and employing a counter measure - designed to neutralise the threat of several tons of snorting horse flesh.

Hatching their plan, the lead elements of the snarling mob ripped the supermarket shopping trolleys from their anchor outside the burning Aldi, and dragged them into the road. Locked together by short chains, the trolleys could only be released by the insertion of a one-pound coin. The sight of this improvised obstacle was demoralising. The act of toppling the trolleys onto their sides, made a long, gleaming wire snake out of the innocent looking wheeled baskets - effectively creating a barrier between them and the looming equine threat.

Behind Jax, the horses slavered over their bits, nodded their big heads and pawed the ground. Whatever tactics their riders had formulated, now seemed temporarily neutered by a set of shopping trolleys held together by around £30 worth of gold-coloured coins. In the absence of a plan, the short shield pushes went on and on, getting as far as the stricken trolleys but no further. By now, elements of the mob were starting to scale low buildings to Jax's left, and were raining down debris from above. *This*, he would later remember thinking, was starting to get fucking serious.

Behind him, one of the mounted officers (later to be commended by the Commissioner) was putting forward an unorthodox plan not included in the mounted branch manual. It was simplicity in itself and was to save the day. Rather than charge their mounts line abreast, he suggested that they split into two columns and circumnavigate the trolley barrier via the narrow corridors either side. The plan agreed, the mounted officers bypassed the metal snake and reformed on the other side. Re-adopting their traditional formation, horses and riders charged the crowd, scattering them before the thundering hoofs.

Public order tactics dictate that once the crowd have

been pushed forward by the horses, men with shields take up the ground taken by them, while the mounted officers re-group. Readying himself for this anticipated move, Jax suddenly realised that another section was overrunning his front line position.

Unbeknown to him, fresh reinforcements had finally arrived in sufficient numbers to relieve both his serial from Kilburn, and the TSG officers. Neil told them that they were to take a break pending further orders, and seating himself atop a ripped out ATM cash machine, he fished out a couple of cigarettes. Lighting one for Bill, and shoving it into the gap of his raised visor, he lit the second one and inhaled deeply. Perched on the most ludicrous seat he'd ever sat on, Jax took in the hell on earth that was Tottenham High Road. Flames lit up the night sky for as far as the eye could see, weary fire fighters dragged hoses along the scorched and ragged tarmac: which looked as though it had been ploughed up by some satanic farmer, and totally exhausted riot officers lay all around. Bill and Paul took war snaps with their phones, but Jax, having left his phone back in his locker at Kilburn took none. He opted instead, to go in search of an alleyway in which to prise his groin guard away and add his piss to the mess that was the Tottenham High Road.

Mounted Branch, had done such a good job of clearing most of the High Road, that the grown-ups took the decision to stand down the original officers. They were directed back to the police station for refreshments. Once inside the safety of the nick, Jax thought the back yard resembled a war zone. Groups of weary officers grouped together, smoking cigarettes among heaps of food either donated by local stores, or liberated from the street. Mostly consisting of chocolate bars, biscuits and crisps, there were also cans of drink - not dissimilar to the ones being hurled at Jax a couple of hours before.

Going inside the unfamiliar nick in search of the

canteen and a hot drink, Jax had been amazed to find the drinks vending machines all smashed open! During the first few hours of the riot - he was told - officers had been so desperate to rehydrate themselves, that they had dashed into the safe territory of the nick, and in the absence of small change; had simply smashed them open and helped themselves. Needs must when the devil drives!

Having survived their first riot, the officers from the Task Force clambered back into their carrier and headed wearily back to Kilburn. They'd answered the call to arms at around 9pm the night before, and it was now 7am. Caked in salty sweat; their faces blackened by the soot of Tottenham's burning buildings, they were elated to have survived unscathed, and with links of camaraderie well and truly forged in the fires of Tottenham, they'd forever share a common bond.

When he thought back, Jax, without a hint of bravado, could honestly say that he hadn't been scared by the mob. Sure, there had been more than one hairy moment, but he had to give the Gravesend trainers their due. They'd instilled discipline and a good knowledge of basic tactics. But more than any of this, they'd pounded him with enough petrol bombs and milk bottles, to give Jax a great deal of confidence in his protective gear.

Given the next day off, they'd re-convened at Kilburn on the Monday. Showing everyone a screen shot from Saturday's BBC news depicting them on the front line, Chloe had grinned ear to ear and announced that: "They were the Famous Five!" Their experiences at Tottenham may have been a far cry from Enid Blyton's depiction of *her* Famous Five, but the name had stuck...

Before Tottenham

Chapter Two

'Any children or pets?'

Simon Coverdale from the Borough Intelligence Unit, locked his computer, shuffled his warrant application papers, and drained the cold dregs from his coffee cup, before getting up with the involuntary groan associated with the middle-aged. In his late forties, he was on the downhill stretch of what had been a full and varied police career. With hound dog eyes and thinning hair that cascaded dandruff over the shoulders of his worn grey suit jacket; he walked with a stoop that belied his six-foot frame. On the rare occasion that he spoke, his deep mournful voice tumbled out words peppered with the flat vowels of his native Yorkshire.

Affectionately known as "Lurch," he'd been a good and steady thief taker back in the day and whenever a new probationer arrived, it had been to Lurch that they were entrusted. Then one day, out of the blue, Lurch had simply had enough of dealing with society's shit. Without telling any of his colleagues, he'd quietly applied for the vacant post of Field Intelligence Officer in the BIU. Nobody really knew why such a good street cop had handed in his cuffs. It may have been following a moment of clarity after he'd copped for the ball of phlegm spat at him by the junkie in the cell; or it may have been that he felt suddenly old and out of touch with the new wave of corporate leadership sweeping the Met. Whatever the reason, he'd managed to hide himself away in the BIU office for the last ten years. There, among the other street-weary cops and civilian female analysts, he counted down his 9-to-5 days until retirement, and immersed himself in intelligence reports, updates on persistent offenders, and crime trends. Lurch's other roles included the compilation of search warrant applications and attending court where, standing before a magistrate, he would swear out warrants.

The search warrant, for which Lurch intended to apply, was covered by Section 1 of The Firearms Act 1968. Normally, this would be earmarked for execution by a specialist firearms unit from CO19, but if he was honest, it was to be more of a fishing trip. The main purpose of the warrant was to gain entry to a certain address. Intelligence had suggested that the occupant may have been holding a firearm on behalf of somebody else and as such, it was believed to be well hidden and so, not immediately accessible for use. The "non-immediacy" aspect of the intelligence had meant that CO19 had turned up their noses at carrying out the search, and so it was to fall to normal borough officers to execute.

The duty inspector was unlikely to want to commit his core team officers to what may well amount to two hours of searching; preferring instead, to keep them on the road and dealing with their everyday calls. He had attendance charter times to make and boxes to tick - whether the calls were to domestics, missing persons or shoplifters. He wouldn't be remotely interested in Lurch's warrant. With any luck, if they weren't tasked to deal with football hooligans, the officers from the Borough Task Force would be available to execute the warrant for him.

Mumbling a barely audible: 'I'm off to court,' to nobody in particular, Lurch descended the grimy staircase of Houndshale nick and made his way out of the grim 1960's building. Finding a spare car in the back yard, he set off for the equally grim magistrates court at Filebridge.

For the uninitiated, the court's exterior Edwardian façade, promised an equally grand interior, but to those unfortunate enough to have to frequent the place, the reality was a jumble of narrow corridors and steep staircases flanked by cubbyholes masquerading as offices.

Despite not being in uniform and in an unmarked car, the gaggle of scruffy Somali youths lounging outside the building quickly recognised Lurch's car as a police vehicle and spat almost as one, in disgust. Lurch was obliged to run the gauntlet of tangible hatred, and stepping over pools of phlegm, with thinly veiled hissed insults invading his ears, he made his way inside.

Once on the threshold, he showed his warrant card to the African security guard before passing through the metal detector arch immediately inside the door. The detector beeped and in a flurry of arm waving from the guard, he was through.

Striding along the narrow corridor in search of the usher, he was once more forced to run a gauntlet of young wasters. England's bright future, dressed in their uniform of jeans halfway down their backsides and grubby hoodies, quietly jeered him as he made his way through the stench of trainer-clad feet, hanging fug-like above their obtuse shaved heads. A couple of them, proudly displayed their plastic curfew ankle tags like some twisted badge of honour.

Pushing through the hostile atmosphere, he eventually found an overworked and world-weary usher: a middle-aged woman with wire-rimmed spectacles dangling from a chain atop her faded gown. Lurch asked whether she would be able to fit him into the busy court schedule. Promising to do her best, the usher consulted her clipboard and swept officiously into the courtroom: her oversized gown billowing in her wake, disturbing the foetid air.

Some courts had police rooms where officers waiting to give evidence could find some respite from the sneers and smart comments of the hood rats. Filebridge afforded no such luxury, and plonking himself into an uncomfortable, plastic cinema-like seat, Lurch settled down to wait. He zoned out the sights and smells of the court and pulled out a newspaper to use as a screen to blot out society's flotsam and jetsam.

*

Three hundred yards down the road at Filebridge nick, the late turn cops of Houndshale's borough task force team UX646, started to arrive and hunt in vain for a place to park. Once the six or so spaces at the front of the station were taken, they'd have to trawl further afield to find a space which: wouldn't piss off the local population *and* would be far enough away from the nick so as not to attract the attention of the local yobs. It wasn't only the local yobs who went in for a bit of cop car scratching - those householders, who were deprived of a parking spot outside their homes, weren't averse to vandalising the cop's cars either. So prolific had this become, that cameras had been set up on adjoining streets in the hope of catching the vandals.

Jax Jackson had been the first to arrive; he usually was: reasoning that the earlier he got there, the better chance he'd have of securing a space. At seven years, Jax was the longest serving member of the BTF. Being practically double the age of his teammates, he'd assumed the role of the old dog reluctant to learn new tricks.

He'd joined the police just on the cusp of change. The politically correct change from the military-like discipline of clean shaven cops, polished boots and ironed uniforms, was gradually being replaced by an "anything goes" culture. The old collective term of "relief" had been replaced with the wishy-washy *all in it together* "team," and bean counters, target chasers and box tickers now reigned supreme.

With fourteen years service - some with Thames

Valley police, and the rest with the Met, he'd forgotten more about police work than most of his BTF colleagues had learned. Six years with a so-called "county force" had imbued him with a good knowledge of the law, especially since any jobs he'd picked up at calls, had been his to keep for the duration. Not for the "county mounties," the luxury of the Met's system of arrest and handover to processing teams. He'd had to combine lengthy and time-consuming investigations with normal patrol. Only serious offences were dealt with by the suits in the CID department - and then begrudgingly!

The other big difference had been back up. Whereas in TVP, support could be in small numbers, and often a twenty-minute drive away; in the capital, swarms of cops would bust a gut to reach beleaguered officers, streaking along arterial routes and bouncing off the ubiquitous speed humps that littered the side streets. An officer requesting assistance would be surrounded by baton-swinging colleagues within minutes, all itching to join the fray. Indeed, it hadn't been uncommon in the ensuing melee, for the cops to end up handcuffing a stray arm, only to find it belonged to one of their colleagues!

Despite feeling more and more de-skilled with every day he spent on the BTF; Jax had decided never to return to core team work and it's ever-changing procedures and form filling. The BTF was simple - you stopped suspicious people and if necessary, searched them. You looked for drug dealers, smashed down doors, held back protesters and got in between rival football fans. You did the occasional suspect interview, assisted with violent prisoners and helped with mental health assessments.

What you *didn't* do was attend domestics to listen to a wife telling you she called police because her husband refused to give her the TV remote control. You didn't go to calls made by single mothers who'd decided that they couldn't handle their eight-year old's tantrums. You didn't attend children's homes to report missing juveniles who'd

- for the third time that week, sneaked out of the back door and not come home for supper. You didn't work the endless queue at the front counter either; where some other unfortunate took reports from those who pretended that their mobile phone had been stolen and who stood there, demanding a reference number to pass on to their insurance companies. And you *definitely* didn't take statements from school kids alleging petty harassment via facebook!

Jax was the team carrier driver - the carrier being a long wheelbase derivative of the Mercedes Sprinter van of the type used by angry "white van man" delivery drivers. The Met police version had had two extra wheels added to the rear axle, and was designed to offer it's occupants protection when ferrying them to and from seats of violent disorder. Equipped with a wire mesh windscreen grille and with the original windows replaced with Perspex to prevent flying glass, it also had manual locking bolts on the inside of the doors to delay those rioters intent on getting inside.

An extra fire extinguisher mounted underneath, and operated by the driver, was optimistically intended to deal with petrol bomb hazards. The seating arrangements on the carrier were fairly cramped with the rear section taken up with storage space for personal protection equipment, and six long riot shields. Another rack held eight short shields and a box of personal fire extinguishers - generally empty - and long since used by bored cops to spray each other with. Overhead compartments designed for smaller items of kit such as hats and jackets, generally tended to be awash with spilled Coke, mouldy sandwiches and rotting apple cores, and every now and then as the driver negotiated a harsh bend, his passengers would be showered with crap from above!

Being the carrier driver had it's perks. It meant that during major operations, such as football matches and demonstrations, Jax got to stay with the carrier - not only

31

to protect it, but also to pick up those members of his team that had spent the day shadowing a march. Of course, this limited the amount of action he got to take part in, but if it was pissing it down or freezing cold, he'd be more than happy to swap the returning cop's war stories for his own uneventful day in the warm!

The other side of the coin however, was having to endure the tirade of abuse traditionally heaped upon a police driver delivering a bunch of fired up and boisterous cops to imminent action. Coming almost non-stop from over his shoulder, it included shouts of: "I wouldn't have come this way!" - When he hit a traffic jam - "Kerbachino!" - When he hit a kerb and: "That was fuckin' close!" when he had a near miss - which when Jax, was driving, happened with monotonous regularity!

Climbing the filthy stairs to the BTF office, Jax idly wondered what the evening would have in store. It was to be an eleven-hour shift and the first of three "late turns" Pushing open the door to the office, he was met by the sight of the team inspector, in what Jax had come to know as his ruminating pose. A keen golfer, the guvnor tended to think things through while swinging whatever golf club-like instrument he could lay his hands on. Today, it had been a pickaxe handle recovered from beneath the bed of a drug dealer - which along with all the other weird and wonderful trophies - had inexplicably found it's way into the BTF office.

Inspector John "The Man" Williams had been known affectionately as "The Man," ever since he'd accompanied the team on an early morning raid. Standing behind the ruins of what had been his front door, the subject of the search warrant; a weasel-like petty thief, had attempted a feeble attack on the officers before being floored and cuffed. Looking up from his filthy carpet, he'd indignantly asked to whom he could make a complaint. At that, and right on cue, the guvnor had stepped into the room and announced that: he "was the man."

Meaning that he was the man to whom complaints should be addressed, it had unintentionally come out more like: "Yeah I'm the man around here, what's the problem?" What had made it all the funnier had been the fact that he was a true gentleman devoid of all bravado. Nonetheless, the name had stuck.

With the look of a genial uncle, the guvnor's stocky frame belied his past as a marathon runner. Laughter lines were etched around his sparkling eyes and he had the relaxed air of a man who had reached the point in his career at which he was happy to remain, while counting down to retirement and a decent pension. Armed with little more than an improvised golf club, The Man would dispense wise advice on both life and the intricacies of police procedure.

Wreathed in smiles, he greeted Jax with his customary:

'Jax Jackson, as I live and breath!'

Putting down his golf club, he perched himself on the edge of a desk and they chewed the fat for a while. The guvnor informed Jax that he'd had a request from the BIU for the team to execute a warrant: saving the finer details until the rest of the team showed up.

Next to show up was the bland Graham "Intel" Clark. In his late-twenties, he was skinny and gangling with an enormous head, which made him resemble a tadpole. At odds with his spare frame, he carried an unattractive paunch; testimony to his lifelong addiction to Kentucky Fried Chicken and full fat Coke. Prematurely balding, he'd resorted to fluffing up what remained of his hair and spiking it up with gel. When he did converse - which was rare, he invariably began his sentences with a reference to police intelligence matters.

True to form, he did no more than nod an acknowledgement to Jax and the guvnor before heading straight for the nearest computer terminal to resume his interminable research, while scratching absentmindedly at his permanent five-o'clock shadow.

Possessing a surly disposition and barely out of probation, the moody Clark was obsessed with the intelligence system known as CRIMINT. It's basically a good intel tool: designed to keep tabs on local criminals and consequently keep the cops informed on the latest comings and goings of the criminal fraternity. It features reports on who's running drugs for which dealer, who's driving what car, and even who still drives whilst disqualified. Some of the information comes from Crimestoppers - the anonymous phone call facility for nosey neighbours, rival drug dealers or disgruntled ex-girlfriends, which serves to provide information to the police. With Crimestoppers, there is also the promise of a reward for information leading to a conviction. Other intelligence is provided by police officers, Police Community Officers, or paid informants.

A good intelligence system in principle, CRIMINT is overloaded with gossip, whispers and rumour. PSCO's in particular love to input such trivia as: "I saw this person talking to this person" and: "today at such and such a time, I saw so and so walking down the High Street." It reminded Jax of the kind of gossip network upon which East Germany's STASI relied during the cold war - 50% bollocks, 40% malice and 10% truth. Jax had secretly dubbed his intel slave colleagues as: "CRIMINT monkeys"

To be fair, among the dross, there is the odd rough diamond to be found and enough information on the same subject can quite easily provide enough information to be put before a magistrate to secure a search warrant.

Clark was one of an amateur intelligence army that slaved over CRIMINT whenever they could get to a computer terminal. They bartered information with all the fervour of young boys swapping football cards, competing among one another for the best and most up to date intelligence. These CRIMINT monkeys even called each other up at home to swap jealously guarded information. They tended to be mainly interested in drug-related reports and would trawl the streets looking for addicts to literally pounce on. If by sheer coincidence the timing was right; the junkies would be caught scurrying home to smoke their pathetic rock of crack.

The intel addicts would then feign friendship with the junkie in order to glean information in relation to the dealers. Now, you didn't need to be Sherlock Holmes to know that junkies don't turn in their dealers any more than turkeys vote for Christmas, but their every word was meticulously recorded.

Through necessity, drug addicts are accomplished liars to the point of actually convincing themselves that they speak the truth. If they thought that they could gain advantage by telling the cops any old shit - they generally did just that. After such encounters, the CRIMINT monkeys would get very excited, rushing to the nearest nick to input what amounted to bullshit, before swapping the so-called hot info in hushed tones with their fellow believers!

As for Jax, he wasn't one to spend too long in front of a computer screen and was happier out on the street generating his own work. The intelligence system did give a leg-up from time to time, but was no substitute for "copper's nose." You never knew where self-generated work would lead, but every now and again, it would turn up something decent and give so much more satisfaction than taking a bag of weed from a school kid mentioned on a CRIMINT report.

The next time the BTF office door swung open, it was to admit Craig "Dynamo" Johnson. Standing at six-foot two, his religion was the gym and diet. Protein mad, he'd been known to consume twenty eggs in one day alone! He carried what was a portable larder - a blue cool bag of gigantic proportions, containing his two-hourly meals. If he were to be parted from his food for a few minutes over his two-hour limit, he'd get very tetchy indeed!

Worshipping at the altar of the gym most days, his biceps bulged and strained against the white cotton of his uniform short-sleeved shirt. So big were Dynamo's arms, the material actually cut into his skin. Filling the large sleeves of a police shirt took some doing - Jax's own sleeves flapped around his arms like bellbottomed trousers on skinny legs! When Dynamo smiled - which was most of the time - his perfect white teeth filled his head and his eyes radiated the playfulness of a puppy dog.

In contrast to Intel, Dynamo's luxuriant head of hair was stylishly gelled into a quiff. Whether it was his intense bodybuilding regime, his huge protein intake, or just a faulty thermostat, the big man was forever complaining about being hot. Whatever the temperature, he was the only cop on the team to wear short sleeved uniform shirts come rain or shine. The minute he entered a room, his first act would be to complain about the heat and throw open all of the windows. While the others shivered in their coats and berated him for admitting what was for him a cool breeze - but for the rest of them an icy blast - he would flash that disarming grin of his and carry on regardless.

Jax, who felt the cold more than the others, would eventually strike a compromise and close the window nearest to the computer terminal where he was working. This normally drew the kind of comments reserved for the oldest member of the team: 'Ah, poor old man, shall I fetch you a nice tartan blanket to put over your legs?' Constantly messing around, you only knew he was serious when he followed up a story with: "and I'm not even joking."

Dynamo's overheating issues didn't end at the office either: once they were all out and about in the carrier, the big man would generally ensure that he sat up front in the operator's seat. This way, he could control the heating system, and not content with turning the heat right down, he'd normally try to sneak the air conditioning on too! His reasoning behind this was to say that; the driver was in charge of the driving controls, while the operator was in charge of everything left of the steering wheel!

He'd been sent home from school on many an occasion: his inability to concentrate misdiagnosed as bad behaviour. No longer a schoolboy, his inability to keep still and low boredom threshold persisted, and there wasn't a lot in life that the big man took too seriously. He was impossibly playful and tactile and once, when he'd met a corpulent superintendent on the stairs, and they'd almost walked into each other while both choosing the same way to go, Dynamo had simply thrown his arms around the startled superintendent and given him a big hug!

Dynamo was great fun to have on the team and with the exception of Intel; he could lighten the mood of the most miserable bastard on the carrier. He was also useful in a scrap, and when the team executed search warrants, there weren't many doors that could defeat him. He simply slogged away until either the door gave way or the masonry surrounding it crumbled!

Hot on the heels of Dynamo came Adie "The Cat" Black. Called the Cat after his main two passions - coffee and tits - Adie was the king of banter. His stock of put down lines seemed inexhaustible. Like Dynamo, The Cat was a gym junkie who liked to dress down in the latest fashion and was on a never-ending quest for worldly information. Another beneficiary of the relaxed height rule, he was a follower of fashion both in the way that he dressed, and the style in which he furnished his home. His house was equipped with the latest TV and audio, and when it came to furniture, Ikea didn't remotely feature. He liked nothing more than to spend hours in front of the TV watching either the Discovery channel or

National Geographic. He could bore for England on air crash investigations, weird and wonderful weapons and ice road trucking.

The Cat suffered from an endearing issue with mispronouncing words almost on par with a victim of metathesis. In his eagerness to repeat knowledgeable quotations, he tended to get them wrong - generally with hilarious results. Words such as "specific," came out as "pacific," while "supposedly" came out as "supposebly."

One of the Cat's more memorable *faux pas* had been when repeating a joke he'd heard previously. It had revolved around the subject of some *persona non grata* with the punch line misquoted as:

'He was left feeling about as welcome as a *lamb* chop at a Bar Mitzvah!'

For all his mispronunciations, he was a likable member of the BTF and pretty good at sarcastic put-downs, be they at the expense of his colleagues, or some half-witted low-level criminal on the street.

Like the guvnor, the Cat enjoyed a game of golf and could often be found on a golf course playing alongside high ranking and influential officers. This was his way of networking, and although this didn't appear to be done out of servility, it left him well placed when certain plum vacancies or more exotic training courses came about.

The more recent addition to the team was Emma "Babes" Cash - so-called after her frequent use of the word "babes." Today, Babes was late. As she sheepishly attempted to enter the room unnoticed and failed miserably, there was a collective ostentatious checking of watches, followed by exaggerated "tut-tutting" and loud calls of: 'Doughnuts!' Cheeks flushing crimson with embarrassment and mumbling something about heavy traffic, Emma agreed to pay the price of being late by way of the traditional penalty of buying doughnuts for the team.

Jax's team had been all male for as the last three

years, possibly - but - wrongly, because there was the perception among female officers, that misogynistic dinosaurs staffed the BTF. This may have been the case in the early years of it's formation, but earlier purges of such people, now meant that a female member of the team - providing she was up to the rigours of Task Force policing - was more than welcome. His sister BTF team - UX647, had recently lost their only female officer, who'd transferred to another borough and pastures new.

Tall and willowy with a lustrous mane of raven hair, and eyes the colour of dark chocolate, Emma had fitted in almost instantly with the team. Apart from sharing the general keep fit ethos and knowledge of sport with the boys, she was adept at banter and generally gave as good as she took. It can't have been easy spending a large portion of your day spent cooped up with six hairy-arsed coppers in the fug of excessive protein-induced flatulence, as they lusted after, and made crude remarks about the rare sight of an attractive woman on the streets of Houndshale.

Emma was attractive in a "girl next door" kind of way and not so outwardly feminine or flirty as to distract and cause rivalry among the boys. This worked well, and to a man, the rest of the team treated her more like a younger sister than a potential conquest.

The skipper - sergeant Ian Jarvis - was also running late, but having pre-arranged to come in an hour late, he wouldn't be joining Babes in the doughnut trolley dash later on. Jarvis had taken over Jax's team a couple of months earlier and he'd been a breath of fresh air. The previous incumbent had done little to foster harmony within the team, having been one hell of a moody, miserable bastard. Besides being another CRIMINT monkey, he had one hell of a problem communicating. As the team assembled for the shift, they'd inevitably find the skipper hunched over a computer terminal - seemingly in a world of his own. The guys had long since given up expecting an acknowledgement to their greetings and a "good morning," was generally ignored. Being alone with him in the car was just as depressing. He'd either sit in silence for the entire shift, or else make lame attempts to ask after wife and kids. Once you answered his rare questions; within the space of a few words, you would be able to see from his vacant expression, that he wasn't listening to your answer! He'd just been going through the motions before sinking back into his own world - wherever that was...

Jax hadn't been able to decide was his issue was - he was either an ignorant twat or else he was so wrapped up in his own little world, that his team were invisible to him. Even on team nights out, the skipper would sit at the same bar table as the rest of them but in a kind of a trance. When out of politeness one would try to engage him in normal everyday conversation with a real life question such as:

'I'm going to Spain on holiday next month, have you ever been?' he would barely look up from his drink before uttering something unintelligible under his breath.

Change that for something like:

'Did you know Abdul is dealing drugs on the Eagle Estate?' and as if by magic, he'd sit bolt upright and be all ears! Jax had likened him to a puppet whose strings would stubbornly remain slack and lifeless until a magic work-related word was uttered in his presence. At this point, an unseen puppeteer would yank on his strings causing his head and torso to jerk upright and restoring animation to his hands and arms. Return to a normal life subject and it was as though someone had cut his strings!

By contrast, skipper Jarvis was gregarious, witty, and enjoyed workplace banter as much as the next man. Take *him* out for a drink and you'd have your work cut out keeping him on the straight and narrow! With his: "Richard Gere for the thinking woman's" looks, he had a keen eye for the ladies and an infectious laugh into which you couldn't help but be drawn. Years of competitive sport had left him with a weak back and if you were driving the carrier with him in the back seat, you would be under strict instructions not to mount the more aggressive speed-humps that abounded at the entrances to Houndshale's housing estates. Forget this and the driver's ears would be assailed with a pained yelp followed by: 'Ouch! My fuckin' back!'

This varied and disparate group completed the members of UX646 of Houndshale Borough Task Force, but left them one short, the vacancy for which was currently advertised borough-wide. Providing the core shift inspectors could be persuaded to give up one of their officers, UX646 would hopefully soon be back up to strength.

*

Meanwhile, Lurch from the BIU waited patiently at Filebridge magistrate's court for the usher to squeeze him into the busy schedule. Then, when he'd been about to give up after two hours of enduring the hard seat in the waiting area, the doors to court two opened silently to reveal the gowned usher gliding towards him. She told Lurch that the court was about to adjourn for lunch, but that the magistrates had granted him an audience before they left for their supermarket sandwich.

Taking his warrant card from him to provide identification for the magistrates, she bade him follow her. Lurch gratefully eased his numb backside from the plastic chair and followed her billowing gown through the thickly upholstered soundproof doors.

Court two was the largest of the four courtrooms at Filebridge. Dominated by the large Royal coat of arms hung above the bench, it was fitted with a public gallery, banks of video playing equipment, and a witness box to the left of the magistrate's bench. Legal books and papers littered the first two rows of official seating and was normally the domain of the clerk, defence solicitors and CPS prosecution lawyers. The court clerk - whose role was to advise the lay magistrates on points of law, was nowhere to be seen. This pleased Lurch, as clerks tended to show off their legal superiority to the three magistrates, that in effect, were ordinary untrained members of the public who had volunteered to sit on the bench. Clerks had been known to be a pain in the backside in their desire to impress the magistrates. They revelled in asking police officers awkward questions in relation to the information upon which the warrant application had been based. The clerks took advantage of the fact, that more tenuous warrant applications made on the strength of so-called single strand information - normally an informant - didn't tend to hold up to vigorous scrutiny.

It wasn't practice for the cops to reveal the source of their information even to the court, but they were expected to elaborate a little on the application.

Directing Lurch to the witness box under the benign gaze of the three lay magistrates on the bench, the usher asked him whether he would swear on oath or affirm. Lurch, like most officers, found the affirmation declaration much more of a mouthful than the traditional religious oath, and so despite being an atheist, he took the proffered bible from the usher and read from the typewritten card she provided. He didn't need to read from the card, having been in the witness box countless times before, but as ever, as part of playing the game, he looked at the card without actually focussing on the words. He cleared his throat before launching into the same archaic mantra that countless criminals earnestly recited once the law had caught up with them. Hearing his own deep voice magnified by the microphone, bouncing off the walls of the almost empty courtroom, he felt as devoid of holy feeling as had the non-religious hypocrites wearing their prison-issue plastic rosaries that had come to the box before him:

'I swear by almighty God, that the information I shall give, be the truth, the whole truth and nothing but the truth.'

Then turning away from the bible to address the magistrates, Lurch continued:

'Good afternoon your Worships. I am police constable Simon Coverdale of the Metropolitan police, currently stationed at Houndshale.'

Passing his warrant card back to him by way of the usher, the second magistrate glanced through the warrant application Lurch had painstakingly typed out earlier that morning. He looked over the top of his gold-rimmed glasses and addressed Lurch:

'Good afternoon officer. I understand you wish to obtain a search warrant?'

'Yes your Worship.'

'I see it's a warrant under Section One. Could you give us a bit of background?'

Lurch rattled off some bullshit about it being information from an informant in the employ of the police and this seemed to satisfy the clueless volunteer. Lurch knew what was coming next. In the absence of a clerk, one of the magistrates - his money was on the one sat to the left - would invariably ask a stock question - the only question that they felt they could ask in confidence - and which would imply they had a grasp on the situation. As the application was passed to the third and last magistrate for perusal, the first - to Lurch's left - asked the oldest question in the book:

'Officer,' he began with a lisp. 'Are there any children or pets at the address?' Smiling inwardly, Lurch feigned sincerity before replying:

'To the best of our knowledge your Worship, the subject lives alone, but in the event of there being young children at the address, we will of course knock on the door first.'

Thanking Lurch, the magistrate in the middle

consulted his colleagues as to where he should put his signature, before uncapping his fountain pen and signing with a flourish. Passing the signed warrant to the usher who in turn passed it to Lurch, the bench rose as one and retired through a side door. Clutching the easily obtained warrant, Lurch flashed the worldly usher a conspiratorial look. She rewarded him with the hint of a wry grin and held the door open for him. Exiting the now deserted lobby, he made his way down the road to Filebridge nick and the BTF office.

By the time Lurch entered the Task Force office, the skipper had joined the rest of his team and already been briefed by "The Man" with regard to their afternoon's tasking. As the door swung closed behind him, Lurch felt a bit awkward as seven pairs of eyes swivelled expectantly in his direction.

Offering the BIU man a cup of tea, they made room for him to log on to a computer terminal and prepare the power point briefing he'd put together back in his office. Forming a standing semi-circle around Lurch's terminal, the assembled team ceased their banter and peered at the small screen as Lurch brought up his pre-planned briefing. This would be a standard presentation using an approved template. Apart from the all-important headings, the standard template would be blank and left for the intelligence officer to complete accordingly. The briefing was mandatory, and apart from being an intelligence briefing, it also served as a kind of safety check and an umbrella for the organisation. For those warrants that were of high importance, such as raids on armed gangs and terror suspects, the entire briefing would be filmed.

They'd sat through countless presentations of this kind before and had also delivered a few themselves. The cops on the ground were only really interested in who the subject was, were there any dogs at the address, what kind of door were they to break down and did it open inwards or outwards. The latter information would dictate which tools they would take along. Nevertheless, they did the BIU man the courtesy of listening to the entire briefing, knowing that however convoluted, Lurch would have to be seen to have delivered the entire briefing and covered all known risks. It would include all of those tedious health and safety and human rights aspects, which potentially - should it go tits up - would negate applications for compensation from both cops and the subjects of the search warrant. Lurch sipped noisily at his tea before putting up his first slide and intoning:

'Information. Source led intelligence suggests that Charlie Barker is holding a Section One firearm on behalf of another. Barker has previously been arrested for burglary and handling stolen goods. Barker is known to stay at the address with his parents and his on/off girlfriend Kerry Brown, who has previous for possession of Class A drugs.

Intention. To execute a warrant under Section One of the Firearms Act 1968, and search the premises and all persons on the premises. To retrieve the firearm, to secure arrests for the offences mentioned, to detect any other offences while at the venue, and to gather information regarding any criminal activity.

Location: 23 Acacia Drive, Houndshale. The property is a semi-detached house situated in a circular cul-de-sac. The property belongs to Barker's parents.'

At this point, Lurch put up a slide taken from Google street view of the address. This new technology gave the cops the opportunity to zoom right in on the target door. It also showed them the layout of the street - which in this case, appeared to not be favourable in the way of concealment. Lurch confirmed this with his next lot of information:

'There are not believed to be any children or dogs at the address, but along with Barker and Brown, it is believed at least one of his parents may be at home.

There is no way of approaching without the possibility of being seen from the address, and so speed will be of the essence. The door is wooden with a small glass panel, and opens inwards.

Method. Uniformed officers from the Borough Task force are to effect entry to the premises and secure all occupants within.

Premises are to be searched and arrests made where necessary.

Appointed person to be responsible for the book 101 and exhibits.

Entry to the address will be with a warrant obtained from Filebridge magistrate's court today.' At this point, as was customary, Lurch handed the warrant to the skipper who passed it around his team. Lurch continued:

'Administration. Houndshale custody is to be contacted direct for any prisoners. EAB statement books to be completed for all arrests and should force be used. 101search log to be completed.'

Sensing the shared glances by officers who hated paperwork, Lurch reassured them that he would be coming along and that he would record the information for any items found during the search. A ripple of relief from the assembled team!

'Risk assessment. All officers must wear PPE (personal protection equipment) and be in possession of personal radios. All officers must be currently officer safety trained (annual handcuffing and empty hand tactics training) and ELS (Emergency life support) trained. When searching persons or premises, all officers are to wear protective gloves, cover cuts and consider sharps, infections etc.' Cue exchanges of "sucking eggs" miming between Dynamo and The Cat.

'Communications. Working channel will be UX despatch 1. PNC checks will be on UX support. CAD to be created.'

Short for Computer Aided Despatch - the latter
46

would create an incident number. CAD was a numeric reference to all incidents, and began at one minute past midnight every day, re-setting to zero, 24 hours later. The CAD number could relate literally to a thousand and one incidents ranging from: "My sister hit me," type of calls, to "I've just stabbed my boyfriend." In the case of search warrants, a CAD would have to be created prior to attending the address, so that the operator knew exactly where the troops were should it all kick off upon entry.

Finally, realising that he had long since lost his audience, Lurch put up the final slide of his presentation.

'Human rights: proportionate - to detecting the offences in question. Legal - by virtue of a search warrant being issued by a magistrate. Accountable - by the intelligence researched and recording of police action. Necessary - to prevent and detect offences.'

Concluding his briefing with: 'Any questions?' he was rewarded by the Cat:

'Yeah, I've got a question - when's Emma gonna' get the fuckin' doughnuts in!'

Through the peals of laughter, Graham did what he did best. He made a droning statement to nobody in particular to show off his intelligence knowledge:

'I read on CRIMINT that Barker was selling weed on the Turpin estate.'

Lurch politely told him that he had no such knowledge while the rest of the team groaned and exchanged bored looks, before strapping on arm and leg guards and then shrugging into their overalls.

Grabbing NATO helmets, UX646, made their way raucously down the steep stairs and to the carrier in the crowded back yard. Once there, they checked the door entry kit: making sure they had the bright red fourteen kilo battering ram - known as the enforcer, the hydraulic rabbit tool and crow bars, a hooligan bar referred to fondly as the "hoolie bar," and finally, a giant set of bolt croppers. Satisfying themselves that they had enough equipment to wreak havoc on whichever door might stand in their way, they set their radios to minimum volume and climbed aboard the carrier.

Chapter Three

'Suck it!'

Acacia Drive was on the extreme borders of Houndshale borough, and in late afternoon school traffic, a good fifteen-minute drive from Filebridge. As the carrier made it's way through tortuous traffic, the banter and anonymous farting began. Dynamo - sitting up front as Jax's operator, took the team's mind off the forthcoming raid with one of his stories. As they overtook a double-decker bus advertising a forthcoming wrestling match, he remembered the time, when as a kid, he'd been obsessed with the colossal wrestlers who strode the canvas of the WWF ring. The conversation had started off between him and Jax, but when the rest of the team overheard Jax laughing, they tuned in to the story.

'What's he on about?' enquired the Cat, who had momentarily torn himself away from "Big Tits.com" on his iphone. He didn't want to miss out on the big man's story.

Glancing at the Cat through the rear-view mirror, Jax grinned.

'No tits in this story Cat - just massive pecs!'

Twisting around in his seat, his massive shoulders filling the gap between the driver's compartment and the passenger area, Dynamo grinned at his audience.

'Anyone remember Triple H?'

'Yeah, I do,' smiled the Cat, big fucker! Wasn't he called Triple H 'cos his first middle and last name began

49

with an "H"?' True to form, Cat pronounced it as "haitch."

'That's him, anyway, that big fucker got me suspended from school and I'm not even joking!'

Dynamo went on to tell his WWF story...

Aged thirteen, he'd been a bit of a handful both at home and at school - not in a bad boy way - more of a: "hyperactive-overgrown puppy-pain-in-the-arse," kind of way. At one point, in a bid to calm him down and get him to concentrate, his parents had sought medical help. A mild case of ADHD was diagnosed and they'd reluctantly agreed to try him on a course of Ritalin. But this was after - and as a result of - the WWF incident.

One Friday, the unexpected absence of a teacher had caused the school to rearrange the last two lessons. It was decided that the scheduled art lesson would be replaced with an ad hoc general knowledge quiz: with the competitors being made up from two opposing teams of girls versus boys. This was to be overseen by the deputy head - an intolerant and out of touch woman who still stalked the archaic world of: "children should be seen and not heard."

The quiz had been a close run thing with the final question set to decide the winning team. Posing a particularly obscure question about law, the deputy head leant back in her chair, a smug grin on her face. Dynamo hadn't particularly taken much of an interest up to this point, staring instead out of the window and happily inhabiting a world of wrestling, racing cars, and pin-up pictures of topless models. Something brought him back to the classroom and the boring quiz. He distinctly heard Miss smug-face asking who knew the age at which a person could be arrested. His dad was a cop and *he* knew the answer to the tiebreaker!

Yelling: 'TEN!' at the top of his voice, pre-Ritalin Dynamo celebrated his winning answer by leaping onto a table inches from the startled faces of the girls on the opposing team. Towering above them, and in true Triple H fashion, young Dynamo triumphantly crossed his wrists and thrust his hands over his crotch. Strutting like a peacock, he bellowed out the accompanying trademark insult delivered by Triple H to his vanquished foes:

'SUCK IT!'

As his innocent exclamation reverberated around the classroom, even the boys fell silent. One of the girls stifled a giggle, and the red-faced deputy head looked as if she may faint. Not being remotely *au fait* with WWF wrestling, the shocked woman had assumed that the crazed kid standing on the table; his crotch inches from the girl's faces, had just invited them to suck his dick! Spluttering with indignation, she'd hurriedly dismissed the class, before commanding the confused boy to follow her to the headmaster's office!

Leaving him outside, she marched self-righteously into the head's office to relate her tale of horror. The grown-ups had kept him standing outside the office while they phoned his parents, and when his bemused mother arrived he'd been wheeled in and informed that he was to be suspended from school for a week!

Through the laughter, her maternal instincts taking over, Emma said:

'Aw babes! What did you mum say?'

Dynamo flashed her a toothy grin.

'She was good as gold. Apart from me, she was the only other person to find it funny! I just stayed at home for a week watching telly!'

Even old Lurch, clutching his warrant papers, cracked a semblance of a grin.

They were nearing their destination now and the skipper quelled the mirth with a:

'OK, switch on now team.'

The skipper's interjection brought the team back to the imminent job in hand. The Cat made last minute checks to the rabbit tool: pumping the handle

51

experimentally to ensure the pressure valve was closed. Graham "Intel" Clark held the enforcer close and patted it like a favourite nephew.

Jax pulled the carrier over just short of the junction with Acacia Drive. Lurch, still in his civilian clothing, and looking like a carpet salesman, got out and made his way on foot to the address. He would make a quick recce of the street to make sure there wasn't anyone outside that could compromise the raid, and then call the team in. Once they'd arrived, he'd point out the front door - this was to avoid the not uncommon mistake, of smashing down the wrong door, resulting in crashing in on an innocent family and costing the Met a fortune in compensation!

Watching the hunched shoulders of the BIU man disappear around the corner, the team donned their helmets and gloves and waited for the call. Jax knew he wasn't alone in feeling the pre-raid adrenaline coursing through his body. No matter how many doors they put in, there was always the anticipation of the unknown; would the door go in easily? Would there be a dog waiting on the other side of the door to maul the first ones in? Would the occupants arm themselves in the heat of the moment? What if the firearm was easily to hand after all...

Talking each other through their entry roles steadied the nerves and helped to quell the jitters. The Cat would carry the rabbit tool, and after using a crowbar to lever the door open just enough to place the rabbit's jaws in the gap, he would silently signal Emma who would begin pumping the hydraulic handle to widen the gap and take the flexibility out of the door. Once the door was groaning under the pressure, Intel would strike it just above the lock with the enforcer carried to the address by Dynamo. Jax would follow up with the bolt croppers and hoolie bar just in case they were thrown a curve ball and the door turned out to be outward opening. They were a tight team and had executed countless warrants. Each knew their role and despite today's batting order, these roles were interchangeable. Everyone got to have a go at the ultimate task - that of wielding the enforcer. Putting the door in with one hit gave kudos. It wouldn't be talked about beyond that particular raid, but take more than three hits, and the ridicule would last for weeks - or at least until the next warrant!

Sometimes, the rabbit - ideal for silent early morning entries - would be sufficient to pop the door open. It tended to cause less damage, but the results weren't quite as spectacular as those offered by the blunt trauma of the enforcer. Drug warrants in particular had to have an element of surprise, and it was no use pumping away with the rabbit for several minutes while the occupants, alerted by the sound of splintering wood or their dog barking, flushed their drugs down the toilet. So, although the rabbit was always carried, if the door looked and felt like as though it would succumb to the enforcer, then, the "big red key" it was!

The skipper's mobile vibrated noisily: it was Lurch giving the green light. With the skipper's urgent hiss of: 'Let's go!' UX646 piled out of the carrier. Forming up in single file, the entry team sprinted into Acacia Drive.

Spotting Lurch around two hundred yards away, Dynamo led the way; the enforcer bobbing around on his huge shoulder like a toy. The big man led the team along a hedge line in the hope of concealing part of their approach for as long as he could, but with fifty yards to go, he was forced to leave it's leafy cover.

Bursting out into the open, he made a beeline for the BIU man standing outside number 23. Next in line was Intel with the Cat and Emma hard on his heels. Then came the skipper, trailed by Jax who, in spite of the urgency of the job, still had to lock and secure the carrier. It may have only been a two hundred yard dash, but by the time they all arrived and took up position next to the front door, they were all breathing heavily into their steamed-up visors and grunting under the weight of the entry equipment.

In the dying afternoon light, the team could just discern the faint flickering of a TV set from behind the net curtains - a sure sign that someone was in. A rapid assessment of the front door by the Cat showed it to be of flimsy wooden construction, and after applying pressure to both the top and bottom of the door he quickly ascertained that there was no top or bottom lock in place. This just left a simple Yale pin tumbler lock to contend with, and providing the Cat took the play out of the door, it would easily surrender to Intel's enforcer strike.

Quietly pointing out where Intel should strike, the Cat sat on his arse and placed his boot flat against the wood. Once in position, he pushed against the bottom half of the door taking out the excess play. Looking up at Intel and praying he wouldn't drop the big red key on his head, he signalled his readiness. Nodding, Intel pulled the enforcer back before crashing it into the space just above the lock.

The stricken door flew open with a satisfying BANG! The locking mechanism inside the door, smashed into the wall behind, sending chunks of plasterwork careering across the laminate wooden flooring in the hallway. Speed, aggression and surprise were now of the element, and with bellowing shouts of: 'POLICE WITH A WARRANT!' UX646 crashed into the lives of the unsuspecting Barker family.

Dynamo was first to enter just in time to see and hear the screaming figure of a woman disappearing into a back room, slamming an internal door behind her. Jax, spotting a giant of a man dressed only in his underpants running up a staircase directly to his front, sprinted after him yelling: 'POLICE! - STAND STILL!' Ignoring him, Man Mountain - over six-feet tall and weighing at least twenty-stones, carried on up the stairs, where he turned right into a bedroom.

Now, it has to be said, that while watching "Come dine with me" on the telly in the sanctity of your own home, one hardly expects half a dozen hairy-arsed coppers -sorry Emma! - to come crashing through your door, but despite the occupant's reactions; the team couldn't afford to take the risk of whoever the occupants were, getting to either the aforementioned firearm, or any drugs. Consequently, until everyone in the house was contained - that is to say - subdued and handcuffed, the momentum of shock and awe would have to be maintained.

To that end, Jax continued to pursue Man Mountain up the stairs to take control of him. This was to prove easier said than done when, twenty stone of practically naked man, insisted on ignoring his commands to stand still! Pushing his visor up so as to actually see what he was doing, the twelve stone Jax, caught up with his quarry just as he stepped into the bedroom.

Downstairs, the team began to clear the rooms in the house. The place rang with the disciplined and practiced shouts of: 'CLEAR!' as they entered, checked and cleared the various spaces.

Meanwhile, trying to grab hold of any part of the man's sweaty, corpulent body that he could, Jax found himself in the undignified position of grabbing the man in underpants from behind. All police textbook grappling moves and holds going by the wayside, he had the man - by now crouched over a bed - in a far from efficient bear hug, nowhere to be found in the officer safety manual! Man Mountain responded by standing up to his full height. Jax's grip somehow transferred itself to his horse-like neck, and before he knew what was happening, he was riding high on the man's back like some mini black-clad ninja, atop a greased hippo!

The drills taught during rapid entry courses in such

situations were unambiguous - should you find yourself alone and outnumbered, or as in Jax's case; grappling hopelessly with a giant - you were to yell: 'SUPPORT!' At number 23 Acacia Drive however, training and professionalism had gone by the wayside and Jax, embroiled in his unequal tussle with underpants man, had completely forgotten to shout for support.

Mercifully, the comical and unwinnable situation was resolved when the Cat, having cleared the first floor rooms, happened upon the bizarre tableau and intervened in Jax's favour. Between them, they managed to subdue Man Mountain and handcuff him. Suddenly compliant, the man started to groan, saying he had a bad back - no doubt not helped by having a riot kit clad copper riding him around his own bedroom!

Leading him downstairs, to the comparatively orderly front room, Jax made the discovery that Man Mountain and his wife were the only occupants of the house: their son Charlie being out and about somewhere.

During the entry, Mrs Mountain hadn't fared too well either. Having seen her disappear into a room and pull the door shut behind her, Dynamo had pursued her, yelling that she should unlock the door and come out. Not knowing what or who was in the room, Dynamo had literally ripped the flimsy door to pieces with his bare hands leaving it a mess of cheap cardboard filling and splintered plywood. It resembled the aftermath of some Tom and Jerry cartoon: with a ragged body-shaped hole bashed through the middle where he'd clambered through to get hold of the unfortunate woman!

Jax sat the man down on a settee next to his wife while the Cat fetched him a dressing gown to drape over his sweaty body, and the search for the firearm commenced. As Jax kept an eye on them, Man Mountain explained that only two days before, a gang had burst into their home in search of Charlie who, it seemed, owed money to a drug dealer. He hadn't been in on that occasion either and his parents, faced with a repair bill for their door for the second time in a week, weren't best pleased with their son!

At the sound of a commotion followed by suppressed giggling emanating from upstairs, Jax left the handcuffed couple in the care of Lurch who was filling out the paperwork. Climbing the stairs, he was met by the sight of Dynamo and the Cat laughing like naughty school kids. The Cat, while searching one of the bedrooms, had found the Mountain's stash of sex toys in a bedside drawer. Chucking an enormous dildo at Dynamo who'd instinctively caught it, he'd darted out of the room to avoid the big man's retribution. Jax was about to tell them that everyone downstairs could hear them, when the skipper entered the room and brought the unruly pair back to order with a hiss of: 'Stop fucking around!'

Tossing Mrs Mountain's "little" helper back into the drawer, the Cat, aided by Jax, finished searching the bedroom while the skipper and Dynamo checked the loft space. Without the help of a search dog, they couldn't be completely sure there wasn't a firearm secreted somewhere, but with no dog available within thirty miles, they had to satisfy themselves with nothing more than a knowledge of the usual hiding places, and a thorough searching technique, honed during countless searches.

Charlie, it seemed, was little more than a casual occupant of the house; using it for not much more than a mailing address, and to satisfy bail conditions whenever he was arrested. He did have his own room there, but apart from a few sets of trainers, a rack of hoodies and a couple of pairs of jeans, there wasn't a great deal to indicate his permanent residence there. The most incriminating item they could come up with was a fluorescent yellow cannabis grinder - which to be fair, was one of the most common things to be found in most teenagers' bedrooms.

Traipsing downstairs empty handed, Jax, the Cat, Dynamo and the skipper, joined the others in the front room. They could hear Mr and Mrs Mountain trading insults in voices that grew louder and louder by the second. By this time, the search of the ground floor had been completed without any significant finds, and Charlie Barker's less than proud parents, had been released from their handcuffs and were having a full blown domestic. Their row seemed to revolve around the smashed front door and their errant son.

According to Man Mountain - by now having made the transition from being subdued and handcuffed, to enraged parent - everyone was: "a cunt." Charlie was a cunt, his drug-dealing mates were all cunts and their neighbours: by now coming out of their homes to witness the commotion - were also cunts. Exasperated by her husband's ranting and embarrassed by his profanities, his missus had thrown up her hands shouting:

'Jesus Christ!'

To which her husband snarled:

'He's a cunt an' all!'

Amused by the man's outburst, but not wanting to involve themselves in what was shaping up to be one hell of a domestic, the cops began to sidle out of the house, leaving Lurch, to attempt to get a signature in his search book from Charlie's warring parents.

Closing the shattered front door behind them, they retreated to the sounds of old man Barker shouting: 'Cunts!' Picking up their entry gear, they waited for Jax to fetch the carrier; still parked out of sight. From inside the raided house, came sounds of the doorbell ringing. The unmistakable "ding-dong," chime was clear as could be. The cops outside looked at each other, puzzled; *they* certainly hadn't rung the bell!

It was Emma who finally resolved the mystery. Doubled over with laughter, and pointing at Dynamo's size eleven boots, she exclaimed:

'Babes! It's you! Look!' The big man looked down at his boot and sure enough, there, stuck to the sole, was the cause of the ding-donging. During the entry, the remote bell push had flown off the doorjamb and onto the ground. Coming out of the house, Dynamo had stepped on it, the self-adhesive had stuck to his boot, and with every step he took, the doorbell ding-donged!

Maddened by the endless ringing of his doorbell, Man Mountain opened his shattered door and stuck an angry-looking red face through the gap.

'It's a bit fuckin' late to ring my bell! You should have done that earlier instead of smashing my cuntin' door in!' he raged. Unsticking the bell push from underneath his boot and trying desperately to keep a straight face, Dynamo handed it to Man Mountain.

'Thanks a fuckin' lot!' was his parting shot as Dynamo, his face crimson with suppressed laughter, turned tail and strode away to rejoin the other cops; who upon seeing Man Mountain emerge like a wounded bear, had scuttled off leaving Dynamo to deal with the bell issue.

Piling back on the carrier, UX646 made good their escape from Acacia Drive before someone called the cops to deal with the domestic their arrival had generated. They hadn't got far before the skipper's phone rang. It was Lurch. 'Fuck!' he exclaimed, in a rare burst of profanity, 'We forgot Lurch!'

The Cat chimed in with: 'He's a cunt an' all!'

With the sound of coarse laughter behind him, Jax turned the carrier around and returned to pick up the hapless BIU man, who by now was trudging unhappily towards them, convinced they'd left him behind on purpose as part of some BTF joke. Assuring him that despite involving them in yet another shit warrant based on the usual poor standard of intelligence they'd come to expect from the BIU; they hadn't deliberately left him behind, they bundled him in and headed to Houndshale nick to drop him off.

*

The London borough of Houndshale lies to the west of the Metropolitan police area of responsibility, and for political and policing purposes, is broken down into wards. At it's extreme east is the genteel suburb of Whistlewick, populated largely by white affluent residents. Professionals and stars of TV and film rub shoulders with head teachers, civil servants and white-collar workers.

Idyllic as Whistlewick is with it's traditional butchers, posh coffee shops and the seemingly endless parade of Bentleys, Ferraris and Porsches; it's residents frequently fall victim to burglars from bordering boroughs who prowl the affluent enclave. It's resident's sons and daughters; distinct in their private school uniforms, and oblivious to the cruel world just beyond their safe borders, provide rich pickings with their iphones and ipads.

The western tip of the borough is Filebridge. The latter is also predominantly white, but the contrast couldn't be starker. Filebridge's inhabitants are a mixture of working class families, teenage single mothers: dressed uniformly in "muffin tops," and feckless youths, all thrown together. They live cheek by jowl in the ugly high-rise blocks and rabbit warren estates with gardens piled high with rubbish and the rusting hulks of cars. The High Street is a pretty good indicator of it's inhabitants, with the most popular outlet being McDonald's - closely followed by the Wetherspoons public house filled with idle and workshy all-day drinkers.

There was an effort by the council to attract higher end businesses, that up to a point succeeded, when a Next store opened on the High Street. Within one day of opening however, their stock was disappearing out of the door at an alarming rate into the arms of delighted shoplifters, and security had to be taken on! A shiny new

Travel Lodge hotel was next to open, but before long, deadbeats placed in the rooms by social services, joined genuine and unsuspecting guests. Soon after this, a group of prostitutes took up residence and simply instructed their clients to come up using the fire escape!

Some enlightened member of the council, had at some point won agreement for a traditional duck pond to be built, but despite the well meant thought; it is now a place for street drinkers - and latterly, somewhere for the newly arrived eastern European immigrants to kill and eat swans, and migratory geese. Wannabe gangsters affiliated to gangs with sinister-sounding names like TAM -Thugs after money - strut the streets, preying on anyone foolish enough to be displaying a mobile phone.

To the north east of Whistlewick, lies Spentford; home to the league one team known to their supporters as: The "Seals." The name is due to the urban myth, dating from the club's conception in 1889, and relates to a stray seal pup making it's way from the mouth of the Thames estuary at Southend, down the Thames to Spentford, where it supposedly hopped up the muddy banks, and came ashore. Local folklore has it that the seal was found by the club's groundsman and taken to the stadium, where the unfortunate animal was paraded for the amusement of the fans.

Spentford is a dilapidated town, earmarked by optimistic property developers for "gentrification." The town is the new destination of choice by those professionals who aspire to living in Whistlewick; but can't afford the property prices. A mess of decaying and derelict industry, it's skyline dominated by hideous tower blocks, Spentford was traditionally home to industrious blue-collar workers, but has latterly suffered from an invasion of listless recipients of welfare, and eastern European street drinkers; who fresh off the coach at Victoria station, thrive as squatters in the numerous derelict buildings.

Driving west, the next suburb of Houndshale is Hazelworth. Sandwiched between the phlegm-spattered pavements of Houndshale town centre, and within hearing distance of the Seal's stadium at Spentford, Hazelworth is mostly known for the large and sprawling hospital known by the locals as "The Florence." This is supposedly due to the passing patronage of Florence Nightingale. It is phonetically by the cops as: "Tango Foxtrot."

Suitably out of sight and to the rear of The Florence, is the mental health section of the hospital, with the innocent and idyllic-sounding name of "The Aspens." This part of the hospital, is attended with monotonous regularity by the cops of Houndshale; either to return the frequent absconders under mental health section, or to deliver those lost souls found wandering around and in need of sectioning - both for their own safety, and that of the public. The latter tend to be assessed by the cops on the street and sectioned using their powers under Section 136 of the Mental Health Act.

Hazelworth is probably closer in posh terms to Whistlewick than Spentford, and is blessed with acres of green spaces and historic buildings, among which are several coaching houses. It has it's fair share of problem families in their tower blocks and 1960's council estates, but doesn't feature too highly when it comes to police attendance.

Houndshale itself is a run down urban sprawl housing shabby discount stores, such as the 89 pence shops - one-pound shops are just too classy for Houndshale! The High Street; with every other building a derelict, and looking much like a row of rotten gums and missing teeth, is home to numerous betting shops inhabited by listless cannabis-selling Somali youths.

Interspersing the betting shops are equally numerous pawnshops and businesses offering pay day loans. The only businesses to rival the prolific bookies and "cash for gold" shops are the ubiquitous fast food chicken shops, African barbers, and Chinese brothels. As for the demographics of the place: it's a melting pot of Africans - all nations - but mainly Qat-chewing Somalis - Indians, Pakistanis, Iraqis, Portuguese, Filipinos, and representatives from every eastern European state you can think of. Among this Labour Party-orchestrated multicultural mistake, wander elderly and confused pensioners, completely taken aback by the speed of which their town has been taken over by people so unfamiliar, they might just as well be from Mars.

Driving west, you come to Cranston, which is little more than an intersection of main roads and arterial routes to better places. Just off these busy roads, lie estates of 1930's houses inhabited mostly by Indian families with their love of gaudy wrought iron gates, and hatred of front lawns. Pretty much every house, has had it's front garden converted to a concrete drive to house status symbols of Mercedes and big BMWs.

Like Hazelworth, a good deal of Cranston is given over to green spaces, and in parts it has a rural feel. Polish families are beginning to flourish in the area too - some hard working - but others, the dross that their country must surely have heaved a sigh of relief to have been rid of. Cranston is also home to so-called domesticated travellers who ply their criminal trade in the form of rogue tarmac laying and "distraction burglaries," talking their way into the houses of elderly ladies before robbing them of their life savings.

Cranston, with it's large Asian population, frequently falls victim to criminals from across London. Indian families tend to keep large amounts of gold jewellery for the purpose of dowries, and it is for this treasure - generally hidden at home - that criminal gangs of Latin Americans, often based in the south of the capital, travel west to steal.

Indian women have been known to be followed

around the streets of Cranston by groups of eastern European opportunists, who have grown adept at squirting ketchup over a victim's clothes, while their cohorts crowd their prey with offers to wipe down their clothing. Before the lady in the sari realises what is happening, her bag has been slashed wide open and the contents removed. Distraught, she then has to use her life savings to fund the cost of another dowry for her future in-laws. The lady may have lived in Britain for the last 30 years, but multiculturalism has meant that she never had to learn how to speak English, and so by the time a police interpreter can be found to explain what happened, the thieves are long gone.

*

Jax had just dropped Lurch off at the nick, and they'd all started the ritual discussion about where and what they were all going to eat, when as one, their radios crackled to life. The strident tones of the operator stopped all talk of food and they all turned up the volume and cocked an ear to their handsets:

'A unit now please for immediate response, High Street Cranston, report of a male exposing himself'

Immediate, or "I" graded calls, always got the attention of everyone with a radio. *Immediate*, meant just that - get there immediately! Other grades of calls were "S" for soon, and "E" for earliest opportunity. All grades of call had a particular stipulated amount of time in which officers were to attend, and could range from: "There's a car blocking my drive," kind of call, to: "My boyfriend hit me but he's since left the house." Any imminent and potential danger, or a call relating to a suspect that was still at the scene of the offence, would be treated as urgent.

In the case of Houndshale, the majority of "I" calls, related to domestic incidents. For some reason, in the whole of the Met, Houndshale seemed to have the lion's share of dysfunctional families! British police had been caught with their pants down in the past, and domestic calls, which while on the face of it hadn't seemed serious, had resulted in death. Since then, all domestic calls were to be treated as "I" grades, regardless of whether a neighbour had heard shouting from next door - which sometimes turned out to be someone's TV! In fact, many operators, aware that domestics weren't popular, would cleverly disguise the fact that it was a domestic by calling it a "disturbance." Once the bait had been taken by a cop anticipating a punch up, the operator would drop in the next piece of damning information that more experienced officers had come to recognise, such as: The neighbour states that she can hear female shouts of: 'Get out - leave me alone!'

Other "I" grade calls included the second most popular of all: that of: "suspects on." This meant that a burglary was in progress and that the suspects were still at the scene. For this type of call, everyone, from miles around with a radio and a vehicle, would bust a gut to get there first. There was no juicier call than a "suspects on," and there was no cop worth his salt who didn't want the kudos of catching a burglar - *absolutely* no one!

Even more than a suspects on call, an officer pressing his emergency button and requesting urgent assistance, would cause cops to drop everything, and through "red mist," risk life and limb in the race to get to the cop in trouble.

The flasher had stubbornly eluded the Houndshale cops for the last month, and having escalated his actions from exposure to touching his victims, he'd become something of a "must nick" suspect. To a chorus of: "Dirty bastard!" Jax punched the big red button on the carrier dashboard that lit up the blue roof lights, and then hit the horn to activate the siren, before heading for the last known location of the flasher. With his passengers clinging on to the back of the seats in front of them, Jax pushed his way through the rush hour traffic, gesticulating impatiently to those drivers who, in a world of their own, hadn't seen the lumbering Mercedes Sprinter bearing down on them in their rear view mirrors.

The name of the game on this call was to ensure that another team unit would go and speak to the victim of the flasher, leaving the BTF to conduct an area search for the man who couldn't keep his dick in his pants. Not for them the drudgery of paperwork - no, they wanted to catch the bastard, nick him, and leave the patrol car to do all the writing!

In the event, a faster and more nimble car beat them to the victim, leaving them to get radioed updates on the flasher's description, and direction of travel. After ten minutes of crisscrossing the immediate area looking for the needle in a haystack that was an Asian male in Cranston, they conceded that he was long gone and resumed their normal patrol pattern around the borough. As they said in the trade - "he'd come again..."

The excitement of the flasher call receding, The Cat broke the silence:

'I watched air crash investigators last night...'

A collective groan ensued as the Cat scanned the carrier for a semi-interested victim upon who he could unload his passion of air crashes. Catching Emma looking vaguely in his direction, he homed in on her and began to drone on about some crash he'd watched on TV:

'Did you know...' he began

Feeling safe now that the Cat had found a victim, the rest of the team went back to discussing where they were going to take "refs" - refs being short for refreshments and being police speak for meal break. Traditionally at the end of the daily briefing, the skipper would run through the call signs and allocate a slot during which individual crews could take refs. The theory behind this was to ensure that not everyone would be in at the same time. In practice, the cops would pay these slots no more than lip service. Getting together over a meal to swap stories was all part of the culture. Of course, should anything urgent come up while they were eating, then all bets were off, and depending on the urgency of the call, fries, burgers and kebabs would be discarded to be retrieved later and eaten via the used and abused communal microwave. Because the BTF travelled as one: unlike their core team counterparts, they generally ate together.

Breaking free from the Cat's enthusiasm of air crashes, fed by his diet of documentaries, Emma opened the bidding on what they were to do for refs:

'I've got soup back at the office, so I'll need to get back to Filebridge to shove it in the microwave.'

'Suits me,' intoned Intel. 'My food's there too.'

Dynamo - who to keep up his calorie intake and maintain his colossal frame had to eat every two hours, joined in with the, going back to Filebridge idea:

'Well that makes three of us - my tuna pasta's there too'

The Cat, sensing his preferred refs of kebab from a Houndshale takeaway joint fast receding, reverted to type and began to moan:

'Why can't you lot bring your food out with you? By the time I get my chicken shish back to the nick, it'll be cold for fuck's sake!'

Jax and the skipper, it seemed, held the casting vote...

'I can pick something up at Tescos in Filebridge'

'Me too,' added the skipper

'Great!' huffed the Cat sarcastically. 'I suppose I'll have to get something there too!'

And so, the age old saga of where and what to eat, was as usual, resolved by majority rule. The *faits accomplis* was celebrated by Dynamo. Leaping up in his seat, he faced the Cat, and with crossed hands thrust downwards, he yelled:

'SUCK IT!

*

The air in the pokey Cranston bedsitting room two floors above Hakim's chicken shop was thick with the smell of stale cooking oil, and the harsh sounds of the Bangra beat that emanated from the multi-occupancy rooms down the corridor. The Bangra mingled with the contrived sounds of synthetic ecstasy coming from room number seven; where sitting on his filthy semen-stained mattress, Balvinder Kapoor had his hand stuffed down the front of his grimy jogging bottoms.

With his rat-like face screwed up in concentration, he stared at his laptop: its screen filled with the grainy image of a fat eastern European porn actress, being skewered by two pot-bellied men. He tried in vain to massage some life into his cock, but it just wasn't happening. He'd already leafed through his used and abused girlie mags: their pages stuck together with the semen of his past ejaculations, but their familiarity bored him. Balvinder's face dripped with sweat at his vain efforts to arouse himself, and the beads of perspiration ran down his forehead, transferring themselves to his greasy, lank hair, before plopping noiselessly onto his grimy duvet cover.

It was no good; porn just wasn't doing it for him any more, he needed to get out and about and bring his fantasies to life. Giving up on the disembodied panting coming from his laptop, he stuffed a wad of toilet paper into his pocket, locked the flimsy door to his room and headed out into the street.

Balvinder Kapoor had a problem - paraphilia - in his case manifesting itself as the insurmountable urge to expose his penis to strangers while masturbating. At 35 years of age, he'd been at it in some shape or form since he was fifteen. He didn't know why he did it, but what he did know, was that it gave him immense satisfaction, a satisfaction that increased in it's intensification the closer he came to being caught - which these days, was damn close indeed.

Twenty years previously, when he'd first embarked on his flashing career, it had been in the school playground with his disinterested audience being Tammy Roberts. Tammy; a girl from the Filebridge tower blocks, had seen it all before - her virginity long since taken - and had roared with laughter, telling him to put it away before a bird swooped down and took it away! Cackling unkindly, she'd told her friends, but not the teachers. Consequently, Balvinder's first clumsy attempt at flashing, hadn't come to the attention of the school authorities, and merely compounded his loner status among his peers.

Balvinder's grandparents: Harpreet and Gurleen had emigrated to Britain in the 1950's. Battling discrimination and racism, they'd settled in Houndshale, where they'd set up a corner shop. Gradually earning the grudging respect of the locals through hard work, they'd built up an empire that included a supermarket, a taxi firm and an Indian restaurant. Over the next fifteen years, they'd recruited half of their native Punjabi village in rural Chogawan to help staff their businesses. It wouldn't be unreasonable to suggest, that Balvinder's grandparents and their hired help, had been among the first to establish what was to become a massive Indian community in the borough of Houndshale: either through imported labour or arranged marriage.

Houndshale's Sikh community had been enlarged when in 1960, Gurleen had given birth first to their daughter Amneet, followed a year later, by their son Anoop. Much to their parent's joy, and in no small measure as a result of their newfound affluence, Amneet had gone on to become an eminent barrister, who later agreed to be married off to a wealthy merchant from Amritsar. Anoop, on the other hand, had strayed from family tradition and fallen for Carol, a local white girl in search of the exotic, and much to his parent's chagrin, had married her within six months of their first date.

Ineffectual, unremarkable and somewhat of a "mummy's boy," Harpreet would privately admit that his son was a "little odd." From an early age, Anoop had developed an obsession with Elvis Presley. Slicking back his greasy black hair in the style of his idol, he'd even grown sideburns to match. Shut away in his bedroom, he'd watched videos of all those dreadful Elvis films back to back, and then played every record the King of rock n roll had ever made. When he looked in the mirror - which was often - he imagined he was Elvis. None of this did him any favours when it came to trying to make friends. As soon he was spotted approaching his peers, they would invariably sneer: "Here comes Paki Elvis!" before laughing and then turning their backs on him.

Anoop had failed to impress his hardworking parents and he'd struggled to make himself visible in stark comparison to his older sister. Uninterested in the family businesses, he'd left school with barely any qualifications and had drifted rudderless, seeking solace from his family's disapproval in the form of hard liquor. All but disowned by his parents and their hardworking community, he'd found no consolation from his new bride's family; who initially welcomed him, but behind his back pulled faces and made cruel comments about the smell of curry that emanated from his clothes and skin.

Anoop and Carol's marriage had been rocky to say the least. Apart from their cultural differences, Carol, a hard-working factory girl, had railed against her husband's fecklessness. By now drinking heavily, her exotic man had done little to impress her. He spent his days in front of the TV, making little if any attempt to find work. When he wasn't glued to the TV screen, he'd shut himself in the kitchen with a bottle of Scotch playing Elvis songs, over and over again. On the rare occasion that he did prise himself from the sofa and leave the house, it was either to sign on at the benefits office, or spend his wife's hard earned money at the bookies. To make matters worse, in 1977, his long-suffering wife fell pregnant.

In 1978, after a difficult labour, Balvinder Kapoor arrived by caesarean section. His father, although in attendance, was half-cut and virtually oblivious to Carol's discomfort and distress. To say that he was indifferent to his son's arrival wouldn't have been far wide of the mark.

Balvinder had grown up in the shadow of domestic violence, interspersed with the music of Elvis Presley drifting from behind the kitchen door. He'd gained some respite with his grandparents who, despite misgivings about their son's mixed marriage, had made an effort to try and instil some traditional values in their grandson. What they hadn't known was that their son had taken to sexually interfering with their grandson from an early age. As is typical with this kind of abuse, young Balvinder had assumed that his father's nightly visits to his bedroom were normal and in his ignorance, he'd submitted to his father's intrusive hands and bitten his pillow while his dad; stinking of Chivas Regal whisky, had brutally sodomised him.

Being such a loner at school, it hadn't been until Balvinder was twelve years old, that he'd begun to realise that what his father was doing to him wasn't normal, and he'd shyly broached the subject with his mum. Carol had gone ballistic and confronted Anoop. Telling him to: "Get the fuck out and never come back," she'd reported him to the police. Anoop's reaction to this had been to go on the run, where he'd spent time first in Bradford with a cousin, before fleeing to a school friend's house in Leicester, following a visit by officers from the West Yorkshire force.

The next bunch of cops to knock on the door of his hiding place had been from the Leicestershire Constabulary. They had made the mistake of not covering the back garden and just before they'd put in the door, he'd flung open the patio doors and made good his escape.

After garden hopping for several minutes, Anoop, feeling like a hunted animal, had emerged into a side-road flanked by blocks of dilapidated garages. Lifting the battered, graffiti-ridden up-and-over door of an unlocked garage, he'd winced as the noise of rusty metal wheels protested and screeched in their warped runners. Grabbing the frayed nylon rope on the back of the door and tugging it back down to the dog shit-littered floor, Anoop stood panting in the gloom of the filthy concrete box. From beneath his ripped trousers, he could feel blood trickling down his shins. He winced from the stinging of his skin; shredded by the barbs of sprawling bramble bushes growing wild in the last garden he'd ran through, before crashing through it's rotten fence and ending up at the garage block.

Later, when the sounds of cop's voices had long since receded, and night had fallen; Anoop warily emerged from his stinking hiding place. During the long hours he'd spent waiting for the sun to go down, it had occurred to the paedophile fugitive, that the overgrown garden he'd last run through, might belong to an unoccupied house where he could hide out for a while. Slinking back over the creaking fence, he'd circumnavigated the vicious bramble bushes and grown-over children's toys, before finding a way into the empty house via the kitchen door at the back. At some point, the local housing authority had half-heartedly boarded up the windows and doors until the money could be found to refurbish the place. All of the windows at the front of the house remained secure, but the sheet of chipboard securing the back door had been ripped off - either by local dossers in search of a dry place to drink their cider - or else by kids, drawn as all kids are, to derelict buildings.

Either way, previous visitors to the house had made it easy for it's latest trespasser to get in: stealthily pushing his way through into the kitchen, his shoes crunching and sliding around on the broken glass that lay underfoot. The un-aired interior was musky with the smell of mould and human faeces, and unable to see past his hand, Anoop lit a match to feel his way through the gloom.

Tentatively making his way up the rotting staircase, Anoop felt his way to the back of the old house, and into what ironically, had once been a children's nursery. Once inside, he backed up to a wall and slid down onto the floor where, with legs drawn up close to his body, and arms wrapped around his bruised knees, he shivered away what was left of the night.

He must have fallen asleep at some point as, sometime in the early hours, when the grey Leicestershire sky began to be suffused with the mauves and pinks of a new day, he awoke with a start to the sound of the only other occupant of the deserted house: a trapped pigeon, cooing and beating it's wings somewhere above him in the exposed rafters.

Rubbing his cramped limbs, Anoop felt wretched. He hadn't eaten for over twenty-four hours and his lips were cracked from thirst. If only those fuckin' bramble bushes had been in season, he could have at least found some consolation from their painful thorns by eating the berries. He decided to at least try and find something to drink, and tentatively descending the stairs, he made his way back to the kitchen and peered out into the back garden.

It was drizzling with light rain outside, and he could hear the drip-drip of water somewhere to his right. Keeping low to avoid being seen by the early morning riser silhouetted in the bathroom window opposite, he sought out the source of the dripping sound. Tripping over rusting and weed-entangled bicycle frames, he triumphantly discovered a water butt still connected to the guttering of what was left of the roof. Ripping off the plastic lid, he plunged his grimy hands into the cool water

73

and scooped it into his mouth. When he'd drunk his fill, he slunk fox-like back to his hiding place where, sitting on an upturned bucket, he took stock of his situation.

He'd run out of places to run to and daren't show himself for fear of arrest. He was hungry, cold and out of options. Even his bitch of a barrister sister couldn't help him now. If caught, he'd be arrested and interviewed, and regardless of whether he gave a "No comment" interview, there was no way he'd get bail; not after he'd done a runner, not when he might pose a threat to witnesses... No, he'd definitely be remanded in police custody while charging advice could be sought from the CPS. Once charged, he'd be put before the next available court with the strong recommendation that he be further remanded.

To be remanded by the court, meant only one thing - he'd be taken by prison van to Wormwood Scrubs or Wandsworth, and once there, he'd be placed on the "nonce's" wing. Word would spread like wildfire that a "kiddie fiddler" had arrived, and he'd be lucky to escape with snot snorted into his food. If he was unlucky, he'd be slashed with a double razor "shank," designed to make a wide wound that would be difficult to stitch. He might even be killed.

The enormity of his situation percolated his brain in acidic little drips, and there, sat on a bucket in the damp gloom of a dilapidated house in Leicester; he buried his face in his hands and began to cry. With tears making salty tracks down his filthy ashen face, his body became wracked with uncontrollable sobbing, and for the first time since he could remember, he wailed for his mother. When the tears and self-pity had subsided, Balvinder's disgraced father made a decision...

Getting up from his bucket, he made his way out of the nursery and onto the landing. Looking upwards, he found what he was looking for. There, yawning above him in the gloom was the open hatch to the loft. Climbing onto the banister, he tottered precariously on the wobbling beam and reached up into the loft-space to grab hold of the wet, slimy hatch frame. His skinny arms trembling with the effort, he hauled himself up into the loft. Once up there, he sat panting from his exertion on a wooden joist. There were enough missing roof tiles to let the watery dawn light into the loft. It pooled balefully on the mouse-infested fibreglass insulation material, allowing Anoop to take in his surroundings.

His eyes settled on a flyblown length of electrical cord, tacked to a rafter, from which hung the remains of a chipped enamelled light shade. Jumping up, he grabbed the shade. With a groan, it gave way, and along with the cord, was ripped from it's rusty and redundant electrical connectors. Staggering under the momentum of the freed cord, Anoop fell backwards, before sitting heavily back down on a joist.

Undoing the screw cap from the crumbling Bakelite light socket, he let the shade fall to the floor, before stripping the rest of the fitting from the cord.

His mind now on autopilot, Anoop tied the cable to the joist nearest the loft hatch opening and tugged on it until the knot tightened. Letting the loose end drop through the hatch, he saw that it was short of the landing below by about six feet. Leaving it dangling, he tightrope-walked along the loft's joists until he reached the brick wall that formed the right-hand apex of the house. Once there, he sat down with his back to the cobwebbed wall and closed his gritty eyes.

Summoning the vestiges of a long-forgotten religion, he recalled the Kirhan Sohila - song of peace and Sikh bedtime prayer, and the last of the Panj Bania or five daily prayers. Gently rocking the top half of his body, he began the hymn:

'God is only one

He is obtained by the grace of the first Guru...'

He couldn't remember the middle part of the bedtime prayer, but continued with the end part...

'I, your servant, pray that

I may become the dust of the Saint's feet - And join the society of Saints...'

Opening his eyes, Anoop removed the Kara from his wrist. A steel bracelet, it was the only part of the five Kakars, or external articles of faith, that he wore. Feeling at peace for the first time in his life, he stood up and walked back along the joists to the hatch opening. Stooping, he pulled the cord back up into the loft space and fashioned a crude loop out of the free end. Sitting on the edge of the hatch, he placed the loop around his neck, then, inching along on his behind, he put both hands on either side of the hatch frame, used them to take the weight of his body, and lowered himself through the hole, supported only by his puny, shaking arms.

Closing his eyes, in one movement, he lifted his hands and drew his arms to his body before dropping down towards the landing below. A millisecond later, the cord around his neck violently arrested his fall, causing his twitching body to swing pendulum-like for a few minutes. With his life force ebbing away, the results of his last involuntary bowel movement: a foul-smelling brown liquid, trickled down his legs and made a plinking sound as it hit a discarded beer can on the dusty floor below before forming mercury-like beads with the dust and pigeon feathers.

*

Twenty-two years after his disgraced father's death, and while UX646 ate their refs in their Filebridge office; Balvinder Kapoor boarded a bus to Hazelworth. The cops were well and truly alerted to his compulsion on the streets of Cranston and it was time to move to pastures new...

Chapter Four

'So, your dad's a Gurkha - and you're a shirker...'

Skipper Jarvis brought refs to a close:

'Right, let's go out and do a bit.'

For the BTF, "doing a bit," meant climbing back aboard their carrier and returning to either their tasking area - if they had one that day - or, to generally resume patrol of the borough. Whilst out and about, they'd look for known criminals to stop and speak with, before making the decision whether to search them or not. In most cases, hands in pockets, was *de rigueur*. Every now and then at least one bag of weed would be found, and if they were lucky, a stolen credit card or weapon of some kind would be unearthed. If they were found to be clean; but stinking of weed, they'd be hauled off to the nearest nick for a strip search.

A rich seam of criminality to be tapped into, were the drug dealers and their runners who operated from betting shops under the guise of ordinary punters. With the help of the CCTV operators, the cops were sometimes lucky enough to blindside the lookouts and sneak up on the dealers.

The main dealers of class A drugs in Houndshale weren't fools, and were well versed with the charging standards required by the CPS. They knew, that in order for a charge of possession with intent to supply to be authorised; not only would large quantities of drugs have to found on them, but the lawyers would also insist on other corroborating evidence of supply.

To get around the risk of a potential fourteen-year prison sentence for supply, they'd make sure that they were never caught with any more than two or three deals: "a bit of personal." The way they tended to operate, was to keep a stash nearby - grill- covered air-conditioning outlets, were favourite - especially as they tended to be hidden down alleyways, away from prying eyes.

Arriving at the betting shop, the addict would be met by the dealer, who would lead him into the alley to access his stash. Once he'd dealt a rock or two and taken the money, he would emerge from the alley clean as a whistle, claiming to have gone there to take a piss.

As the twenty-pound notes mounted up in his pocket, the dealer would launder them through the bookie's shop, exchanging them for fifty-pound notes. As most single deals were of the twenty-pound variety, this was yet another tactic employed to frustrate the cops and prevent them gathering evidence of supply. Sometimes a dealer would keep a couple of deals to hand, and if the cops appeared, he'd simply put the wraps in his mouth.

If he had to, he would swallow them and retrieve them later. He may even keep them up his arse - after all, crack addicts are desperate people, and non too fussy about where their fix had been!

UX646 had barely left the back yard, when the Cat, oblivious to the moans and groans of his captive audience, embarked on one of his soliloquies:

'I watched air crash investigations the other night...'

Before he realised what he'd done, Jax, who'd seen a documentary on the Busby Babes' air crash, in which most of the Manchester United team were killed at Munich, chimed in with:

'Did you see the Busby Babes thing?'

Seeing the triumphant glint in the Cat's eye, he could have bitten off his own tongue. The rest of the team heaved a sigh of relief when they realised that they could now ignore the Cat: Jax having well and truly taken the bait. *Of course* the Cat had seen the Busby thing!

'Why the fuck did I ask you that?' asked Jax miserably as the Cat, laughing out loud, went on to tell Jax all about the properties of aircraft black boxes.

'Do you know Jax, that black boxes aren't black at all - guess what colour they are?'

'Just tell me Cat, I can't bear the suspense any longer!'

'Yellow - you know - so they can be easily found. Actually,' he continued, 'there was a crash back in 1987, where the black box was never found...'

Mercifully, Jax was spared any more on boxes, black or otherwise, by a shout from Intel: 'There's Dhama!'

Dipendra Gurung Dhama was a Nepalese heroin addict, and son of an ex-Gurkha soldier. The actress Joanna Lumley: whose father served as an officer in a Gurkha regiment during the Second World War, fought and won a campaign to allow ex-Gurkhas and their families to settle in Britain. Well meaning as she'd been, it was a sentimental and naïve venture.

Old Gurkhas back in Nepal were misled by the rumour, that all they had to do was to literally arrive at Heathrow airport, where they'd be met, given a house and immediate access to benefits. Understandably, they flocked to the UK, only to find there was no such provision in place, and a great deal of them ended up thousands of miles from home in dire straights.

Houndshale had it's fair share of these brave old warriors, and quite a few young Nepali families too. Away from the strict upbringing of their homeland, the Gurkha kids roamed the streets of Cranston in gangs. It was more a case of safety in numbers than being part of some violent gang, and when stopped by the police, they were politeness personified. Unfortunately, and inexplicably, a lot of the kids trapped between the traditions of their fathers' and life on London's streets, turned to heroin.

While the old and bold soldiers sat at home trapped in a world that to them, might just have well been another planet, their kids roamed the rat-infested streets of Houndshale in search of something to help them escape the reality of their situation.

Intel may have been largely devoid of personality, but he had a good memory for names and faces, and upon his shout, they'd piled out of the carrier to stop Dhama. Dynamo was first out and put the stop in.

'How's it going Dipendra?'

Looking sheepish, the young Nepali cast his eyes downward.

'OK sir.'

'You got anything on you, you shouldn't have?'

This was the usual prelude to a search, and was usually trotted out by the cops upon stopping known players. Regardless of whether there was anything to be found, it was mostly answered with a "no"

The law dictates, that upon announcing a cop's intention to search someone or their vehicle, the mnemonic GOWISELY must first be employed. That is to say that the grounds and object of the search must be announced, a warrant card for non-uniformed officers has to be shown, and identity given. The station to which they are attached must also be given, followed by the information that they are entitled to a copy of the search record. The legal power used has to be stated and the subject must also be informed that: 'you are being detained for the purpose of a search.'

Some cops trotted this out easily, some fitted it into the general conversation, while others: struggling with a reluctant detainee - or even chasing them down the street, didn't bother to go beyond telling them they were being detained.

During the general preamble, along with asking Dhama what he was up to, Dynamo asked him if he was still at college or whether he was working. When he gave the stock Houndshale reply of 'Not at the moment', the Cat seized his chance for a quip. Quick as a flash, before Dynamo could begin his search, he chipped in with:

'So, your dad's a Gurkha - and *you're* a shirker!'

In the event, apart from the twenty-pound note he'd yet to spend on "brown," with which to escape the drudgery of Houndshale, Dhama appeared clean and so was spared the ignominy of a strip search and sent on his way. Dynamo was feeling philosophical:

'We've no idea what a desperate life these junkies live really,' he said to nobody in particular.

'Yeah,' mused Jax. 'It's bad enough running out of smokes!'

'Someone like Dhama,' continued Dynamo, 'Ever since opening his eyes in the morning, his every waking hour revolves around getting his next hit. So, he pawns another bit of his mum's jewellery, gets twenty quid, and contacts his dealer. After being fucked around for an hour by the dealer, he manages to get a bit of brown and hurries home along the backstreets to smoke it. Even before he takes it, he's euphoric to have it in his pocket - the anticipation of his high is almost as good as actually getting high. All he's thinking about is getting home, finding a bit of tin foil and smoking his way to heroin heaven.'

No one interrupted Dynamo's soliloquy. Jax merely nodded; trying to imagine what it must be like for hopeless addicts such as Dhama - what they must go through every day: that frantic, desperate need to get enough cash to get that first hit. The all-consuming need to get that shit into your system at all costs...

The big man continued thinking aloud. 'So there you are, almost home when boom! - around the corner comes the Old Bill! You didn't have time to swallow it and before you know it, coppers who know you're a smack head surround you. They're holding your arms and going through your pockets. They find your wrap of brown, nick you, slap the cuffs on and take you in. One minute you're imagining your high and the next minute you're in a cell with some fucker looking up your arse and under your bollocks! They've snatched away your gear and left you in a cell clucking and wishing you were dead. And I'm not even joking!'

There were a few nods, but Emma was the only one who could think of anything to say.

'Yeah babes,' she called from the back seat. 'Fuck that!'

Trundling along the backstreets of Cranston in search of the elusive Asian gold burglars, Jax and the team went into carrier mode. This was a mixture of cyber loafing cops hunched over their iphone screens, conversations that inevitably revolved around the subject of sex, and sneaky anonymous farts. The latter would be released to shouts of: 'Dirty bastard!' and the sound of windows and side door being opened. If the fart had been proudly laid by the Cat, and identified by his giggles, windows and doors usually weren't enough to dispel the foetid results of his protein shakes, and Jax would have to switch on the extractor fan to expel the persistent fug.

Every now and then, a car featured in the daily briefing would be spotted and pursued by Jax. This would put the team on alert and cause the Cat to reluctantly close down the website featuring celebrity tits and Emma would end her domestic tiff over the phone. Intel would be inputting the car's details into his palm held device, while Dynamo would sigh and put away his plastic box, from which he'd been shovelling pasta and tuna into his mouth.

Today, the car "put up" by Jax, was being driven by Albie White: a prolific offender when it came to all things motoring. He was always worth a stop, but stopping him usually came at a price. Once he'd got behind him, Jax put on the blue lights and gave a quick burst of siren.

As with all those indignant about being frequently

stopped by the police, Albie braked violently before swerving into a bus stop. True to form, he immediately leapt out of his car. Puffing out his pigeon chest, while doing a good impression of a man carrying carpets under his skinny tattooed arms, he made a feeble attempt at emphasising non-existent *latissimus dorsi*, and strode angrily towards the carrier. 'What! Why are you always harassing me?' The diversionary tactics had begun...

By the time cops, who'd not come across him before, had spent just two minutes listening to him whinge and complain about being stopped, they tended to regret ever having seen him:

'Haven't you got anything better to do than stop me? Shouldn't you be catching burglars, rapists, child molesters?'

The litany of outrage seemed endless, but to those conversant with the ways of Albie White, his aggressive behaviour was recognised as being part of his game - mostly a smokescreen to try and divert the cop's attention from what he was up to. What he "was up to" today, was driving around in a death trap of a car displaying a tax disc clearly issued to another car, but with his own registration crudely written over the top. Had Albie been bright enough - and nobody could accuse him of being bright - he'd have chosen an out of date tax disc to tamper with - that way, he wouldn't have been committing fraud.

Crime of the century it wasn't, but given the lack of burglars to catch, Jax decided to take him in:

'I'm arresting you on suspicion...' he began. Albie, his voice, filled with indignant disbelief interrupted:

'You're havin' a fuckin' laugh aren't you officer? Aw c'mon guv, don't nick me for that, it's bullshit!'

'...Of fraud,' continued Jax while taking out his handcuffs and putting the protesting Albie into front stack. He wasn't a happy bunny. Jax continued with the official part of the arrest:

'You do not have to say anything, but it may harm your defence if you do not mention when questioned something which you later rely on in court. Anything you do say may be given in evidence'

'Right, I want a solicitor and I'm goin' no comment!'

Jax had heard it all before: it was all part of the game. 'And...I want to see a fuckin' doctor, I've got a heart condition!' Albie was pulling out all the stops, in a last ditch attempt to be let off. This was criminal speak for: "I'm going to be a right royal pain in the arse, so you might as well let me go!"

'Whatever Albie, get in the van'

Securing a place at Houndshale custody suite over the radio, and putting the offending tax disc into his pocket, Jax drove the protesting Albie to the nick where he'd be booked in, processed and interviewed.

Just as he drove the carrier under the barrier pole and manoeuvred it into a vacant space, his radio squawked to life:

'No units shown free on the RDW. A unit now please, for an immediate fear for welfare. LAS report a male seen self-harming at 60 Finch Close Spentford. More to follow. Units on the "I" India please'

There had been no other takers for the call generated by the London Ambulance Service. All other units were either busy at other calls, in having refs, or else ignoring the radio. The resource display window on the radio operator's screen was blank - ostensibly; there were no more troops left in the box.

In such cases, when there was nobody else to run to "I" calls, the BTF tended to help out, and having no particular desire to assist Jax with his gobby prisoner, they put up for the call.

Hustling Albie out of the carrier, the skipper took Jax's place at the wheel and left him to escort his prisoner into the custody cage in the back yard. Jax just about heard Intel chime in with: 'There's a CRIMINT on for

Finch Close...' before his monotone voice was drowned out by the skipper sticking on the carrier's "blues and twos." Shooting out of the back gate in a cloud of choking diesel smoke, UX646 quite happily left Jax to deal with Albie alone.

Once in the cage, Albie became a bit more cooperative, and realising that having a solicitor would delay his interview and eventual release, he told Jax that he now wanted neither legal representation nor medical attention, and was there any chance of a quick smoke? Jax rewarded Albie's compliance with a cigarette, upon which, the grateful Albie sucked while standing underneath the No Smoking sign. Jax settled in for the wait while a cop with an earlier arrest stood before the custody sergeant's desk and waited to bail his prisoner.

Peeking through the yellow bars that led into the custody area, Jax realised with dismay, that the custody skipper on duty was sergeant Blake. He was a nice enough bloke, but God, did he take his time. He procrastinated over every procedure and didn't seem to be able to concentrate on any one thing. Rumour had it - although Jax had never witnessed it - that Blake, was a victim of narcolepsy and had been known, without warning, to take an impromptu sleep during the booking in procedure! If he did manage to stay awake, he'd often excuse himself halfway through, announce that he was off to: "feed the chickens," before wandering into the back yard for a smoke!

As he waited to be called in, Jax heard the rest of his team TOA at the self-harm call. TOA meant time of arrival at an incident, and upon arriving at a call, TOA was generally put up over the radio so that a box relating to response times could be ticked.

More importantly: this quick radio transmission let the operator know that a unit had arrived at what potentially could be a dangerous situation. TOA also served to tell other units where their colleagues were should they shout for back up.

More cynical cops, mindful of what could be a pain in the arse call, would let it "marinade" for a few minutes until someone else got there. Once TOA was broadcast; secure in the knowledge that traditionally, the first to arrive would be lumbered with the jobs' paperwork, they'd turn up - blue lights blazing - as though they had just busted a gut to arrive first. In this case though, there had been enough cops on scene, in the form of UX646.

Stuck in the custody cage at Houndshale, Jax wished he hadn't been saddled with Albie and his fraudulent tax disc. The self-harm call sounded a lot more promising than spending the next couple of hours processing his prisoner.

Skipper Blake cut into his reverie with a cheery: 'Ok Jax, bring him in,' and pushing open the heavy yellow cage door, before the skipper changed his mind and went out for a smoke, Jax ushered his prisoner inside and Blake began his booking-in pre-amble:

'I am the custody officer. I am independent of the investigation and responsible for your welfare whilst you are at this police station. This officer is going to tell me the reason for your arrest. I will listen to the officer's account and then decide whether it is necessary to detain you further at this police station'

Blake looked up from his computer screen. This was Jax's cue to give the circumstances of the arrest - or "circs" - as it is known in the trade. The spiel would begin with an outline of the offence for which the suspect had been arrested, the time and place of arrest, and the officer's justification for not dealing with the offence out on the street. The latter was a multiple choice option from the SOCPA menu and included such reasons as: "to enable the name of the person to be ascertained, to prevent loss or damage to property, to prevent the prosecution from being hindered by the disappearance of the suspect et cetera." The main catch-all favourite, and the easiest to remember, was: "to allow the prompt and effective investigation of the offence." Jax rarely deviated from this reason.

Taking the incriminating tax disc from his pocket and putting it on the custody desk, Jax began:

'Sarge, this is Albie White' - not that Albie needed introducing to any of the Houndshale cops. 'I stopped him driving a car in which he was displaying a fraudulent tax disc.'

Skipper Blake nodded affably while making scribbled notes, and Jax was about to continue, when quick as a flash, Albie shouted: 'what tax disc?' before grabbing the circular piece of paper, putting it into his mouth, and chewing furiously before swallowing the evidence with a painful-sounding gulp! The skipper, head down in his note writing, didn't appear to notice what had happened until Jax, caught out by the oldest trick in the book said in a deadpan voice:

'Sarge, he's just eaten the tax disc.'

Sergeant Blake, looked up from his notes, managed to utter a: 'what...?' before opening and closing his mouth like a beached trout. Flushing crimson, he scratched his grey head and rummaged in his shirt pockets for cigarettes. Jax offered a silent prayer that he wasn't about to go and feed the chickens!

It hadn't been the first time that a prisoner had seized the opportunity to swallow an unwary officer's exhibit, and rookies the land over, had learned the hard way to keep evidence well and truly out of reach. Jax should have known better - this was day one stuff! It was just as well it hadn't been a wrap of class A - that would have meant a trip to accident and emergency and a lengthy and miserable wait while doctors gave the all clear. In the event, he'd actually found the whole thing quite comical - what with the look on the skipper's face, and the absurdity of the situation; it had taken quite an effort not to have burst out laughing!

His composure restored, the skipper continued with his booking-in questions:

'Have you been arrested before?'

Albie's mouth may have still been dry from his snack on the Queen's stationary, but not so dry that he couldn't manage a quip or two: 'I've been nicked loads of times sarge - I've done more porridge than the three bears!'

'Are you dependent on drugs or alcohol?'

'What - like sniffing glue you mean? Nah, fuck that, I'd only come to a sticky end!'

Albie, happy in the knowledge that he'd eaten the evidence, was on good form. 'Get us a coffee will ya officer? I've got a mouth like the bottom of a budgie's cage!'

Entertaining though his prisoner was, Jax was beginning to tire of him and just wanted to get his arrest notes written up and get back out. 'You can have a coffee Albie, but not until you've been booked in, so let's stop mucking around and crack on.'

'Alright guv, but you might as well let me go; you ain't got shit on me now!'

'Albie,' began Jax wearily,' this custody suite is wired for sound and vision and your actions are recorded on CCTV. Furthermore, your dodgy tax disc will not only be recorded in *my* statement, but also in the statements of at least four other officers.' Alfie shrugged.

'Whatever officer, can I have a coffee now?'

*

While Jax wrote up his arrest notes on Albie's heinous tax disc offences, UX646 were outside 60 Finch Close, working out the best plan of approach. The latest over the radio had suggested that a male inside was armed with a knife and was intent on harming himself. He was said to be at the back of the apartment in the kitchen.

The address was a first floor maisonette with the

entrance at the rear and accessed via a flight of wooden steps that opened out onto a kind of decked area on stilts. From the decking, the kitchen window: which was without blinds or curtains, was clearly visible. Loud music in the mournful form of REM was heard coming from inside and the skipper sent Dynamo up the steps to investigate.

Keeping as low as his bulk would allow, Dynamo sneaked up the steps and peered tentatively through the window. He'd seen some weird and wonderful sights in his time, but this topped the lot: there, dressed in tight skirt, pretty blouse, and wearing a blonde wig: was a *man*. If Dynamo had been in any doubt as to his gender, this was immediately dispelled when he saw what the cross-dresser was doing.

His skirt hitched up, he stood close to a worktop traditionally used to chop vegetables on. But... there wasn't a carrot in sight! Instead, the man in a skirt, was holding his penis down on the worktop with one hand, while with the other, he was sawing at it's base with a knife! Tearing himself away from the eye-watering sight, the big man turned to his expectant audience below and shouted: 'He's doing it! He's cutting his knob off!'

With a collective exclamation of: 'fuck me!' UX646 scrambled for the carrier and while the Cat and Emma unloaded a couple of long shields, the others hastily donned gloves and as much protective gear as was immediately to hand. Dynamo, the silence of his initial approach abandoned, clattered back down the wooden steps and grabbed the enforcer from the back of the carrier. Hastily putting a plan together, the skipper tasked Dynamo with putting the back door in and then instructed the Cat and Emma to link shields and burst into the kitchen. Once inside, they were to rush and subdue the cross dressing lunatic. When he'd been secured, Intel and the skipper would handcuff him and they'd take it from there.

Dashing back up the steps, with the Cat and Emma in tow, Dynamo was about to swing the enforcer when the skipper hissed: 'Try the door handle.' You never knew whether a door might be open. In the heat of the moment many an unlocked door had been trashed! Sure enough, as soon as Dynamo wrenched the handle down, it flew open almost causing him to fall flat on his face inside! Standing aside, he let the shield entry team fly past him and into the kitchen. The music had been turned up so loud, that man/woman appeared to have been taken completely by surprise. Cannoning into him, Emma and the Cat pushed him away from the worktop and up against the nearest wall. In the process, his penis whipped off the worktop, adding grazes to the cuts he'd already made. The knife clattered to the floor where it was instinctively kicked away by Dynamo. The skipper yelled at the man; his ashen face squashed flat by the plastic shield:

'Put your arms out to the side! - Do it now!'

'OK, OK!' the female wannabe wailed. 'Tell your gorillas to let me go, they're hurting me!'

'Put your arms out to the side and we'll take the shields away.'

Lifting his arms, lady/man complied with the skipper's instructions, and slipping a cuff onto his left wrist, he signalled for Emma and the Cat to release the pressure just enough to get him turned around. With his face against the wall, the skipper could now grab his other hand and cuff him in a rear stack. Withdrawing slightly, the shield team held their shields at the ready while Dynamo, who had just returned from the heavily perfumed front room, where he had been figuring out a way to silence REM, joined up with Intel to give the man a thorough search.

With matey now out of danger, the next thing to do was to work out what powers of detention to use to get him to a place of safety. They'd entered the apartment under Section 17 - to save life or limb - and although the obvious thing to do under these circumstances would have been to section him under Section 136 of the Mental Health Act and take him to hospital; 136 is a power that should only be used in a public place, as oppose to inside a dwelling.

They were just considering employing the fictional "ways and means act," to drag him outside in order to section him in a public place, when Intel - who else - remembered a newly introduced piece of legislation designed for such cases. The Mental Capacity Act stated, that if the police or ambulance service are of the opinion that someone needs to see a doctor but refuses to do so, it can be assumed that their ability to use reason is impaired. They can then be detained against their will and taken to a place of treatment. Once outside, Section 136 can be brought into play - job done!

With Cat and Emma taking the cross dresser out to the carrier, Dynamo and Intel went through the apartment to make sure that they were leaving it secure. In the bedroom, they found what could only be described as a do it yourself surgeon's kit. In a black plastic box, they found a selection of surgical grade knives, saws and pliers-type implements. It later transpired that the man in a dress: who had been turned down for gender reassignment, had previously castrated himself. He'd used the surgical kit to slit open his scrotum before removing his testes and flushing them down the toilet! Little wonder, the reassignment shrinks had found it necessary to reject his application pending psychiatric tests!

Sitting forlornly in the back of the carrier, his wig askew, man/woman was a pitiful sight. It wasn't too difficult to sympathise with his predicament. After all, the cops of UX646 - as happily heterosexual as they come - could have no idea of the mental torment of someone who agonised daily over being a woman trapped in a man's body. The Cat summed it up succinctly, with: 'If I had a pair of tits *and* a cock, I'd be in heaven!'

With the heady perfume of their 136 patient filling the carrier, and mercifully masking the Cat's farts, they drove the couple of miles to Hazelworth and The Florence, where they hoped to deposit their detainee at one of The Aspens' mental health wards.

Theoretically, providing the paperwork was all in order, The Aspens were duty-bound to admit those sectioned by police under Section 136. In practice, however, they would find all manner of reasons not to take on the extra work. The nurses had been known to meet the cops at the entrance to the wards, with a device not unlike the ones used by the cops, with which to measure the level of alcohol in a potential patient's body. If they could get away with it, they would try and say that the detainee's behaviour was down to nothing other than the influence of alcohol.

In the case of man/woman: although he'd certainly had a few drinks, attempting to give himself a sex change was beyond the actions of a sane person. Whether he was pissed or not, and despite the nurse's triumphant declaration that he was under the influence of alcohol, the skipper had sent her off to get a manager. Shrugging haughtily, she'd gone off to find one.

When he'd finally been persuaded to leave his warm office, the manager of Robin ward hadn't been much more helpful than his nurse had been. Latching on to the fact that man/woman was bleeding, he stated flatly, that he wouldn't be admitted on to his ward without first being treated for his self-inflicted injury. This meant that the cops would now have to escort, and then stay with their charge until such times as he could be seen by one of The Florence's overworked doctors.

Given no choice but to take him to A&E, the skipper acquiesced and drove around the block to the main hospital entrance. The only advantage to being a cop in these situations was that hospital staff allowed them to bring a patient directly to a cubicle instead of waiting in line in the reception area. Going through the side entrance reserved for ambulance crews and emergency patients, UX646 settled down for the long haul.

It was at this point that man/woman started to become a pain in the arse, and once they had transferred him to a cubicle and onto a trolley, he began to complain and try to leave the hospital. In handcuffs, he didn't present too much of a problem, but handcuffed or not, he still made several lame attempts to get off the trolley. It was all for show of course, and presumably, he'd hoped that his latest self-surgery exploits would get back to the psychiatrists who would ultimately make the decision on his sex change op. Privately, the cops had known, that far from accelerate his operation, his actions on that day would more than likely delay - if not permanently - shelve his aspirations to become a female.

It hadn't taken more than two cops to keep him pinioned to his trolley. They worked out a rota system of twenty minutes on restraint duty, and forty minutes off. Waits in A&E had been routinely known to last up to four hours or more, and their improvised shift system, had made it just about bearable. After a couple of hours though, it began to dawn on them that although they'd dropped Jax and his tax disc prisoner like third period French; he was probably the one who'd ended up with the better deal.

*

Back at Houndshale nick, Jax, had been interviewing Albie. Due to the fact that the interview was tape recorded, he hadn't had his radio turned on. He'd been oblivious to the trials and tribulations of his comrades, and once he'd bailed Albie, he'd decided to get a quick bite to eat before settling down to complete the prosecution file that would accompany Albie to court.

Climbing the stairs to the canteen, Jax pushed open the double swing-doors and entered to the sound of Sky news and the relaxed banter of cops on refs. Cut backs had ensured that the actual canteen had long since closed down, sending the jovial and long-serving West Indian serving ladies off to join the unemployment line. It was still known as the canteen, but was now little more than an eating area with a TV and microwave. Vending machines dispensing decidedly unhealthy fare such as crisps and chocolate, lined the back wall along with machines that for 50 pence, would dole out vile-tasting dishwater - not remotely related to the coffee beans so attractively depicted on the front of the machine.

Apart from the odd health-conscious calorie counters with their Tupperware boxes of tuna and rice, the majority of meals in front of the cops were of the polystyrene takeaway container variety. Big Mac boxes competed with Subway and KFC wrappers, while the soggy white paper that had held kebabs and fries, lay discarded on grubby tables - the same tables, upon which, officers wrote up their notes and bagged up the kind of exhibits not entirely conducive to food hygiene: smelly training shoes, sweaty hooded tops and used hypodermic needles.

In the far corner, sitting among the ruins of a chicken carcass, Jax spied the self-styled "Kenyan cowboy." Billy Kimathi was from the Kenyan Kikuyu tribe and was always good for a hilarious story from his days as a cop back home. Built like a brick shithouse, Billy had a broad forehead, criss-crossed with scars, and a nose that was practically flat against his face. It seemed as though he couldn't decide which hairstyle to adopt - alternating between shaved to the bone, and wild, unkempt Afro. It had to be said that, the Kenyan Cowboy really didn't suit an Afro - that just made him look crazy!

Flashing Jax a huge grin, that revealed an unfeasibly

94

large gap between his two front teeth, Billy pulled out his ipod buds. Interrupting the flow of his beloved country and western music that had been piping into his ears, the big African beckoned him over:

'Jaarx,' he drawled. Jax clapped him on the shoulders: 'What's that shit you're listening to Billy?'

'George Strait - he's good man' - and before he could stop him, Billy launched into the lyrics to his favourite song:

'All my ex's live in Texas,

And Texas is a place I'd dearly love to be.

But all my ex's live in Texas,

And that's why I hang my hat in Tennessee...'

The Kenyan cowboy did *not* have the voice of an angel! Jax pulled a pained face. 'Yeah Billy - that's very good. You should be on stage - sweeping the fucker!'

Beaming, the Kenyan randomly asked: 'Do you know what to do if you see a leo-paard?'

'No mate, what should I do if I come across a leopard on my way home?'

His answer, when it eventually came, was as enigmatic as most of Billy's advice tended to be:

'Well...' he began. 'If you have a dog with you - you're fucked!'

'Hmm... I'll be sure to bear that in mind Billy!'

Leaving the Kenyan cowboy mangling George Strait's lyrics, Jax went over to the drinks machine, put in a coin, then watched in frustration as the machine - quite clearly out of cups, dispensed his tea down the drain. Trying his luck with the neighbouring coke machine, he stuck his ready meal into the microwave and watched the clock count down before fishing out the lava-hot Sicilian pasta. By the time he had managed to get a drink and heat up his refs, Billy had gone back out on patrol and returning to the table, still strewn with Billy's chicken bones, Jax sat down to his meal.

His scalding hot meal wolfed down and washed the

rest of it's way into his stomach with burp-inducing cola, Jax took out his phone and checked out the latest ramblings on facebook. Scrolling through updates posted by those who felt the need to constantly let everyone know what mood they were in, he was pleasantly distracted by Houndshale's fragrant-smelling queen of the rumour mill: Becky Thomas.

'Y'awight Jax?'

In possession of the largest surgically enhanced breasts Jax had ever seen, Becky may have been full of rumour and gossip, but with those assets, she could have told him any old shit. More than just a heavy flirt - and to quote the Cat - 'That girl knows her way around a cock,' she was a welcome distraction from the requests for "likes" on facebook.

Jax looked up, but as usual didn't get much further than her neck. He addressed her weapons of mass destruction: 'Yeah, I'm alright Becks - you?'

'I see Porridge Face is coming to your team'

'Really?' This was one rumour he hoped she'd got wrong. 'Who told you that?'

'He told me himself, reckons he had the nod from your guvnor.'

'Yeah, right - if *he* told you that it *must* be true!'

Jax had good reason to be cynical; Tam "Porridge Face" Morris, never let the truth get in the way of a good story - if you told him you'd been to Tenerife - he'd been to Eleven-erife. He could have easily been known as Billy Liar, but it was his face that had given birth to his nickname of Porridge Face.

A bad bout of teenage acne had left scars on his face that made his skin look not too dissimilar to a bowl of cold lumpy porridge. On any given day though, if asked, he was capable of producing a whole host of reasons for the state of his face. These ranged from: It had been caused during the Iraq war, while he shielded a woman and her children from an exploding grenade - to:

his face had been dragged along the road while hanging on to the fender of an armed robber's getaway car following a bank job.

While he was digesting Beck's latest unpalatable rumour, the rest of UX646 - finally released from The Florence, trooped in and when he finally managed to drag the Cat's blatant attention away from Becky's tits, he passed the rumour on. Almost as one, their mouths fell open accompanied by disbelieving shouts of: 'You must be fuckin' joking!'

'I heard he was on the waiting list...' chimed Intel.

All eyes swivelled to the skipper. Emma, not in the least bit impressed by Becky's breasts, was the first to speak: 'Skip - we can't have that tosser on the team! You're gonna' have to speak to The Man!'

Putting up his hands to quell the growing outrage, skipper Jarvis assured them that he would take it up with the guvnor - but could everyone *please* get on with writing up "use of force" notes for man/woman?

Dynamo sat in the seat vacated by the Kenyan cowboy, and took out his two-hourly meal of chicken salad.

'You missed out on a right twat with him Jacko - he was trying to cut his cock off, and I'm not even joking!'

Becky giggled and wandered off to spread alarm and despondency elsewhere while Jax sat back to listen to the team's stories about the man who wanted to be a woman and had flushed his bollocks down the drain to prove it. Once they'd regaled him with tales of self-surgery, Jax told them all about Albie and how his appetite for tax discs had almost put the custody skipper into cardiac arrest! Emma thought it was hilarious.

'Babes! That's priceless! - I bet he went straight out to feed the chickens!'

'Fuckin' bloke's a nightmare! Still think I got the better deal though - spending a few hours in A&E holding down a man in a dress, really *isn't* my idea of fun!'

While UX646 had been dealing with the man in a wig and the tax disc muncher, Balvinder Kapoor had been lurking in a Hazelworth bus shelter waiting for some unsuspecting female to appear. His paraphilia was progressing. Flashing from a distance wasn't satisfying his urges anymore, and the need to be up close and personal with his victims was beginning to overwhelm him.

He'd sat on the cold hard plastic seat at the bus stop on London Road waiting until a lone female appeared. There had been plenty of college girls waiting to catch a bus home, but to his frustration, there had been equal amounts of boys too. After an hour, he'd given up on that particular bus stop and moved on to a more secluded one on the Waterfield estate.

All of the windows of the shelter had been put in by the local yobs and the wind whistling though the broken frames made his slight body shiver. It hadn't been too long before a peroxide blonde from the estate wandered up to the shelter. Dressed in figure-hugging jogging bottoms bearing the stains of a week's wear, the girl, in her late teens, was glued to the screen of her phone. Sitting down heavily on the seat next to Balvinder, she continued to pump out text messages oblivious to his stare; fixed on her fleshy breasts spilling over her low-cut top.

Surreptitiously slipping a grubby hand inside his jeans, he grabbed hold of his cock and began to stroke it. Once he'd massaged it into an erection, he stood up and whipped it out. Making a "Psst" sound, he turned and faced the girl, who reluctantly tore her gaze away from her phone. Moving towards her, Balvinder grabbed her shoulder while hoarsely whispering: 'Touch it lady!'

Shaking herself free of his hand, the girl screamed, pushed him away, and fled back into the estate. Running all the way home, it hadn't been until her mum came home from work and called the police, that the authorities had been alerted to Balvinder's latest victim of exposure. By the time he'd been circulated over the radio, he'd long since gone home to flash another day.

*

By the time UX646 had finished their notes for the man/woman incident and Albie White's prosecution file had been completed; there wasn't much of the shift left to do. Seeing an opportunity to maintain his caffeine uptake, the Cat suggested they go and get a coffee - not just any old coffee from the machine - no, the Cat had expensive tastes and his latest fad was the "flat white."

'Yeah,' he enthused, 'I discovered it the other day in town. Do you want to know what it is?'

Nobody really did want to know, but in keeping with his tradition of ploughing on regardless, he switched to soliloquy mode:

'Well,' he began, 'The flat white originated in Australia and New Zealand - which by the way, is why it's normally finished off with a fern pattern in the milk...'

A soliloquy it may have been, but the Cat liked to draw his audience in - 'Jax, you're well travelled - you know the fern I'm talking about don't you?'

Fuck! Thought Jax despondently, he's dragged me into it! And with what he hoped was a non-committal 'hmm...' he realised that the Cat had well and truly reeled him in by flattering him about his worldliness. But there was more, the devious little bugger had found a way to involve Dynamo too:

'Big fella, you like your rugby don't you?'

The big man sighed and looked up from his iphone screen. 'What the fuck are you on about now?'

The Cat, his face glowing triumphantly at the thought of having involved at least two people in his flat white story continued:

'Well, you know the New Zealand All Blacks rugby

team?'

'What about them you irritating little twat?'

Not put off by the insult, the font of all trivial knowledge thought he'd found a way to turn his quest for coffee into something of a team quiz:

'Who knows what the emblem of the All Blacks is?'

The team heaved a collective sigh and as one shouted:

'A fuckin' fern, now stop going on about bloody coffee!'

'Exactly! A fern - and that's why it's on the top of a flat white - cos it originated from that side of the world! Anyway,' he continued to no one in particular: 'A flat white is espresso-based but with less milk and no froth. It has two shots of espresso as oppose to the one in a caffe latte. Also, it's made from full fat milk - and do you know what temperature it's heated to?'

Blatantly ignoring him by either staring out of the carrier windows or pretending to be absorbed in their 'phones, the Cat's captive audience refused to play his game any longer. Stony silence met his question about the temperature of a flat white. He was going to tell them anyway!

'The milk is heated to 120 Fahrenheit! And - guess what? There's a new *Starbucks* drive through just off our patch - can we go there skip?'

Skipper Jarvis, happy to agree to anything that had a chance of keeping the Cat quiet for a few minutes while he drank his coffee, acquiesced. Unfortunately, there was little chance of that, and as they drove past a dress shop; the Cat spotted a couple of naked female mannequins in the window. It looked as though they had been recently stripped in preparation for re-clothing in new outfits.

'Look at the tits on those dummies!'

Skipper Jarvis shook his head in disbelief. 'You certainly live up to your name Cat - all you think about is coffee and tits!'

Emma giggled. 'Babes - you need to see someone. I reckon you're addicted to sex!'

The rest of the carrier joined in the laughter, and as Jax pulled into Starbucks, he thought with a smile that, the Cat might be irritating at times, but he was good for morale. Sipping their coffees, UX646 toasted the end of what had been an odd day - not that it was unusual to have odd days; in fact most days were, but it had been the first time they'd prevented a man from emasculating himself, and Jax's first tax disc eater...

Chapter Five

'Don't you think that's strange?'

The only attractive feature of Houndshale's Club 101 is the fact that it remains open long after the rest of the bars in the area have closed. It can be reached - not that you would want to reach it - by taking a risky walk down one of the rat-infested alleyways off the High Street. A source of drunken late night fights, it tends to be a right royal pain in the arse for the cops. Sloshing with *Sambuca* shots, 101's female clientele totter in wearing skirts so short, they are little more than belts.

Scoop tops spill cleavage regardless of the weather as they balance precariously on six inches of heel. Appearing to be on the verge of falling over, they resemble kids who've sneaked out of the house wearing their mother's high-heeled shoes for the first time.

The men, and hopeful suitors of the shot-swigging women; are a mixture of swaggering Jamaicans: dripping with gold and attitude, white trash from Filebridge, red-faced eastern Europeans in their cheap leather jackets - already tanked up on cheap Polish lager - and the odd good Muslim boy playing away from home.

Prowling the outer edges of the inevitable roped off area that marks the queue, are brash-looking Somalis peddling weed, and furtive Indians palming wraps of coke. Should a passing police patrol appear, the Jamaicans suck their teeth contemptuously while the dealers - like a shoal of fish threatened by hungry tuna - dart away to

102

hide in corners; their wares hidden inside their mouths or up their arses.

Doormen, with their thick tattooed necks and uniform of black Harrington bomber jackets control the queue. Leering at the scantily clad girls, they wave them through while making ridiculous judgements on the men's dress code. It's the 21st century, and despite the shit hole of a club they police, they still stick to the laughable tradition of the "no trainers allowed" rule.

Should you be unlucky enough to pass their scrutiny, the next person you'll need to get past is the woman at the desk just inside the door. Taking an extortionate fee in exchange for a crude ink stamp on the back of the hand, you are now admitted to the gloomy antechamber where yet more staff insist on your attendance at the cloakroom. Here, your jacket must be exchanged for a ticket of the type used in church raffles before you can progress into the pulsating interior.

This particular Friday night saw Angie Brown exchanging her faux leopard skin fur coat for an orange cloakroom ticket. Pushing open the batwing doors, she entered the beer-soaked maelstrom of Club 101. The wall of sound that greeted her, masked the cloakroom girl's sneering aside of:

'There goes mutton dressed as lamb.'

It would have been fair comment, to remark, that the skimpy black cocktail dress which clung to her body, was more suited to a woman a decade younger, and she was easily old enough to be mother to the spiteful twenty-year old handing out the cloakroom tickets.

At thirty-seven years old, Angie was a peroxide blonde who, with the clever use of engineered uplifting underwear, had curves in all the right places. Loose-limbed, she had great legs, which she loved to encase in silk stockings. Her emerald-green eyes shone from an elfin face, framed by trendy glasses. Just a hint of fresh citrus perfume made her sexy and attractive rather than naturally pretty. Her workaday attire was generally smart business suits of the kind that make a woman look sexy without being trashy, and she still managed to turn heads when she entered a room. For all her attractiveness, she had two failed marriages and a string of disastrous and abusive relationships behind her. When it came to men, she always picked the wrong ones and had long since resigned herself to being left firmly on the shelf.

She didn't really do night clubs, but upon a whim, she'd decided to take up the offer of a girl's night out to relieve the routine of working, eating and watching trashy TV soaps, before going to bed and waking up to do it all over again.

Angie Brown worked on the third floor of Houndshale nick. She'd worked there for the last five years, sharing the floor with the officers from the criminal investigation department - most of who she was on first name terms with. Angie was employed as a civilian crime analyst and her job was to monitor crime trends and predict emerging patterns. As such, she had the same level of security clearance as the cops she worked alongside, and was privy to most operational decisions made on the third floor.

A lifelong smoker, she shared the area set aside for the tobacco addicts who trooped down the stairs for their nicotine fix throughout the day. That smoky corner of the back yard; unfurnished save for the overflowing pedestal ashtray, was home to both CID and uniformed officers. It formed the setting for exchanges of gossip and rumour - who was sleeping with who, marks out of ten for the latest recruits to arrive at the nick - so and so were getting a divorce... In unguarded moments, whispered semi-secret details of the next drugs raid could be overheard.

The girl's night out had started off in a civilised enough way, in the form of dinner at an Italian restaurant chain. Pasta, pizza, mozzarella salads and tiramisu, were all washed down with a few bottles of white and followed by happy hour at a cocktail bar, where they'd sunk several cut-price mojitos.

Fuelled on mint-infused white rum and brown sugar, the girl from the station's mailroom had suggested they move on to Club 101. Unused to drinking the quantity of alcohol she'd put away in such a short space of time; Angie, along with Karen who'd suggested the club - there were no other takers - found herself saying: 'what the hell,' before draining her fifth mojito, and heading to the rest room to redo her makeup.

Inside Club 101, Angie strained to adjust her eyes to the random bright lights of the dance floor that pierced the otherwise murky interior. Coupled with her alcohol intake, the disorientating effect of the lights made her feel suddenly giddy.

Making her way unsteadily to a corner table, she sat down to wait for Karen, who she'd left outside taking a call from her babysitter. The leather seats were soft and low and each time she moved, she'd had to tug the hem of her dress down to cover the tops of her thighs. The sexy stockings and suspender belt, pulled on in the privacy of her bedroom, just weren't designed for low-slung nightclub furniture, and she felt awkward.

A few moments after she'd sat down, Karen appeared from out of the gloom. Showing none of the reticence of her work mate, she practically threw herself down beside Angie; lifting and spreading her legs in a full frontal display of black lacy thong and freshly waxed bikini line.

'There you are!' she shrieked. 'Let's get some bubbly!' Tugging at the sleeve of an unsuspecting passer by, she thrust out a hand and shouted over the music for him to give her a hand up. The guy: a tall sinewy Jamaican, flashed the girls a brilliant white smile, took the proffered hand, and pulled Karen to her feet.

With a drunken shout of, 'Oops a daisy!' she stumbled off in the direction of the bar, returning after what seemed to Angie like an age. Giggling, she tottered unsteadily over, balancing an ice bucket, a bottle of cheap Prosecco, and two fluted glasses on a tray.

A couple of glasses later, Angie had ceased to pull at her hemline and was well into the swing of things. Karen on the other hand, held her head in her hands in a vain effort to stop it spinning. Telling Angie in a weak little voice that she felt sick, she staggered as urgently as she could towards the rest rooms, bouncing off tables and revellers along the way. Watching her, Angie giggled like a schoolgirl. Karen reminded her of a pinball, propelled violently upwards by the operator's flippers, before rebounding off the electrified bumpers and whizzing around the machine all over again! Poor girl! She felt sorry for her, but not sorry enough to accompany her to the toilet and hold her hair back while she spewed up!

Waiting for her sick friend to return, Angie suddenly felt her age. What the hell was she doing in this dive anyway? She'd long since outgrown such places. Left all alone, surrounded by drunken teenagers and throbbing dance music, she longed to be back at home, curled up on her settee with her cat and a cup of tea.

She'd been just about to go in search of her friend, when the guy who'd pulled Karen to her feet, sidled over. Flashing her a smile that would melt an ice cap, he asked if he could sit down.

In contrast to most of the other men in the club, Calvin Anderson was well dressed, over six feet tall, and powerfully built. This guy - mused Angie dreamily - is charm personified. With shaved head and small, but perfectly formed ears; he had the sleekness of a panther. Close up, there was something magically alluring about his musky smell, and when he asked for her name and then repeated it, his West Indian lilt was so entrancing, that she forgot all about the cat waiting for her to come home.

Although the idea of care in the community for mental health patients had been around since the early 1950's, it wasn't until 1983 that the government of Margaret Thatcher made it a reality. Large Victorian mental health institutions were closed down and their inmates farmed out into the local community. Whatever the principles behind this - be it well meaning or a cost saving exercise, it inevitably meant huge numbers of patients with mental health issues would now be housed among the community. Some were placed under the care of home treatment teams who would make occasional visits to ensure compliance with the taking of medication, while other more vulnerable and difficult cases were placed in small units staffed by live-in carers.

This all seemed very well in principle, but where the police were concerned, it created an additional responsibility to clear up the mess when it all went wrong. Of course, there are still mental health wards in existence, but these only provide temporary care for those unable or unwilling to cooperate with the regime of medication.

The police have Section 136 of the Mental Health Act at their disposal, and can utilise this particular power when dealing with those who are quite obviously in need of professional help. Under Section 136, officers can - providing the subject is in a public place - section a person, and take them to a place of safety; i.e. the local hospital, where they can be further assessed.

For more difficult cases, mental health teams consisting of doctors and social workers will visit the patient at their home and carry out a mental health assessment. Depending on their findings, either a course of home treatment is agreed upon, or else a decision to section is made. The latter will involve a stay in hospital for anything up to six months, where the patient will be administered drugs - sometimes forcibly - and their behaviour monitored. In more severe cases, the decision to section will be taken in absentia, and the doctor will come armed with a warrant to detain: negating the long and difficult process of consultation with a patient, who is way beyond reason.

This system works well on paper, but in reality, after a few stable days on medication, patients are often granted permission to either go out into the insecure garden to smoke, or else given home leave, or permission to go to the shops unsupervised. This of course, is on the condition that they return. Inevitably, at least once a week, there are several "escapes" made from the smoking area, and a handful of non-returnees from home leave and shopping. It is at this point, that the ward managers wash their hands of their patients and call the police to track down their errant charges.

Once the ball has been passed to the cops, they reluctantly assume full responsibility for finding the missing patients before they can do harm to themselves or others. All of this has long since been accepted as another part of the job; but for home visits to either assess, or execute a warrant, mental health teams routinely request the attendance of police officers to physically restrain and forcibly remove the unfortunate person from their homes. This naturally puts a strain on an already overstretched police service and so, when it came to requests for assistance with mental health assessments, the remit fell firmly with the borough task force.

After all, if not committed with something, they provided a ready-made team of seven officers trained in rapid entry, and in possession of entry equipment should the patient decide not to play ball. Waiting discreetly in a hallway, they could provide instant physical aid to the mental health team should it become necessary.

Attacks on doctors, paranoid patients arming themselves with all manner of weapons, and refusal to cooperate, were sadly commonplace, and when the wheels came off, the BTF were there to restore order, and enforce compliance with the doctor's decision.

If the original plan had been to save money by housing patients in the community, there were those who often wondered just how cost-effective the whole thing was. By law, the recommended composition of a mental health team visiting a patient with a view to section has to consist of two doctors and two mental health social workers. In addition to this, there are normally representatives from the home treatment team, sometimes a student social worker, a locksmith to drill out and replace locks, and police officers varying in number from four to seven. The process can take as long as three hours, and assuming a decision is made to section the patient; an ambulance with a crew of two has to attend for transport to the hospital.

It was under their mental health remit, that UX646 answered the call to attend 11 Thirlmere Crescent in Hazelworth. They'd been asked to assist in the sectioning of Roger Beeston. Upon receipt of the assignment, Intel trotted out one of his habitual observations. Addressing the Cat: who was a wannabe CRIMINT monkey, he intoned:

'Wasn't Ibrahim Mahmoud supposed to be dealing from Thirlmere Crescent?'

Of course, the Cat had no idea, but he nodded sagely in agreement, hoping Intel wouldn't expand on the matter.

Turning into Thirlmere, Jax pulled the carrier up short of number 11 so as not to spook Beeston. They didn't want him to spot them and disappear out the back door. As was usual with these assessments, the BTF tended to arrive before the mental health team assembled, and so cutting the engine, Jax settled down to await their arrival. Normally, when they did arrive, they had the habit of congregating right outside the patient's door where they would hold a case conference. Apart from the fact that this served to announce their arrival to whoever was inside the house, Jax never really understood why they hadn't met up at the office to discuss the case they were about to make a decision on.

First to arrive was Jill Lomax - or whispering Jill - as she was known to the BTF. A middle-aged spinster, she tended to turn up in her soft top Audi, before breezing up to the carrier window and briefing the cops about the patient's mental health history. Long past her sell by date, Jill spoke in a conspiratorial breathy whisper at all times. She appeared to have a soft spot for skipper Jarvis, and when around him, she was blatantly flirty and tactile. It had long been a joke among the team that she wanted the skipper to "slip her a length," and although flattered by her attentions, he normally tried to avoid dealing with her if he could help it. He'd try to hide in the back of the carrier, leaving Jax to deal with her, but wickedly, when she sidled up to the window, he'd ask her if she wanted to speak to the skipper! The issue forced, skipper Jarvis would reluctantly climb out of the carrier and suffer the knowing looks of his team while she simpered and held on to his arm.

A sound, not unlike a swarm of wasps trapped inside a bean can accompanied by a cloud of blue smoke, announced the next arrival. Astride his ancient Lambretta scooter, was Doctor James Pigeon. Regardless of the weather, his attire was consistently that of: faded jeans, dirty training shoes, and an old waist-length *Barbour* waxed jacket. Dismounting, he pulled his crash helmet up over his forehead, leaving it perched atop a head of unruly blonde curls, and fumbled around for his glasses. Putting them on, he approached the carrier, said something about the traffic, and much to the skipper's relief, went into a huddle with Jill.

Of all the doctors they came into contact with, Doc Pigeon was undoubtedly the BTF's firm favourite. Unlike

110

the doctors who were dragged unwilling from their warm wards, Doc Pigeon was freelance. Attending several jobs in a day at around £200 a pop; he was coining it in at the expense of a national health service already groaning at the seams. With Doc Pigeon, it was a case of quantity rather than quality.

Armed with a stock of questions with which to grill patients that wouldn't have stretched the brains of a layman, he was in and out in a flash, scribbling his rationale on section papers and zooming off to his next appointment before the rest of the team had realised what had happened! This suited the BTF, releasing them as his decisions did, long before Doc Pigeon's contemporaries had even got done with introductions! 'Ooh, that doctor Pigeon,' Jill would whisper, 'He's so naughty!' Then flashing Skipper Jarvis a knowing look while grabbing his forearm, she'd add: 'He likes a quickie - in and out just like that!'

Outside 11 Thirlmere Crescent, the team watched as the mental health team assembled. True to form, they made their way outside the house where they entered into a huddle to discuss the case of Roger Beeston.

Recognising the risk of flight, the skipper sent Emma and Intel around the back of the house to prevent potential escape. Whispering Jill had already informed them that she was in possession of a warrant to detain Beeston, so should he try to sneak off, they could nab him without any legal issues. Meanwhile, the locksmith, who would get paid regardless of whether his services were needed, sat in his van eating a sandwich.

Taking his cue from the huddle breaking up, the skipper turfed the rest of the guys out of the warm carrier and went to join the Doc and his team on Beeston's front path. Jill proceeded to try and brief them all over again, but after a few minutes, Jarvis politely cut her short, examined her warrant, and followed the Doc down the path. Once there, Pigeon stepped aside to allow Jill to make contact with Beeston.

Lifting the flap of the letterbox, she introduced herself and asked him to let her inside. In response, Jax, who was at the Doc's side, heard Beeston bark: 'Fuck off and leave me alone!' Jax was just thinking that this wasn't such a good start to proceedings, when Jill tried again:

'Roger, I'm Jill Lomax from Houndshale mental health team, can you let us in? I'm here with Doctor Pigeon and we just want to come in and have a chat. Can we do that?' The letterbox flap flew open making Jill jump back in alarm.

'That cunt Pigeon?' bellowed Beeston. 'Last time I saw him the bastard sectioned me! Fuck off the lot of you!'

Jax recognised the signs, and the signs were, the softly-softly approach just wasn't going to work. Gesturing for Jill to step aside, he took over letterbox duty.

'Roger! Open the door and stop fuckin' around. We've got a warrant, so just let us in.' Silence.

Then just as Jax was peering through the letterbox, the door opened just a crack, and a dishevelled Beeston; his scruffy beard stiff with the grime of the unwashed, hair jumping with lice, appeared between the door and it's frame.

'I'm coming!' he bellowed, in the best impression of a parade ground sergeant major Jax had heard since his army days. Peering through the letterbox, he hadn't expected Beeston to appear inches from his face, and what with his bellow and his sudden appearance, he drew back, startled.

Regaining his composure and realising at once that old man Beeston's bark was worse than his bite, he kept up a tone of domination tempered with reason.

'Roger, let the doctor in; there's a warrant anyway and we don't want to damage your door. OK?'

Leaving the door ajar, Beeston muttered something

about needing to collect his stuff, and disappeared into the gloom accompanied by a curious scuffling sound. Taking advantage of the partially opened door, Jax decided to push it open and enter the house, but when he pushed against it, the door offered a kind of spongy resistance. The stench of rotting food, stale cooking oil, coupled with the general smell of unwashed body odour, made him recoil, but with the rest of his team taking a back seat having watched him assume control, he was on his own.

Upon further investigation, he found that the reason for the door not yielding to his push, were ceiling-high columns of old newspapers. They literally filled the entire house, and by opening the door as far as he could - little more than six inches - Jax could see that Beeston had left no more than a literal tunnel in the newspapers, through which to crawl. This was what the scuffling noise had been. Roger, inhabited a world of newspapers, though which he had to crawl in order to get anywhere around his house. He'd become a tunnel rat in his very own version of the Vietnamese tunnels of Cu Chi.

Much scuffling later, Roger reappeared, and forcing his way out through the front door in a much-practiced manoeuvre, he emerged blinking in the daylight. Jax appraised him for any risk. Dressed in a pair of greasy grey suit-trousers, topped off with what had once been a white shirt, upon which ink blotches competed with the remnants of countless breakfasts; the old boy proudly thrust the back of his neck against a grimy collar, specked with dandruff, and looked belligerently around. Roger's sleeves were far too long for his short spindly arms, and to keep his cuffs from falling over his gnarled hands, he wore a set of old-fashioned, sprung sleeve holders. A set of fountain pens and biros jutted out from his breast pocket, and he looked for all the world like a 1930's newsroom editor from some seedy New York newspaper. Despite his bellicose manner, he cut a sad figure, and Jax

113

wondered about his past and what had caused him to be in such a state.

Doc Pigeon attempted to quiz him on his lifestyle, teeing him up for one of his favourite lines: 'Roger, why have you filled your house with newspapers?'

He was rewarded with a: 'Fuck off Pigeon!' to which the doctor came in with his favourite question. It was more of an observation than anything else. In fact, when Dynamo - who was like a mynah bird when it came to impressions - mimicked the Doc, it was always this particular line that he used. Sure enough and to the delight of the waiting cops, he didn't disappoint them:

'Don't you think that's strange?'

On this occasion, Doc Pigeon hadn't needed to employ the rest of his stock questions; the warrant to section Roger was already in place, and so all he needed to do was to make a few hastily scribbled notes, before mounting his trusty scooter and zooming off in a cloud of smoke to his next appointment.

Taking hold of Beeston's arm, Jax said: 'C'mon Roger, lets go.'

Shaking him off, the tunneller of Hazelworth strode proudly to the waiting ambulance and climbed the steps.' You!' he said, addressing the bemused paramedic in his parade ground bark; 'When I get there, I want the Wall Street Journal, The New York Times and the Financial Times. I've got to check my shares!'

Watching the doors close behind him, Jax wondered sadly; not for the first time, what turned ordinary people into basket cases.

As with all mental health assessments, a police escort had to be provided for the ambulance and generally, depending on the wishes of the crew, an officer would sit in the back with the patient until they arrived at the ward where they would accompany the patient inside. In Roger's case, he was more verbal than violent, but nonetheless, the Cat had been designated to escort Roger to The Aspens.

With a face like a smacked arse, the Cat knocked on the ambulance doors and followed Roger inside. Later, he would regale the others with Roger's antics in the back of the ambulance. Once the Cat had sat down, Roger had demanded his name, police collar number and - bizarrely - his marital status! He'd also reiterated his request that financial newspapers be made available to him upon his arrival on the ward!

*

Angie Brown had thrown a sickie. It wasn't like her to cry off work; but here, with the late afternoon sun streaming through the half-open venetian blinds; all thoughts of work and duty were forgotten, as she lay back on the settee, in a post-coital reverie. She was enchanted by the tiny dust particles swirling around the room. The bright specks of dust rode the golden sunbeams, which as though thrown from a movie projector, illuminated her naked body. Just as she'd done as a schoolchild, in a rare sunlit classroom, when bored by an inadequate teacher, she blew into the dust swirls, disturbing their natural descent, and scattering the tiny specks around the room.

It had been half an hour or more since the ebony Adonis that was Calvin Anderson had pulled on his jeans and left her apartment. Stretching like a contented cat, she closed her eyes and recalled the events of the night before.

On Calvin's suggestion, she'd ushered the wasted Karen into a cab and gone back inside Club 101 to rejoin Calvin on the settee. Beaming up at her, he'd held out a hand and pulled her down next to him. Giggling, she'd fallen into his lap, where he'd put his arms around her and looked solemnly into her eyes. He'd uttered a deep belly laugh that had sounded like the muted rumbling of a freight train rushing through a darkened tunnel; getting ever nearer as it reached a crescendo, before bursting

115

delightfully from his lips. He'd gently tugged on her hair and kissed her full on the mouth. The heady mix of Prosecco, Calvin's musky smell, and the awakening of a dormant stirring between her legs, had dissolved her inhibitions. She'd given in immediately and returned his kiss, exploring his mouth with her tongue. They'd stayed there on that couch, bodies entwined in lust, until the lights had come on and the doormen began their mantra of: 'Finish your drinks now ladies and gentlemen, the club closes in fifteen minutes.'

Angie had wondered where the evening had gone; one minute she'd been laughing at Karen bumping off the furniture, and the next, she'd been swept off her feet by a stranger, who had not only made her feel horny as hell, but had also told her she was beautiful. Nobody had ever said that to her before. Sure, she'd been told she looked "pretty" on her wedding day - and yes - men had told her she was sexy and they'd like to fuck her, but until that night in Club 101, she couldn't recall ever being told she was beautiful.

On her settee, Calvin's sweat still wet on her body, she dreamily recalled the moment they'd burst through her front door before ripping each other's clothes off. She'd ran her hands over his body. Whipcord tight, his torso was ridged with unfeasibly defined abdominal muscles, and sliding her hand around his back and grabbing his backside, she'd felt his buttocks. *My God*, she'd thought, he feels like a wild stallion!

Kissing her way down his chest, the irresistible musk emanating from further down his body, drove her wild and sinking to her knees, she'd kissed his taut stomach before taking his hard cock into her mouth. Calvin was big, probably the biggest Angie had ever seen outside of a porno film with the girls from the office, but she didn't care; she wanted it inside her, thrusting and driving deep into her.

She'd been wet, wetter than she could remember,

116

and kissing her way back up Calvin's body, she'd led him into her bedroom, pushed him onto her bed and straddled him. Guiding him into her velvety wet pussy, she'd gasped at his size and then moaned as he'd entered her fully. She'd taken the full length of that magnificent cock and ridden him like a gypsy's pony. Just as she'd climaxed in hot beautiful waves of euphoria, he'd grabbed her arse, pulled her closer, and shuddering, he'd come like a train, his searing hot semen lancing deep inside her.

She'd rolled off him and into his strong arms. Falling into the kind of delicious sleep denied to her since God knew when, she'd not stirred until her alarm had gone off with the strident, grating buzz which usually told her it was time to get ready for work.

Disentangling herself from Calvin's embrace, she'd sighed, shaken her head in a vain attempt to clear last night's Sambuca's, and then donned a silk robe, before stumbling into the bathroom. Throwing water onto her face, she'd scraped her hair into some semblance of order, dragged her toothbrush across her furry teeth, and gone through to the kitchen to make some coffee.

Before her ancient and noisy percolator had dripped enough coffee to fill a quarter of the pot, Anderson had appeared behind her. Slipping his arms around her waist, his rough hands making the silk rustle, he'd kissed her neck and moved his hands over her hips, pulling himself close. Angie could feel his hard cock against her arse, and despite her raging hangover, felt herself getting wet. She pushed back against him, and turning around, her lips found his and they kissed with as much passion as they had the night before. This time though, it had been Calvin who had taken her by the hand and led her into her front room and towards her settee.

The sun was beginning it's climb across the early morning sky, and turning her around, Anderson had undone the tie of her robe, before pushing her down onto her knees. Grabbing hold of Angie's breasts, he'd kissed her back, moving downwards to her arse. Parting her cheeks, he'd licked first her anus, then her vagina, before taking hold of his rock-hard cock and guiding himself into her, thrusting deep inside with long urgent strokes.

Despite her soreness from the night before, Angie thrust back matching his urgency. Waves of ecstasy rolled over her and she climaxed for the second time in six hours. Pouring with the kind of excessive sweat born of a hangover, she panted and bit into the embroidered cushions she'd inherited from her aunt. Letting out a cry, Calvin's strong fingers clamped onto her stiff nipples as he burst inside her, his seed filling and spilling out of her before dripping onto the carpet. Pulling himself free, he sat down on the settee, opened his arms to admit her to his embrace. Watching her still gasping for breath, he pushed the hair plastered by sweat from her forehead and laughed his deep, throaty, freight train laugh.

When they'd finally got around to drinking the coffee from the long since filled pot, he'd looked at the gold-strapped watch that hung loosely from his wrist and announced that he had to go. He'd disappeared into the bedroom and emerged a few minutes later fully dressed. Not wanting him to walk out of her life just yet, Angie had ferreted in her handbag and pulled out a business card. It had read:

Angie Brown, Crime Analyst, Metropolitan Police, Houndshale. Underneath her job description, were telephone numbers for both her office and her cell phone. Calvin hadn't offered her his number, but reading her card, he'd given her a barely perceptible curious glance, before tucking her card into his wallet, pecking her on the cheek and walking out of her apartment.

It hadn't been the fact that she'd been barely able to walk that she'd called in sick, or even that her knees were red raw from carpet burns. She'd just thought: 'fuck it, I'm never going to make it to work on time, my mouth feels as though I've just eaten a handful of talcum powder, and I'm really not up to analysing anything today!' Staggering back to bed, she snuggled back under the duvet and pressed her nose into the pillow vacated by the head of her ebony Adonis.

'Well fancy that Angie Brown,' she mused just before she drifted off: 'Someone thinks you're beautiful!'

*

Mobile again after dropping off Beeston, UX646 resumed their patrol. Intel, who'd spotted a likely looking-car, broke the silence and requested information from the dispatcher at Uniform X-Ray.

'VL check please UX.'

A VL check, or "known to CAD," related to any information held on the system with regard to any given registration plate. It could range from the owner reporting damage to a car, to being the victim of crime. It may even be on the system because it's driver had caused an obstruction of the highway, by simply blocking a neighbour's drive. If a CAD had ever been created in relation to the vehicle, it would show up on the system.

Previous stops, where the driver had been found to be uninsured, or in possession of drugs, would all trigger a "known to CAD" report. If they got lucky, the cops would have their VL check come back as something juicy, such as: the vehicle was believed involved in burglary or drug dealing.

There was a great deal of banter around "putting up" cars, which turned out to be innocent members of the public, and so finding a "good one," just by appearance of car and driver, was a respected, if sometimes lucky art. The operator's remote voice crackled through the cop's radios:

'Vehicle very well known to CAD. Standby...'

As one, the occupants of Jax's carrier fell silent, looked up from their iphones and turned up the volume of their radios expectantly. Now that there was a hit on CAD, Jax closed the gap between his carrier and the suspect car, making sure no other vehicles got in between them should it turn into a pursuit.

"Very well known to CAD," was usually a good indicator that the car and it's occupants were no strangers to law breaking; but often, despite it being known multiple times, the end result might well come back from the operator as a: "satisfactory stop." This meant, that although the occupants were clearly up to no good, they'd managed to evade the law by either appearing legitimate, or by cleverly hiding whatever contraband they'd been in possession of. The stop would generate yet another CAD, with the "suspects" allowed to go on their way.

In such fruitless situations, Jax, when in conversation with the suspects, was in the habit of repeating an old Irish Republican Army maxim; learned during his days in Northern Ireland, where "known players" would tell him:

'You have to be lucky all the time - we just have to get lucky once.'

Back then, it had related to the ever-present threat of concealed explosive devices or sniper rounds, but he liked the simplistic truth of the phrase, and it had followed him from khaki uniform to the blue of the Met.

The operator's voice boomed around the carrier:

'You should be looking at a VW Golf GTI, black in colour. The vehicle is involved in armed robbery, and must not be stopped without Trojan assistance'

This got their attention. Trojan assistance meant that the vehicle could be followed from a distance, but armed officers from CO19 would have to be called out to put in the stop. Just because it had allegedly been in some way associated with an armed robbery, didn't automatically mean that the current occupants were armed; but the MET is so risk averse, as to practically facilitate the getaway of such criminals, rather than have them stopped by patrol officers. Trojan were spread pretty thinly and their units tended to satellite certain areas such as south or north London, where gun crime tends to be more prevalent.

Normal procedure dictated that if a Q car was available, it would be dispatched to take over the follow from the marked vehicle, thus giving a better chance of going undetected by the suspect. Q cars are unmarked vehicles equipped with sirens and concealed blue grille and roof lights, but the only one available on the borough that day, had been the task forces' own Vauxhall Zafira, currently in the back yard at Filebridge

Dropping back and leaving room to get away from any potential armed threat, Jax did his best to remain inconspicuous - no easy task in a marked police carrier! Observing protocol, his operator Emma, switched her commentary from the local channel to the "main set." This was the radio set fitted to the carrier with a default channel, on the other end of which, was an operator dedicated to monitoring pursuits London-wide. The operator was known simply as MP. If the follow became an actual pursuit, the powers that be back at headquarters, would demand constant updates on the situation. They needed to know the class of driver engaging in the pursuit, road conditions with regard to weather, and density of traffic, along with updates on speed and direction of travel. Should the situation escalate into a pursuit, and the "bandit" vehicle looked like becoming a danger to other road users or pedestrians, it was likely that the pursuit would be called off.

Seasoned criminals knew that if they were to go around a roundabout the wrong way, or better still drive the wrong way down a motorway, the pursuit was be sure to be called off. At the risk of losing a bandit vehicle being driven dangerously - regardless of the skill of the police driver - the order to terminate the pursuit would be given, in order to prevent potential death to innocent bystanders. If the helicopter was available, the cops had a good chance of catching the criminal, but if not, frustrating though it was, they'd have to concede defeat.

On this day, the nearest available Trojan unit was twenty minutes away at the extreme edge of the Met, in Bromley - and that was on blues and twos. Despite this, they were duly dispatched, and UX646 settled down for the long haul. If the driver of the Golf GTI got spooked and put his foot down, there would have been no way that Jax, in the lumbering carrier would have been able to keep up. In the event, the Golf kept to the speed limit. The driver could be seen making regular checks in his wing mirror, and his front seat passenger had lowered his sun visor and appeared to be checking out the cops through the vanity mirror in the visor.

A Trojan skipper came onto the radio. Jax could hear his driver's siren in the background of the transmission as he asked for more details and current location of the Golf. He was, he said, fifteen minutes away from Houndshale. Calmly, the driver of the Golf, signalled left and turned into a residential side street. Heart thumping, Jax followed while Emma updated the main set operator, who relayed the information to Trojan.

Halfway down the street, the Golf pulled over. Jax stopped short and waited.

'Vehicle stopped outside number 38 Prince Street,' said Emma into the main set. They heard the operator calling Trojan.

'What's you're ETA Trojan Seven-Zero?'

'Ten minutes.'

Then to Emma:

'Confirm vehicle stopped?'

'Yes, yes over.'

'Do not approach the vehicle'

'*Obviously*,' retorted Emma rolling her eyes - but into the radio: 'All received MP.'

After a couple of minutes, the driver's door of the

Golf opened and a skinny white male climbed out. Emma relayed the update to MP:

'Driver is out out MP.'

'Confirm driver out of the vehicle Uniform X-Ray 646?'

'Yes, yes - it's a white male, slim build, around 6 feet tall and dressed in black clothing over.'

'That's all received Uniform X-Ray 646, keep the commentary coming over.'

'Stand by.'

Through the carrier's grimy windshield, all eyes were now on the driver of the Golf. After a glance back at his vehicle, the driver turned around and began walking towards the carrier.

'Male on foot towards us MP.'

'ETA Trojan Seven-Zero?'

'Approximately four minutes MP.'

'Too fuckin' late,' mouthed Jax as the driver of the Golf approached his window. Muttering: 'Fuck It!' Jax made a decision. Opening his door, he climbed down, drew his baton and faced the armed robbery suspect.

'Stand still! Keep your hands where I can see them!' he barked.

Throwing his arms theatrically into the air, the driver complied. By now, Dynamo, the skipper and Intel had exited the carrier and joined Jax on the pavement. While Jax kept him covered, Intel and the skipper moved forward and put the bemused man into handcuffs before searching him. Still in the carrier monitoring the radio, Emma updated channel one.

'Male detained and in cuffs.'

'Confirm all officers safe and well?'

'Yes, yes.'

The wail of Trojan's sirens began to get louder as they raced to the scene. Seconds after the suspect for the armed robbery had been handcuffed, they screeched around the corner and piled out of their BMW X5. Their skipper didn't look impressed at having raced across London only to find that the task force had initiated contact with the suspects. Consoling himself with the fact that the Golf's passenger was still uncontained; he marshalled his men and cautiously led them towards the Golf. The passenger had tried to tough it out and had locked the car doors, but two MP5 semi-automatic rifles pointed directly at him, concentrated his mind and unlocking the door, he was yanked out before he could even get his hand on the door handle. Within a second he'd been dragged bodily from his seat, was kissing tarmac, and trussed up like a turkey in cable tie plasti-cuffs, before he could say: 'what the fuck?'

A search of him and the Golf revealed nothing more than a small bag of weed, and clearing their weapons, Trojan left the scene, heading south and back to more bountiful hunting grounds.

The owner of the Golf had only bought it a week before, and had been blissfully unaware of the CAD marker on his newly acquired pride and joy. Both the driver and passenger had petty criminal records, and aware that they were being followed, the driver had pulled over and brazenly approached the carrier with the intention of cheekily asking what the problem was. This was quite common among the bolder members of the criminal fraternity who, bored with being followed, would initiate contact with the cops and seek a confrontation. Jax didn't suppose he was expecting to be cuffed and stuffed while his mate was slammed into the deck by gun toting cops!

Issuing the passenger with a warning for the cannabis, UX646 dusted them both down and sent them on their way. The tension broken, they piled back into the carrier. The Cat sneaked out one of his vile farts, got punched by Dynamo and requested a drive to Starbucks for his beloved flat white. It was almost home time, but feeling indulgent after his team's hairy encounter, skipper

Jarvis acquiesced and treated them all to a coffee on the way back to the office. To the sound of groans, Intel said something about how he'd seen the Golf on a neighbouring borough's briefing.

'Yeah, well done,' answered Jax sarcastically, 'You've not been speaking to Porridge Face have you? He probably *wrote* the fuckin' briefing!'

'Speaking of which,' added the skipper, 'As of tomorrow, he's on our team.'

UX646 were still debating the merits of having a "Billy Liar" on the team, when they arrived at Starbucks, and to no one's surprise, the Cat was first out of the carrier and at the counter queuing for his flat white.

Chapter Six

'Is it because I'm black?'

Arriving at Filebridge for late turn, Jax pushed open the door to the BTF office to be confronted with the concrete evidence so casually relayed to him by Becky Thomas in the canteen at Houndshale, and more recently by Jarvis. There, large as life and twice as ugly, sat PC Tam Morris - aka Porridge Face. Wearing a supercilious look, Porridge Face swivelled in his chair to greet Jax:

'Yaw-wite Jacko?'

The mockney accent immediately wound Jax up, and as he took in the legend-in- his-own-lunchtime that was Tam Morris, he thought - not for the first time - you're one ugly fucker!

Apart from the lunar landscape that was his face, Morris had the unfortunate additional curse of practically being a hunchback. His head, a mass of dark curls - much like a white man's afro - seemed to sit on top of his shoulders without connecting to his neck: which appeared nonexistent. This gave the impression that his torso was abnormally short. His belly stuck out like that of a heavily pregnant woman. Despite his outward appearance of a hunchbacked egg on legs, Porridge actually fancied himself as a bit of a ladies man, but really, he was all retch and no vomit.

'Hello Porridge.' Then lying like a crack addict, Jax continued: 'Welcome to the BTF.'

Morris's ugly mug cracked into a grin and uttered

126

his first lie of the day.

'Cheers mate; I expect it's a bit like the TSG this job. I used to be in the TSG you know'

Jax looked around the room; now that Porridge Face had an unwilling listener in the form of Jax, everyone else could breathe a sigh of relief and leave him to listen to the bullshit stories. He noticed Skipper Jarvis look subtly heavenwards in the way he did when faced with a fool, and he heard Dynamo and the Cat giggling at his expense from behind the lockers.

'Did you hear about what happened to my TSG unit?' continued Porridge Face unrelentingly.

Jax tried desperately to find something to busy himself with, but the trap had been sprung and he was at the mercy of his new teammate's bollocks until such time as he could feign an important call on his phone. Knowing that whether he answered Morris's question or not, he would still receive the unwelcome answer, Jax grimly prepared himself for the verbal diarrhoea which would surely follow. He fervently hoped, that for that day's shift he would be driving the Q car and not the carrier. He felt sure that if it were to be the latter, the rest of the team would be sure to stitch him up by quickly piling into the back; leaving the operator's seat vacant for Porridge Face.

'Well...' continued Morris, 'our skipper died after he fell off a cliff. Everyone said it was an accident, but I reckon the yardies were after him after he got one of them convicted. Anyway, being senior PC on the unit, I was chosen to stand in as skipper...'

Jax didn't know whether to laugh or cry. If he hadn't been the only other person in this crazy conversation, it would have been priceless!

'As soon as I took over as acting skipper, I laid the law down and told the team that things would be very different with me in charge. I told them I wanted more results. More stops and more arrests. They respected me of course, everyone knew I'd been in the SAS and I know how to lead from the front.'

The giggling from behind the lockers intensified, but Porridge Face didn't appear to notice. He ploughed on:

'Anyway, after just a couple of weeks, our results were so fuckin' good, we were the best in the Met. We caught armed robbers, broke up an international drugs gang, *and* rescued a kidnap hostage.'

At this point, the Cat, deciding to have some fun and extend Jax's torment, chipped in with: 'Then what happened?'

Foolishly thinking that the Cat had unwittingly taken his place as listener to Porridge's crap, Jax was about to walk away, when he realised that the Cat had dashed straight out of the office leaving Jax to continue with his ordeal.

'Well,' droned Morris; 'our results were so good, that we started to embarrass the other TSG units, and one of the inspectors - who's a freemason - by the way, met up with the commissioner at one of their Mason's Lodge meetings and told him to disband us!'

A voice inside Jax's head screamed, SHUT THE FUCK UP YOU TWAT! He felt as though he was on the verge of releasing his inner voice while strangling Porridge. He was relieved when skipper Jarvis put an end to his misery; firstly by calling them all together for the day's briefing, and later, by informing Jax that he was to be posted to the Q car along with the Cat. The skipper would drive the carrier for a change and this announcement put paid to any ideas the others may have had with regard to Porridge Face being operator. Along with being tasked to hunt down the flasher, the Q car was to operate in and around Houndshale town centre, with a view to bringing down the number of robberies that had been on the rise since the beginning of the month.

Breathing a sigh of relief, Jax headed down to the

back yard to prepare the Q car, which currently, was a silver Vauxhall Zafira MPV. The cops tried to switch the car around with neighbouring boroughs every so often, but it never took long before the baddies on the street got to know it. What didn't help, in a diverse borough like Houndshale, was the fact that invariably, a white male accompanied by a white front seat passenger drove the Q car! A male/female combination helped preserve anonymity for the initial glance, but it wasn't an advantage that lasted any more than a few seconds.

He found the Cat already down there and promptly called him a wanker for encouraging Porridge Face's tall tales. If he thought Jax was going to take him to Starbucks after that stunt, he had another thing coming!

He went through his checks of the Q car. After ensuring all the standard lights worked, he flicked a concealed switch that illuminated blue lights hidden in the windscreen, front grille and rear lights. A press on the vehicle's horn activated the siren, with a further press alternating the tone from a steady rise and fall wail, to the more urgent repeat tone used when approaching areas of dense traffic, red lights and junctions. Once he found all lights and sirens worked to his satisfaction, he flicked another hidden switch to turn on the vehicle's main set, which he ensured was set to channel one.

Opening the trunk, he next made sure there was a first aid kit and police cordon tape in the back. Throwing his yellow hi vis jacket into the trunk in case they should have the misfortune to stumble across a road traffic accident, Jax filled in the log book detailing his call sign of UX11, and jumped in beside the Cat, who was busy booking them on with the local channel.

As they began to drive out of the back yard, Jax caught sight of Emma waving him down. Winding down his window he gave her a smile.

'Babes,' she began. 'You'll never guess what Porridge Face just said!' Grinning broadly, Jax said:

'I bet I will!'

'Honestly Babes, he's doing my head in already! He reckons he's a descendant of King Arthur!'

Jax shook his head in disbelief but it was the Cat who quipped:

'You sure he didn't mean Richard the third? He was a fuckin' hunchback too!'

Looking in his rear view mirror, Jax spotted the so-called heir to the British throne, and as he loomed large, fearing he may again fall victim to the lunatic's bullshit, Jax engaged first gear, gunned the engine and abandoned Emma, still helplessly laughing at the Cat's joke. She was just about visible through the cloud of black diesel smoke left behind in the ageing Zafira's wake.

*

It had been almost a week since Balvinder Kapoor's encounter with the blonde in the bus shelter, and apart from visits to the local gurdwara where he could get one free meal a day, he hadn't ventured out properly since. Emboldened by the passage of time and drawn back outside by the urge to show his cock to a stranger, he caught the bus into Houndshale.

Mooching around in search of suitable prey, he trawled the backstreets near to the bus station. Settling on a likely victim - a middle aged Polish woman dressed in a tight denim skirt, he was just about to approach her, when he noticed a police patrol car turning into the street just ahead of him. His heart in his mouth, he reluctantly let the fortunate woman pass by.

The patrol car was being driven by a team officer from core shift. He was alone - or single crewed - as it was known in the jargon of the job, and he was on his way to keep one of several low-grade appointments assigned to him by the control room.

The appointments car was an unpopular posting among the cops and was usually reserved for those basic drivers, awaiting response courses. The shift would be taken up with those mundane appointments deemed routine enough not to warrant an immediate response and today, PC "Chalky" White, was on his way to deal with a neighbour dispute: something about an overgrown Leylandii tree which was blocking the sunlight from the adjoining garden.

Houndshale had had it's fair share of flashers; in fact, barely a week went by without a report of someone or other getting his knob out. In Balvinder's case however, the thing that had alerted the suits upstairs in the CID office, had been the fact that their flasher had progressed from merely exposing himself, to actually touching his victims. Fearful of an escalation beyond that of the usual cases, they'd got the girl from the bus stop to come in and give a statement. Grudgingly, the girl from the council estate had agreed - providing the officers visited her at home.

She was, she said, far too busy - presumably collecting her welfare cheque - to come to the station. With her reluctant help, the detectives had drawn up an e-fit of Balvinder. Mind you, had he seen it, he would have been safe in the knowledge that even his mother wouldn't have recognised him from the detective's efforts!

The image of an Asian male with shoulder length hair, and non-descript electronically generated features, was duly circulated among the cops at Houndshale; though in a town predominantly inhabited by Asians, the chances of actually pinpointing Kapoor were slim to nothing.

Chalky White had read the briefing when he'd come on duty, and skipping through the dross, he vaguely remembered the e-fit and an Asian guy with long hair. He idly speculated whether this might be Houndshale's latest flasher.

In no rush to get to the Leylandii dispute, he slowed the car and pulled up alongside the now sweating

Balvinder. Opening the window, he greeted him with the stock 'How you doing? Do you live around here?'

'Hello officer, I live in Cranston, but I'm on my way to sign on at the job centre.'

'Just wait there for me.'

Parking his car, Chalky got out and wandered over to where Balvinder was obediently waiting.

'We've had a flasher in the area recently and we're speaking to anyone in the area.'

Balvinder feigned disgust. 'That's bad officer, I hope you catch him.'

Chalky pulled out his hand held PDA and logged in to the PNC page before asking another stock cop question: You known to police at all?'

'No officer, I'm a good boy.'

'That's good, what's your name then?'

Quick as a flash, Balvinder came up with a well-practised alias name.

'Harpreet Singh officer.'

He knew full well, that giving a name such as that, accompanied by a spurious date of birth, would bring up all manner of Singhs known to PNC. Sure enough, Chalky's PDA screen lit up with dozens of Harpreet Singhs, only one of which was shown wanted by police. Seeing the "whiskey mike' marker, which indicated persons wanted or missing, Chalky, like all cops, became a lot more interested than he'd been when first encountering Balvinder. Adrenaline flowing, he subtly closed the distance between them, while noting any potential escape routes. He clicked on the wanted Singh.

His PDA screen filled with the details of the wanted Singh, but disappointedly, this man lived in Birmingham and was a good ten years older than the man stood before him. At that, Chalky lost interest, and thanking Balvinder for his patience, he said goodbye and hopped back into his car. On the way to his neighbour dispute, he made a mental note to compile a CRIMINT to the effect that he'd stopped a long-haired Asian by the name of Harpreet Singh in the vicinity of the bus station - just in case any victims reported a flasher in that area at that time. In the event however, by the time he'd spent eight hours reporting absolute shite, he'd gone home without logging onto CRIMINT.

For Balvinder's part, feeling rather pleased with himself and more than a little excited, he'd simply gone to the bus station and caught a bus to Spentford, where he'd planned to go in search of another victim. Once on the bus, he climbed the stairs to the top deck; where apart from a couple of old age pensioners on their way back from the post office, he found that he had the deck to himself.

Sitting down at the rear of the bus, it's windows scarred with graffiti, the Polish woman in the tight denim skirt, combined with the close encounter with the cop, began to make him feel horny. Hidden from the pensioner's view by several rows of uncomfortable seats, he began to play with himself. Closing his eyes, he imagined ripping off the woman's skirt, grabbing a handful of her hair and forcing her to suck his cock. Within seconds, flinching with ecstasy and arching his back up against the hard seat, he ejaculated all over the seat in front of him. Putting his prick away, Balvinder pressed the button for the next stop. Leaving his semen running down the seat and onto the floor, he stood up and prepared to get off the bus.

The relief, which came from his act of public masturbation, had left him suddenly bereft of the urge to seek out a victim in Spentford. By interrupting Balvinder and diverting him to pastures new, it seemed that Chalky had inadvertently spared the Polish woman the ordeal of seeing Balvinder's cock - or worse. Unknowingly, by forcing Balvinder to leave the area on a bus where he'd pleasured himself, the cop had carried out one of the basic roles of policing - that of directly contributing to community safety! And so, some unsuspecting female in Spentford, would today be spared the attentions of the Houndshale flasher...

*

Not long after Balvinder Kapoor's encounter with Chalky White, Jax and the Cat drifted into the town centre in search of the flasher. During the drive from Filebridge, Jax had made the schoolboy error of mentioning that he'd seen a newspaper article about the founders of Costa coffee: Bruno and Sergio Costa.

At this, the Cat had become animated, opening up a debate on the merits of Costa coffee over those of Starbucks. The latter: he said with authority, had come into being for the American market and their coffee, as a result, was sweeter and milkier. The Cat, warming to his subject, elaborated:

'The Americano was created for the American taste - espresso topped up with hot water 'cos Italian coffee was too strong for them.'

Jax groaned inwardly and cursed the moment he'd let down his guard and given the Cat *carte blanche* to wax lyrical on his second favourite subject! He'd only meant to make small talk while they had been stuck in traffic, but to his operator, this was manna from coffee heaven! It could have been so much worse though, he mused, I could have been lumbered with Porridge Face! He consoled himself with this, but nevertheless, tried desperately to switch off. But the great forced coffee debate continued:

'And do you know why I prefer Costa?'

Jax gave up on trying to screen the Cat out, hoping something would happen to make him abandon his coffee comparisons. Anything would do, even a shit call over the radio; but it wasn't to be.

'Go on then, surprise me.'

'Well, Starbucks use coffee from a machine, whereas

Costa load the grounds into a scoop and force water through the grounds. It's all in the grind Jax!' he announced triumphantly.

Jax recalled a scene from the film Blackhawk Down; in which coffee aficionado Ranger John Grimes played by Ewan McGregor says:

'It's all in the grind, Sizemore. Can't be too fine, can't be too coarse. This, my friend, is a science. I mean you're looking at the guy that believed all the commercials. You know, about the "be all you can be." 'I made coffee through Desert Storm. I made coffee through Panama while everyone else got to fight, got to be a Ranger. Now it's "Grimesy, black, one sugar" or "Grimesy, got a powdered anywhere?"

The Cat; who would probably have been more aptly known as Grimes, was just about to launch into telling Jax how there were only three master Italian coffee roasters in the whole of the UK - all of whom are employed by Costa, when the sound of a car horn distracted him. He saw group of four black wannabe gangsters, dressed in un-coordinated colours so outrageous, they looked like they'd stepped off the set of the film Warriors. Coming from the direction of the large open recreation area known locally as Lambton park, they wore their baseball caps back to front and had gang-style bandanas hanging from the back pockets of their low-slung jeans. One of them even wore a single leather glove in the style of a shooter; but the sinister hit man connotation was at odds with his bright blue sneakers.

Trying to be ultra-cool, one of their number: dressed in a flamboyant brown leather jacket with a tiger's head emblazoned across the back, had stepped off the kerb and walked straight into oncoming traffic. He'd presumably assumed that the car with the blaring horn would make way for him and so show his friends that nobody messed with him. It had backfired spectacularly when the turbaned driver of the Nissan Micra, had simply maintained his speed and heading, given him a blast of the horn and remonstrated loudly, before screeching off and leaving the very un-cool gangster scuttling for the safety of the pavement!

'What a bunch of twats!' exclaimed the Cat, bursting into laughter, and mercifully for Jax; becoming totally distracted from his coffee monologue. Jax had to agree with the sentiment. They didn't recognise the group to be locals, but there was certainly nothing subtle about them. The only thing needed to complete the 1970's look, would have been a ghetto blaster hoisted upon a shoulder, pumping out Dj Kool Herc.

A short time later, and after a circuit of the backstreets behind the shops, Met call's Houndshale operator crackled through their radio sets:

'Units now for an immediate response. Robbery in Lambton Park details to follow.'

The Cat keyed his radio mic. 'Show uniform-x-ray one-one'

'Thank you one-one, that's all received. Descriptions to follow.'

Jax heard several other call signs adding themselves to the list in search of the robbery suspect. Flicking the switch to activate the blue lights and siren, he slewed the Zafira around and headed for Lambton Park.

'UX from UX11,' began the Cat. 'What time did this call come in over?'

'Call made at 1656 hrs.'

'That's ten minutes ago,' commented Jax cynically, 'they'll be long gone by now.'

'All units standby for description of suspects...'

'More than one suspect?' exclaimed the Cat. 'Well, if they're still in the park, and there's more than one, at least they'll be easier to spot.'

The radio operator boomed out of Jax's and Cat's radios: now turned up to maximum volume to compete with the wail of the Zafira's sirens.

'Four suspects described as IC3 males aged around
136

eighteen to twenty-years old. One described as being dressed in a brown-coloured leather jacket with some kind of animal motif on the back, and another wearing blue sneakers. The property taken is a Blackberry'

'Fuckin' hell!' exclaimed the Cat. 'It's those fuckers from earlier!'

Jax nodded enthusiastically. 'Oh yeah, the idiots from the Warriors!' Just then, Dynamo's voice joined the airwaves, announcing that the carrier had done a sweep of Lambton Park with no sign of the suspects.

'I reckon,' said Jax, 'that when we saw them earlier, they must have just done the robbery; that's why they're not in the park. Let's have a quick look around for them.'

Spinning the car back around, Jax turned off the lights and sirens so as not to alert the robbers should they still be in the area. He could hear several units, already bored with what was believed to be just one more unsolved robbery. One by one, they called up with: "Area search no trace." This was cop colloquialism for a fruitless search, and was usually declared before they broke away and carried on with patrol.

'Area trace no search more likely!' muttered Jax cynically. Then, just as he too was beginning to think the robbers were long gone, he spotted them! All four wannabes, still together and swaggering along the High Street as if they owned it, were just yards away on the other side of the carriageway. Walking past a series of fruit and vegetable shops with their wares piled up in pavement stall displays, they were laughing and joking: seemingly without a care in the world. Met call rejoined the fray:

'Units looking for the robbery suspects, the victim's family are reported to have sighted the suspects and are following them.' The Cat responded:

'High Street, junction with Pearl Road, four suspects. Appear ident over.'

'All received, confirm ident over?'

'Yes, yes.'

The operator addressed UX646. 'Did you receive that 646?'

Intel's voice filled the Q car. 'Yes, yes, ETA four minutes over.'

'That's received by uniform- x-Ray, all units stand by.'

Just for a moment, Jax thought about how the two of them would intercept the four suspects without it getting messy. The Cat, having radioed Dynamo and the rest of the team and established that they were a few minutes away, broke into his thoughts:

'If we don't stop them now Jax, they'll be into the Park Estate and away.' Jax nodded in agreement.

Trying to remain as unobtrusive as he could in what to the criminal fraternity was blatantly an unmarked police car, Jax abandoned the Q car at a bus stop opposite the fruit and veg stalls. With the Cat at his heels, he crossed the busy road as nonchalantly as he could and approached the lead robbery suspect.

So busy had they been with their horseplay, the suspects hadn't noticed the cops closing in, until Jax was upon them. Grabbing hold of the guy in blue sneakers, Jax bellowed 'POLICE!' before cannoning the startled robber into a shop window. The Cat followed suit and wrestled another to the ground. Of the two remaining suspects, one walked away, but the other made the decision to go to the aid of his captured cohorts. Alternating between Jax and the Cat, he battled to try and free his accomplices from the cops, kicking punching, pulling and pushing, all the while screaming: 'Run nigger! Run!'

The Cat still held his man on the ground, who for his part, appeared to have given in. Sensing this, the Cat drew his Asp and kept the aggressor at bay by making short threatening dashes towards him. Jax however, was finding it harder and harder to keep hold of his suspect.

The kid's sweaty body made him slippery as an eel. Every time he got a hold on him, he managed to get free. Jax, in comparison to his lightly- dressed detainee, was wearing a hoodie over his stab-proof vest, below which was his heavy utility belt. He was melting. He could smell the kid's acrid sweat and stale tobacco on his breath, as he twisted and turned like a fish on a hook.

Turning his attention away from the baton-wielding Cat, the would-be rescuer ran over to Jax who by now had employed a non-police approved headlock on his prisoner and had him fairly secure. Pulling at his clothing, and kicking out at Jax, the third suspect was on the verge of freeing his buddy from the hated cop. The Cat was back on the ground with his man, and was in the process of handcuffing him, and so wasn't able to come to Jax's aid.

After what seemed like a breathless eternity, the embattled Jax could hear the carrier's sirens in the distance. If only he could hang on to blue sneakers for a few seconds more, he'd be OK. The third suspect, also hearing the ever-closing sirens, ran off and Jax's man redoubled his efforts to get away from his grip. He almost managed, before Jax got angry. Fuck this for a game of soldiers he thought grimly. This guy's taking the piss!

Kneeing him in the balls, in yet another unapproved police move, Jax grabbed a handful of clothing, spun his man around and brought him crashing down; right on top of a fruit and veg stall.

The stall collapsed like matchwood, scattering pineapples, melons and mangoes, and sending oranges rolling down the street. On the pavement, surrounded by the mess that had once been an orderly stall, Jax lay on top of his man's back, gasping and wheezing for air, as only a forty-something man could, after a prolonged tussle with someone less than half his age. His captive was still struggling and ignoring Jax's orders that he put his arms out to the side for handcuffing. Turning his head to one side, he had managed to get up on all fours and was writhing around like a man possessed.

Skipper Jarvis vaulted the metal barrier between pavement and road to come to his aid, but even their combined efforts failed to subdue the robber. Jax, tiring of the whole thing and wanting to bring the matter to a conclusion, thought: fuck this! Punching him on the back of his head, he drew his CS spray and emptied most of the can into his face.

Coughing, spluttering and streaming snot, the fight gone out of him, Jax's man finally gave up and offered his arms to be cuffed. There was no way this joker was suitable for front stack, and determined to secure his man once and for all; Jax wrenched his arms tightly behind him, forced the backs of his hands together, and snapped the cuffs on.

Along with skipper Jarvis, he hauled blue sneakers unceremoniously to his feet and pushed him face first against a wall to await the van. Jax took in the scene. The Cat - still holding his man on the ground, had been joined by the robbery victim's enraged mother who, while screaming obscenities at her son's attacker, bizarrely picked up melons, mangos and pineapples, from the ruined stall, and hurled them at the prone robber's head!

Meanwhile, just across the street, Jax saw with some satisfaction that Intel had tracked down the third suspect. After learning that he'd attacked his fellow cops, Intel struck him with his baton, took him to the floor and trussed him up like a turkey! The fourth and final suspect, who appeared somewhat shocked by the cops' shock and awe, gave himself up to Dynamo without a fight.

Even as the cops began to withdraw with their prisoners, the stallholder was calmly re-stacking his shattered stall with produce which, when bought and consumed, would have a curious peppery taste after being marinated in Jax's CS!

Marching his prisoner - who funnily enough turned

out to be in possession of the stolen Blackberry - across the road to the waiting prisoner van, Jax thrust him into the cage and slammed the doors shut. He was just about to walk away when the kid called out to him.

'Officer!'

'What?'

'Is it because I'm black?'

Shaking his head at hearing what along with: "I bet you were bullied at school" - was a common accusation, Jax opened the cage door. The kid's mucus glands were in full flow. Snot dripped onto the floor of the cage and his eyes streamed.

'No - It's because you're a fuckin' robber!' Then, slamming the door, which shut with a satisfying metallic clang, he crossed the road to the Q car he and the Cat had abandoned when they'd first spotted the suspects. The sweat on his face mingled with the remnants of CS spray, making his skin sting and his eyes water. After years of being exposed to much higher and more potent strains of CS in the military, Jax had built up a lot more resistance to the stuff than his robber ever would!

The scene began to clear of curious onlookers, police vehicles, and fruit-throwing relatives. All four suspects had been rounded up and the fruit and veg man had just about finished restacking his CS-contaminated fruit. As the High Street resumed an air of normality, it was now time for Jax to leave and re-join his suspect at the nick where he would be waiting in the van to be booked in. Once all four wannabes were safely in their cells, it would be time to slow down, take stock, and fill out the reams of paperwork required to hopefully bring the suspects before the court. Before all this though, Jax was in need of a well-deserved smoke. Heading back to the station, he got himself a brew from the vending machine and sneaked off to the darker recesses of the back yard to get his nicotine hit.

Once he'd had his brew and a smoke, Jax queued up

in the custody cage to book his man in. Once he'd given the custody skipper the circumstances of his arrest, he requested a strip search. Having become compliant, at some stage - probably while Jax had been having a smoke - the officer who'd escorted his suspect to the custody cage, had removed the kid's cuffs. This was fairly normal, but depended on whether a detainee had passed the "attitude test." In this case, the van driver, keen to get back out on the street, had taken the kid out of his van and led him into the custody cage until Jax arrived. He'd agreed to ease the pain that came with back-to-back restraint by removing his cuffs.

Dynamo appeared in the custody area just in time to help Jax with his strip search, and heading down the narrow custody corridor to a cell, they sat the now subdued kid on the wooden bench.

Watching him closely, the cops got him to systematically remove his clothing. It wasn't long before Dynamo - characteristically sweating buckets in the confines of the cell - noticed the suspect having difficulty taking off his tee shirt. They'd started with getting him to remove the blue sneakers: which had given him away in the first place, followed by his socks. The kid's trousers had been next, the pockets of which hadn't yielded anything contentious. It had been when they told him to take of his top, that something hadn't seemed quite right. He was holding his left arm stiffly to his side and seemed reluctant to remove his tee shirt. Fearing he may have been concealing a weapon, Dynamo quickly took hold the kid's right wrist in a vice-like grip while Jax grabbed his other arm and barked:

'Don't fuck about mate, what have you got under your arm?'

Realising that it was futile to hold out any longer, the kid shrugged before shifting his arm slightly and allowing something to drop onto the cell floor. Pushing him back down onto the bench, the cops took a step backwards and Jax stooped to pick up the object from the floor. The kid obviously hadn't anticipated a strip search; reserved as this kind of search was for drug addicts. What he'd been at pains to conceal was another Blackberry phone. Jax guessed that the van driver, having taken the cuffs off, must have taken his eye off the suspect, giving him time to secrete the phone under his armpit. Running the IMEI number of the phone through his PDA, Dynamo quickly established that it had been stolen in east London the week before, during yet another robbery.

Placing the Blackberry into a self-sealing evidence bag, Jax further arrested the kid on suspicion of the east London robbery, before taking him back before the custody skipper and resuming the booking-in process. The search over, Jax now released the now profusely sweating Dynamo from custody. He smiled while the big man gratefully rushed off in search of cooler climes.

Once he'd booked in his prisoner, Jax headed off to the writing room to begin the long process of recording his evidence and putting the robbery case together, before hopefully, handing the case over to the robbery squad.

The writing room served as a space where officers could access the mind-numbingly slow computer terminals - assuming there were more than a couple that worked. The centre of the room was crammed with rickety desks, at which officers either hand wrote notes, bagged property, or ate kebabs. Houndshale wasn't equipped with a room in which victim statements could be taken, and so among the detritus of fast food wrappers and Coke cans, you could sometimes find wide-eyed victims of crime reliving their ordeal for the purpose of an evidential statement, laboriously written up by some pen-chewing cop. When this was the case, the banter, which was undoubtedly liable to offend the innocent, would be contained, and all farting activity curtailed.

Pushing open the door to the writing room, he found the rest of UX646 compiling their notes on what had already become infamously known as: "The great fruit and veg incident." The Cat was sipping on what he bemoaned as: "shit coffee," Intel - losing no time in updating the Met's CRIMINT monkeys - was adding a report of the event to the system, and Dynamo - who from somewhere, had secured a small electric fan with which to cool himself - was tapping out his statement via a grimy keyboard. The big man's chunky fingers flew over the keyboard with a dexterity, which belied his size and Jax reflected, not for the first time, on the speed and skill of his computer-literate colleagues, at odds with his antiquated paper and pen method. Watching this - his limbs already starting to ache with the efforts of rolling around with teenage robbers - he suddenly felt his age.

Long since having given in to the embarrassment of having to correct his ageing eyesight with glasses, he fished them out, perched them on his nose and sat down to write his arrest notes. Somewhere among the background noise and banter, he could hear Porridge Face telling a tale - to nobody in particular - about how when he was in the TSG, he'd single-handedly fought off four robbers armed with shotguns and machetes!

Smiling wryly to himself and determined not to catch Billy Liar's eye, and so become the foil for his latest bullshit story, he settled down to recording the events of the fruit and veg stall. He'd been making some progress, when he was startled by Dynamo yelling in frustration. The fan, which he'd liberated from some desk jockey on the second floor, had clearly done little to cool the big man's brow.

Striding over to a window in a desperate attempt to bring down his temperature, he'd grabbed the handle to wrench it open. The plastic window; installed cheaply by the Met, had been no match for Dynamo's heat rage, and when it had at first refused to yield to his pulling on the handle, he'd doubled his efforts and pulled the whole window clear of it's frame!

When Jax looked up from his notes to see what all the commotion was about, he witnessed Dynamo looking sheepish; still holding the window by it's handle and with a "what the fuck" expression on his face. The writing room erupted into laughter as the big man carried the window back over to the jagged opening and tried in vain to refit it! Skipper Jarvis did one of his skyward glances while Porridge Face droned on about how his brother was a window fitter. Shaking his head in wonder at Porridge's seemingly innate ability to manufacture lies to suit all events from thin air, Jax went back to his notes.

Apart from writing notes, putting on a crime report and preparing a handover for the robbery squad, the suspects would all need to be fingerprinted, photographed, have their DNA taken and be tested for the presence of narcotics in their bloodstream. Once that had been done, the suspects would be stripped of their outer clothing and footwear, which would be seized as evidence, before being painstakingly bagged up into paper evidence bags. Replacing the suspect's clothing with a one-size-fits-all paper suit, the cops had to seal, label, and document what was to become an exhibit. This was done not only to match the victim's and witness description of what the suspects had been wearing at the time of the crime, but also in order that it could be sent off to the lab for forensic testing.

Before seizing the suspect's clothes, they would be photographed wearing it. Confiscating a criminal's treasured sneakers was a task that was both smelly and rewarding. Apart from seizing his cash, there was nothing the suspect of a crime hated more than to have his sneakers taken away for what could easily be months.

Routine for those arrested for crimes of theft, was for their homes to be searched under Section 18 of The Police and Criminal Evidence Act. The more accomplished criminals tended not to give their real address for fear of having it searched. The usual way of thwarting the cops, was to give a parent's address, which although they hardly ever occupied, would often be as good as it got for the officers.

The cop's regular clients generally tended to have been brought up by one-parent families. Nine times out of ten, the parent was the mother, and on visiting the address supplied by the suspect, they'd be greeted by mum. She either backed her kid's story up; or on occasion, having had her fill of police officers traipsing through the house, she'd deny all knowledge of her offspring living with her. When this happened, Jax had never known a parent to give away their kid's actual address.

Out of loyalty, they would feign ignorance. No address, theoretically meant that the suspect would be remanded in police custody until such times as he or she could appear at court, which unless a Saturday afternoon, or the eve of a bank holiday, would be the next day. In order to prevent the suspect from being remanded, mum generally told the cops that although her little darling didn't actually live there, she would allow her address to used as a bail address. Sometimes the cops got lucky and a possible address would be found by trawling the intelligence system. If this were the case, and the arresting officer had been fortunate enough to find a set of keys in the suspect's pocket, then they just may get lucky...

All of this took long enough for one prisoner, but to process the entire gang of robbery suspects, would take the rest of the shift. The BTF were both fortunate and unique in that, compared to the usual partnering of two, which was common with team officers; they routinely had up to seven pairs of hands to make lighter work of prisoner process.

Normally, by the time an arresting officer had emerged from booking in his prisoner, the others would have fingerprinted and photographed, taken DNA, put on the crime report and logged any property. If enough of them were in, two or three would go off to carry out Section 18's. The Cat often volunteered to go off and search houses, knowing that this would give him the opportunity to stop off somewhere along the way for a coffee!

In the case of the great fruit and veg stall incident, UX646 were sure to be tucked up for the rest of the shift. While most of them were sent off to carry out house searches, Jax would be spared the distractions of the usual writing room banter, but more importantly: Porridge's seemingly endless supply of tall tales. Getting Emma to pick him up some food from wherever they decided to go, Jax settled in for the long haul.

Chapter Seven

'You don't half talk some shit babes...'

Nadine Cousins had been a pretty baby. Even the triangular birthmark on her left cheekbone hadn't spoilt what, to her parents had been perfection. Her eyes, the colour of cornflower, blinked out at her new world from under strawberry blonde hair, and her smile had been divine. Her parents; both Francophiles, had settled on the French version of Nadia, meaning "hope," when coming up with a name for their newly born daughter.

In adulthood, there hadn't been a lot of hope in Nadine's life. All that remained of that pretty little baby was her birthmark. Her clear blue eyes, had long since lost their sparkle, and her hair was greasy and as devoid of shine, as that of a peroxide madam at a brothel. Mr. and Mrs. Cousins' little girl was hopelessly addicted to crack cocaine.

Short of murder, there was absolutely nothing she wouldn't do to get hold of enough dirty white rocks to get her through the day and fill the pipe that she'd fashioned from an old water bottle.

Making a hole in the neck of the bottle, she'd stuck a cut-down straw into it and sealed it with gum. She'd substituted the bottle's cap with a nest of wire wool, which formed the pipe's bowl, and had had to cut the straw right down because of the short amount of time that crack smoke remains potent. The downside to the shortness of her pipe was evident on her blistered and cracked lips; caused by routinely pressing a hot pipe to them, as she greedily sucked up the noxious fumes which within nineteen seconds, would take her on a short-lived trip to crack heaven. With the effects of the nasty little drug being so short lived, but providing such an intense high; her entire day revolved around how she would get her next hit.

Even when using the vile stuff, she suffered auditory hallucinations, hypertension and even tactile hallucinations, like the feeling of bugs crawling all over her sallow skin. This prompted her to ceaselessly scrape her filthy fingernails through her lank, greasy hair in search of non-existent creepy crawlies. Her paranoia made her hear non-existent sirens, music, and even people talking. As early as an hour after her hit, Nadene would "ghost bust" the grotty carpet in her bedsitting room.

In desperation, on her hands and knees, she would pick up stray lint or anything remotely crack-coloured, in the vain hope that she'd dropped a fragment. If in the next few hours, she failed to secure another rock, depression would set in and she'd start to feel remorseful and even suicidal. Scouring her room for non-existent things to pawn and finding nothing of value, she would be forced back out on to the street to either run rocks for a dealer or prostitute herself.

Now in her twenty-first year, Nadine's life hadn't always been so hopelessly wretched and her rotten, crack-stained teeth had once been white and healthy. Born to hard-working middle class parents, she'd enjoyed a normal childhood and had been a popular kid at her Hazelworth school. But on the day the head teacher Mrs. Shelby, had come into Nadine's art class and quietly ushered her out of the room; everything changed. Sitting the girl in her office, Mrs. Shelby had given her a glass of water and put a maternal arm around her shoulders, before delivering the earth-shattering news, that at the

149

tender age of fourteen, poor Nadine had become an orphan.

Ironically, her parents had been rushing back from a wedding anniversary lunch and had been making their way to Nadine's school. Still a long way from home, they'd realised too late that the one last drink in the country pub had made it impossible to keep their promise of collecting their daughter for a dentist's appointment. They didn't normally fuss over her, and she was usually quite happy to make her own way home from school. That fateful day had been different though; petrified of the dentist, her mum had agreed to pick her up, and having taken the day off work to celebrate their anniversary, her dad had agreed to go along to provide further support.

It was a lovely sunny day and with the roof of their convertible lowered, they'd hurtled along unfamiliar country lanes, while laughing, joking and reminiscing over the ups and downs of eighteen years of marriage. Feeling nostalgic, and laughing like kids, Nadine's mum had slid a Dire Straits CD into the player, and they'd sung badly along to "Walk of life."

Rounding a bend, they'd suddenly come across an unmanned rail crossing. Red warning lights were flashing and an alarm heralded the train, which was about to flash past the crossing on it's way from Birmingham to Marylebone.

There hadn't been any other cars at the crossing and the last pint of beer, combined with the music of his youth, had made dad feel heady. Like a teenager once more, and to the shrieks of his wife, he stamped on the gas pedal and headed straight for the crossing. When they'd been kids and still courting, he'd run the odd railway crossing just for the hell of it, and to hear her squeal her reproach.

The beer, hand pulled from the cellars of the Stag Inn, had dulled his senses. He didn't have the reactions he'd possessed as a kid, and with high hedgerows either side of the approach to the crossing, it was plain stupidity to attempt to outrun a train, the approach of which he couldn't even see.

By the time the dull black snout of the express train burst into view from behind the hedge, the anniversary couple were at the point of no return. Vainly stabbing at the brake pedal only had the effect of bringing the doomed car to a screeching stop right in the path of 129 tons of iron, glass and steel. So sudden had the car appeared on the crossing, that the driver hadn't had time to react. At 70MPH, his train smashed into the side of the couple's car; instantly converting the outside shell to a wreck of twisted metal, and the interior into a meat grinder, where flesh and bone merged with smashed door panels, flying glass and gearbox components. Finally coming to rest a quarter of a mile down the track, the wreckage of what had once been a man's pride and joy, see-sawed on the tracks, before slowly rolling down the steep railway embankment, where it's ungainly fall was eventually arrested by a wild entanglement of thorny brambles and stinging nettles.

With no immediate family to step into the breach, social services had taken on Nadine's case and placed her into a children's home. Cherry Tree House, in Spentford housed adolescents who for one reason or another were unable to lead normal family lives. If you spoke to a social worker, they would tell you that Cherry Tree House was home to the "most damaged kids" in the area. In reality, this meant that children from abusive backgrounds - both physical and sexual - rubbed shoulders with the likes of those kids who'd become petty criminals and or drug addicts, and the likes of Nadine; who'd found herself there by cruel circumstance.

Not differentiating between kids of entirely different needs, social services mixed the good the bad, and the downright ugly with the carelessness of a novice keeper of tropical fish who, while well meaning, really didn't have a clue as to which fish mixed together harmoniously.

The inadvertent but disastrous result was; that traumatised kids got bullied by their peers, while vulnerable kids were led astray, and into a world of crime or drugs, by those more streetwise than themselves. Nadine had enough about her not to be bullied, but after a few months, she began to fall into the category of being led astray.

Teaming up with a girl of her own age: who not only smoked weed, but drank vodka and flouted every rule the staff tried to enforce, she went from model resident to rebel in a short space of time. Before she'd met Vicky - her new street-hardened friend, Nadine had never so much as put a cigarette to her lips. She had drank no more than the half a glass of wine allowed by her parents on the odd occasion when they'd gone to the pub for Sunday lunch. Apart from the odd awkward fumble with a boy at the school disco, she'd not had any sexual encounters. Now though, with her new friend, she began to skip school and stay out beyond the time when the doors at the home were locked for the night.

The staff at Nadine's care home were a mixed bunch with their own and different agendas for working there. Some - the agency staff covering sickness in particular - were motivated by the lucrative nature of the work. Those staff from the agency could almost double the wages earned by the regular staff. Others seemed to enjoy the power they exerted over their charges, and then there were those who were idealistic and worked there to try and improve and educate the kids.

Unfortunately, well meaning though they were, these people just didn't get the fact that the majority of their charges were beyond normal middle class parenting. This group fared the worst and was the most resented by the kids. A thirteen-year-old girl, who had been abused since she could walk, just wasn't interested in the old maxim of "if you don't finish your dinner there will be no pudding." They certainly didn't give a toss about being told to keep their elbows off the table, or being told off for leaving the table half way through the meal. So, when the kid from the council estate; used to eating pizza in front of the TV, told dear old Liz Browne to "go and fuck herself," before storming out of the house, it should not have come as a total shock. The tragedy was, that to Ms Browne, it came as a massive shock every time it happened. Although the foul insults varied from child to child, it did happen, with monotonous regularity.

The staff at Cherry Tree House were bound - or more accurately - hamstrung by the Children's Act. This pretty much ceded all the power to the children and the kids knew it. In fact, for those who could read, the Act was available in a child friendly booklet, for them to do just that. Knowledge is power, and armed with this, it wasn't any wonder that the more informed kids ran rings around the authorities. They knew full well that if they didn't want to go to school, nobody would make them.

Don't want to get out of bed all day, don't! Can't be arsed to make your bed in the morning, tidy your room, help with chores? Then don't! What are they going to do - withhold your pocket money? I don't think so! In fact, the hierarchy at Nadine's home, out of desperation to get the kids to do anything at all, had introduced incentive money. So - get up in the morning, tidy your room, help lay the dinner table, go to school, don't swear at staff - and there was a small fortune to be made!

The Children's Act also meant that the kids couldn't be physically prevented from leaving the house, even if the staff knew that they were going out and putting themselves in danger. They'd come up with the plan of locking the front door at ten pm, but those bent on doing their own thing, simply went out *before* ten, and stayed out. Sure they'd be reported as missing to the police, but unless a patrol bumped into them, they'd not be caught, and it didn't take much to outwit those making only a token effort of searching for them.

Nadine's friendship with Vicky had proved to be an ill-fated union. Her friend was already in the clutches of a cartel of Pakistani taxi drivers; all good Muslim boys of course, and loyal to their veiled wives at home. Playing away with white infidel girls, it seemed, didn't count as adultery, and they preyed accordingly on young girls such as Vicky. Starved of affection, such girls thrived on the men's pseudo affection. Never having been called pretty before, or bought expensive gifts, they soon succumbed to the men's charms. In order to hook and reel the girls in, the men would encourage them to experiment with crack cocaine.

After a couple of hits, the white trash was putty in their hands. Thereafter, the compliments and gifts ceased and were replaced by rough demands for disgusting sex - blowjobs mainly. Not content to use and abuse the girls themselves, the cartel began to farm the girls out to other drivers and takeaway workers. When they'd baulked at going down on some of the older men and recoiled at the stench from their piss stained underpants, they'd been slapped and had their crack withheld. Given the choice of suffering horrendous withdrawal symptoms and blowing the disgusting driver in his stinking cab, the hapless girls normally acquiesced.

So it went; the never-ending cycle of abuse of young girls, let down by a system of weak legislation. In the case of some of the boys in care, known burglars had been known to pick the lads up from the home and make use of their size and fearlessness to squeeze them through small windows. Their Fagin-like controllers fed them the line that as children, nothing would happen should they be caught. They were usually right. The only people gaining from the whole rotten system were, it seemed, criminals, agency workers, and the firm that charged social services fifty quid just to change a light bulb; thanks to unwieldy health and safety legislation dictating that members of staff weren't allowed to change light bulbs.

Aged eighteen and hopelessly addicted to hard drugs, Nadine left the home and went into assisted living. This involved being given a flat within the grounds of the home and daily visits by staff who would give her tips on how to live independently, how to budget, get your laundry done and generally care for oneself. What they didn't do was tell her how to feed herself or buy washing powder, once she'd spent her weekly allowance on crack.

The taxi drivers had long since tired of her and abruptly stopped her supply, cruelly mocking her desperate pleas. They'd dropped her in a heartbeat and moved on to groom the next young waif and stray from the seemingly never-ending supply of kids in care. Once the care home staff had patted themselves on the back in the mistaken belief that they had prepared young Miss Cousins for the real world, she was released from care and given a council flat on one of the rough tower block estates in Houndshale.

She still got handouts, but these now came in the form of welfare benefits. Panic attacks and addiction had meant that she also qualified for incapacity benefit and could not therefore, be expected to find work. She spent her days and most of her nights cooped up in her tiny flat, and acquired a taste for cheap cider. Such was her need to smoke crack that she'd resorted to prostituting herself. She brought tricks back to the flat, where, kneeling in front of the one bar electric fire underneath the solitary bare light bulb, she'd blown a procession of men in exchange for twenty quid to buy the yellowy-white rocks, she depended on so much.

Calvin "Spoons" Anderson was Nadine's main supplier. Passed on to him by the taxi cartel, he'd first joined the list of people who'd sexually used and abused her, before identifying her as a potential runner.

Initially using her to run the odd rock and bag of

weed, she'd built up enough trust to be used to ferry around larger quantities from one safe house to another. Sometimes, he even used her to move uncut crack from further up the drugs chain to one the many Houndshale addresses he used for cutting up and onward distribution. Spoon's advanced network was such, that he no longer dirtied his own hands with the merchandise. He had cultivated a network of runners and coerced several down and out addicts with their own council houses and flats, into allowing their addresses to be used for the cutting up, weighing and packaging of his poisonous, but highly profitable merchandise.

Among Anderson's network of runners, no one really knew why he was known as "Spoons." The rumours which abounded on Houndshale's streets, included those that told of the time, when as a juvenile offender back in Kingston, Jamaica, he'd dug his way out of his cell at St Andrew Juvenile remand centre using a spoon. A more sinister explanation for the moniker; had been that he'd gouged out the eye of a rival drug dealer using a sharpened teaspoon. Either way - without exception - his runners were all shit-scared of the nasty Jamaican.

Nadine's drug-raddled body wasn't much in demand in the way of prostitution these days and she was heavily reliant on Spoons for her daily fix. He scared her to death, but needs must when the devil drives, and she'd found herself making the daily pilgrimage to wherever his chosen meeting point was to be. The cops were getting quite cute at interrupting the Jamaican's activities of late and he'd had to come up with more and more ways of thwarting them.

He preferred using female runners, and encouraging them to dress smartly, one of his ruses was to walk arm in arm with one of them; seemingly out for a stroll along some riverbank or other. Having had a stash dropped off at some rural location, he would take his accomplice along and in the guise of perambulating lovers, he would make sure the coast was clear before sending the girl into the bushes to retrieve the goods. Of course, he could have just sent her there alone, but for the purposes of exerting total control, he would always want to be present to make sure his junkie runners didn't literally run off with his stash. Once his gear had been safely picked up, he would leave the scene; negating any possibility that he may be pounced on by any watching cops, who may have been tipped off by colleagues on surveillance.

Another of his methods was to dress in sportswear and send a runner in to collect his stash, while he ran up and down in the area of his merchandise, posing as a jogger, all the while keeping an eye on his runner. Sometimes, he would throw his hands around as though he were a boxer in training.

Today, it was Nadine's turn to play a bit part in his charade, and telling her over the phone, that she was to dress smartly, he gave her instructions on where they were to meet. From a distance; wearing a smart, if threadbare business suit, her greasy hair scraped back in what the cops mockingly called "a Filebridge facelift," and her blistered lips smothered in lipstick, Nadine could easily pass as one of many commuters heading into the city for a day at the office.

Clucking desperately for her morning fix, she made her way to the area of an underpass, which ran under the three-lane carriageway linking the borough of Houndshale with central London. The underpass, which facilitated access for the people who lived on one side of the main road, to the commuting tube station on the other side, was flanked by an area of sparse woodland. It was this woodland that had been chosen by Spoon's supplier to hide his latest pre-paid consignment - 50 wraps of brown (heroin) and 50 white (crack). With a combined street value of around £2000, it was a drop in the ocean for the likes of Anderson, and would be

157

scarcely enough to keep his regulars going for the day.

Meeting Nadine at the tube station entrance to the underpass, Anderson - dressed in his running clothes, sent her up on to the railway embankment and followed closely behind at a slow jog. Once she was up on the bank, he overtook her, stopped a few yards away and went into his shadow boxing routine. As Nadine passed him, he indicated a supermarket carrier bag suspended from a tree branch and hurriedly whispered that she was to unhook the bag and return to the underpass. Once she had reached the other side, he would call her with further instructions.

Unbeknown to the pair - but always suspected by Anderson - their charade had been witnessed by two officers in plain clothes; who, acting on a tip off from an informant, had hidden in among the trees and settled down to wait. The cops, from a neighbouring borough, hadn't informed their counterparts at Houndshale, and consequently had no back up to intercept Anderson and his runner.

Once Nadine had collected the carrier bag, they called up over Houndshale's radio channel with a less than clear message about suspects, drugs and underpasses. By the time Houndshale's officers had unravelled the enigmatic radio message, Anderson had jogged off and disappeared into the station, leaving Nadine to make good her escape.

Among the cops rushing to the area of the underpass, were Intel and Emma who had been posted to the Q car for the day. Eventually managing to get a description of Nadine and her direction of travel, Emma headed to the affluent estate opposite the tube station into which she hoped their suspect was heading.

'What do you reckon babes?'

Intel, at a loss what to think without being in front of his beloved CRIMINT, but wanting to sound knowledgeable nonetheless, scratched at his stubble.

'Try the Lakes estate, I read on CRIMINT that a female runner lives there.'

Smiling to herself, Emma pointed the Zafira in the direction of the Lakes estate just off the London Road. In the event though, it was the unlikely intervention of the heavily accented Indian police CCTV operator that gave them a positive lead.

Paid peanuts by the council to scan Houndshale's streets for those up to no good, the band of unintelligible African and Indian operators, though well meaning, were mostly reactive as oppose to proactive. Most of what they scanned for was after the event. On one memorable occasion; when asked to try and locate a reported hunger striker on the High Street, the operator triumphantly announced that he had found the man in a bus shelter, excitedly adding: 'He's definitely not eating!'

Today though, the CCTV man had come up trumps. Through his thick accent, he managed to convey that a female matching that given by the plain-clothes cops at the station; was walking along London Road, Hazelworth in the direction of Summersby Park. Hearing this and being only a couple of blocks from the Lakes estate, the cops in the Zafira felt their adrenaline begin to flow. With the familiar fluttering of excitement generated by the sighting of a suspect - and, not wanting other officers to get to the scene before her, Emma spun the Zafira around and screeched westwards to intercept the suspect.

Putting on her blue lights, she made sure not to activate the siren lest it spook the girl. She cursed softly when she heard the distant wailing sirens of other cars; driven by cops desperate to get out of whatever mundane assignment they'd been previously tasked with. Potentially, it had been a good call to go to and so, as tradition dictated, all assigned calls were temporarily abandoned in favour of flooding the area.

Then suddenly, they were upon the suspect who

was just about to cross the road opposite the park to which the Zafira would have no access. Dramatically slewing the car across the width of the road, Emma tore at her seatbelt fastening before shoving the door open and leaping out. Intel raced around the car just as Emma got "hands on." There was always something satisfying about beating Intel to a "body." His physique belied the speed with which he could move when scenting the opportunity of an arrest.

For her part, Nadine remained cool and feigned surprise. 'What's going on officers?'

'Keep your hand out of your pocket!' shouted Intel as she instinctively reached for her jacket pocket.

'Alright, alright, keep your hair on darlin'!'

Other cars started to arrive, their occupants spilling out to join the fray. Once they realised Emma had hands on, and they would have to carry on to the shitty call they'd been assigned to in the first place, they made unconvincing offers of help, before skulking back to their cars to resume their journey to the dreary call they'd put on hold.

On this occasion, Intel's hours of trawling CRIMINT seemed to have paid off.

'Hello Nadine, you still running for Spoons?'

If Nadine was surprised by Intel's accuracy, she didn't show it. 'No darlin' I haven't seen him since he beat me up. I'm just on my way to a job interview. That's why I've got me suit on.'

Emma put a stop to Intel's gloating. 'Babes, I'm going to search you under section 23 Misuse of Drugs Act. Do you have anything on you that you shouldn't have?'

'No love.'

'Any sharps or anything that might hurt me?'

'I don't inject if that's what you mean love.'

'OK, give me your handbag.'

Passing Intel Nadine's bag to search, Emma began

to search through Nadine's pockets, but apart from her crack pipe, she didn't find anything incriminating. Similarly finding nothing in her handbag save for a can of cider, a list of names and mobile numbers, a bunch of keys, used tissues and a week's supply of condoms; Intel handed her back the bag.

'Babes, I believe that you may have drugs on you and for that reason I'm detaining you for a drugs search.'

'What - a strip search you mean? I've got nothing on me love, if you take me to the nick for a search, I'll be late for my job interview!'

Intel had heard it all before; the only pressing engagements crack heads ever had were those relating to scoring crack.

'The decision's been made Nadine,' he interjected. 'Now the quicker we get you to the station and give you a search, the quicker you can get back out and go about your business'

Putting the girl into front stack, Emma ushered Nadine into the back of their car. Intel made sure the door child locks were engaged on her side before sliding in beside her to prevent her from getting up to anything. He'd long since learned the hard way. When left alone in the back of police vehicles, it was quite common for suspects - despite being in handcuffs - to manage to ditch drugs, stolen credit cards, mobile phones and even weapons. It wouldn't be until they were long gone that someone would find contraband either stuffed down the back of a seat or even underneath a front seat: dropped in a rear foot well before being kicked out of sight.

Just as they were driving away, another of Anderson's runners: Muhammad Kaar emerged from the park riding an undersized BMX bike. Circling the car, he peered inside, made a gun out of his fingers, and pointed it at the cops within. Winding down his window, Intel challenged the Somali, who cycled off laughing.

As Nadine had been detained for a search and

wasn't under arrest, she would have to be taken into an interview room outside of the custody area where she would be strip-searched. This was never a pleasant experience at the best of times. Junkies, whose lives tended to be chaotic, often neglected their personal hygiene, the result of which manifested itself in smelly feet, bad body odour and soiled underwear. The cops knew, that despite being dressed smartly, Nadine would be no exception.

The officer on duty at the front counter buzzed Emma into the interview room while Intel went in search of another female officer to assist with the search. Finding only men in the writing room, Intel climbed the stairs to the canteen where he found Becky Thomas - of pneumatic breasts fame. Interrupting her gossiping, he addressed her breasts and asked if she would help Emma with her search. Feigning reluctance, but as ever, up for getting involved with something that may facilitate some gossip at a later date, she skipped down the stairs with the lascivious gaze of Intel firmly focussed on her backside.

Knocking on the interview room door, Becky was admitted by Emma and the strip-search procedure began. Telling Nadine to sit down, Emma put on latex gloves and offered a pair to Becky, before asking Nadine whether she'd been strip-searched before. Assuring her that they would respect her dignity and be as quick as they could, she removed Nadine's handcuffs, warned her against any sudden moves and instructed her to remove her jacket.

Keeping an eye on her suspect, Emma passed the proffered jacket to Becky who began to go through the pockets before patting down the lining in search of anything that may have been concealed within. Becky pulled out yet more tissues, a couple of grimy elastic hair bands, a small set of electronic weighing scales and a mobile phone, which had began to ring incessantly.

'Someone's keen to get hold of you babes,' remarked

Emma. Glancing at the phone's screen, she could see seven missed calls: all from Spoons.

'Thought you didn't have anything to do with Spoons babes?'

Nadine remained silent and the search continued. Becky put Nadine's jacket on the table.

'OK babes, take your tee shirt off.'

Nadine stood up and peeled off her tight-fitting, and once white tee shirt, which she handed to Becky before sitting back down. While Becky turned the tee shirt inside out in search of hiding places, Emma told Nadine to remove her shoes. Baulking at the smell of long-unwashed feet, Emma passed them to Becky who had finished searching Nadine's top.

'Socks off now babes; turn them inside out, show me your feet and put them back on.'

Revealing her slimy grey feet, Nadine, for the first time showed some embarrassment.

'Sorry love, I haven't changed my socks for a few days, can't afford to buy any more.'

'Don't worry babes,' she soothed, recoiling from the stench. 'We've seen worse. You can put your socks back on now, but I'll need you to take your bra off next.'

Nadine unclipped her stained black bra and passed it to Emma. She cut a pathetic figure as she sat in the interview room; shivering while trying to protect her modesty by folding her skinny arms across her abused and shrivelled breasts.

'Stand up babes, lift your arms, and let me see under them.'

Nadine complied and lifted her mottled and bruised arms above her head.

'Turn around.'

Her eyes downcast, the wretched girl turned around and showed the cops her back. As relieved as their detainee to have got the first part of the search over with, Emma passed Nadine her bra and tee shirt which she gladly put back on.

'Right babes, take your trousers off.'

With tears running down her face, Nadine pulled down her trousers, and as she did, the supermarket carrier bag, which until recently had been hanging from a tree, fell from her waistband.

Picking it up from the interview room's threadbare carpet, Emma placed it out of Nadine's reach and onto the table.

'What's in the bag babes?'

Nadine, softly sobbing, made no reply, and while Becky took a step forward to pay more attention to Emma's detainee, Emma opened up the neck of the carrier bag. Seeing what was obviously a substantial amount of what appeared to be class A drugs, Emma turned back to face Nadine,

'I'm arresting you on suspicion of possession with intent to supply. You do not have to say anything, but it may harm your defence if you do not mention when questioned something which you later rely on in court.'

With that legal mouthful out of the way, Emma and Becky continued with their search. The atmosphere in the interview room had turned from being chatty and informal to one of increased vigilance. Getting Nadine to remove her knickers, Emma instructed her to squat down while Becky went about the distasteful business of searching through Nadine's stained panties. Checking Nadine's orifices for concealed items and coming up negative, Emma told Nadine to get dressed.

The silence while she dressed was broken by her battered mobile phone, buzzing away on the table with an increasingly anxious Spoons on the other end. Emma made a mental note to seize the phone as evidence when she booked her in to custody.

Taking the crestfallen Nadine through to custody, Emma thanked Becks and left Intel - who'd posted himself outside the interview room, to scurry off and update CRIMINT. Emma called after him to get hold of the rest of UX646 and ask them to organise a Section 18 search of Nadine's address.

Once in front of the custody sergeant, Nadine broke her tearful silence to assert that the 50 brown and 50 white were for her own personal use. This was standard practice among the runners who, petrified of their dealer's wrath, would always trot out the tired old mantra that the gear belonged to them and them alone.

After she'd been booked in and had her fingerprints and photo taken, Nadine had a cotton bud shoved into her mouth to collect enough saliva for a sample. As was common practice with those arrested for either acquisitive crimes or drug supply: a COZART test would be carried out to check for the presence of opiates, cocaine or amphetamine. If the test proved positive, the suspects would be offered a chat with the on-hand drugs worker before being given a mandatory appointment at the addiction clinic. Those that failed to keep the appointment were liable to arrest. In theory, this was to give addicts a chance to come into contact with professional drugs workers in an effort to get them off the gear and onto something legal.

In the case of heroin addicts, if they agreed to stay clean - and actually managed, they would be prescribed a daily dose of methadone. In addict parlance, being on methadone was known as being on a "script." The well-meaning idea was that the addicts would start on so many millilitres a day, with the plan that they would reduce their intake over a set period of time. Most junkies - with some justification - argued, that this was even more addictive than the heroin it was replacing. At the beginning of a script, the addict attended the clinic every day, got handed their methadone and, like a child taking medicine, they suffered the ignominy of being supervised while they drank the foul tasting green liquid.

Perversely, those trusted with collecting their

165

methadone to take at home; at times enough to last the weekend, quite often sold it to other junkies who in turn, provided the hard cash for the seller to buy actual gear. It wasn't uncommon for cops searching a suspect's house, to find an entire stash of methadone - sometimes up to a dozen bottles - mostly with the label bearing the original patient's name, removed.

With the COZART test revealing cocaine in her bloodstream, Nadine's custody booking in procedure was all but complete and after an appointment had been made for her to attend the clinic, she was led to a bleak cell where she settled down to await interview and the arrival of police doctor. Shivering under a scratchy blue blanket, she hoped and prayed that the doctor; who would hopefully give her the medication she needed to settle her down, wasn't at some nick the other side of London. Nadine knew that she'd be in that cell for a long time and she was going to need something to prevent her clucking for the duration of her incarceration. The wretched girl also knew that Kaar had seen her with the cops, and when Spoons got hold of her he was going to kill her...

*

Ending his call from Muhhamad Kaar, Calvin Anderson wasn't happy. That fuckin' stupid bitch had allowed herself to be nicked with two grand's worth of *his* gear. Not only was he now out of pocket, he also felt that Kaar had enjoyed telling him about it. The Somali would undoubtedly take great pleasure in regaling his shitty little cohorts with the news that Spoons had been had over by the cops. It wasn't so much the money - a couple of grand was chicken feed for him and his Yardie cartel. No, it was a respect thing - he couldn't have snotty little bitch junkies making him look out of control. He'd have to fuck her up. Actually, come to think of it, his safe houses and runners seemed to be getting targeted on a regular basis - and what was today all about? How the fuck did the Met pigs know where he was picking his stash up from today? He'd heard the sirens just before he had got the fuck off that embankment. It smelt like the work of on informant to him; a dirty fuckin' snitch.

Now that the Met had switched to digital radios, it was virtually possible to monitor their activity. They'd been pretty much the last force in the country to switch, and when they did, the O2 mobile network had been more than happy to provide a service that would guarantee a hefty income from all emergency services well into the future. In the good old days, people like Anderson had been able to monitor the pigs using a fifteen-dollar frequency scanner. Feeble British legislation had made it an offence to monitor cop channels, but not to own the device, and the petty criminal fraternity had always been one step ahead. Anderson himself; had simply paid a woman who lived opposite the nick to report not only extraordinary police movements, but to also scan their channels. The police did have access to military radios, which encoded transmissions, but these had only been available to squads combating major crime. There *had* to be a way; he had to prevent the raids, which right now were damaging both his business and his reputation.

Lighting his last cigarette, he crushed the empty carton and headed off to what, until previously, had been the Blacksmith's Arms. Along with numerous other 1950's public houses in suburban London, the Blacksmith's had now been converted to a Tesco Express convenience store. He normally sourced his smokes by the hundred from back street bootleggers, but on this occasion he was completely out. For once, he'd have to swallow the every day exorbitant prices that most other people had to pay. Not only had he lost two grand's worth of gear, he was now about to cough up almost £8 for smokes.

Standing in line at the tobacco and lotto kiosk -

lately equipped with roller shutters to hide the contents in a vain effort to prevent kids from seeing glamorous cigarette packaging and so deter them from smoking - Anderson pulled out his wallet. Tugging out a credit card, he dislodged a business card, which fluttered to the floor. Stooping to pick it up, what passed for a smile, played at the corners of his cruel thin lips. The card read: *Angie Brown, Crime Analyst, Metropolitan Police, Houndshale.*

*

Nadine Cousins hadn't bothered with a solicitor; she'd just wanted to get her interview over with and get the hell out of her cell. Meanwhile, having trudged up the stairs to the CID office, Emma and Intel had been met with the usual suits' apathy and spurious reasons to get out of having the job handed over to them. It was the usual barrage of excuses: too busy, tied up with another big job, only two detectives on, "it's probably only enough for possession," etc etc...

Possession with intent to supply cases, supposedly, fell within the remit of the CID; but depending on which duty detective sergeant the uniformed cops went to, would determine whether his department would take the job on. Often, when faced with the inevitability of taking a body, the suits would go through the motions and always find the path of least resistance.

This meant either getting a suspect to accept a caution - thus negating any further avenue of investigation - or in the case of drugs offences: rather than spend time packaging and sending drugs off to the lab for forensics, they'd simply decide that it was a case of possession, rather than intent to supply. A junkie caught with enough gear to supply his street for a week, would happily agree to possession and so incur no more work for the CID than was strictly necessary. Rather than take it up with the inspector, the BTF cops decided to keep the job, and to at least try and secure a conviction.

Checking on the result of the EDIT test - a chemical test kit that determined the nature of the drugs she'd brought in from the strip-search; Emma noted that they were indeed crack and heroin. Next, she borrowed the gaoler's medieval-looking bunch of keys and went to collect Nadine from her cell.

Getting the custody skipper to sign her over for interview, and into her care for the duration, Emma took Nadine into the windowless room that was furnished with no more than a bolted down table, three chairs and a cabinet, upon which sat a twin deck cassette recorder.

Struggling to remove the tapes clinging cellophane wrappers, she inserted two tapes into the antiquated machine. One would be the master tape - sealed in the suspect's presence - while the other, would provide a working copy for the typists upstairs to compile a ROTI - a record of taped interview; which would be added to the file. Should the suspect wish, they could take away a further copy, but should the need arise; it would be the master copy that would be played in court.

Glancing down at her scribbled notes and making sure that exhibit EC/1 - the 50 white and 50 brown, and EC/2 - the weighing scales - now sealed inside evidence bags - were safely tucked away under her chair, she inserted the tapes, closed them up inside the machine and pressed record. The tapes began to spool and a warning buzzer sounded which would cease once the recordable part of the tape went through the recording heads. The buzzing stopped; Emma cleared her throat and began to read from the aide memoire taped to the table in front of her.

'This interview is being tape-recorded and it may be given in evidence should your case be brought to trial. At the end of the interview, I will give you a notice explaining what happens to the tapes. I am PC 1190UX Emma Cash, stationed at Houndshale. We are in interview room number two at Houndshale police station and I am interviewing...'

She glanced up at Nadine. 'Can you state your full name and date of birth for the tape?' Nadine had been here before, but as with most suspects, she solemnly played the game.

'Nadine Cousins, twelfth of January 1992.'

'Thanks Nadine. Can you confirm that besides me and you, there are no other persons present?'

'Yes.'

Emma gave the time and date and reminded Nadine that she had the right to free and independent legal advice. 'Do you want to speak to a solicitor?'

'No love.'

'You don't have to tell me; but is there any reason you don't want to speak to a solicitor?'

'I don't think I need one.'

Emma cautioned Nadine once more and confirmed that she understood the caution. Not for the first time, she thought about how much longer the whole preamble took, compared to the actual questioning of a suspect such as Nadine. With the formalities over, she reverted to her habitual form of address.

'OK Babes, you were arrested earlier on suspicion of possession with intent to supply.' Reaching under her chair, she pulled out the evidence bag. 'For the tape, I'm showing Nadine exhibit EC/1. Nadine, can you confirm that this was found to be in your possession during a strip search?'

Nadine looked at her feet. 'Yes love, you know it was.'

'I just have to ask you for the tape babes. Can you confirm what's inside the bag?'

Nadine shuffled her feet and made pretence of examining the bag as though it were the first time she'd seen it. 'Blast.'

'Do you mean crack babes?' prompted Emma softly.

Nadine nodded.

'For the tape please...'

Barely audible, Nadine confirmed that she'd meant crack.

'What else is in here babes?'

The girl opposite Emma took a sip of water from her plastic beaker.

'A bit of brown.'

'Heroin babes, yeah?'

'Yes love.'

Emma continued to prod:

'How much is in here Nadine?'

'About fifty of each.'

'Fifty rocks of crack and fifty wraps of Heroin?'

'Yes.'

Putting the bag safely back beneath her chair, Emma pressed on.

'Can you talk me through the events that led up to you being stopped by officers?'

Of course; Emma knew exactly the sequence of events, but in order to get an account from a suspect in order to later challenge it, she would have to go through the pretence of not knowing about what had happened a couple of hours earlier.

At training school, cops were taught not to ask closed questions such as: *Did you do it?* The preferred method; was to skirt around the issues, asking seemingly un-related questions in order to close down any defences in advance. Once the suspect's account had been summarised and read back to them, it would then be the turn of the interviewer to challenge the account.

All angles, no matter how ridiculous or insignificant would have to be covered, so that once the case came before a magistrate, there wouldn't be any surprise defences with which the defence solicitor could ambush the officers.

So for example, where fingerprints or traces of a suspect's DNA were found at the scene, the officer wouldn't say: *your fingerprints were at the scene so you must have done it.* Rather, the interviewer wouldn't reveal the presence of such evidence, before asking whether there was any reason for the suspect's fingerprints to be at the scene. Of course, if the suspect was smart - and thankfully, the low level criminals dealt with by the uniformed cops weren't known for their guile - the suspect would simply say, that of course his fingerprints were found at the scene of the burgled shop - He'd popped in there to buy some cigarettes the day before. The reason his fingerprints had been found on the wrong side of the counter; was because a coin had rolled under there and he'd gone around the other side to pick it up - using the counter to pull help pull himself back to his feet. *Bad back you see officer...*

In Nadine's case however, there were no such machinations; she just wanted to get the interview over without implicating Spoons, and get the hell out of there. For Emma's part, the main thrust of her questioning, would be to try and prove possession with intent to supply, rather than the much lesser offence of possession. She'd learned the hard way that, in order for the CPS to agree to a charge of supply, the quantities and the fact that electronic weighing scales had also been found, would be irrelevant. There had to be some other corroborating evidence such as a deal being witnessed, or fresh evidence being turned up during the Section 18 of the suspect's address.

Sadly, Emma had already been made aware that her team had drawn a blank at Cousin's address. She felt some sympathy for Nadine. It was the likes of Anderson that the cops wanted to nail, but so far, by using his addicted runners, he'd always been one step ahead.

Nadine began to falteringly trot out the now-familiar story - long since accepted by court jurors:

'You know I'm an addict love,' she began. 'Well, I get through a lot of gear and it's cheaper for me to buy in bulk.' Slumping back in her unyielding plastic chair, Nadine fell silent. Emma reached between her legs once more and brought up the bagged scales, holding them up for Nadine to see.

'I'm showing Nadine EC/2. What are these babes?'

'You know what they are love.'

'Just for the tape...'

'They're scales.'

'And can you confirm they were inside your jacket pocket when we searched you earlier?'

'Yes, they were, they're mine too. Like I said, I buy my gear in bulk and I carry the scales around with me so I can weigh the gear and not get ripped off.'

Emma smiled, if she could have a pound for every time she'd heard this story - inside and out of a courtroom - she'd be rich enough not to have to sit in this dingy airless room inhaling the repellent odour of this junkie's feet! Despite having heard it all before, she scribbled some notes for effect, before bidding Nadine to continue with her well rehearsed story.

'Where had you been before you were stopped by officers?'

'*You* were there love, I told you.' She began to fidget. 'How long is this gonna' take officer?'

Emma knew that the doctor hadn't made it to see Nadine before she'd booked her out for interview, and she looked like she was starting to cluck.

'I know you told me earlier babes,' she said soothingly, 'but I need to get it on tape. We're almost done. Just tell me where you'd been.'

'I went to meet a friend.'

Emma nodded. 'Where was that babes'?

Nadine hesitated; she didn't know how much the cops knew about her meeting with Spoons.

'Umm... just up by the tube station.'

'Which station babes?'

'You know, the one up by the Lakes estate.'

'Bosterley?'

Nadine nodded. 'Yeah, that one.'

Knowing that her next question was a waste of time, Emma ploughed on just the same.

'What's your friend's name Nadine?'

'I - er... don't really know his name; he's more of a friend of a friend really...'

'Why did you go to meet him?'

Nadine's pale cheeks flushed red. 'I owed him some money, so I went to meet him to pay it back.'

'What did you owe him money for babes?'

Nadine looked at her feet and fidgeted. 'I'd rather not say, I just wanted to give him the money and get him off my back.'

You'll never get that bastard of your back babes, thought Emma *not until you're six-feet under.*

'OK Nadine, then where'd you go?'

'Nowhere really love. I was just on my way to my interview when you stopped me.'

Emma wasn't even going to go into the fictitious interview; there was no point. So far, she reckoned there wasn't a lot more than possession on the cards for this one, and realising she was flogging a dead horse, she ran through her last few stock questions; the answers to which she'd wearily predicted before they were even uttered.

'Where did you get the gear from babes?'

'A bloke on the street, just around the corner from the Lakes.'

'Does he have a name, this bloke?'

'We never ask that love, dunno' who he is.'

'How much did you pay?'

'A couple of hundred up front and the rest on tick.'

'Where'd you get the money from, are you working?'

'Some from my mum, and the rest I saved from my bennies.'

'Really babes? How do you manage to save money

from your benefits?'

'I get quite a bit; I get bennies for unemployment, housing allowance and disability 'cos of my addiction.'

One day, thought Emma; *someone is going to surprise me with a different story.* It was time to wind the predictable interview up.

'OK babes, you do realise that possession of class A drugs without lawful excuse is an offence?'

Nadine, knowing the interview was coming to an end brightened up.

'Yes love.' She smiled, revealing her heavily stained, rotten teeth. 'But I'm a crack head, what can I do?'

Emma glanced at the aide memoire. 'Is there anything further you want to add or clarify?'

'No love.'

'In that case,' sighed Emma, getting Nadine to sign the tape label; 'interview concluded at nineteen-thirty-five hours on the same day.'

'You don't half talk some shit babes,' she smiled, having switched off the tape recorder and removed the tapes. She looked up from wrapping the sticky sealing label around the master tape. Nadine shrugged her shoulders.

'Come on then, I'll take you back to your cell while I speak to the skipper...'

Booking Nadine back in with the custody skipper, Emma went in search of a gatekeeper. This was a sergeant, with who she would have to sit down and outline the case and what had been said in interview. Despite the track record of CPS lawyers when it came to charging standards, Nadine had certainly been arrested in possession of enough gear to constitute an intent to supply charge, and she could only hope for the best. The uniformed skipper she found in the writing room agreed with her and suggested she bail Nadine and seek CPS advice on the matter.

'Send me the MG3 and I'll write it up.'

The MG3 is one of a set of repetitive forms which, when completed by the investigating officer, makes up the physical file, that forms the prosecution case. It basically sets out the history of the case, including what was said in interview. The MG3 allows gatekeepers and the CPS to decide on whether a case can be successfully run or not. Cops like Emma; after spending hours putting a file together, have long since learned to keep a spare copy. Emma had lost count of the times she'd got to court only to be told by the CPS prosecutor, that the file had gone missing.

Procedure adhered to; Emma went back through to see the custody skipper and arrange a date for Nadine to return to learn her fate.

By the time she got back in there, the skipper was in the middle of booking in a drink-driver, the procedure for which was going to be lengthy. Unwilling to lose her place to the next prisoner to come through the door, she settled down to wait. By the time the skipper had finally got done coaxing the pissed-up driver to provide a couple of samples of breath on the machine, half an hour had passed and Emma's stomach was rumbling.

Finding a date for Nadine to return for her bail wasn't straightforward; the bail diary was pretty full and they had to agree on a day, which coincided with Emma being on duty. Eventually settling on a date two months into the future, Emma went down to Nadine's cell, swung open the heavy door, and told her she was going to be bailed.

Bringing the now severely clucking crack head before the skipper, Emma went into the store room to fetch Nadine's meagre belongings - less the gear, weighing scales and her mobile phone - and waited for the ancient printer to churn out several copies of Nadine's 47/3 bail sheets.

Nadine nodded solemnly in all the right places as the skipper warned her about not returning for bail, and reminded her to keep her appointment with the drugs clinic. She signed to confirm she'd received her copy of the bail notice, before being led from the custody suite, and out of the front door.

Intel was still lurking around the writing room. 'Took your time with her didn't you?' he asked. 'You ready to go back out now?'

'Intel - you can fuck right off! - Eaten *your* food have you? Well, *my* stomach feels like my throat's been cut, and I'm going nowhere until I've had something to eat! And *then* - I've got to send the MG3 to the gatekeeper to do his bit - unless you want to do it for me?'

Intel hunched his shoulders and raised his hands in a defensive gesture; accentuating his tadpole-like head.

'Whoah! Don't want to get in the way of a girl and her food! Let me know when you're ready to go out.' And with that, he went back to his beloved CRIMINT while Emma went out on to Houndshale High Street in search of a takeaway.

Chapter Eight

'Flashes everything but C'

Released From custody without her mobile, Nadine Cousins was desperate for a smoke. She couldn't call anyone until she got home and found her old address book containing the numbers of fellow addicts who could hopefully spare her a rock or two. Unless, of course the old bill had taken it away as evidence when they'd been to do their Section 18. Thinking about it though; if they *had* been able to unearth her tatty old book from beneath the piles of dirty clothing, old magazines, food-encrusted plates and mouldy food; the cop who had interviewed her - the one that called everyone babes - would surely have produced it from under her chair along with the other exhibits.

Rushing home to her scabies-infested bedsitting room behind the bookies, she pushed open the front door and climbed the stairs to her room. She was seriously clucking by now; shivering, but at the same time covered in a film of sweat. Against all odds, she imagined finding a fragment of a rock somewhere on the floor, and just as soon as she could get into her room she'd be on her hands and knees ghost busting.

The flimsy door usually yielded without too much pressure. It's lock long since ruined, just had to be shown to key to pop open. She'd never bothered to get it fixed and the landlord never came around. As long as he received his monthly direct debit from the council on

Nadine's behalf, he didn't give a toss about the state of his buildings.

Reaching the second floor landing, she turned right along the corridor to her room. Nadine was panting, her stomach was cramping, and tunnel vision had set in: distorting the distance between floor and ceiling. She was on the verge of a panic attack.

If only she'd insisted on seeing a doctor before she'd been interviewed, she might have been given some meds to see her through to her next fix. The custody skipper had given her the option, but she had been desperate to get out of her cell and just hadn't thought it through. The babes cop had wheedled and coaxed her through the whole process with promises of a quick interview. She'd told her that she wouldn't be there long, and that was why she hadn't seen a doctor or consulted a solicitor. By the time Nadine had been released from custody, she'd been there for over three hours.

Feeling her way blindly along the wall, she reached her room. Fuck! Fuck! Instead of her battered door, she came up against a solid sheet of ply board, screwed across the doorframe!

Not wanting to leave Nadine's room insecure after they forced entry, for the 18, some well-meaning cop had called in the boarding-up firm who'd nailed her door shut, and the bastards hadn't bothered to tell her! Attached to the door was a sheet of police memo pad with a CAD number scrawled on it and the instruction to call the police operator; who in turn would call out the boarding up people to allow her access to her own apartment!

How the fuck was she going to call the cops - or anyone for that matter without her phone! She was going to have to go back to the nick and wait in a queue to speak to the officer on the front counter, before she could even think of getting back into her room. It could take *hours*.

Sinking to her knees, Nadine beat at the board

covering her door. Her fingers bled with her frantic, but vain efforts to dislodge the screws keeping her from her address book and crack heaven. Tears running down her face, and desperate to smoke a pipe, she made an irrational decision; she was going to have to go and face Spoons...

*

By the time Emma had finished writing up her notes and emailed her MG3 to the skipper, there was less than an hour left to the end of her shift. Intel - had left her to it, dropped off the Q car back at Filebridge, and jumped on the carrier with the rest of UX646, who; since doing the Section 18 at Nadine's and waiting an hour for boarding up, hadn't really got to do much patrolling.

They'd done a couple of stop and searches, but apart from issuing a cannabis warning to a spaced out Polish guy, their patrol hadn't been particularly fruitful. That was the way of it sometimes: all or nothing. Returning to Houndshale nick, they picked Emma up and set off for the office at Filebridge.

They'd almost got back. Driving over the railway bridge leading to the nick, Jax had to slam on the anchors to avoid hitting an obviously drunk man who'd staggered out into the road in front of him. Winding down his window Jax shouted: 'Get off the road you idiot!' Instead of complying, the man - a white Filebridge chav, in vest, shorts, and covered in tattoos - stood his ground and flipped the cops the bird!

The Cat and Porridge jumped out to remove him from the road while Dynamo logged back into the MDT so that chav could be put through the system. Dragging him from the road and onto the pavement, the Cat was eventually able to get the belligerent swaying man's details, which he relayed to Dynamo to feed into the MDT.

The chav had certainly done enough to warrant

being arrested for being drunk and disorderly, but this close to the end of the shift, the last thing the cops wanted to do was delay their journey home for the sake of a pisshead. The only problem was, that in such a state, if left alone, he was bound to create havoc for someone else to deal with. Even if they could encourage him to stagger home; should he get there, collapse and drown in his own vomit; it would be counted as a "death in custody" The system was such, that should a person die within 24 hours of any police interaction, questions would be asked and pensions lost.

Mindful of the risks, and to the groans of his team, skipper Jarvis got the Cat and Porridge to drag the chav on board the carrier while they established who he was and where he lived. Characteristically, the MDT was playing up. Lack of O2 coverage in what was an established black spot, it was now on what was known as: the "go slow." Dynamo was still working away at the screen and keyboard, but to save time, Intel put the chav's details up over the radio and requested a name check. It came as no surprise to find that their man was well known to the PNC system.

Although not currently wanted, his warning signals "flashed": Mike for mental, Victor for violent, Alpha for alleges, Delta for drugs and Echo for escaper. Intel remarked that he flashed everything but C - for contagious.

'No, hang on Intel!' shouted Dynamo triumphantly. 'I've just found him on the MDT and he *definitely* flashes C!'

Having got the MDT screen to come to life; unbeknown to the rest of the team, Dynamo had been busy searching the map database for the north Lincolnshire town of Scunthorpe. Zooming in on the town's name, he continued to zoom in until the only part of the word Scunthorpe showing on the screen, and now filling it: had been the word "CUNT."

'Yep, there you are buddy!' he announced to peals of laughter from the rest of the carrier. The newly dubbed "cunt," tried to focus his drink-befuddled brain on what was so funny. Driving him home and establishing that his unfortunate girlfriend was in the house, UX646 dumped him unceremoniously at her feet before driving back to the nick without further incident.

*

Calvin Anderson was a contented man. Despite the money he raked in from the drug trade and his small time protection racket, Anderson lived at the taxpayer's expense: in a subsidised council flat in Houndshale town centre. He even had the nerve to draw unemployment benefit, and from his sixth floor balcony, he could look down on the dark warren of alleyways to the rear of the High Street's shops.

The alleys - not covered by the town centre CCTV - hid his runners from view and served as a rat run that branched off in several directions. It enabled them to make good their escape, should they be pursued by the cops.

His non-descript apartment door opened into a living area furnished with expensive leather furniture and modern kitchen fittings. The interior was filled with the sound of music and film, piped from state of the art cinematic surround sound that had cost several thousand pounds to install.

There in his practically rent-free apartment, he lounged around in designer tracksuits and trainers, king of all he surveyed. He was a very big fish in a small and stagnant pond. Anderson's influence over those who strived to make a living in Houndshale was plain for all to see. He could be frequently found lounging around in Club 101; being waited on hand and foot, and dressed in tracksuit and training shoes.

Meanwhile, doormen; shit-scared of the nasty

Jamaican, turned away those paying customers who had the temerity to try and get past them wearing the very same footwear worn by the seemingly untouchable Anderson. The club's archaic dress code didn't appear to apply to someone who collected protection money from it's owners.

He knew that the cops were aware of his activities, but he'd either not been deemed enough of a priority to spend precious tax dollars on, or else the word on the street about Houndshale's new borough commander was true.

Besieged by the grown ups at Scotland Yard, he'd given in to cutting his borough's appalling burglary figures, to the detriment of allowing his officers to get to grips with what was an equally appalling drugs problem. The fact that drug addiction directly affected his burglary statistics, didn't feature in his borough objectives, and so to the delight of Anderson, he was more or less left to his own devices. It had been left to the quasi-freelance cops of the Borough Task Force to target - as best they could - the borough's drug dealers.

There was only so much they could do in relation to targeting the likes of Anderson. Without a proper surveillance job being set up on him, they'd had to satisfy themselves with intercepting his runners in the hope of catching him out or - more fancifully, getting them to turn informant. The word among some circles, even suggested that he may have been a police informant - such was the difficulty experienced by the ordinary cops on the street, in trying to nail him.

Anderson's intercom buzzed. Picking up the receiver, he listened to a tinny and disembodied voice from below his eyrie.

'Spoons, it's me Nadine. I need to see you.'

Angrily gripping the receiver in anticipation of learning about her capture, Anderson's cruel mouth twisted into a sneer. He barked into the mouthpiece.

'What the fuck do you want? I told you never to come here you fuckin' stupid bitch! Get your skinny white arse around the block and check for feds. You get me?'

The small trembling voice confirmed she'd understood his order and Anderson slammed the receiver back onto it's cradle. Going out onto his balcony, he scanned the immediate area below the block looking for cops.

Ten minutes later, and the bitch was back, buzzing his intercom.

'There's no old bill out here Spoons, please let me up, I'm dying!'

Reluctantly buzzing her up, Anderson lit a smoke and paced up and down while the junkie rode the lift to the sixth floor, hope brimming against all odds in her tortured soul.

Nadine tapped nervously on Spoon's door. A malevolent eye peered at her through the spy hole before bolts were drawn noisily back to admit her into the flat. She'd never had the nerve to call on Spoons before and when he admitted her inside, the clean and orderly interior was in sharp contrast with her filthy and disorganised bed sitting room.

Striding across the hallway, Spoons didn't stand on ceremony. Sparks flew from his unfinished cigarette as he stabbed it into Nadine's forehead making her scream in pain and terror. Her hands flew to her head; nail-bitten fingers exploring the pink watery blister which had blossomed instantaneously.

'Where's my fuckin' gear?' he snarled.

'The old bill...'

Grabbing a handful of her greasy hair, Anderson stopped her next words with a hard punch to the stomach. Squealing in pain and fighting to regain the breath so brutally knocked out of her body, Nadine sank to her knees.

'Please Spoons!' she gasped, 'I couldn't help it; they must have been waiting for us!'

'Whaddya mean *us*?' he screamed. 'They followed *you*!'

Nadine, in the vain hope that Anderson wouldn't hit her again, stayed on her knees. His rant had sprayed her face with tobacco-laced spittle and she felt a droplet of it coursing it's way down her cheek, mingling with her tears.

'I'm begging you Spoons! Give me a smoke! I'm fuckin' dying!'

Anderson bent down, his eyes blazing. 'You!' he hissed sibilantly, 'owe me two fuckin' g's! How you gonna' pay me back?'

'I will Spoons! I swear!'

'You're gonna' have to go back to sucking cock, cos' you're finished with me,' he snarled.

'The next time I see you, it had better be to give me my dough back cos' I want fuck all else to do with you! You get me?'

'I'm begging you Spoons! Please hit me up! Please!'

Anderson's face softened, but his eyes betrayed an evil intent that the clucking Nadine failed to interpret.

'I'll tell you what Nadine,' he said, gently cupping the back of her head and using her name for the first time since she'd entered his flat, 'I'm gonna' to do you a favour...'

Nadine's heart leapt. Spoons was going to give her a couple of rocks after all.

'Actually,' he murmured inaudibly while stroking her hair; 'it's more of a favour to those losers whose cocks you're gonna' suck.'

Then suddenly, without a hint of warning, Anderson gripped the back of Nadine's head, stooped, drew back his arm, and savagely punched her in the face with all his might, smashing her rotting front teeth clean out of their sockets. He laughed, a laugh completely devoid of humour; like the braying of a donkey.

'There,' he shouted, spittle flecking his thin lips; 'Now your punters won't have to worry about infecting their cocks on your rotten fuckin' teeth!'

Nadine's head spun, her vision erupting in a stabbing myriad of shooting stars against a descending backdrop of black as she struggled to remain conscious. She gagged on her smashed out teeth, the splintered bone threatening to choke her. Spitting them out of her blood-filled mouth, she crawled into a corner and curled up into a defensive ball; but Anderson wasn't finished. Snarling hatred, he rained kicks on her head, back and ribs.

Scrabbling on her hands and knees, Nadine reached the front door. Grasping the handle, she pulled herself upright and fumbled frantically with the locks, her bloodied hands slipping on the brass fittings and leaving dark smears on the woodwork. Finally dragging the door chain free, she heaved the door open and fled along the corridor. Anderson's cruel laughter rang in her ears.

*

It had been more than a month since Angie Brown's incredible night of lust-soaked passion with Calvin Anderson, and after a few days of compulsively checking her phone's message box to no avail, she'd given up on ever seeing him again. She'd written it off as yet another one-night stand, after which the male of the piece usually awoke, fucked her once more and in the cold hard light of day, moved on to someone younger and with less baggage.

Waking up one morning, five weeks after her night at Club 101, she'd unplugged her mobile from it's overnight charge and turned it on to find a text message from an unknown number. It had simply read: "Missed you baby, call me? C. xx"

Her heart raced and she felt a warm glow spreading between her legs. It had to be Calvin! Ignoring the obvious fact that as he hadn't bothered to contact her in the last five weeks, his text wasn't worth acknowledging, Angie stared at the short SMS before punching in a reply.

"Missed you too sweetie. Drink? x" Agonising over how many kisses she should add to her reply, she moved the blinking cursor to the solitary kiss she should have sent, then added two more.

She thought briefly about the old adage so often repeated by her old school friend that: men should be treated mean to keep them keen. Well Michelle Patterson, she said out loud. That's all very well, but your advice never really worked for *you* did it? Smiling at the schoolyard memories, of her regularly dumped friend, Angie Brown pressed send and off her message went; kisses and all! This was one hot guy she didn't dare treat mean! But meanwhile, it was time to get her arse in gear and get ready for work.

Dreamily, she showered. Under the jet of hot water, she rubbed gel suds over her body, pausing when she got to her breasts and lingering over her nipples, which stiffened to her touch. With eyes closed, memories of that night of lust with her ebony lover, flooded deliciously back.

Sliding a hand down her tingling body, her fingertips found the coarse hair between her legs. She began to caress herself, easing a finger between her lips and teasing her clit. Feeling her own velvety wetness, she moaned and slid a second finger inside; slowly, but rhythmically rubbing her clit while her other hand tweaked and pinched at her nipples.

Imagining Calvin entering her with his huge cock, she began to rub harder and faster, her hips thrusting against her hand, while her arse bucked and the rest of her body trembled with pleasure. Groaning: 'Christ!' she felt a stab of white-hot heat, and shuddering, her knees buckling, she came like a train.

'Oh yeah baby,' she said out loud. 'Missed you too you horny bastard!' Closing her eyes, she shuddered anew as she slowly pulled out her fingers and sucked her juices from them.

Towelling herself dry, Angie was still weak at the knees. Wiping the steamed-up mirror with her towel, she looked at herself in the misty mirror. Grinning like a teenager at her self-indulgence, she addressed her flush-faced reflection.

'Angie Brown,' she giggled - 'you are *such* a slut!'

Wandering back to her bedroom to get dressed, she couldn't help picking up her mobile. Unlocking the screen, she saw with excitement that Calvin had already replied.

"See at the 101, Friday night, around 7:30 for an encore? xxx"

He'd matched her three kisses! She keyed in her reply: "See you there hot stuff! xxx"

Friday! That gave her a week to get her hair and nails done and get waxed to re-establish her overgrown Brazilian, at the Polish-run beauty salon on the High Street.

Drying her hair, she dressed and left for Houndshale nick for another day of compiling crime statistics among the suits on the third floor. She'd have around an hour to go over last night's crime stats before presenting her graphs and flow charts to the detective chief inspector. In turn, the DCI would make a presentation of her findings to the senior management team during their daily meeting - also known as "morning prayers."

Arriving at the station, she swiped her card at the back gate and entered the yard. Muscular arms folded across bulky ballistic vests, she saw two heavily armed cops leaning on the hoods of their armed response vehicle, which was lined up by the gate and ready to go.

The Trojan cops had Glock side arms strapped to their thighs and MP5 carbines slung from their shoulders. Their gun ship's tail pipe emitted plumes of smoke as the engine idled in the cold morning air. The smoke; with hardly a breeze to disperse it in the stillness of that cold morning, wreathed the men, partially obscuring their features and making them appear like heroic wraiths coming out of the mist in some Arthurian movie. If Angie Brown hadn't been so smitten with Anderson, her body still tingling from her self-pleasure, she would have found the sight of the armed cops quite erotic.

Plain-clothed officers scurried around loading polythene and paper evidence bags along with plastic weapons tubes, into the trunks of unmarked cars. Angie heard the harsh barks of general purpose Alsatians coming from the back of a dog van; dominating the lower, more playful yaps of a Spaniel drugs dog running around the yard in search of a playmate.

Among others, she recognised the unmistakable figure of Dynamo. His bulk squeezed into flame-retardant overalls, he was effortlessly shouldering an enforcer, while carrying a heavy canvas bag containing crowbars and a rabbit tool. Tossing the kit into the back of a carrier, he flashed Angie his trademark grin, all teeth and mischief. She gave him a wave.

Angie greeted one of the plain-clothes officers puffing on an electronic cigarette: 'Morning Jimmy. Big op today?'

Jimmy, a lifelong smoker trying to kick the habit, sucked the last remaining wisps of nicotine-laced vapour from his plastic smoke. 'Mornin' Ange, yeah, drugs warrant on the Lakes.' She knew better than to ask whom the intended subject of the raid was, but wishing him good luck, she swiped into the building and climbed the stairs to begin another day of analysis.

Once the cops had loaded up their kit, they crowded into the writing room where Simon Coverdale waited to brief them on the warrant. Last to enter the crowded room, were UX646.

Laughing raucously at some crude joke the Cat had

189

just cracked at the expense of the plump female station officer they'd passed on the way in, they piled into the room under the scornful gaze of the supercilious Trojan officers. Shooting his team a look which said: "stop embarrassing me," skipper Jarvis looked heavenward with his, "sorry, but what can I do" look, and apologised to Lurch for their late arrival.

Not given to wasting words on youngsters who refused to take the job seriously, Lurch merely nodded, cleared his throat and put up the first slide of his briefing. His assembled audience had heard such briefings many times before, but as ever, they did the old warrior the courtesy of feigning interest - apart, that is from the Cat, who along with Porridge face - was tucked away in a corner of the room, hunched conspiratorially over his iphone, checking out "rack of the day."

'Information. Source led intelligence suggests that Terri Porter is holding a large quantity of class A drugs at her address on the behalf of Calvin Anderson.'

The very mention of Anderson's name got the local cop's attention; even tearing the Cat away from electronic breast ogling.

'Apart from a caution for shoplifting five years ago, Porter has no previous, but...' Lurch tailed off and looked at the Trojan skipper before continuing.

'Information has been received, that along with holding Anderson's stash, Porter may be also holding a revolver.'

The Trojan skipper chimed in.

'Any idea of where it may be hidden?'

'The source suggests it's only being stored at the address and not readily to hand. If there at all, it's believed to be concealed under the floorboards.'

The Trojan skipper nodded and Lurch continued his monotone briefing.

'Intention. To execute a warrant under Section 23 the Misuse of Drugs Act, and to search the premises and all on the premises. To retrieve the drugs and secure evidence, to make arrests for the offences mentioned, and to detect any other offences while at the address.

Location. The address is on the Lakes estate - 41, Challis House, Peterlee Road, Spentford. The property is a ground floor flat at the southern end of the street.'

Next, Lurch put up the now obligatory Google street view slide - more for the benefit of the dog handlers and Trojan, than for the locals.

'There are not believed to be any children at the address, and Porter is understood to be the only occupant, although her boyfriend is known to stay over at weekends. A leaflet drop in the street yesterday, suggests that there is at least one dog.'

At this, Simon looked meaningfully at the dog handlers, before continuing.

'The address can be approached without being seen, as long as all vehicles are parked around the bend in the road, just short of the block. There's no back entrance and only two windows facing the street - the front room and a smaller bathroom window, which is frosted. The door is UPVC, with hinges on the left. It opens inwards into a small porch, where there is another wooden door.

Method. Officers from the Borough Task force are to effect entry into the premises and secure all occupants within. Once all occupants are secure, the dog unit is to carry out a search; with arrests made where necessary. Appointed person to be responsible for the book 101 and exhibits.

Entry to the address will be with a warrant obtained from Filebridge magistrate's court yesterday.'

Lurch handed the warrant to the officer nearest him, who, after a perfunctory glance, passed it around the rest of the room. He continued:

'Administration. Houndshale custody is to be contacted direct for any prisoners. EAB's to be completed for all arrests and any force used.'

191

Lurch glanced at the BTF contingent.

'Sergeant Jarvis to nominate an officer to complete the book 101.'

At this point, Jarvis, already irritated by the Cat's lack of attention to the briefing, nodded in the direction of his coffee and tits obsessed subordinate, who huffed and puffed silently while the BIU man continued.

'Risk assessment. All officers must wear PPE and be in possession of personal radios. All officers must be currently OST and ELS trained. When searching persons or premises, all officers should be aware that drug addicts are unpredictable, and are to wear protective gloves, cover any cuts, and consider sharps, infections etc.'

'Communications. Working channel will be UX despatch 1. PNC checks will be on UX support. The CAD number for this operation is 1671 of today's date.'

Finally, Lurch went through the human rights spiel, asked for any questions, and left the cops to sort out who was doing what. The Cat, his face like a smacked arse, went in search of a book 101, while skipper Jarvis allocated roles for his team's entry.

41 Peterlee Road, formed part of a grey concrete structure, which housed twenty other apartments not much bigger, than rabbit hutches and not too dissimilar to look at.

The block predominantly housed single mothers and welfare claimants - the majority of whom, stayed up late annoying each other with loud arguments, even louder trashy music, and the incessant barking of status dogs wallowing in their own shit and piss. Not much more than kids, the residents of Challis House - apart from signing on day - would linger in bed until lunchtime and even then, remain in grubby nightwear for most of the day, watching reality shows without recognising the irony, that they were existing in their very own real-life episode of Jeremy Kyle.

Lurch, crammed into a tiny Vauxhall Corsa, led the

way into Peterlee Road, stopping short of the bend in the road. The BTF's carrier pulled up behind the Corsa, with Trojan and the dog unit close behind.

The BIU man stopping was UX646's cue to don NATO helmets and gloves in preparation for the entry. It also heralded the cessation of all piss taking and got the adrenaline coursing through the veins in anticipation of the unknown. Once suitably attired, professionalism took over the banter, and UX646 focussed on the roles they'd been given by Jarvis as they piled out of the carrier and onto the street.

Lurch shambled ahead of the BTF with the intention of identifying the right door for them to put in. Hard on his heels was the Cat; who, after the last door he'd attempted and failed to smash open, had pride at stake, and had been allowed the chance to redeem himself. Intel was next in line and was carrying the enforcer to prevent the Cat from tiring under it's weight on the sprint to the address. Jax came next, carrying the rabbit tool, followed by Dynamo wielding the hoolie bar. Bringing up the rear were Porridge Face, Emma and the skipper. With the firearm having been assessed as not ready to hand, Trojan remained in their vehicles on standby, to examine and make safe the revolver, should it be found.

The dog handlers, on the other hand, formed up behind the BTF, fire extinguishers and dog catching loops at the ready. "Bite Back" spray - a costly dog deterrent - hadn't yet been approved by the Met's costing department, and it would take a vicious attack on officers later that year, to usher it in. Meanwhile, the dog handlers relied on Halon fire extinguishers, of the type used by cops in riot situations to put out petrol-bombed colleagues. A blast of Halon, designed to take out the oxygen feed at the seat of a fire, also had the effect of taking - quite literally - a dog's breath away too. A quick blast of this was usually enough to distract a furry land shark, just long enough to get a loop pole around it's neck.

The Cat took over the enforcer from Intel and stood back while Jax jammed a pry bar into the gap between the door and it's frame. Prising an opening big enough to take the closed jaws of the rabbit tool, he took up the tension on the pry bar using his thigh and inserted the expanding jaws. A look over his shoulder confirmed that Porridge Face had hold of the pump handle at the other end. He nodded at Porridge, who acknowledged by pumping hydraulic fluid through the armoured hose, expanding the rabbit's powerful jaws. Jax removed the pry bar, took hold of the retaining rope that prevented the rabbit tool from crashing to the ground, and stood back ready to direct the Cat's enforcer blows.

With every pump of the handle, the gap between door and frame yawned wider. The cheaply made UPVC doorframe began to buckle. Jax, seeing it about to splinter and so lose all tension, recognised the danger, and signalled for Porridge to stop pumping. With the door straining against it's locks and taut as a funeral drum, Jax stepped aside and pointed out the best area for the Cat to strike. The Cat, his face a mask of concentration and with everything to prove, swung the enforcer back before smashing it into the door just above the handle.

The door flew open with a satisfying crash. The Cat, his chest puffed with pride after his one hit enforcer blow, joined Jax, who had already stood aside; leaving Dynamo to deal with the flimsy inner wooden door. As with pretty much all entries, the cops: in their eagerness to get the job done, generally didn't tend to check whether a door was already unlocked before setting about it. This was the case with Terri Porter's door and Dynamo, not checking the handle, booted it with his size eleven's, smashing out the plywood panel, which went slithering along the hallway.

Trying the handle as an afterthought, he flushed red

as it swung open, before, along with the rest of the team, he sprinted into the apartment screaming: 'Police with a warrant!' Dropping their tools, the Cat and Jax, brought up the rear.

The tiny apartment rang with shouts of: "Clear!" as each room was cleared, found to be unoccupied, and made safe. Of Terri Porter and her dog, there was no sign. A fug of cannabis smoke indicated that the cops hadn't missed her by that long, and the remnants of dog food in a plastic bowl confirmed the usual presence of a dog. With Porter's apartment cleared, the assaulting officers relaxed and called in the dog handlers who set their eager spaniels to work.

Police Dog Rosie's stubby little tail wagged ten to the dozen as she raced here and there, snuffling into every nook and cranny. Calling her away from the resident dog's food bowl, her handler diverted her attention away from the food, whereupon she darted into the one and only bedroom and disappeared under the bed.

Emerging covered in fluff and dust, she was directed into a wardrobe where she happily stuck her wet nose into every corner, her paws scattering clothes and empty trainer boxes all over the room, before jumping out without a find. Then, just when Rosie's handler had written the whole thing off, his dog trotted into the bathroom and sniffed noisily in the area of the bath panel before sitting down and wagging her little tail like crazy. Once she had sat down, her handler knew, without a doubt, that something juicy was hidden behind that panel, and prising it off with a screwdriver, he was delighted to discover two polythene bags stuffed beneath the bath.

Calling skipper Jarvis into the bathroom, the dog handler showed him Rosie's finds before making a huge fuss of his dog and rewarding her with a treat and her favourite toy.

Pulling on a pair of bright blue latex gloves, Jarvis

dragged the bags out and examined their contents. One bag was filled with around a kilo of brown powder, which he provisionally identified as heroin, while the other bag was crammed with banknotes. Calling out: 'Find!' Jarvis summoned Intel to photograph the bags in situ before removing them and taking his exhibits into the tiny front room where, the Cat - who up until now had been spared the effort of writing in his book 101 - reluctantly recorded the skipper's exhibits.

Lurch, hovering in the background, typically showed no more excitement other than to say quietly: 'That's a bit of alright isn't it?' as though commenting on a pint of his favourite Yorkshire ale.

Porridge Face looked over the Cat's shoulder as he laboriously recorded Police Dog Rosie's find.

'That's fuck all!' he sneered. 'When I was in the army, I was attached to the Special Boat Squadron off Jamaica and we fast roped from choppers onto a container ship in the middle of the Caribbean Sea.'

Not put off by the groans and rolling of eyes from his colleagues, UX646's very own Billy Liar continued relating his fantasy.

'Yeah, on my way down, I took out two bad guys with my pistol and we found two tons of cocaine hidden in the hold.'

The groans of his fellow cops grew in volume, but Porridge was in full swing now: glassy-eyed and completely oblivious to all around him.

'And you know what?' he asked of his captive audience, 'I was put up for a Victoria Cross for that job, but they only decorated the fuckin' Ruperts. Tossers!'

It was the Cat who shut him up:

'I bet you had a Bowie knife between your teeth too!' he laughed humourlessly, tossing him an evidence bag. 'Well you're here now hero, with the Met's finest. So do me a favour, shut the fuck up you ugly twat, put the gear in there, and get writing on it before the café stops serving breakfast and starts serving fuckin' dinner!'

Porridge, mistaking the Cat's vitriol for banter, caught the bag, called the Cat a wanker, and began dutifully scribbling on the bag while Jarvis gave another of his heavenward looks.

The intelligence regarding the revolver being under floorboards was disregarded once the cops discovered the floor beneath the grubby carpet was concrete. With no other hiding places uncovered, the Trojan skipper gathered his troops, jumped back into his car and zoomed off to the next job.

The only other find of note was a book containing runner's street names and punters' phone numbers. Next to some of these, in a margin, were amounts of cash: presumably owed to Anderson for gear taken on credit. Not only had the BTF struck gold with the heroin and cash, but Intel was positively slavering over the potential intelligence he could share from Terri's notebook once he could get logged into CRIMINT!

Eager to get his team and the exhibits back to the nick to begin the long process of recording evidence and writing notes - via the café for breakfast - Jarvis called in a favour from the safer neighbourhood team skipper, who he'd served with on the TSG some years earlier. The SNT skipper, after some mock indignation and sucking of teeth, agreed to provide a couple of Police Community Support Officers to secure the property until the boarding up company arrived.

Once the PCSOs turned up, UX646 jumped back aboard the carrier and decamped to their favourite breakfast spot - a café, on one of Filebridge's industrial estates, named The Hidey Hole.

The Hole - as it was affectionately known - was ably run by an enterprising Portuguese family, who were GTP. This meant that they were, "Good To Police." The GTP label simply meant that they offered the cops a discount.

Most nicks had had a canteen for as long as even

the most senior PC's could remember, but hit by swingeing cuts to the Met's catering services, the canteens had been the first to go. The lovable Asian and African canteen ladies, who called everyone "darling," started to disappear from all but the large central London stations. This left the cops to forgo their privacy, and eat their bacon and eggs among the public at large; who regarded the sight of uniformed cops tucking into breakfast as something of a novelty. Offering a decent cut price breakfast for the cops, the Hole provided a damn good breakfast for under a fiver, and consequently, with the amount of police vehicles outside every morning, it was undoubtedly the safest café in the whole borough!

*

Jerking himself off, Balvinder Kapoor lay on his semen-stained duvet, bathed in sweat, and stared at the grainy image paused on the screen of his out of date laptop. He'd done little more than pull his jogging bottoms down around his ankles, followed by his grimy y-fronts.

Staring back at him, wriggling and on all fours: was a bound and gagged eastern European woman. She had a full, but cellulite-ridden arse, which she thrust out provocatively, while her pendulous breasts swung in small circles beneath her.

A heavily tattooed and bare-chested, man stood over her; his head covered with a hood. A fistful of heavily dyed, jet-black hair in one hand, he had her head jerked back, while he struck her face with the open palm of the other. This was Balvinder's favourite part of the video, and on freeze frame; it provided him with the necessary stimulus to get himself off. He longed to get hold of the real deal; a compliant bitch, with whom he could do whatever he wanted. Just getting his cock out, no longer did it for him in quite the same way that it used to.

Ever since the cop had stopped him before he could

198

flash that whore - with the exception of sneaking out to the gurdwara for free food - he'd rarely ventured out during daylight; preferring instead, to spend his days alone, watching porn on his laptop.

He'd got hold of a clapped out old bike, long since abandoned outside the gurdwara. When night fell, he'd taken to prowling the area of Southwick market, on Cranston's borders, where it was well known that you could pick up a whore from pretty much any street corner. He imagined that he was really riding a motorcycle, just like the one his idol rode in his favourite Elvis movie: Roustabout.

The majority of those who plied their trade in the shadows cast by the miserable sodium lamps of Southwick were from eastern Europe. Girls, bought from families and smuggled from Romania; their pinched, pale faces raddled from slugging cheap vodka and crack abuse, had long since given up on their master's promises of a new life in Britain, where a good job awaited and the streets were paved with gold. With their passports confiscated by brutal pimps, they were condemned to walk the miserable streets of Southwick and neighbouring Houndshale looking for tricks. The girls, who hailed from surroundings equally as grey, wet and depressing, had resigned themselves to spending their nights blowing or dispensing hand jobs to disgusting men of all shapes and sizes for twenty quid a go - seventy-five percent of which, would have to be paid to unscrupulous gang masters.

So far, Balvinder's night time sojourns to Southwick hadn't involved any contact with the short-skirted women who inhabited the shadows. He'd been content to cycle slowly past, staring at the flesh on display while fantasising about what he would do to them if they were ever unfortunate enough to spend any time with him. The girls had got used to seeing the grubby looking Indian guy with the sly look in his piggy eyes, and despite being desperate for the cash, whenever Balvinder appeared on his rusty old bicycle, they'd all silently prayed that he didn't approach them.

Staring at the frozen frame from his favourite movie, he mechanically went through the motions of jerking off, but even the bound and gagged woman with the big tits, wasn't doing it for him anymore. He just *had* to get hold of the real thing. *He* would be the man controlling that bitch, slapping her, fucking her up the arse and then making her suck his cock.

Pulling up his pants and jogging bottoms, he got up from the bed, removed the paused image on his laptop with one press of the mouse, turned it off and closed the lid. Slinking downstairs, he grabbed his bike, lugged it outside and set off into the night towards Southwick.

Through force of habit, he stuck to side roads and alleyways. He didn't know whether the cops had his description, but in any case, a cyclist out at night, always provided them with a reason to stop and search; such was the volume of crime committed by elusive suspects riding bikes. If you were to commit a robbery or burglary and you knew your way around the borough's interconnecting alleyways - *and* you had access to a bike - you were almost certain to outsmart the cops who, sutured to the seats of their nice warm cars, were reluctant to get out and walk.

Tonight, as he emerged from an alleyway opposite the BP petrol station, which marked the border between Southwick and Cranston, Balvinder spotted a girl coming towards him from the forecourt of the BP. Unwrapping the cellophane from a packet of cigarettes, she discarded it on the ground, took out a smoke and paused to light it. Passing him with barely a look, the girl wandered off in the direction of Southwick market.

Giving her a head start, Balvinder cycled slowly after her, watching as she flicked the stub of her smoke against a wall, creating a shower of sparks. She was dressed like all the other whores in the area: a skirt so short it could be mistaken for a belt, and stockings embossed with lacy, oversized roses. From beneath a mini leather jacket, he could see that she wore a scoop necked top, out of which spilled her milky white tits. She walked awkwardly in vertiginous heels; like a kid who'd borrowed her mum's shoes to dress up in. The heels had the effect of making her arse sway provocatively, and Balvinder was mesmerised.

He couldn't help but follow her, and couldn't believe his luck when he saw her stop and go inside a heavily graffitied bus shelter, well known as a pick up point for the market whores. Balvinder - anticipation starting to swell in his groin, decided to take a closer look. After all, if she was a hooker, she couldn't exactly complain, could she?

Hearing the sound of un-oiled chain whirring over a worn-out sprocket, the girl looked up to see a dirty looking long-haired Indian in stained jogging bottoms with a disturbing leer on his face. The guy on the bike made a slow pass before turning around and coming back. Feeling inside her handbag, her hands closed over a pair of scissors, which she pulled out and hid in the palm of her hand. This time, when he was level with the bus shelter, he stopped and looked her up and down.

'Hello lady,' he said lasciviously, 'you waitin' for a bus?'

She didn't really want to talk to him, but had the feeling that speaking to him was probably the only way she'd get rid of him. He seemed a bit simple, but she still felt freaked out by the look he was giving her.

'Um... sort of.'

As she spoke, she revealed front teeth, which looked so white and perfect as to appear false, and as he looked closely at her thin face, he could see a triangular shaped birthmark just under her left eye.

'There's no buses stop here this time of night lady,' he said wagging his finger. 'You're not really waiting for a bus are you, you naughty girl?'

Just then, there was a flash of headlights and a patrol car turned into the estate car park next to the bus stop. The girl put her scissors back into her bag and turned around to face the crude graffiti on the back of the shelter. She took a mobile phone from her jacket pocket and feigned a call. The cops, getting out of their car, ignored her and raucously sharing a private joke, they made their way towards the entrance of an apartment block. When she turned around, the leering Indian on the rusting bicycle had gone.

Chapter Nine

'First gear, and... vroom!'

It was to be an easy day for UX646. As was usual on Tuesdays and Saturdays, during the football season, they'd been assigned to policing supporters at the local club. The policing operation was on nowhere near the same scale of the Premiership teams that Jax and the team were sometimes called upon to police; but even small teams like the Seals, have an up and coming thug element - known in police parlance as "risk."

Mostly kids, some as young as fifteen, the risk group try to emulate the old traditional firms from clubs like the Chelsea Head Hunters, and Millwall's Bushwackers. The Seal's risk element, have even adopted Millwall's chant of: "No one likes us and we don't care!"

Much improved police intelligence and planning, along with the wide use of CCTV, has recently resulted in football hooligans being caught and sent down for long stretches by no nonsense crown court judges. Those still intent on fighting amongst themselves now resort to arranging a "meet" in some neutral location, where they can meet up and have a good old punch up away from the Old Bill. Spentford's youth, however, are still dumb enough to try and have a go at the supporters of visiting teams and for this reason; UX646 had been deployed to the football ground. What made it an easy day, was the fact that once the match was over and the supporters had dispersed, they wouldn't generally return to normal patrol

203

duties, meaning a half-day and then home for a beer.

The trick was to follow the risk group around, keeping them buttoned down tight during both the build up and aftermath of the game. The risk group made this fairly simple, as they tended to roam around in a pack looking for lone visiting supporters to prey on and pick off. Once inside the ground, Section 23 of the Football Spectators Act 1989, armed the cops with the powers they needed to eject and arrest any unruly element within.

Intel had reported sick and so it had fallen to the core team skipper to nominate a replacement. Jax was pleased to see that Intel's replacement was to be the big Kenyan, Billy Kimathu. Jax was out in the back yard at Filebridge sorting the carrier out, when Billy sidled over and greeted him with his gap-toothed grin and customary: 'Yes Jaarx!'

'Hey Billy, how's it going?'

The Kenyan clapped Jax on the back. 'Awright moit,' he drawled in his best Kenyan/Cockney. 'You can relax Jaarx, you got the Kenyan cowboy watching your back today!'

Jax grinned back at him and went upstairs to pick up his kit and let skipper Jarvis know the carrier was ready to go. Pushing open the door to the BTF office, Jax was greeted with the sight of Dynamo and the Cat involved in some sort of competition involving the team's enforcer.

Bright red and looking like he was about to burst a blood vessel, the Cat was futilely attempting to match a grinning Dynamo in bicep curling eighteen kilos of red metal, while skipper Jarvis looked characteristically heavenwards.

The Cat dropping the enforcer to the floor with a crash signalled the end of the game. Picking up their kit, UX646 trooped downstairs and joined the Kenyan cowboy in the carrier.

They'd not long left the nick, when the operator at

Met call, announced a robbery at Cranston Country Park. The core team skipper transmitted that he had no one to send, and after some debate, about how they were within three minutes of the robbery call, skipper Jarvis; to the muted protests of the Cat, put his team up to deal.

Jax punched the big red 999 button on the carrier's dashboard. Blue lights came on, and a stab on the centre of the steering wheel activated the wail of the siren. Apart from the description of the robbery victim and his location in the park, the information regarding the robbery was typically scant, putting UX646 on alert for anyone running away from the immediate area of the park.

As they approached the scene of the robbery, Jax went for the so-called silent approach. Had it been a report of a fight, he'd have left the siren blaring to scatter the protagonists and so save them from a whole heap of unnecessary paperwork, but given the circumstances, he double pressed the horn for a silent approach, so as not to scare off the robber.

A height restriction at the entrance to the park meant that they would have to look for the victim on foot, and as soon as the carrier had come to a stop, everyone piled out. Last out were Jax and his operator for the day, Billy.

Skipper Jarvis led the team along the main path of the park while Jax and Billy took a right fork, which led to a car park. As they did so, the radio operator added an update to the CAD, stating that the victim was in the car park. She added the details of the car so that it could be easily identified. She'd no sooner finished transmitting; when Jax and Billy were hailed by a distraught Indian man, who appeared from inside a misted up Nissan Micra and came dashing towards them waving his arms around.

His head weaving from side to side in a pretty good impression of a snake charmer on the streets of Mumbai, the heavily accented man: obviously not long in country and known colloquially by his peers as a "Freshie" - fresh from India - eventually managed to convey what had happened.

His wife had sent him out to do the weekly shop at Tesco's and on the way; passing Southwick market, he'd been flagged down by a scantily clad female who'd asked him for a lift. Flattered, he'd agreed, and once inside the car, she'd slid a hand onto his thigh and told him she liked him.

The little Nissan filled with the girl's heavy scent. Coupled with the feel of her hand on his thigh, her perfume had made the freshie forget all about Tesco's and the wife who back in the Punjab; had been party to their parent's arranged marriage. Stroking his thigh, the girl had suggested they drive to nearby Cranston Country Park for a "chat."

His mind a whirl of heady perfume and promises of what was to come, the freshie drove to the park and reversed into a space away from the other cars. Once there, rather than continue her caressing of the freshie's thigh, the girl had snatched his wallet from the car's console, opened the door and done a runner!

His hard on instantly diminished, the freshie had let out a wail of indignation and given chase, only to see her disappearing through a gap in the shrubbery, taking with her the money his wife had given him for Tesco's! Years of a diet involving vast quantities of ghee, had made chasing after the girl and his wallet impossible, and after a short dash, his face flushed and his heart pounding, the freshie had given up, returned to his steamed-up car, and called the police.

Billy Kimathu, a veteran of "writing off" jobs that in his opinion would result in no more than a shit load of paperwork with no suspect in custody to show for his efforts, took the man by the shoulder and walked him away from Jax.

'That girl,' he began earnestly, looking into the

freshie's distraught face. 'Do you know what she was?'

'No sir,' replied the unfortunate man.

Billy looked around and leaned in close. 'She was a pwostitute!'

As usual, failing to pronounce his "R's," He spat out the last word like a Spanish inquisitor interrogating an unbeliever.

The man's head bobbed from side to side. 'Yes please...'

Billy continued. 'Do you want your wife to know what happened - that you picked up a pwostitute?'

The freshie began to cry. 'But sir, she took my wallet!'

Billy was adamant he wasn't going to take a dead end report and pressed on.

'What will happen if you go home and tell your family you went with a pwostitute?'

Not wanting to return to his wife with a tale of how he had lost their grocery money to a whore who he'd picked up not more than two streets from their home, the wretched man acquiesced. With a: 'Thank you please,' he trudged miserably back to his car.

Billy walked back over to where Jax was waiting. 'Well Billy - what's the suspect's description? Which way did they go?'

The Kenyan laughed. 'Jaarx, don't worry about it man, it's all sorted!'

Jax wasn't convinced, but if Billy was happy to put his name to the write off, that was fine with him.

'Hmm... well OK, as long as you call up UX to write it off...'

Billy merely laughed his deep rumbling belly laugh, and clapped him on the shoulders while Jax called up the others to rejoin them by the gate. Back on the carrier, skipper Jarvis asked Jax what had happened in the car park.

'Ask Billy skip, he dealt with it.'

Jarvis looked over at the Kenyan who turned his bulk around in the operator's seat to face the back of the carrier.

'Yes, skippah, he decided that because he'd been robbed by a pwostitute, he didn't want to take it furtha.'

Knowing Billy to be Houndshale's king of job write offs, Jarvis shrugged. 'Just make sure your name is all over that!'

'No worries skippah!'

He turned back and addressed Jax:

'Do you know what Jaarx?'

'What's that Billy?'

'The same thing once happened to me!'

Jax glanced over, waiting for another of the Kenyan cowboys stories. 'Go on...'

'When I first came to this country, a girl stopped me in my car and asked me for a lift. She kept looking at me and smiling. She told me that she liked me and she was very nice Jaarx!' Jax grinned, 'yeah Billy, carry on'

'This girl said that she knew a nice park where we could go and talk. I liked her and she liked me, so I agreed. When we arrived at the park, she started talking about money and then I understood! I had to think of a way to get rid of the girl!'

The big man looked serious for a moment. 'Do you know what Jaarx? She was a PWOSTITUTE!' He spat the last word out, spraying Jax with indignant spittle from between the wide gap in his front teeth. Jax brushed it from his sleeve.

'How much did it cost you then Billy?'

The Kenyan looked offended. 'Fark all Jaarx! I said to her, look; in my country, when a girl likes a man, she goes to a certain tree, collects some leaves and takes them back to the man.'

Billy's face was one big grin. 'So I told the girl, look over there, that's the kind of tree. She got out of the car and went she went to pick the leaves.'

Jax was grinning too now. 'So then what did you do?'

'Jaarx,' he said pointing at the carrier's gear stick.

'First gear, and... vroom!'

Billy was pissing himself laughing at the memory. 'She ran after the car shouting and throwing leaves! She was shouting: you fuckin' bastard!'

Jax laughed so much; he had to pull the carrier over. 'I bet she was!'

Porridge Face had been listening from the back seat. As soon as he opened his mouth to speak, everyone pretended to look busy, either looking out of the windows or checking their phone screens. Not put off by this blatant display of bullshit story avoidance, Porridge launched into a tailor-made tale.

'When I was in the army...'

'Here we fuckin' go,' muttered Jax. 'The SAS again, I suppose...'

Porridge continued. 'We were in Belize and patrolling deep in the jungle. Suddenly, we came to a clearing in the middle of nowhere, and found a straw hut. I pulled the pin on a grenade and was just about to sneak around the back and check it out for bad guys, when this bird comes out, stark naked! And guess what?'

The carrier remained silent, nobody was foolish enough to respond to his question and so become a target for his stories for the rest of the day. Porridge wasn't put off and continued his story.

'She was stark bollock naked, she had the hugest set of tits I've ever seen!' He glanced over at the Cat, hoping that the very mention of tits would snare him, but the Cat didn't take the bait.

'Anyway,' Porridge said, 'she was clearly a prostitute and wanted to fuck the whole patrol for a Dollar each!'

He hadn't given up on piquing the Cat's interest just yet.

'Hey Cat - I bet even you've never seen nipples like

she had. Like Scammel wheel nuts they were!'

The Cat steadfastly ignored Porridge's tactics, staring at the screen on his phone like his life depended on it, but when Emma rescued him with talk of coffee; he seized her lifeline like a drowning man.

'Hey babes, I had one of those flat whites the other day. It was lush and really silky!'

'I wouldn't call it silky Emma, I think of it as velvety... Skip, can we get a coffee?'

As they neared the ground, they passed groups of Seals fans, cans of cheap lager in their hands. They were chanting the same old tired crap - 'Oh west Lon-don... is won-der-ful!... Oh west London is wonderful! (This to the tune of: "When the saints come marching in...") Then, when they came across groups of rival fans - today it was Brighton - they launched into a homophobic chant (this time to the 1970's tune of The Village People's: "Go west.")

'Stand up, cos you can't sit down...stand up cos you can't sit down...'

Jax wasn't particularly a fan of the game, much less the Seals, and their fan base, but he was philosophical about it. All the cops had to do, was to keep fans apart before the match, sit like school prefects during the game - telling off those who hurled insults and made obscene gestures to the opposition - deal with any ejections the club stewards made, and then after the match; with the help of "spotters" from the away teams local nick; they simply had to identify potential trouble makers and escort them to the train station and onto the trains. Once they had all been seen off from the area, a quick tour of the local bars was all that was required before they would be released and return to Filebridge for an early finish. Provided of course, that they didn't come across something on the way back to the office...

When he was driving; which was pretty much all of the time, Jax tended to stay in the carrier for as long as he could before going inside to join the others. Sometimes, he managed to stay out of the ground until half time, when the loud speakers *always* blared out the Beatles "Hey Jude." He never did know what the Jude connection was, but he hated going inside and watching grown men - accompanied by small children - making masturbatory signs towards opposing stands.

Sometimes, when they didn't agree with the referee's decision, the dads would break into a chant of: "The referee's a wanker!" This crass display of stupidity, ensured that the next generation would take their father's places on the terraces, and so keep the hatred going ad infinitum.

The only excitement during the game had been when some drunken fans pushed one of their number over the barrier and on to the pitch. The grass, during a game was hallowed territory, and the clubs stewards - with their earpieces and beer bellies - rather than recognise the pitch invader as the victim of his mate's idiocy, swung into action. Sprinting over, they grabbed the inadvertent invader, placed him in a headlock and between them, carried his writhing body to an exit where he was dumped at the feet of the cops.

Skipper Jarvis detailed Emma and Porridge Face to deal with the ejected fan. Theoretically, Section 23 made pitch invasion an arrestable offence, but unless it was a blatant case of a pissed-up fan leaping over the barrier and sprinting up and down the field and interfering with the game; the cops tended to do no more than obtain personal details, search him, then inform him that he was to be banned from the stadium. Providing the football thug's drug of choice - usually cocaine - wasn't found, and he wasn't shown as wanted on PNC, he'd then be free to go.

The pitch invader dealt with, Emma and Porridge rejoined UX646 and the Kenyan cowboy, who were just exiting the ground and lining the route outside in preparation for keeping departing fans apart.

As was their routine, once the bulk of fans had left, the cops followed groups of away risk as far as the railway station, where they would wait for the trains to arrive and depart. Once the platforms were clear in both directions, their work would almost be done for the day. This was also Jax's cue to jump in the carrier and drive up to the station to collect them.

Once he'd picked them up, they made one last tour of the bars to make sure there were no troublemakers around and Jax set off back to Filebridge. They'd just joined the east/west three-lane carriageway, when Dynamo pointed out of the window and burst out laughing. Following his pointing finger, Jax looked down at a little red Toyota Yaris. At the wheel was an Indian, beaming up at the cops in the carrier. He looked very pleased with himself, and on closer inspection, Jax could see why. Strapped to the side of his head with an elastic band was a mobile phone! Laughing, Jax wound down the window. 'Nice hands free!' he grinned.

Smiling up at Jax, his head weaving from side to side, the inventor of the world's first non-Bluetooth hands free kit, waved at the cops, closed his window and continued jabbering into the mouthpiece in excited Punjabi. Jax gave him a salute and overtook him while the rest of the carrier rolled around laughing.

A big BMW streaked past the carrier. 'Cheeky bastard!' retorted Jax, before hitting the 999 button and giving chase. Had Intel been there, he probably would have recognised the driver of the BMW, but in his absence, Billy put the car's plate through PNC.

By now, Jax had caught up with the BMW. It was held at a set of red lights and he pulled alongside to allow Billy to speak to the driver. Even before Billy could get a response from PNC, he recognised the belligerent looking guy behind the wheel. Looking hatefully up at the cops as if he had no idea why they were pulling him over,

Calvin Anderson stroppily shouted: 'Wot?'

Billy indicated a petrol station just ahead. 'Pull into there, I want to speak to you.'

Anderson's response was to suck his teeth Caribbean style, before muttering something about Babylon. When the lights changed to green, he drove aggressively away tyres screeching, but nonetheless, complied with Billy's request that he drive into the station.

Anderson invariably presented what was known by the cops, as a resented stop, and today was no exception. Full of attitude, he climbed out of the car, slamming the door behind him. His usual tactic was to try and intimidate any cop who stopped him, by getting right up into their faces and continually demanding to know why he'd been stopped. He was never willing to listen to the explanation, and would just shout over their voices, before claiming racism.

Now, the big Kenyan had spent months out in the bush tracking down bad guys and getting into firefights with Somalis up on the Kenya/Somalia border. He wasn't cowed by the likes of Anderson and, what was more, old Billy couldn't be accused of racism either! His big hand thrust out in front of him, Billy pushed Anderson back out of his personal space and up against the carrier.

'Don't fuck me around man,' he hissed sibilantly. Anderson made a token attempt at saving face, but managed little more than petulantly puffing out his chest and trotting out the same old line.

'If you weren't in that uniform...'

'Hey man, it comes right off,' said Billy, his eyes bulging. He started to remove his jacket. Anderson backed down, choosing instead, to spit in a final gesture of defiance rather than take on the crazy-eyed Kenyan. Jax, standing next to Anderson's open window called over to Billy.

'Stinks of cannabis in here Billy!'

Hearing the magic words, which heralded a search of Anderson's vehicle, the rest of UX646 piled out of the carrier and began to carry out an extensive search of the BMW. Seeing the cops clambering all over his precious car, Anderson protested and made a move towards them. Quick as a flash, Billy, eyes blazing, grabbed his arm and pushed him back up against the carrier. 'Stand fuckin' still moight, until I say you can move!'

Of course, someone like Anderson wasn't likely to be caught with anything illegal, but it eased the cop's frustration with someone like him, just to pull his car to pieces. Once that was done and all his stuff had been haphazardly chucked back into the car, Jax came over to him and searched his pockets while Billy kept a firm hold of him. That done, Jax warned him about his driving.

'Thank you Mr. Anderson, have a nice day won't you.'

Scowling, his eyes spitting hatred, Anderson sucked his teeth, got back into his car and drove away, tyres squealing. 'Another satisfied customer,' laughed Emma. 'He's one nasty bastard babes,' she added, walking over to the carrier with Billy. He flashed her his gappy smile.

'He knows not to fuck with the Kenyan cowboy!'

Once they were all back on board, the Cat rubbed at non-existent stubble, mimicking the absent Intel.

'So, Spoons has got himself another car eh? That's going straight on CRIMINT!'

Porridge retorted: 'Yeah, I knew straight away that was a drug dealer's car. My brother used to run a BMW garage. He reckons all drug dealers drive beamers. I knew, as soon as I saw it. He's probably got a secret compartment underneath. If I'd had my brother's special BMW tools, I'd have been able to get it open.'

The others studiously ignored him, but he continued. 'I bet he had a massive stash under there, I could tell by the way he was acting. Shitting himself, he was. Whaddya reckon Billy? Did you have that in Kenya?

Bet you did. I was in Kenya with the army, slotted a few Somalis up on the border, I did...'

Billy, a veteran of such real life skirmishes, just smiled the smile he normally reserved for idiots, and like everyone else on the carrier, ignored the bullshit streaming unabated from the lips of the ugly little man with no neck.

'Mjinga,' he said quietly to himself, reverting to Swahili and calling Porridge an idiot.

For the journey to Filebridge, Jax stuck to the main roads to try and ensure an uninterrupted journey back to the office. Along with the rest of UX646 - determined to make the most of an early finish - he drove with his blinkers on. It wasn't often they got to finish early, but on football days, provided all the fans left early without any trouble, it was back to the ranch for an early off, then home for a few beers. Fingers crossed, they wouldn't come across a traffic accident, a blatantly drunk driver, or some member of the public flagging them down to report some crime or other. Football days, when for all intents and purposes they were off the borough's radar, were definitely a perk - which, quite unashamedly, they wanted to make the most of!

In the event, they managed to get back to the office unimpeded, dump their kit and make it out of the gates and into a world where drunks didn't fall over, husbands didn't batter their wives, cars didn't crash, and radios couldn't call them to arms.

*

It had been one shitty week for Calvin Anderson. First, that useless bitch Nadine had got herself nicked carrying two grand's worth of his gear, and now the feds had smashed Terri's door down and had it away with ten G's worth of brown and five grand in cash. He was beginning to think there was a leak. There was no way, those dumb assed cops could have struck it lucky *twice* in one week without the help of some fuckin' snitch. The sooner he enlisted the help of that stupid horny bitch that worked at Houndshale nick, the better...

As for the unwitting subject of Anderson's thoughts; Angie Brown had impatiently counted the days, and now that Friday was here, she let herself into her apartment, slipped out of her work clothes and stepped into the shower in preparation for her date with her ebony Adonis.

Under the shower, her week at the office swirled down the plughole with the soapy water running off her body. Feeling intensely alive, she sang the snatches of Shania Twain she could remember, and hummed the bits she couldn't.

'Oh, oh, oh go totally crazy-forget I'm a lady...'

Towelling herself dry, she looked into the mirror, winked at herself and exclaimed: 'Man! I feel like a woman!'

Wandering naked into her bedroom, she blow-dried her hair before covering every inch of her body with moisturiser to combat the drying out effects of hard London water. Next, she sprayed herself liberally with Burberry Weekend - including, with a cheeky grin - between her legs. The Burberry had been a recent buy, especially for tonight. It was a bit more youthful than the perfume she normally wore, but it went with her mood, and what the hell, lately; she felt ten years younger!

Ditching her glasses, she popped contacts into her green eyes and thickened her lashes with Clinique mascara - it claimed to double lash thickness, and it certainly made a difference to Angie's fair lashes, making her look vampish and feisty. She felt a bit like a child, experimenting with her mother's make up, but loved the transformation.

Next, she sat on the edge of her bed and rolled on nude silk stockings, which she hooked to a garter belt. Feeling wicked, she'd forgone knickers and gone commando. Wiggling her hips, she pulled on her favourite cream belted miniskirt. Pleated, in the style of a tennis player's skirt, and worn without underwear, it made her feel sexy as hell. Cupping her breasts inside a lacy Victoria's secret push up bra, she shrugged into a tight fitting leopard print blouse and sat back down on the bed to slip into her shoes. Four-inch anthracite Manolo Blahnik sling backs, with woven cage detail: these shoes had been an impulse buy.

Out in town for daytime drinks with her best friend, she ought not to have wandered into Liberty's after an afternoon of champagne, but feeling fuzzily rebellious, and tempted over to the Manolos on sale range, she'd spotted the Fertillia sling backs, tried them on "for a laugh" and instantly fallen in love. The fact that they were on sale and down from £563 to £227, had made it a done deal, and before you could say: 'That'll do nicely sir!' she'd whipped out her Barclaycard and walked out of Liberty's carrying her first ever Manolos; beaming like a Cheshire cat.

Arranging for a cab to pick her up in an hour, Angie poured herself a glass of Prosecco and sat at the table to put on her nail varnish. Agonising briefly over the colour, she settled for Cotton Candy. Taking a sip of ice cold sparkly, she dipped the brush into the little bottle, and squinting, began to spread the bright pink varnish over her nails.

By the time the cabbie called her mobile to announce he was waiting outside, she'd put away two glasses of Prosecco and was feeling pleasantly heady. Jumping in to the back seat of the cab, her nostrils were assailed by the characteristic smell of all cabs - stale sweat, kebabs, and the lingering smell of the driver's stale cigarette smoke.

Feeling as though the very atmosphere of the cab would ruin all her efforts to be sweet smelling, she tried to hover, rather than sit on the stained seat. In an attempt to circulate some air around the inside of the pungent cab, Angie opened the window - not too low - for fear of messing up her hair in the wind; but just low enough to get some air. The driver, a bearded Pakistani with prayer beads hanging from his mirror, was curtly polite. He was most likely disappointed in picking up short a short fare, when he could have been plying his trade in and around the more lucrative area of the airport.

With a quick leering glance at his rear seat passenger, he swung violently out into the evening traffic, cutting up other vehicles and leaving honking, protesting drivers in his wake, in answer to which, he muttered something unpleasant sounding in Urdu. Pulling up at the end of the alleyway that led to Cub 101, the cabbie grunted the price and made no effort to get out and open the door for Angie to get out.

The click-clack of her brand new Manolos echoing off the walls of the grotty, cigarette butt-strewn alleyway, Angie mused that Club 101 wasn't the ideal venue for an intimate date, but it was early days, and rather than suggest an alternative, she was happy to go along with Calvin's choice. Once she arrived, she began to understand his choice.

Joining the end of the roped-off queue, it wasn't long before a doorman approached her and asked her name. Bemused, Angie complied with his request, at which the doorman told her to accompany him to the front of the queue. Walking past people who'd waited up to an hour to be admitted, she sensed their hostile eyes spearing between her shoulder blades. One leather-jacketed Albanian looking guy went beyond hateful staring; spitting vehemently as she passed.

Feeling bewildered, Angie followed the doorman inside, where she was fast tracked past the giggling cloakroom girls and into the dimly lit club. With a nod of his shaved head, the doorman indicated a cubicle to the right hand side of the as yet deserted dance floor, before leaving her.

Smoothing the material of her skirt against her bare buttocks, she plonked herself down on the deep red velvet bench seat. As she did, she enjoyed a brief feeling of sensual pleasure as her stockinged legs brushed against the soft material of the bench. Sitting there in the gloom, she enjoyed an exquisite moment of flashback to the last time she'd been at the club when she'd met her Jamaican Adonis. And suddenly, there he was! Edging into the cubicle, carrying a bottle of Moet Chandon inside a clinking ice bucket, was Calvin Anderson.

Feeling like a teenager, Angie's heart skipped a beat. Christ! he looked good! His musky smell mingled with that of sandalwood from Hugo Boss and filled the cubicle. Dressed in low cut Armani jeans, a heavy gold chain peeped out from within his black open necked Dolce & Gabbana shirt, and his diamond white smile made her go weak at the knees. He sat down beside her, leaning over close and kissing her full on the lips while his hand gently cupped the back of her head.

'Hey baby! Looking good girl!'

Angie blushed, but eagerly returned his kiss. 'Looking pretty good yourself sweetheart,' she breathed. She thought for a moment that she wished she'd been a bit more imaginative with her response to his compliment. "Looking pretty good yourself sweetheart." *Sweetheart?* That was pure cheese! She seemed to have got away with it though. Still smiling broadly, Calvin popped the cork on the champagne bottle and slowly trickled the deliciously expensive liquid into two frosted flutes.

'What was with the doorman escort? Do you know him?'

Calvin just smiled in response.

'No, tell me, how come I got the VIP treatment out there?'

Chinking his glass against hers, he took a swig of bubbles. 'Let's just say, he replied enigmatically, 'the

219

owner's a good friend of mine...'

'Well,' she said, raising her glass; 'Here's to friends in high places!'

'Yep.' He grinned, thinking exactly the same about friends with benefits...

While they sat there in the cubicle, her looking adoringly into his eyes, and him smiling and laughing his deep belly laugh, she hardly seemed to notice the screen on his mobile blinking almost constantly. Every now and again, under the guise of going to the bar for more drinks, he'd get up and go to deal with the many calls a major dealer of class A drugs has to contend with. When she did mention his frequent trips away from the cubicle, he charmingly apologised, saying his brother had been rushed to hospital the day before with appendicitis. The reason he had to keep dashing off, he said, was that he was having to field phone calls from concerned friends and relatives back in Jamaica.

'Oh babes, I'm so sorry! And here's me taking you away from your family duties!'

'Oh, he's fine, anyway, I wasn't going to not see you just because I'm playin' daddy to my kid bro!'

Angie smiled, cuddling up close and stroking his thigh.

'Tell me all about Calvin Anderson.'

He laughed. 'Tell you what, tell me all about Angie Brown and then I'll tell you all about Calvin Anderson.'

'Not a lot to tell sweetie,' she said suddenly feeling boring. 'I'm just an office girl really.'

Calvin moved his hand down under the table and placed it on her stockinged legs, mirroring her own thigh stroking. Angie almost groaned in anticipation.

'Not *just* an office girl baby,' he wheedled, 'I've got your business card remember? Now, what was it I read? *Crime analyst Metropolitan police.* That doesn't sound like an office girl to me! I bet your job is really important.'

For the second time that evening, Angie flushed red.

This man knew just what to say and she was basking in his compliments.

'Well...' she said, taking a sip of her champagne, 'I suppose it's quite an important job, I just get bored working with those CID dinosaurs. They're all job pissed.'

Calvin leaned closer to hear her above the house music, now pumping out from the giant speakers. 'Job pissed?'

'Sorry!' she laughed, 'that's police speak for someone who has no life outside of the police, can only talk about job-related stuff, and would spend the night in the office if they could.'

'Yeah,' Calvin probed, 'but it must be exciting getting to know all about what happens and who's raiding who when?'

'I guess so,' she admitted, 'I do get to hear some things I suppose. But enough about me,' she murmured, nuzzling ever closer; 'what do you do, apart from keeping that gorgeous body in shape?'

Anderson stroked her hair, pulled her close and kissed her long and hard. Angie felt herself getting wet.

'Well, baby,' he said kissing her nose; 'I guess you could call me a businessman. You know, a bit of this, and a bit of that, but mainly selling cars.'

'What, you *own* a garage?' she asked, becoming more and more impressed. 'What kind of cars?'

'High end, usually: Beamers, Mercs, Porsches, Astons, that kind of thing. My clients are usually eastern Europeans, so I source them here in the UK - mostly from auctions. With the recession, there's plenty of bargains around. It's one thing to buy a posh motor, but running it; that's a different matter. Every month, I ship them over to Romania or Bulgaria, where there's plenty of new money. I tell you baby, those eastern Europeans love a German motor!'

'Very impressive Mr. Anderson,' she purred, rubbing her leg against his. 'When do I get to see this garage of yours?'

Anderson laughed. 'There's no garage honey, I work from home and store the motors at a mate's nearer the docks. That way, I got no overheads.'

'Gorgeous *and* shrewd,' she simpered. 'Where *have* you been all my life?'

Calvin threw back his head and laughed. 'Fancy another?' he said indicating the empty bottle. 'This one's dead - you *do* like your bubbles don't you girl?'

Angie smiled contentedly. 'Oh go on then,' she sighed. 'You know how to spoil a girl!'

Smiling, he got up and she watched the glory of his tight arse as he disappeared behind the veil of fog pumped out by the DJ's dry ice machine. The intense strobe lights cut through the fog, making it look as though her lover was dancing his way to the bar. For the first time in as long as she could remember, Angie Brown felt content and utterly at peace with the world.

The second bottle of Moet finished, Angie was all but wrapped around Calvin's body. He kissed her neck, she felt shockwaves of ecstasy all over her body. Unable to keep herself from ripping his clothes off right then and there, she evoked that famous line from Top Gun, when Carole feels horny and wants a piece of the Goose. Hoarsely, she whispered into his ear.

'Hey Calvin, you big stud! Take me to bed or lose me forever!'

'You are one crazy woman Angie Brown - c'mon then, let's blow!'

Angie giggled. What was she thinking? She really was the queen of cheese tonight! What with calling him *sweetheart* and then quoting from Top Gun! Just as well he hadn't seemed to mind.

They stood up and holding him real close, she could feel his hard cock, pressing urgently against her knickerless pubic mound. Nope, she thought, he *definitely* doesn't mind my cheesy lines!

The cab ride home was a blur, and fumbling with her front door keys, she giggled drunkenly before finally getting the door open, and going inside. She was just about to kick off her precious Manolos, when Calvin stopped her.

'I want you to keep them on baby...'

'Ooh, alright then, you naughty, kinky man!'

They never even made it out of the hallway before Calvin grabbed her hair and tugging it, began to undo her blouse. The buttons undone, Angie shucked out of it and let it float to the floor. With one hand around her waist, Calvin expertly unhooked her bra. Shrugging out from the restricting straps, she pulled it off and threw it onto the floor. Stopping him as he began to nuzzle her breasts, she pushed him away and began unbuttoning his shirt: all the while looking seductively up at him.

Dropping his shirt onto the ever-increasing pile of discarded clothes, she kissed his smooth muscular chest while pulling the bulge of his cock against the wetness between her legs. Arching her back and throwing her head back, she now allowed him to tease her erect nipples with his tongue. Shuddering uncontrollably, she held his head as his tongue licked ever downwards: first over her belly and then inside her belly button. Kneeling, Anderson undid the belt of her skirt, unbuttoned the solitary button and pulled it over her hips. Groaning, she wiggled until the pleated skirt was around her ankles, then lifting her feet, she allowed him to unhook it from her 4-inch heels and toss it aside.

Calvin moved his face to her crotch. Sniffing deeply, he grabbed her garter belt, ripping her stockings from their fasteners and laddering the sheer material. Thrusting his tongue deep inside her, he found her lust-engorged clit and noisily sucked on it.

'Christ!' she groaned, gripping his head and bucking her hips against his tongue. 'Don't stop, please don't fuckin' stop!'

Unable to stand it any longer, she came within seconds; wave upon wave of sheer unadulterated ecstasy. So intense was the feeling that she almost fell over and actually cried. His tongue still worked on her clit. She felt as though an electrical current was being passed through her body.

'Stop baby, stop!' she cried, shuddering, shaking, and completely and utterly helpless. Calvin finally relented and she sank to the floor, the smooth wooden floor, making her slide around on her stockinged knees.

Anderson had only just got going and he wasn't about to show any mercy to the orgasm weakened Angie. Face wet from Angie's orgasm, he kicked off his boots, unbuckled his belt, and undid his jeans, kicking them into a corner.

Angie, her head spinning from champagne and her mind-blowing orgasm, needed time to get her self together, but Calvin was having none of it. Taking off his boxers, he sank to his knees, pushed Angie up against the wall, spread her butt cheeks and violently entered her from behind. Had she not been so drunk or soaking wet, his uncaring entry would have caused her pain, but with her face up against the wall, the room spinning, she could only manage a feeble: 'Easy tiger!'

He ignored her plea and thrust even harder. His fist clenched a handful of her hair, and he violently yanked her head back. She felt rough as rats and just wanted him to get it over with. Mercifully, Anderson grunting like an animal, came in seconds, released the painful hold on her hair and pulled out, before lying on the floor, panting like a dog.

Angie didn't have the strength to get up, and remained on her knees, Anderson's semen dribbling out of her and onto her ripped stockings before pooling on her laminate floor.

Anderson wasn't happy. The stupid bitch had flaked out on him just when he was getting started. In that state, she was worse than useless to him. At this rate, she was going to fuck up his plans. When she started to gently snore, he scooped her up in his arms and carried the comatose woman to her bedroom. Save for making those sleepy little noises made by the half awake, she didn't stir. He dumped her inert form on the bed, took a noisy piss, then opened her window and smoked. He wasn't about to give up on his plan just yet. Let the bitch get some sleep and he'd try again.

She didn't know how long she'd been in the hallway, but opening her eyes and adjusting to the dark of her bedroom, she awoke to find herself on her bed. Feeling around, she found that Calvin was beside her. Her clit was still throbbing, and when she moved her hand down there, she could feel the Brazilian strip of hair, matted and encrusted with dry semen.

'Hey baby,' he said in a sugary voice, 'you OK?'

The rough, violent sex of a few hours ago forgotten, she smiled weakly. 'I'm fine hun, what happened? I must have passed out! How did I get to bed?'

Calvin, his mask back in place, propped his head up with his arm and looked at her through the darkness of early morning. 'You were a bit pissed baby, we had one hell of a fuck and then you passed out on me!'

'Sorry babes, you must think I'm a right lush!'

'Well...' he replied, the hint of a smile playing on his thin lips. 'You can always make it up to me. Calvin feels horny as fuck right now, you ready to go again?'

'I want to babes, honestly, but I'm not quite with it just yet. Shall we get some sleep and try again in the morning?'

Anderson bit back his anger, but his words were saccharine sweet.

'I can't stay much longer baby, but I've got just the thing to get you horny again!'

Angie wasn't so sure. She didn't really want to fuck again so soon, but also didn't want to risk him leaving unsatisfied, never to come back again.

'What do you mean sweet, what you got?'

Rolling off the bed, Anderson snapped on the bedside light. Rummaging in the pockets of his jeans, he pulled out his wallet and phone. From his wallet, he pulled out a small snap bag containing white powder.

'Sit up baby,' he coaxed. 'You ever done a line?'

'What... coke you mean?'

'Yeah baby, this stuff will fix you up in no time!'

Angie wasn't too sure about the way things were going. She'd never done more than the odd spliff as a student *and* she worked for the police! But the heady effects of champagne, drunk a few hours earlier, still clouded her judgement...

'Calvin, you know I work for the police. I'm really not sure...'

'Oh baby,' he wheedled, 'well who's gonna' know?' He grinned down at her.

'I don't kiss and tell, c'mon, give it a try. You'll love it!'

Angie, well and truly hooked by the man sat on her bed, thought, what the hell; I'm big enough and old enough to try a line for once in my life and after all, most of her non-police friends regularly did the stuff.

'Erm... OK,' she said. 'I'm up for it! And I *do* owe you a good fuck after I crashed out on you! You'll have to show me what to do though. I'm a cocaine virgin,' she giggled.

Anderson couldn't believe the stupid bitch had given in so easily. He could barely conceal his jubilation! 'Of course baby,' he said soothingly. 'Calvin will take good care of you.'

Angie watched as Calvin took a twenty-pound note from his wallet and rolled it into a tight straw.

'So people really *do* use banknotes?'

He flashed her the kind of look normally reserved for young children. 'Oh yeah sugar! Watch and learn...'

Opening the snap bag, he carefully poured out a small pile of the snow-white powder onto Angie's bedside table. Next, he took out an American Express card from his wallet and chopped the powder into four equal lines.

'You ready for this baby?' he grinned. Angie giggled again: suddenly unsure.

'I don't want to get addicted sweetheart,' she said, a frown creasing her forehead.

'Don't be silly baby, this is Charlie, not smack!'

Angie felt foolish, like way back in the day, when she'd been a kid worrying about her mother smelling the tobacco of her first illicit cigarette on her breath.

'OK, you go first, show me how it's done.'

Putting the rolled up twenty to his nostril, Anderson put it at the end of the first line and sniffed nosily, hoovering up the powder. It reminded Angie of the wind blowing away a chalk line she'd made on the road for hopscotch, when she'd been an innocent, pigtailed girl back in primary school.

Calvin exhaled, a grin spreading across his face as he passed her the rolled up twenty. 'Your turn baby girl.'

Hesitantly, she took the note from him. Placing his hand over hers, he guided her fingers to the end of the second line. 'Take it in baby!' he coaxed.

Sniffing deeply, she followed the ever-diminishing line as it entered her nasal linings and rushed into her bloodstream. Apart from making her sneeze, she didn't feel anything apart from a light dizzy sensation. Anderson looked at her, a look of anticipation on his smooth face.

'Well?' he asked.

'Dunno babes, not sure,' she replied.

'OK, I'm doin' another, give us the twenty.'

Taking the note from her, he sniffed up the penultimate line before falling back on the bed. 'Yeah baby! yeah! That's good shit! Do the other one!'

A warm feeling of wellbeing spreading through her body; Angie thought: what the fuck, and snatched the twenty back from him.

'Wait baby, wait!' he urged.

'What, what's wrong sweet?' she babbled, suddenly feeling inexplicably euphoric.

Getting up from the bed, Anderson switched on the room's ceiling light, grabbed his mobile and switched it to the video function.

'What are you up to you naughty boy?'

'Calvin's gonna' record baby girl popping her coke cherry!' He laughed. 'Do it baby! he urged, do it!'

Giggling, Angie put the twenty to her nose. 'Look up here baby! Here's goody-goody Miss Brown doin' a line of coke!'

Looking into Anderson's camera lens, she hoovered up the last line - this time without sneezing. Giggling, she threw the twenty on to the floor and lay back: her head spinning pleasantly. Babbling away, she wouldn't shut up. 'Oh coke, oh cokey-wokey,' she gabbled. 'Where have you been all my life?'

Angie felt on top of the world. She felt invincible and the sudden urge to talk nineteen to the dozen. Mostly though, she felt horny as hell!

Anderson, feeling very pleased with himself, put his phone down, but left the video running.

'And now, Mr. Anderson,' she trilled, 'I'm ready for a good hard fuck! But first, I want to suck your beautiful hard cock!'

Still standing, he reached down to the bed and pulled the cocaine virgin to her feet before pushing her down on her knees in front of him. Putting her hand around his hard cock, she licked the tip and took it in her mouth. Looking down at her, his plan almost complete, he reached for his phone and pointed it at the top of Angie's bobbing head.

'Look up here baby!'

Angie Brown, crime analyst at Houndshale police station, her mouth full of cock, pupils wide from the coke and her libido off the scale; looked up at Anderson. Strands of hair, wet with sweat, covered her eyes. Gently pulling her hair away from her face, he resumed his damning video commentary.

'And here, is Miss Brown of the Metropolitan police, sucking Spoons Anderson's black cock. Suck it hard slut! You love cock don't you, you slut?'

Angie, cocaine playing havoc with her inhibitions: removed his cock from her mouth and smiled for the camera. 'Mmm... You know I love it!' Then she took it back in her mouth, sucking noisily.

His film in the can, Anderson put down his phone. The excitement of having snared himself a crime analyst coupled with having a coke crazy bitch attached to his cock, made him feel an ache deep in his balls. He was about to come and this whore was gonna' swallow his load. Grabbing her hair, he buried himself right up to the hilt inside Angie's willing mouth. She choked at his length and gagging, tried to pull away.

'Oh no, you don't baby!' he snarled. Keeping hold of her hair, he twisted it savagely between his fingers, trapping her and stopping her from pulling away. Shouting: 'Yes!' he made one last deep thrust before spraying Angie's tonsils with white-hot semen and instantly filling her mouth with his sticky, salty gloop. Feeling as though she was about to choke, the pressure on her head immobilising her, she panicked and swallowed hard. Just as she did, he pulled his still dribbling cock from her mouth and pushed her away, making her fall backwards.

Gasping for breath, she wiped his stickiness from the side of her mouth. Looking up at him with hurt in her eyes, she asked:

'Why so rough baby, you nearly choked me!'

He sneered, his face twisting into an expression, she'd never seen on his face before. 'Yeah,' he sneered, 'but you love it, don't you bitch?'

The euphoria of her first coke hit, was waning. She didn't understand his sudden hostility towards her. What had she done wrong? Why was he so aggressive? She picked herself back up from the bedroom floor to see Anderson pulling on his pants.

'Where you going babes? What did I do wrong?'

Anderson lit a smoke; he didn't bother to open a window this time. Then, cold as ice: 'I fuckin' told you didn't I? I can't stay, I've gotta' go.'

Angie, her mind a whirl, sat down on her bed, tears streaming down her face and watched him dress in silence. When he'd pulled on his boots, he simply said:

'See you around,' and without so much as a kiss, turned on his heel and stalked out of her apartment, slamming the door behind him.

Walking back to his own apartment, Anderson was feeling very pleased with himself. Who'd have thought it would have been so easy to get himself a sleeper right in the heart of his enemy's camp - and it had only taken two dates with the bitch to seal the deal! The stupid old bitch had fallen for him hook line and sinker, and she'd not given bad head either. His hand went to the lump in his jacket pocket, and affectionately patting the phone: it's sim card crammed with incriminating evidence, his face twisted into an evil smile...

The first grey light of a weak and watery Houndshale dawn was beginning to creep into the room. Slumping back on her bed, Angie Brown, hugged her pillow and quietly cried herself to sleep. It wasn't until she awoke six hours later that the enormity of what she'd done began to seep into her throbbing consciousness.

The lines of coke, which she'd snorted earlier, had increased her brain's natural supply of dopamine. But now, coming down, her brain was suffering a sudden depletion of the stuff, leaving her feeling sad and depressed. Along with her Moet hangover and the memory of being filmed snorting coke and giving head,

Angie was feeling pretty down. Her emotions were all over the place.

*

Nadine Cousins owed her new, but rapidly yellowing Hollywood smile to the generosity of the National Health Service. Upon visiting her dentist and displaying Spoon's handiwork, it had been decided that her quality of life would be improved by the fitting of dental implants. Her official status of unemployed and on benefits meant that the treatment would be free of charge. Naturally, after being shown the dentist's handiwork in a small hand mirror, she'd feigned sincerity and assured Dr. Shah that she would change her lifestyle and look after her new teeth. True to form though, just as soon as the Novocain had worn off, she'd gone in search of a rock and crack heaven. She'd not gone to Spoons of course, she was done with him - more accurately - *he* was done with her.

Rather than take the risks associated with the running of drugs, she'd taken to walking the streets on Houndshale's borders where she ran less risk of being recognised by the local cops. In order to finance her habit, Nadine now joined the other streetwalkers who leant on the open car windows of prowling kerb crawlers. After some pretty unsavoury encounters: including one during which she'd been raped at knifepoint, she'd befriended a Hungarian girl, who'd suggested she join the escort agency that she herself was signed up with.

Nadine's life now revolved around her cheap mobile phone and taxi rides to filthy apartments where she gave head, or anything else demanded by panting, sweaty men. The work was regular if nothing else, and even after she'd paid the agency their cut, there was enough money left over to feed and clothe herself. More importantly however, her agency work ensured that she could sustain a crack high and numb herself while she was pawed and penetrated by an unpleasant variety of sexual deviants.

Chapter Ten

'Dismissed with thanks'

UX646 had been detailed for aid - that is to say, they were to be taken off borough duties for the day and seconded to Westminster. Aid, was assistance to those Met boroughs that had major events planned, but needed additional resources to facilitate them. It could be anything from a premier football match: such as Chelsea, to a gig at Wembley stadium.

Jax's team tended to only assist in level two aid - sometimes fully kitted up in flame proof overalls and protective armour - but mostly dressed in normal uniform with level two equipment readily to hand. Level three aid was a more mundane affair and carried out by officers who hadn't been through POTC - the public order training centre at Gravesend.

Today, as Serial 990B, they'd been called upon to police the ongoing demonstration by hundreds of supporters of the Sri Lankan Tamil Tigers, who were currently camped out in large numbers in Parliament Square. They were there in the vain hope that Britain's politicians could somehow prevent the Sri Lankan army from massacring the last of the Tigers, now hunted down and hemmed in between the Sri Lankan army and the ocean.

Parliament Square has long since been favoured by anyone who wants to display a grievance; situated as it is, opposite the nation's seat of parliament. In fact, at any one time, there are at least two disparate groups in semi-permanent shanty-type constructions, displaying any number of protest banners. One particular occupant of the square had been there ever since the start of the Iraq war. Leaving only to use the toilet and have the odd wash, he relied on supporters to temporarily take over his tent and arrange for his welfare cheque to be paid to him.

What Sir Winston Churchill: his bronze statue, watching impassively over the comings and goings of the great unwashed, must think; God only knows. London, it seems, is the protest capital of the world and on any given day, at least, one group protests about something in some God-forsaken country in an otherwise unknown corner of the globe.

Jax had been off on leave for a week, and while he'd been away, there'd been a change in the dynamics of UX646. Intel, characteristically failing to inform anyone, had applied for and been given, a position in Houndshale's BIU. Working alongside the taciturn Simon Coverdale, he had been posted with immediate effect, and without ceremony, had left the team and was now in CRIMINT heaven! It was probably fair comment, that his bubbly personality wouldn't be particularly missed. His replacement was already in place.

Arriving for the Tamil aid, Jax went up to the BTF office and found his team busying themselves getting their level two kit together. Pushing open the door, the first thing he noticed, was the new addition to the office of a dartboard fixed to the back wall. Negotiating the chaotic piles of overalls and ballistic armour being stuffed into kitbags, Jax was hailed by the others with a mix of greetings and sarcastic comment about the week he'd spent away from the office.

Responsible for the newly installed dartboard, was darts fanatic Ollie "Bullseye" Knight. A popular character among the cops at Houndshale, Bullseye was an area car driver. That is to say, he was a class one advanced driver, authorised to drive one of the borough's two high-powered BMW's.

Area car drivers were normally called upon to pursue equally high-powered bandit cars, driven by criminals who would do anything to evade capture. It was the job of the area car driver to take over a pursuit from level three response drivers; who although authorised to initiate a pursuit on blues and twos, would, in the case of a prolonged chase, ultimately have to hand over to the likes of Bullseye.

To qualify for the privilege of an area car course, a PC would have to have proved their mettle on the street, be industrious, proactive and a good thief taker. He or she would be an experienced cop, looked up to by their peers and expected to be a stand-in in the eventuality of a skipper's absence. Bullseye came with the added advantage of being a carrier driver, which Jax welcomed. It would be nice not to have to drive *all* the time.

Jax wandered around to the back of the office and an area partitioned off by steel lockers, to get changed. The only other person in the cramped space: an area smelling of farts - and conversely - deodorant, was Ollie Knight. With his back to Jax, Bullseye faced the tin mirror on the inside of his locker. With a brush of the kind your sister might have had back in the 70's in one hand, he fastidiously patted strands of thinning grey hair into place with the other. He was fond of proudly telling anyone who took the piss out of his grooming habits, that he'd had the same brushed back hairstyle for the last thirty years.

Permatanned, Bullseye was around the same age and height as Jax. He wasn't tall in the way that tourists to the capital may have expected him to be, and his ready smile seemed at odds with his pugnacious reputation. His filthy mind, ramrod straight back and trim figure, were testament to his past employment.

Bullseye had sailed around the world with the Royal

Fleet Auxiliary, been an airman with the Royal Air force, spent time as a cop in the Ministry of Defence police and been a radio dispatcher for Jax's old force, over at Thames Valley.

His grooming complete, Bullseye turned away from his locker and gave Jax a nod and a smile. 'How's it going Jacko?'

'You alright Ollie? When'd you start mate? I see you brought your dartboard with you!'

The very mention of darts - or arrows as they were colloquially known - lit up Bullseye's teak-coloured face. 'Oh yeah!' he exclaimed excitedly, 'I've got the whole team into it! D'you play?'

'It's been a while mate; not since the army, but I'll have a go - I'm sure my misspent youth will come flooding back in a trickle!'

Bullseye grinned. 'Nice one, no time today though, apparently the Tamil Tigers have stopped play!'

Once he had got changed and gathered his level two kit together, Jax logged on to a terminal and checked his emails for the week he'd been away. Disregarding most of his mail as the usual dross, he checked the operation order for the day's aid. Scanning the names on his serial, he saw that Bullseye was second on the list after the skipper. Traditionally, the PC listed after the skipper's name, was the allocated driver for the day. This meant that for a change, Jax got to chill out in a passenger seat while the new addition to the team took the strain of London's frustrating traffic. He'd also have to endure all of the other occupational hazards of a police driver, tasked with ferrying bored cops to seats of potential disorder. This normally came in the form of good-natured insults and questions about his qualifications to drive.

A serial is basically one of three others, which make up a police support unit. The skipper of each serial, when booking on with the central operations radio channel - or

GT, as it is known to the cops - normally waits until they are on their way into town, before calling up with the serial's status.

If the serial is the "A" serial of a three serial PSU, this will include an inspector, sergeant and seven PCs. So an "A" serial skipper will call up on the radio and say: 'GT, from serial 1234A Alpha.'

GT responds with: 'Go ahead 1234A Alpha.'

'Full compliment of one, one and seven, leaving Filebridge en route for feeding at Buck Gate.'

This meant, that one inspector, one sergeant and seven PCs were on their way to the allocated feeding and briefing centre. In most cases, this was a hall on Buckingham Gate, Westminster - known fondly by the cops as Buck Gate, and latterly, Michael Messenger Hall (Shortened affectionately to Mick Messenger.)

Leaving the back yard, skipper Jarvis called up GT, informed the operator that serial 990B were en-route, and confirmed a full compliment. Bullseye pulled into a garage to fill up, while Emma and the Cat went inside to optimistically buy newspapers, they hoped they'd be able to read during down time. After a few seconds of agonising, Dynamo - who never passed up the opportunity to buy food - followed them in. He emerged grinning a few minutes later clutching a couple of packs of cooked chicken - just to: "supplement my lunch."

They drove in silence for a few minutes, before Bullseye looked across at Jax. He wore an odd, thoughtful kind of look on his tanned face. Then, worryingly, he proceeded to express the way in which he would like to die.

'I want to die peacefully in my sleep, just like my grandad,' he began. Jax, not sure where this was going, and wondering why the new guy was sharing such personal information with him on day one, looked over at him, but stuck for words, said nothing. Bullseye continued.

'Yep, just like my grandad - but *unlike* his passengers, who died screaming in terror!'

Jax grinned. With that kind of sense of humour, the new man looked like he'd fit in well with the team.

In 1912, the modern day police briefing centre had formed part of the London Scottish regimental headquarters. Today, the feeding centre is housed within what used to be the drill hall. It's claim to fame, is that it was used to host the British wreck commissioner's enquiry, reporting on the tragic loss of the Titanic.

The modern day interior looks pretty much as it did back in 1912 - save for the addition of a kitchen from where Met-catering staff doles out pre-deployment meals to hundreds of cops.

Row upon row of large dining tables fill the echoing interior; the narrow spaces between them, patrolled by no nonsense West Indian dinner ladies. These fierce women make sure all spaces are filled before the dining cops are allowed to move on to the next table. Like kids in a school dining hall, everyone wants to sit with their own serial and not find themselves among strangers and unknown banter. Sulkily though, in the end, they inevitably comply with the dinner ladies who would have easily felt at home on an aircraft carrier, organising returning fighter jets to the flight deck!

Once fed, junior representatives from each serial file down the narrow corridor, which leads to the exit. There, from within a dimly lit cubbyhole, a scowling pipe-smoking man: most of his face hidden by a luxuriant handlebar moustache; hands out enough snacks and bottled water to theoretically see the cops through the rest of the anticipated eight hour shift.

The man with the smelly pipe isn't known for his imagination when filling the snack bags, and if you're not on the ball, you'll end up with nine egg and cress sandwiches, nine bags of ready salted crisps, nine identical chocolate bars and nine bullet-hard apples. You could, if brave enough, haggle with him and get him to part with a bit more of a mixture, so saving yourself from the wrath of nine dissatisfied cops. As for the pecking order, when snacks are handed out on the carrier: if there isn't an inspector on the serial, the skipper traditionally gets first choice, followed by the driver.

Fed, watered and snacks collected by a grumbling Cat, serial 990B, headed back to the carrier to wait for skipper Jarvis, who'd stayed behind to be briefed. Just like the hungry caterpillar, the moment Dynamo got back onto the carrier, he grabbed his snack bag and wolfed down the contents before you could say egg and cress sandwich. His reasoning was, that firstly, he may not get another chance to eat it and secondly, it wouldn't stay fresh for long in the hot, fart-laden atmosphere of the carrier.

Bullseye clambered into the driver's seat and Jax joined him in the front to act as operator for the day. There was a lot more legroom in the front of the carrier, but if you volunteered to be operator, you risked having to navigate under the pressure of a blue light run, to whichever far-flung corner of the capital the serial might be despatched to. Jax had taken this into consideration, but knowing that Bullseye was legendary among the cops for his encyclopaedic knowledge of the capital, he didn't anticipate having to do too much map reading.

In the event, once skipper Jarvis briefed them on the day's deployments, Jax found that they were to drive all of a quarter of a mile to Parliament Square, where they were to spend the rest of the day. If the experience of those officers who had done the Tamil aid before was anything to go by, Jax and the other Houndshale cops were in for a long day. Word had it, that twelve hours was the minimum tour of duty for this one.

The Tamil demonstrators had set up their noisy camp on the lawn opposite the houses of parliament, some weeks before Jax and the team were called upon to assist. Their tents, banners and flags filled the entire square and their occupation was 24/7. During the day, they maintained a presence of a few hundred, but later on; once school was out, their numbers would swell with children and mothers. As night fell and people finished their working day, they too would arrive, adding hundreds more to the protest.

Given the day and night nature of the protest, the cops were stretched, and because of the up until now peaceful nature of it, not nearly enough resources had been thrown at the demo. This meant that the few serials deployed would have to have all available cops out on the ground at all times. To cops like Jax, this actually meant standing in front of the protestors without a break for either food or toilet for as long as their shift lasted. Dynamo must have anticipated this when he'd eaten his snacks!

The only possible option open to the serial skippers was that of allowing two people per serial a ten-minute break every two hours. With the nearest toilets being over the road in the Palace of Westminster, this meant no real time sitting down at all. Even without getting to sit down, the biggest relief was getting away from the constant, but limited repertoire of the protestor's chants: shouted at full volume inches from the cop's ears.

The cycle began with a swipe at the then prime minister:

'Gordon Brown, Gordon Brown! Open your eyes!'

Then a go at the media for underreporting the Tamil issue:

'BBC! BBC! Open your eyes!'

'Media media! Open your eyes!'

Then it was a few minutes of:

'Tamil tigers - freedom fighters!'

And to end that particular cycle of chants:

'Tamil Elam!'

This was the crowd's cue to raise banners depicting

the Tamil commander who was under siege five and a half thousand miles away. At this point, the noise usually grew in intensity as they screamed:

'Our leader! Our leader!'

This particular chant appeared to last the longest and seemed to be the favourite of adolescent girls, who screeched hysterically, inches from Jax's ears. To him, this felt like torture, and on his feet for hours and hours, he longed to be just far enough away to not to endure the full, relentless volume.

There were a couple of tents at the front of the square. Inside one of these, was a demonstrator who had taken it upon himself to go on hunger strike in the hope that the government would do something about his homeland. Once a day, paramedics from the London ambulance service, would arrive to carry out a medical examination of the man, who to Jax; looked the picture of health. There was nothing Gordon Brown or anyone else in a position of power in the country could do about the Sri Lankan army purging the country of terrorism, but what they could try to avoid was the embarrassing prospect of a hunger striker dying outside parliament. To that end, the hard pressed men and women of the LAS had been instructed to make bizarre daily house calls to the man in the tent.

Incidentally, the hunger striker never did manage to starve himself to death. Unsubstantiated rumours abounded among the police serials with regard to mysterious cheeseburger wrappers supposedly seen at the foot of his deathbed. Word had it among the cops, that this information had been passed on by the paramedics, but as good a rumour as it was for the provision of entertainment for bored cops on aid, it was never actually confirmed.

Every now and then, badly made up casualties would be borne through the camp on a makeshift stretcher to represent wounded tigers. The quality of the acting was reminiscent of a school play, but at least it gave the weary cops something to look at!

It was dusk. Jax and serial 990B had been in the square for around ten hours. There was to be no late turn to relieve them - the Met just couldn't afford the numbers. They would have to hang on until night duty serials came on, and that wasn't for a few hours yet.

His ten minutes of sitting in the carrier over, Jax wandered wearily back to the endless chanting. He was almost back at the police line, when the occupants of the square suddenly surged forward as one. Jax looked on in amazement as the double barrier line erected to stop the demonstrators from spilling into the road, was sent skyward, landing in a pile in the middle of the busy road, and resembling a metallic equivalent of palm trees, smashed and tossed aside by a tsunami.

The Tamil's numbers; swelled by kids, housewives and men who'd finished work for the day, now numbered in their thousands. The human tide was absolutely unstoppable and the cops; taken completely by surprise, had no alternative other than to scrabble out of the way and allow them to achieve their coordinated ambition of blocking the busiest road junction in Westminster.

Completely filling the road opposite parliament, they surged on to Bridge Street, occupying the first half of Westminster Bridge. Double decker buses, black cabs, couriers and tourist buses swerved and screeched to a halt, their progress abruptly halted by the human tide of chanting Tamils. The cops, completely outnumbered, switched their attentions from Parliament Square to Whitehall, where the Tamils could theoretically besiege Downing Street. They managed to hurriedly regroup, and using carriers supported by cops on foot, they hastily threw a cordon across the junction of Parliament Street and Bridge Street. That they were allowed to do this, was purely due to the fact that the protestors had quite simply run out of people to move that far west.

Once they'd filled the junction, the demonstrators simply sat down in the road and refused to budge. Cynically, the leaders placed women and children on the periphery of their mass so as to avoid heavy-handed tactics of removal by the cops. Some of their number triumphantly shinned up lampposts, from the top of which they flew their red Tamil Tiger flags.

A group attacked a stranded bus, smashing all the windows and laying underneath it to prevent it being moved. The idea behind this tactic was to incorporate the bus into their human barricade. A couple of enthusiastic men lay underneath it's wheels to discourage it from being moved, while some bright spark decided to deflate it's tyres. Given the fact that their comrades were underneath the bus; letting it's tyres down, was probably not such a genius idea, but inflamed with passion, they did it nonetheless.

Standing just across the road from the stricken bus, Jax stood in a cordon in front of Bullseye's carrier. Almost driven mad after hour upon hour of relentless chanting, his stomach rumbling and his water long since drunk; he watched as some young Tamil men began to throw things at the cops, before disappearing into the crowd.

Jax, near snapping point, scanned the crowd and tried to pick someone out who he'd seen throwing things. It was one thing to hold a peaceful - if futile protest - but now they were attacking police lines.

He'd had a gut full. He was tired, hungry, thirsty and irrational. It was through this mist of irrationality, that he managed to identify a protestor hurling a traffic cone at his cordon. Quick as a flash, determined to grab his man before the tide closed back around him, Jax committed the cardinal sin of rushing into a mob. So sudden had his decision been, that he hadn't informed the cops to his left and right of his intention. Sprinting forward, he reached his target. Grabbing a handful of shirt, he hauled him out from the crowd and dragged him kicking and screaming back to the safety of the police lines, before enlisting the help of a bemused Dynamo to take him to the rear of the carriers.

Jax could smell whiskey on his prisoner's breath. He'd obviously been caught up in the moment, fired up with passion for the Tiger's cause, with alcohol clouding his judgement. He hadn't seriously resisted Jax's efforts to detain him, in fact, he looked pretty sorry for himself and Jax guessed he wasn't someone who'd done this kind of thing often - if ever.

The big man looked at the panting, but satisfied Jax and beamed his toothy grin.

'Fuck me!' he said laughing. 'You've caught a tiger by the tail!'

Jax, still high from his adrenaline-fuelled charge into the crowd, grinned back. Once he'd helped put Jax's prisoner into a front stack, Dynamo returned to the cordon.

Filling a gap in the line next to the Cat, he took a swig of tepid water filched from one of the other serial's unlocked carriers, before passing it down the line.

'What the fuck was that all about?' asked the Cat.

'What - Jacko? Oh yeah, he just got himself a tiger by the tail - and, I'm not even joking! Mad bastard!'

Porridge Face, just as sick and tired as the rest of them, took it out on an innocent Japanese tourist who'd made the mistake of asking him directions to the Science Museum. Pointing a stubby finger at his cap badge, which incorporated the monarch's cipher of EIIR, he replied:

'This says E to R, not A to Z!'

The rest of them looked away in embarrassment while the ugly little man with no neck laughed at his own joke. The Japanese tourist smiled uncomprehendingly, and skipper Jarvis, his face like thunder, pointed him in the right direction before telling Porridge he was in line for the next shitty job.

By the time, Jax had processed his now subdued and apologetic prisoner at Belgravia nick, dragged on a long awaited smoke and written his notes, the protest organisers had signalled for their followers to return to the square.

Road sweeping vehicles, their brushes whirring, cleared away the debris of the Tamil occupation, an army of council cleaners picked up discarded placards and traffic cones, and the constant stream of traffic returned to normal as though nothing had ever happened. This was to be the first of many such surges in the days and weeks that followed. It was this mass occupation of Westminster's arterial route that finally forced the Met's commanders to deploy more resources. This would at least benefit future level two serials and hopefully give them more than ten minutes off every two hours.

For today though, the PSUs took their places back in the square, the chanting resumed and the cops wondered wearily whether their night duty relief would ever arrive.

Jax, the decision made for his prisoner to receive a caution, begrudgingly hitched a lift from Belgravia back to Parliament Square. Rejoining his weary serial to calls of: "you took your time," he joined the cordon for another couple of hours chorus of: "Our leader!"

Over the radio, he could now hear night duty units calling up to announce their arrival at Buck Gate. Forty minutes later, they began to arrive to relieve the serials in the square. Jax and 990B happily handed over their cordon position to night duty, and with mutterings of: "thank fuck for that" they clambered onto the carrier.

Seventeen hours after their arrival, with newspapers unread and food long since eaten, the best-loved transmission in the Met came over the radio:

'Units stand by for dismissals...'

Every cop in the square strained to listen to the radio over chants of "Gordon Brown open your eyes," and then it came - the long awaited second part to GT's dismissal transmission.

'Serial 990A Alpha receiving GT?'

'Go ahead GT.'

'Serial 990B Bravo receiving GT?'

'Go ahead GT.'

'Serial 990C Charlie receiving GT?'

'Go ahead GT.'

'Serial 990A Alpha, 990B Bravo and 990C Charlie - you are all dismissed with thanks.'

Otherwise known as: "dismissed with *spanks*," the last radio transmission raised a ragged cheer from within Jax's carrier, and without further ado, Bullseye threw the carrier in gear, floored the gas pedal and headed at speed for Buck Gate.

With the grown ups realising that the troops had had nothing to eat or drink for several hours, they were directed back to Buck Gate for a hastily prepared supper of burger and chips while they compiled notes to cover any use of force that may have been used during the long day. The only person who had anything to write about was Jax, and to the relief of his serial, he'd already written his notes at Belgravia nick.

All that remained, was for 990B to scoff down greasy chips and a burger containing around ten percent meat and ninety percent gristle, before heading back to Filebridge and then home for a few hours sleep before coming back in for whatever the following day had in store...

*

It had been two weeks since Angie Brown had been filmed snorting coke and giving enthusiastic head to Calvin Anderson. Even had he made contact, she'd resolved never to see him again. Actually, it had been more a case of *dreading* hearing from him. Once she'd come to on her bedroom floor after that awful night; her

245

hair matted with Anderson's semen and her mouth sticky with his seed, the reality of what she'd done drip-dripped into her mind like Chinese water torture. Her head had reeled from a monstrous hangover and her brain wallowed in the depression of a cocaine comedown.

Every day she'd sat down at her desk, mentally flinching with every drug- related report she compiled. She avoided all unnecessary contact with the cops; thinking that if she spoke to them, they would somehow guess her guilt. Her job, which she'd once loved, now threatened to drown her in guilt.

She'd resisted the overwhelming urge to feed Anderson's name into the CRIMINT system, fearing an intelligence audit would lead a snail trail to her terminal. Questions would be asked as to her interest in him. Then, one morning, after the daily intelligence meeting, her mobile buzzed and blinked on the desk beside her keyboard. The words: "Calvin A text message," struck dread into her palpitating heart.

Feeling contaminated by those four little words, she shoved her phone into her handbag, pushing it deep down under her makeup bag, house keys and Marlborough Lights, before placing her bag under her desk; as if being out of sight, it would somehow go away.

Seconds later, from the depths of her handbag, she felt her mobile buzz once more against her leg. She decided to ignore it. Ignore it and it will go away, her mother used to say. But what if he called her, what if the bastard called her up, right there in her office, the office on the same floor that housed the offices of the detective chief inspector, the detective sergeants and the detective constables of Houndshale CID? What if she ignored his texts and calls and he turned up at the nick to ask for her? She admonished herself: he's *hardly* likely to actually turn up here, is he?

Angie couldn't take it any more. Scooping up her handbag, she got up from her desk and walked along the corridor to the ladies. Passing the main office, she forced a smile and returned the cheery greetings called out from within. For fuck sake! She felt so damn guilty! Get a grip girl!

Going into the bathroom, she was startled to see Janet from admin, who was reapplying her lipstick in front of the mirror. Choking down panic and resisting the urge to turn tail and flee, she made a beeline for the cubicle and smiled a mirthless smile.

'Hi Jan, dodgy curry last night, desperate!' Janet turned up her nose in mock horror.

'Oh dear, I'd better leave you to it then!'

Entering the cubicle, Angie locked the door and sat on the toilet seat. Hearing Janet depart, she fished her mobile from her bag, unlocked the screen and clicked on the dreaded message.

Hey baby! Long time no see! How is the part time porn star? Done any lines lately? I've been thinking, maybe I'll upload our movie; make Angie Brown, crime analyst a YouTube star. What do you think? Ironically, Anderson finished his nasty little message with a smiley face icon. She felt as though her pounding heart would burst right out of her chest.

Putting her phone away, she flushed the toilet for the benefit of anyone who may have been listening and walked shakily back to her office. Closing the door, she sat down at her desk. The mug shots on her wall depicting the faces of menacing-looking criminals of interest undulated and swam before her eyes. She thought she would pass out. Opening her window, she took a deep breath and tried to pull herself together.

Her office window looked out over Houndshale's dreary High Street, and from her vantage point on the third floor, she could see rows of boarded up shops interspersed with cut-price stores, bookmakers and pawnshops. Threading their weary way along the street, she saw the grey flotsam and jetsam that made up the High Street's clientele: some in search of a cheap, made in

China bargain, while others listlessly smoked bootleg cigarettes and whiled away the hours of yet another day without employment.

Going downstairs for a smoke, she found that the yard was mercifully free from fellow smokers, and after chain-smoking two Marlboroughs; she steeled herself and resolved to call the bastard's bluff. She decided to reply to his text, warning him that if he contacted her again she'd report him for harassment.

She was aware that if someone were to pursue a course of conduct; likely to cause harassment, alarm or distress, they would be liable to be prosecuted under the Harassment Act. Of course, this was subject to the victim first informing the offender, that their attentions were unwelcome, but any further contact after that, would constitute a course of conduct.

Yes, you callous bastard! She though vehemently, this crime analyst knows the law! Feeling confident, she keyed back a reply right then and there in the back yard. She told him that she wanted nothing more to do with him and threatened to make a complaint if he didn't leave her alone.

Pressing the send button, she put out her cigarette and made her way back upstairs to her office. Once back at her terminal and feeling rebellious, Angie logged onto CRIMINT and tapped in the words Calvin Anderson. To her horror, within seconds, her screen lit up like a Christmas tree.

In fact, the message that the hit count for her enquiry had exceeded limits, indicated one hell of a list relating to her former lover. This message basically meant that there were so many entries, not all of them could be displayed at the same time. The system commanded her to refine her search, and in a state of shock, she limited the search parameters to the last two years. It got worse.

Most of the entries for Anderson were highlighted in red, the main body of the text invisible. This indicated that these entries related either to material supplied by an informant, or that the intelligence related to an ongoing investigation by some one much higher up the food chain than her. Those older entries, which were viewable by her, screamed words like firearms, extortion, GBH and drug supply. Her blood ran cold.

Suddenly paranoid and not daring to read any further, she closed down the system, switching her screen back to the mundane but innocuous excel spread sheet still in the background. The spread sheet detailed crime trends that she'd been working on before she'd received *tha*t text, before she'd dared to research the bastard who had insinuated himself into her life. What is it with me, she thought bitterly. Why do I keep falling for such bastards? Why don't you *ever* learn you stupid bitch?

When after a week of not hearing from Anderson, and with her French polished nails bitten to the quick, Angie fell into an uneasy state of dread. Like a patient with a terminal disease who every once in a while remembers they're going to die; the fear of what would happen should Anderson ever rear his ugly head again, came and went in waves.

And then it came; as she'd always known it would. His text message was short on preamble and shockingly to the point: "Look out of your window bitch. Yeah, you see me? That's me with the red cap and guess what? I'm on my way to speak to the Feds. All about you!"

Angie, a cold hard knot of fear pulling at her insides, pulled up the blinds and peered out. There, on a bench next to the bookies was the unmistakable figure of Anderson; a bright red Ferrari cap on his close cropped skull. She dropped her phone. It bounced on the floor, the back cover and battery flying off, before it came to rest underneath a chair. In a panic, and desperate to prevent him coming in to the station, she dropped to her knees, scrabbling around to retrieve and reassemble it.

With shaking hands, she slotted the battery back in

and turned it on. She exhorted the phone's screen under her breath. Come on! Come *on*! To her relief, the phone powered back up, and after what seemed like an eternity, the home screen appeared. Going back to Anderson's message, she tapped the call button, and with her heart in her mouth, listened to the tone. Looking out of her window, she felt sick. She could no longer see the red cap; he'd been replaced by the town dosser, with the inevitable can of cider clasped to his emaciated chest.

To her immense relief, after a few rings, she was connected with Anderson. He didn't mince his words.

'There you are!' he spat. 'All cosy in your nice little pig office? You wanna' keep your job bitch?' Angie reeled from his nasty tone.

'What do you want from me?' she asked quiet and submissive as a mouse.

'Well,' he laughed, 'it ain't your dried up old cunt you bitch!' Angie shook with indignant rage at his insult, but didn't dare terminate the call.

'What is it that you want Calvin,' she asked, a tremor in her voice.

'I'm coming to your place *tonight*. Seven o'clock - and don't bother dressin' up!' He laughed again. It sounded more like the bray of a donkey than an expression of mirth. 'Be there bitch or else...'

His shock announcement was followed by a beep-beep in her ear, indicating that he'd terminated the call.

Walking home in a daze, Angie felt just about as wretched as she'd ever done. Cheating husbands, abusive boyfriends - they couldn't hold a candle to the devil that was Calvin Anderson. At times, on her way to meet whatever destiny the bastard had in mind, she was tempted to throw herself under one of the ubiquitous red double decker buses that thundered by, leaving clouds of stinking diesel smoke in their wake. She glanced up at the top deck of one of the lumbering beasts and saw indifferent multinational faces looking back at her -

staring right through her miserable soul, each with their own tale of woe.

No, she thought, I just don't have the courage. Knowing my luck, I'd end up maimed and in a wheelchair for the rest of my life.

On and on she went; the normally long and tedious walk seemed to be over in minutes, and before she knew it, she was fumbling for her front door key and letting herself into what had been the scene of her crime.

Gathering up the junk mail from her doormat, she was on automatic pilot. Tossing the letters aside without a glance, she went into the kitchen, opened the door to her kitchen cupboard and pulled out a bottle of vodka. Pouring herself a bigger measure than even the most liberated European bar tender served her on holiday; she took the bottle into her front room, sank into the cushions of her settee and swallowed the lot in one gulp.

By the time her front door bell rang to announce the arrival of the bastard, she'd drained the vodka bottle and was feeling numb. She had no sooner opened her door, before Anderson pushed past her, leaving a trail of Hugo Boss in his wake. He wore an expensive looking leather man bag strapped across his body, and without waiting for an invitation, sat himself down on her settee.

Angie followed him in, her arms folded defensively across her chest. Looking at the cruel twist of his mouth below his wicked glittering eyes, she thought that he resembled a rattlesnake. For the life of her, she couldn't imagine why she'd fallen for him. Perching on the edge of an armchair, she felt like a stranger in her own home. He didn't beat about the bush.

'Not putting our little movie on You Tube's gonna' cost you,' he said, his face a mask of malevolence.

Angie averted her eyes, looking instead at the rug on her floor. So it was money the bastard was after. 'I don't have any money Calvin,' she said quietly. She looked up at him. 'What did I ever do to you? Why are you doing this to me?' she asked pleadingly.

He sucked his teeth and laughed that deep belly laugh that had attracted her to him, but now filled her with revulsion. 'I don't need your money bitch!' and with that, he got up from the settee and strode over to her armchair. Angie recoiled in fear at his sudden move and slid back in her chair, cowering, her hands spread before her protectively.

Anderson viciously slapped her hands aside. She felt the thin skin on the back of her hands sting and she screamed. His arm snaked towards her, his hand gripping her chin. She glanced at the empty vodka bottle on the coffee table. If I could just reach it, she thought, I'd smash it over the bastards head!

It was fanciful thinking of course, Anderson had her completely at his mercy and the look in his eyes scared her to death. Tears welled up in her eyes, rolling down her cheeks. He thrust his face close. She could smell stale tobacco smoke on his breath, and when he spoke, he sprayed her with his spittle.

'Shut the fuck up bitch and listen!' he hissed. 'You're now working for me!'

Her mind reeled. 'But I've got a job Calvin.' He laughed again.

'I *know* that,' he said, his voice laced with sarcastic undertones - 'but from now on, I want information. I want to know all about when the feds are planning to raid my yard. In fact, I want to know about every raid in this town; you get me bitch?' Angie's eyes were big as saucers.

'But...' she stammered, 'If I get caught I'll be in big trouble! I'll lose my job and might even get arrested for giving out that kind of information!'

His grip on her chin tightened causing her to wince. 'If you don't do this for me, you're fucked anyway,' he hissed. 'Don't forget our little video clip - that's enough to get you sacked and arrested. If you're a good girl and don't fuck up, Calvin won't share the video.'

He let go of her face, stepped back, and returned to the settee where he delved into his man bag and took out a mobile phone box. He tossed it over to Angie. 'Calvin's bought you a little present. Open it.'

Angie's shaking fingers fumbled with the flap of the box. Pulling it open, she saw a cheap Nokia phone nestling in it's cardboard cradle.

'What's this for?'

'Switch it on. In the address book is a number that you can use to call me on. It's the only number in there and you're only to use that phone to call me.'

With that, he stood up, slung his bag around his shoulders and walked towards the front door, pausing by her chair.

'Look at me,' he demanded.

Reluctantly, Angie met his gaze. His eyes bored into hers chilling her to the bone. He bent down, his muscular arms gripping the arms of her chair.

'Don't you *ever* fuck with me - I'll slit your fuckin' throat! You get me?'

She felt like a rabbit caught in the headlights. Her throat constricted and her mouth felt as dry as if she'd eaten a mouthful of talcum powder. Unable to reply, she nodded vigorously, he head bobbing up and down like a cork on stormy seas.

Anderson straightened up. 'The minute you get any information about raids, you call me. Understand?' She nodded again. With one last withering look at his prey, Anderson sucked his teeth and walked out of Angie's flat leaving the door swinging open.

It must have been ten minutes or more before she moved from her chair. Staring at the magnolia coloured wall in the corridor through her open door, she sat transfixed by the thought of what she'd been asked to do. Slowly, locomotion returned to her muscles. Shakily, she arose from her chair, closed the door and slid home all the bolts, as if to shut out the world and prevent anyone

253

from ever coming into her home again.

What the hell was she going to do? Should she just go to the DCI and confess? Maybe she could do a runner, move away. Where the hell would she go? Whether she came clean or moved away, she felt sure that the bastard would track her down. Anderson's words reverberated around her head. *I'll slit your fuckin' throat! You get me?*

She went over to her settee and lay down. The cushions next to her face seemed to be impregnated with the bastard's lingering scent. She curled up and fell asleep.

Her phone rang, dragging her from her fitful nap. Her heart in her mouth, she scrambled for her handbag. She felt sure it was Anderson, and full of dread, she picked it up.

To her immense relief, the screen was filled with the smiling face she'd assigned to her friend Karen. She'd taken the picture in the wine bar on that fateful night before she'd met Anderson at the 101 Club, and hadn't seen her friend since. She pressed the green button.

'Hey Angie baby!' trilled Karen. 'Fancy a girlie night out this weekend?'

Angie almost burst into tears at the sound of a friendly voice, but didn't think she would be able to face going out ever again. She forced a lighthearted tone.

'Oh hi Karen. I'm not feeling too good babes. A touch of the flu I think. I'm going to stay in with a box of tissues and a black and white movie.'

'Poor you! Shall I come over and keep you company?'

Angie really didn't want to see anyone. She wanted to shut herself away from the world for as long as she could while she got her head together.

'No babes, I don't want you to catch my lurgie! Another time?'

'Well if you're sure... let's meet up soon though, I want hear all about that new stud of yours!'

Angie shivered involuntarily at the very mention of

the bastard. She forced a bit of joviality into her voice. 'I never kiss and tell Kaz!'

Karen laughed. 'Yeah, whatever you dirty mare! OK, catch you later Ange. Get well soon!'

Chucking her phone onto the coffee table, she grabbed the Nokia. The very sight and feel of it made her heart beat faster. Stamping on the empty box as though it were Anderson's face, she chucked it into her recycling bin, threw the stubby little phone into a kitchen drawer, and tried to forget all about it. Next, marching back into her front room, she grabbed the Hugo Boss infused cushions, ripped off the covers and slung them into the washing machine.

The very act of stamping on the bastard's phone box and erasing every trace of his scent felt liberating. Deep down though, she knew it was nothing more than symbolic, and when the poisonous little Nokia summoned her, she knew she'd have no choice but to succumb...

Chapter Eleven

'Could you start me off?'

The wheezing putt-putt of Doc Pigeon's ancient scooter announced the arrival of the last member of the mental health team. Whispering Jill and her social workers had arrived some ten minutes earlier and had briefed UX646 on the patient they'd all gathered to assess. Porridge Face wasn't in that day. He was at Filebridge magistrates' court, where he'd no doubt be regaling defence and prosecution lawyers with whatever fantasy he'd concocted with regard to the arrest of the drink driver, now before the court.

In his absence, and while the BTF had been waiting for Doc Pigeon, Dynamo had regaled them with a story he'd heard about their very own Billy Liar.

'So,' he began. 'You know why Porridge is in court don't you?'

Blank faces and the shaking of heads indicated that this particular Porridge story was as yet unknown to them.

'It's from that time he nicked a drink driver on his way to work.'

'Really?' asked the Cat. 'Who told you this then?'

'Some matey I know from team who turned up to rescue him. Apparently it went a bit wrong. He spots this bloke swerving all over the road. He stops at the lights in front of Porridge, who thinks the driver must be pissed up. Porridge gets out of his own car, flashes his warrant card, and takes the bloke's keys from the ignition!'

'Nice one,' said the Cat. 'What did he do then? Tell him he was a secret agent?'

Dynamo laughed. 'He didn't get the chance. The driver - a massive wowski - gets out of his car and starts throwing punches at Porridge.'

'Fuckin' hell!' said the Cat, impressed. 'Didn't the Polish geezer know not to mess with black-belt Morris?'

'Porridge must have left his ninja powers at home, 'cos when the wowski started swinging, he ran away along the line of cars at the lights, banging on windows begging to be let in - and I'm not even joking!'

'Then what?'

'Well, what would *you* do if you saw that ugly bastard tapping on your car window?'

'I'd lock the doors babes!' said Emma from the back of the carrier.

The big man suddenly had a fit of giggles, which lasted so long, the others thought they'd never get to find out what happened next. Eventually, Dynamo regained his composure long enough to tell the rest of the story.

'The lights have changed to green, the cars are starting to move off and Porridge is still being chased down the road. He manages to stop a van at the end of the line and shows the driver his badge. Matey stops and Porridge jumps in and locks the doors!'

'Didn't he call the Old Bill?' asked the Cat. 'I'd have phoned up as soon as I was thinking of stopping anyone.'

'This is Porridge we're talking about here,' said the big man. 'You know what he's like; he lives in a world where he's indestructible. A legend in his own lunchtime!'

'True...'

'Anyway, once he's safely in the van, he dials 999, and team come to his rescue. The wowski gets nicked and Porridge goes off to rewrite history!'

The carrier erupted into laughter. Skipper Jarvis spotted Whispering Jill coming over and he called them all to order. The subject of Doc Pigeon's team appeared to potentially pose a bit more of a threat to those assessing him, than UX646 were used to.

Quite often, they'd be called upon to stand in the background while the mental health team assessed what was invariably a relatively harmless person of advanced years. Every once in a while however, the patient was young, strong and obstructive. The majority of mental health assessments involved those who had been released into the community on the back of a promise that they would comply with home visits and continue to take the drugs that kept their unfortunate conditions under control. As such, having not taken their medication for some time, they tended to be unpredictable and in some cases very dangerous. This was where the police came into the equation.

In most cases the patient could be persuaded to voluntarily attend hospital for treatment, but sometimes, once the announcement had been made that they were to be sectioned and would have to remain in hospital for several weeks, they reacted badly. The cops were also there should the need arise to force entry to the property. It was in those few cases, that Jax and the team would have to get involved with putting the door in, restraining the sectioned patient and removing them to hospital against their will.

Jax had an inkling that this was to be a difficult case, as soon they'd been admitted into the patient's house. The guy Doc Pigeon had come to assess was a powerfully built man in his twenties. Once his mother had granted them access, they'd gone in to find the guy sitting in a back room, which led out onto a garden patio area. He was sitting in a chair with a glass table in front of him. He had his back to the patio doors and wore a vacant look on his face. The sound of him grinding his teeth filled the room; accentuated by the clenching and unclenching his fists. Every now and then, he'd nod; seemingly in relation to whatever the voices in his head were saying. Then he'd smile disconcertedly to himself.

His mother had gone off into the kitchen to bring the mental health team a pitcher of cordial, and outwardly, the scene seemed civilised enough. The pitcher and several tumblers were placed on the glass table and the team took up positions in chairs and a settee either side of the patient. Jax, however, took one look at the guy in the back room and felt rather than saw, the tension emanating from him. He hadn't taken his medication for several weeks and his mother; concerned about his increasingly erratic behaviour, had called in the professionals.

To Jax, the whole set up; with glass table, glasses of cordial and no space between patient and assessors, looked like a disaster waiting to happen. Seemingly unaware of the tension, the assembled professionals duly sat back, politely sipped at the cordial, and with Doc Pigeon directly facing his patient, they began their assessment.

The rest of the BTF, who like Jax had picked up on the patient's hostile vibes, split up and tried to remain inconspicuous. Jax and Dynamo went into the adjoining kitchen, from where they would be able to access the garden and from there, the patio doors at the back of the patient's room. The rest of the team remained as subtly as they could on the fringes of the assessment, ready to react should it become necessary.

From the kitchen, Jax could hear Doc Pigeon going through his stock questions. Were voices in the patient's head telling him to do things? Was the television urging him to act on it's commands? Then he hit him with his favourite.

Didn't he think it *strange* that he spent all day staring at the wall? Jax had heard it all before. He had yet to hear something from the room next door to give him reason for concern, so he relaxed slightly; grinning as Dynamo pulled a face and quietly mimicked Doc Pigeon's: "don't you think that's strange?"

Suddenly, all hell broke loose. Jax heard shouts from the cops in the room next door and the sound of the glass table being upended. True to their plan, he and Dynamo rushed through the kitchen door and raced around to the patio doors to cover the rear. When they got there, they were dismayed to find that the previously unlocked patio doors had inexplicably been locked by the patient's mother!

Their faces pressed helplessly to the locked doors, they saw that the previously orderly room was now trashed. Spilled cordial seeped into the carpet from upended tumblers and mingled with the shattered glass of the tabletop. The mental health team was cowering at the back of the room, and blood was pouring from Doc Pigeon's nose.

The Cat, who'd been at the back of the room, had heard the doctor announce to the patient, that he was now under mental health section. He watched in horror as the sectioned man jumped up from his chair and lunged at Doc Pigeon. Too late to prevent the doctor taking one in the face, he'd dived over the table, cannoned into Doc's patient, and in the tight space between table and locked patio doors, he'd managed to take him down.

Jax and the big man rushed from the garden and into the room just in time to see the rest of the BTF piling on top of the reluctant mental health patient, while his mother screamed hysterically in the background. Emma took mum into the kitchen while her son, by now subdued by the cops, but smiling enigmatically, was put into handcuffs and pushed back down onto his chair. He'd be held there until a van arrived to transport him to hospital.

When the caged van arrived, the Cat was delighted to see that it was crewed by Becky Thomas of the bolt-on-breasts fame. Greeting her enormous tits rather than her, he hauled the patient into the back of her van. Slamming the door, he grinned like a halfwit. 'Alright Becks?'

'Hi Adie,' she grinned. 'Stop staring at my tits!'

The Cat flushed bright red. He was in tittie heaven. 'One day Becks, I'm gonna' get my hands on those puppies!'

Becky laughed. 'In your dreams Adie, in your dreams...'

Doc Pigeon came out of the house holding a handkerchief to his nose followed by an ashen-faced Jill. He handed the Cat a sheaf of notes to take to hospital, which confirmed the patient had been sectioned.

'You OK Doc?' he asked chirpily.

'I'd like to say it's an occupational hazard,' he said ruefully, 'but that bloody well hurt! Thanks for jumping in though'

Whispering Jill approached skipper Jarvis, laid a hand on his arm, and looking coquettishly up at him, she simpered: 'Goodness me Ian, your boys are so brave!' Although Jarvis didn't like to admit it in front of the others, he was always quite flattered by Jill's flirtatious manner. Flushing with pride, he quickly glanced around, to make sure he wasn't being watched, before smiling at her and patting the hand that still lingered on his arm. It wasn't that he fancied the woman, but old habits die hard, and when attention of the female kind was directed his way, he just couldn't help but to reciprocate. 'That's OK Jill, anytime...'

Looking over at the departing van, he could see that the Cat had needed no encouragement in escorting the patient to the Aspens. He'd jumped straight into the back from where he could look over Becky's shoulder at her breasts. Giving his trademark look to the heavens, Jarvis bade farewell to Jill, gathered his team and jumped on to the carrier to escort Becky's van and her passengers - one certified lunatic - and one breast-obsessed cop.

261

Balvinder Kapoor had become somewhat of a recluse. Twice in the last week, he'd watched a patrol car pull up outside his apartment block in Cranston. On both occasions, the feds had got out of their cars and knocked on the front door at the bottom of the shared stairs. Nobody had admitted them and they hadn't been too persistent, leaving after a few desultory taps. Paranoid that the cops were closing in on his flashing activities, he'd taken to mostly staying indoors; playing Elvis songs.

He now spent his day calling sex chat lines and leafing obsessively through worn out porno mags. The only time he furtively ventured out during daylight was to sign on at the job centre once a week, and to collect his benefit cheque. He had even stopped going to the gurdwara for free meals, existing instead on take away chicken from Hakim's below.

He'd never been in any danger of having his benefits stopped due to not attending job interviews as he was now registered disabled. He'd been to see his doctor: who hard pressed, jaded and totally disillusioned with his profession, had written him a note with the minimum of fuss declaring Balvinder to be suffering from agoraphobia. With his rent and council tax paid by the state, his spartan lifestyle ensured that he didn't spend too much money. This meant that he had plenty of disposable income to spend on cheap lager and sleazy sex chat lines.

Then one day, he crept down the stairs to find a leaflet pushed through the letterbox advertising local escort girls. The girls, the leaflet announced: "visit you in the privacy of your own home." Scurrying back upstairs, leaflet clutched in his grubby hand, he went back up to his foul-smelling room and pored over it.

The very thought of getting a woman to come to his room and what he would do to her, excited him. Sitting on his grimy bed, he stuck his hand down his pants and stroked his rapidly hardening cock. He quivered at the thought of getting hold of a flesh and blood woman to reenact his porno film fantasy. He was so fired up by the notion, that he didn't need the usual stimulation of film or magazine. Undoing the zip of his pants, he breathlessly pulled out his cock and for the second time that day, jerked off.

His nightly visit to Hakim's complete, he devoured his chicken and tossed the empty box into a corner where it joined the pile of festering bones now steadily piling up and attracting rats from miles around. Wiping his greasy fingers on his duvet cover, he picked up the escort girl leaflet and fished out his mobile.

Dialling the number, he heard it ring a couple of times before his call was gruffly answered by a heavily accented eastern European man who answered with the name of the innocent sounding agency:

'Sweet Dreams Escort Agency.'

Balvinder bottled it and couldn't speak. Not used to actually communicating with people, he froze and didn't know what to say. The guy on the other end of the phone didn't have the patience for timid callers.

'Hello? Hello? Kurs tas ir?'

Getting no reply to his question as to who was calling, the Latvian quickly became abusive:

'Izbeidz!' he shouted, slamming down the receiver.

Had Balvinder understood Latvian, he'd have realised that the impatient receptionist for Sweet Dreams had just told him to *fuck off!* His heart pounding, he redialed the number.

'Sweet Dreams Escort Agency.' intoned the man.

Balvinder didn't really know what to say so he just blurted out:

'Can you send me a girl?'

Sensing money to be made, the Latvian guy feigned politeness.

'Yes of course my friend, what kind of girl would you like to fuck?'

He laughed the kind of mirthless catarrh-laden cackle, which typified a smoker of forty cigarettes a day. The effort made him cough, and placing a meaty paw over the phone; he hawked up a ball of phlegm and spat it into a wastepaper basket.

Balvinder, his initial reticence overcome by the excitement of what he was about to initiate, now spoke confidently.

'I don't want an Asian girl and I don't want a black girl,' he stipulated, the image of his favourite movie firmly in place.

The Latvian laughed again. 'You want a nice Polish girl?' he asked. 'Big tits, nice arse?'

Balvinder didn't want a skinny-lipped Polish girl. Too dominant, he thought.

'Do you have any English girls?' he asked hesitantly. He was a bit worried that the rough-sounding Latvian might take offence at his unwillingness to accept an eastern European girl, but fuck it, he thought; I'm paying for the bitch.

'An *English* girl?' he asked incredulously. 'Don't you know this is Houndshale my friend?' He laughed again.

'Yes,' replied Balvinder. 'I only want an English girl.'

There was a pause. On the other end of the line, he heard the sound of a flint being struck against a wheel followed by the sound of smoke being sharply inhaled.

'OK my friend, OK, No problem...'

He tailed off. Balvinder heard the Latvian exhale forcefully before being taken over by a coughing fit.

'Hello?'

'Yes my friend, let me check. OK, I have a lovely English girl for you. She loves to fuck. Nice tits and juicy arse, but she's not here until tonight. You want me to send her round?'

Balvinder very much *did* want her to be sent over!

'Yes, send her tonight.'

'Your phone number my friend?

Balvinder rattled off his number. 'What time can she come?

'About eight o'clock my friend - she will call you first. Her name is Nadine. Enjoy your fuck my friend, but don't forget to pay.'

He didn't laugh this time, but what he said next, put the wind up Balvinder.

'Yes, enjoy her, but if you don't pay, I will find you my friend and give you the kind of fuck you don't want!'

Bizarrely, the Latvian signed off with a cheery: 'see you later alligator! And with that, the phone went dead.

In eight hours time, Balvinder would have his very own girl to do whatever he liked with. Powering up his aging laptop, he clicked on to his favourite movie and watched rapt while for the hundredth time since he'd watched it, the masked man grabbed the bitch's hair and smacked her in the face.

Baring his yellow teeth in an expression of sexual ecstasy, he jerked off for the third time that day: but with the renewed vigour of anticipation.

Kneeling on the dusty bare floorboards before his bed, he positioned his laptop in front of his flushed face. Fixating on the paused frame of the girl's cellulite arse now filling his screen, he came in seconds, his hot spunk jetting in spasms and spraying the junk and detritus under his bed.

*

It wasn't that Jax was particularly unhappy on the BTF, but one morning, when scanning the force jobs bulletin, his attention was drawn to the vacancy section of Special Crime Directorate Eleven. SCD11 is the Metropolitan Police's surveillance department and vacancies have practically trebled in the wake of Islamic terrorist activity on the United Kingdom's mainland.

The post, which caught Jax's eye, was for the technical department. Their role, the ad said, was to place and remove tracking and listening devices to vehicles and buildings and to monitor the traffic generated by them.

The idea behind applying for the technical post was the potential of becoming a fully- fledged surveillance officer somewhere down the line. Jax had a rudimentary knowledge of the role, through work he'd carried out in Northern Ireland.

While there as an internal security soldier, he'd spent a few days at a time watching the houses of both known players, and their potential victims. It had been quite routine for Jax and his patrol to spend the night dug in around a house or farm belonging to either a contractor who carried out work for the security services, or a part time soldier in the then, Ulster Defence Regiment.

Jax made a phone call to the detective inspector who ran the technical surveillance unit. After a brief chat, the DI said: 'Hmm... so, you're a middle aged white bloke?' He paused. Jax didn't really know whether to answer what was a rhetorical question, but assumed that this was the DI's blunt way of telling him he hadn't a hope in hell! The DI continued: 'Well - we have a use for them too - I'm sure...'

On one hand, Jax had been appreciative of some straight talking. In a job dominated by political correctness, it had been a welcome, if disappointing reaction. In retrospect though, in a world stalked by Islamic extremists, he was hardly likely to blend in among those he sought to monitor. Despite this, he was still hopeful that a position could be found for a "middle aged white bloke," and he arranged for a day's attachment with the unit. In the event, he'd been made very welcome and managed to glean a fair amount of information with regard to the department. He also knew, that to go on attachment would place him at the forefront of the DI's mind should he get an interview.

Skipper Jarvis granted him a couple of hours in the office, and in the quiet vacuum left by his raucous team mates, Jax sat down to compile his application and to reacquaint himself with the relevant legislation, he'd need to know should he qualify for an interview.

This mainly revolved around the Regulation of Investigatory Powers Act of 2000, but he'd also be expected to be conversant with stated cases and any case law, which had come about through prosecutions brought as a result of evidence gathered through the use of surveillance.

He was aware that most interview boards consisted of an inspector, sergeant and a representative of the Met's human resources department. The latter - apparently to justify their existence - usually sat on the panel and questioned the candidates on all matters corporate.

The technical and legal aspect of what Jax had to study was of genuine interest to him, but bored to tears by the corporate stuff, he did little more than pay it lip service. He'd be expected to be able to recite the Met's strands of diversity - age, gender, sexual orientation etc. He'd also have to learn the Metropolitan Police Service priorities values and mission. Phrases such as: *Increasing public confidence and satisfaction, improving quality of service, being efficient and effective;* were included in a long list, that for the life of him, Jax just couldn't get to stick in his head. Resolving to cram this dry subject on the eve of his interview - should he get one, Jax concentrated instead, on the world of RIPA and stated cases.

His application form completed and checked by the skipper, he passed it on to inspector "The Man" Williams, who would add a few comments: hopefully recommending him for the job.

A few days later, all the boxes complete, he sent it off to be scrutinised. The first part of the process was contracted out to a civilian firm, which sifted out those applications that didn't meet the criteria.

Wrong font, boxes too full, not full enough, structure not adhered to, bad sickness records, outstanding disciplinary matters...

Just one example of non-compliance with the demanded format, would be enough to get the candidate rejected before anyone at SCD11 got sight of the application. The next part of the paper sift would be undertaken by the candidate's potential employers at SCD11.

A week after the closing dates, Jax was summoned to the Man's office and officially informed that his application had been successful. He'd been granted an interview, scheduled for the end of the week. Going back up to the BTF office, he told the others that he'd got through the first part of the application process. The first to react to his news had been Porridge Face.

'Did I tell you about that time when I was in the TSG and I was part of a surveillance team?'

Jax groaned, desperately casting around for some support among the others. But with Bullseye solidly burying treble twenties into the dartboard with unerring accuracy, and the others tactically tucking their heads into non-existent paperwork, computer screens and iphones, he was alone. Not for the first time, he found himself at the mercy of Billy Liar. He sighed resignedly.

'No mate, you didn't.'

'Fuck me Jax - this was the big one. Thought I was gonna' get blown away. Proper big boys we were following. Some gangsters from up north; tooled up and everything they were!'

Porridge was very pleased with himself. He'd managed to get hold of a captive audience in the form of the unfortunate Jax. His little piggy eyes lit up, brimming with pure rapture.

'We'd been following these blokes from Manchester for months. Of course, 'cos of my special forces training, I was selected to infiltrate their gang and I had a 9 mil in my shoulder holster - you can't fuck about with these people Jax - one false move and I reckon I could have taken them all out. I'm pretty shit hot with the old pistola you know.'

Jax repressed the urge to scream: "shut the fuck up!" but instead, he widened his eyes in mock admiration and just hoped that some kind of divine intervention would silence the lying bastard! Thankfully, Porridge didn't elaborate much more.

'Anyway mate,' he said. 'I can't tell you much more about the job, it's top secret.'

He tapped his nose knowingly. 'Anything you need to know about the old surveillance though; I'm your man.'

Winking enigmatically, Billy Liar abruptly got up and strode towards the office door to the sound of the Cat muttering: 'Porridge - you're my hero!'

Porridge spun on his heel and fired off a parting shot:

'Fuck you Cat! Oh, what will *you* tell your kids when they ask: daddy, daddy! What did you do in the war?' And with that, he flounced majestically out, the door slamming with a petulant bang behind him.

Dynamo took one look at the red-faced Cat and burst out laughing. 'Yeah Cat,' he said. 'What *did* you do in the war? Make coffee?'

'No babes,' laughed Emma. 'He was too busy looking at tits!'

The day of the interview found Jax dressed up in collar and tie, riding the train to Clapham and going over the dreaded HR questions. So far removed was he from all things corporate, that the printed page just stared back at him. Putting it down, he tried to control the waves of dread that always accompanied the anticipation of a job interview. He was simply no good when it came to creating first impressions and throughout his working life, the fact that he was unable to be himself when faced with

269

a situation of formality, had been a perpetual curse.

He was pretty sure that with his life experience, he could do the job for which he was applying, standing on his head, but to his unending frustration, once he was up in front of authority, he tended to freeze. He called to mind the words of a leftie schoolteacher who had once told him that should he ever come up in front of self-important people, he should imagine them naked. A staunch anti-royalist, she'd often told her pupils that the Queen wasn't special at all. To prove it, she'd suggested they all imagine her Royal Highness sat on a very different kind of throne - namely the porcelain one, into which she had to take her daily dump!

When he arrived at the TSG base at which the interviews were being conducted, he found that he was third in line, and seating himself in the canteen among confident looking candidates, he tried once more to swat up. The words swam before him and giving up, he went downstairs for a smoke. Two cigarettes later, he went back upstairs, just in time to hear his name being called.

Going into the room, someone invited him to sit down in an oversized armchair that sunk almost to floor level when he sat in it. He felt like Ronnie Corbett. A pitcher of water and a plastic cup were placed before him. Drinking nervously, he looked up from his low down position and took in the scene.

Three people faced him from across the table. An inspector - seated in the middle - smiled benignly, while a sergeant to his left appeared to scowl. To his right sat the dreaded HR woman. Totally unsmiling and seemingly devoid of any character, she was dressed in a frumpy outfit and appeared to Jax to either be radiating hostility, or the discomfort of being sandwiched between two uniformed police officers. Jax couldn't figure out which of the two emotions she was displaying, but she made *him* feel uncomfortable.

The inspector kicked off with a question about why

270

he wanted to enter the world of surveillance and Jax, who felt a genuine desire to enter that world, was able to give an impassioned answer containing the truth. This seemed to impress the guvnor and Jax relaxed slightly. Next came a couple of technical questions from the unsmiling sergeant. Unfortunately, Jax hadn't prepared himself for the depth of these questions, and although he'd stumbled through them, he felt as though he'd given it his best shot.

The skipper then gave a sidelong glance at the HR woman. She took her cue, and looking down at her crib sheet, asked him what the Met's strands of diversity were and how he felt he'd implemented them. Jax scoured his mind for the elusive corporate questions that he'd been dreading. Some of the strands came to him, but try as he might, he just couldn't recall all of them. He mumbled something about how he had respected the needs of a Muslim prisoner who had asked for a halal meal in custody... and then froze.

Recalling his teacher's words of advice, he stared at the woman in her frumpy outfit and desperately tried to imagine her naked. He'd only got as far as imagining her saggy breasts, when he was jerked back from his reverie by the sound of the fully clothed HR woman asking him the next question on her list. It was the big one, the one he'd dreaded most of all.

Putting her sagging breasts firmly out of his mind and making a mental note never to heed his old teacher's advice again, he asked her to repeat the question.

'Can you tell me, PC Jackson,' she said with a trace of impatience in her voice, 'what are the Met's priorities and values?'

Can I fuck Miss; was what he actually wanted to say, but instead, feeling like a drowning man, he took another sip of water in the hope that he could somehow stall the woman's line of questioning. Perhaps, he thought vainly, she'll suddenly drop dead right here in front of me and I won't have to answer her fuckin' irrelevant questions!

Jax, although not much interested in the corporate side of policing, had put a bit of effort into learning the jargon. He believed that if only someone could start him off by giving him the first sentence on the list, his memory would be jogged and he would be able to rattle off the rest. Assuming correctly that he hadn't made much of an impression on the board so far, he gambled all. Desperately swigging another mouthful of tepid water, he looked the woman in the eye and asked:

'Could you start me off?'

The looks that passed between the guvnor and the skipper were priceless. For the first time since he'd walked into the room, Jax saw the skipper smiling. Whether this was because he'd found Jax's bold request funny, or outrageous, Jax didn't know, but at least the bastard had smiled! As for the HR woman, she looked fit to burst - clearly, no one had ever had the audacity to ask her to: "start a candidate off!"

Confronted with such an unorthodox approach in what must have been a very mundane and orderly existence, she cleared her throat and actually gave Jax the first sentence on the list!

'PC Jackson,' she intoned. 'Our mission is working for a safer London. What does this mean?'

This hadn't quite given Jax the kick-start he'd hoped for. Bewildered, he blurted out: 'Umm... being efficient and effective?'

HR woman nodded almost imperceptibly, but totally without encouragement. The guvnor and skipper looked away in the way that a squeamish viewer might hide their face from a gruesome part of a horror film. Jax knew he was sunk. He shrugged.

'Sorry, it's just not coming to me.'

The woman looked incredulous and swiveled her eyes over to the guvnor in search of some kind of intervention. He smiled his benign smile and looked at the squirming candidate in the low chair.

'Thank you PC Jackson. Do you have any questions for the board?'

Jax suddenly wanted to be far away from that room. Red-faced and sweating, he forced a weak smile.

'No guv. Thanks for the opportunity.'

'In that case,' said the guvnor, coughing nervously and shuffling his papers, 'that concludes your interview. Thank you for coming and we'll be in touch.'

Fleeing from the torture chamber, Jax made his way disconsolately out of the building pausing only long enough, to have a quick smoke in the yard. Walking back to the train station, he reflected unhappily that he probably just wasn't cut out for the surveillance world after all.

Settling down on the train, he began to relax and the thought of the naked HR woman with her sagging breasts and silly questions brought a smile back to his face.

It came as no surprise to Jax, when a fortnight later, he received a rejection email from SCD11. He didn't really need to read the part that detailed what he'd fallen down on - that had been obvious! Putting what had been the disaster of his first police board down to a steep learning curve, he vowed to be a little more corporate minded in the future. Those that knew him, however, would say that this was unlikely to happen.

Putting the image of the naked HR woman with the saggy breasts out of his mind, he returned to the fold of the BTF.

Six am on the first day after his board, found Jax along with UX646, crowded around a computer screen at Houndshale nick. As was often the case, the large screen onto which the briefings were normally projected, wasn't working.

Tapping away self-importantly at the keyboard was the latest addition to the BIU. Graham "Intel" Clark looked skinnier than ever. The spiky gelled hair on his tadpole-like head seemed to have receded even further since his old team had last seen him. The most perfunctory of nods in their direction, confirmed that he hadn't developed a personality yet either.

Satisfying his caffeine addiction, he slurped noisily from a Coke can before looking up from his screen. Leaning back in his swivel chair, he cracked his fingers and prepared to deliver his briefing on the warrant, for which they had all dragged themselves out of bed to execute.

In the absence of any grown ups or officers above the rank of sergeant, Intel mercifully cut the health and safety and human rights part of the briefing, and got down to the juicy bits. He recognised that all the cops really needed to know, were the basics. The address, the subjects and their warning signals, type of door, best approach route, and whether there were likely to any dogs at the address; was about the only information that was required.

As was mostly the case, Intel's warrant was under Section 23 The Misuse of Drugs Act. The address was a terraced house - 61 Roberts Drive Filebridge, which for a change, was situated in one of the more affluent areas of Filebridge. The subject of the warrant was Ricky Timms - previously unknown to the police.

A source had given information to his handler, that the address was used to store class A drugs on behalf of Calvin Spoons Anderson. This name concentrated the minds of the listening cops. Anderson - or more accurately, his name - had become quite prolific over the last few months. Everyone knew that he was a big league player on the borough, but to date, he'd evaded all attempts to snare him.

Intel brought up a Google Maps image of the address and zoomed in close enough for them to see the door, through which they intended to smash their way into the house. It appeared to be made of wood and although it appeared substantial, it was far more preferable to UPVC.

Intel said, that in the guise of a leafleter, he'd managed to get right up to the door. It was definitely wooden and opened inwards. He added that he had heard at least one dog inside the house, which had barked when he'd shoved a leaflet through the letterbox. Although he couldn't really say what breed the dog was, he did say that it had a rough, deep bark as opposed to a lap dog yap.

This particular piece of information - which to be fair to Intel - had been intended to be helpful, was greeted by the Cat with a derisory: 'Thanks for that Doctor *Doolittle*!'

Ignoring what had been intended as a double-edged barb, Intel passed the magistrate's warrant around to confirm it's existence. Once it had come full circle, he retook possession of it, and walked over to a table next to the window. Perching on it, he cast an imperious look around the room and asked if there were any questions.

'Yeah,' shouted the Cat, determined to get a rise out of the surly Intel.

'You actually done any work since you left us?'

His reference to Intel's new job of sitting on his arse behind a desk finally drew an irritated response.

'A damn sight more than you Cat - there's more to police work than coffee and tits you know!'

With that, he gripped the front edge of the table, raised his skinny behind from the surface and swung his body backwards, banging himself back down on the back of the table. This act of uncustomary belligerence had a dramatic effect on the table, which had been moved to the side of the room pending repair. Some bored wag had removed the screws fixing the top to the base and Intel's sudden movement had been catastrophic.

The instant his arse hit the back of the table, it tipped backwards, and like some magician's prop; once Intel had been unceremoniously dumped head first on the floor, the top swung back onto it's frame hiding it's victim from view. The only thing to indicate there was anyone behind the table, were a pair of wriggling, oversized boots sticking out from between the gap between wall and table. A muffled commotion from underneath, signaled that Intel was still alive, and once the uproar in the briefing room had subsided, and Emma had rushed to the toilet on the verge of wetting herself, skipper Jarvis and Dynamo dragged the treacherous table to one side and pulled the puce-faced Intel to his feet.

Once the skipper and a giggling Dynamo had dusted Intel down, he handed Jarvis the now crumpled warrant, and limped indignantly out of the briefing room. The skipper called them all to order and they sat and planned their entry.

As Bullseye was driving, Jax was to get the rare opportunity to wield the enforcer, while Porridge Face, the Cat and Emma were detailed to operate the rabbit tool. Once the Cat had done his bit with the placement of the rabbit's jaws, he was to take charge of the team's newly acquired Bite Back spray.

As they piled boisterously out of the briefing room, Jax noticed the crime analyst, Angie Brown. She seemed skinnier than he remembered and appeared flustered. When Dynamo had flung open the door, he'd almost knocked her over. She'd made some remark about needing to use the briefing room for a meeting and was checking if it was occupied.

Jax, who only really knew her enough to say hello, wondered briefly what she was doing in so early. The third floor didn't usually show until around seven-thirty at the earliest.

'She's in early,' he remarked to the Cat.

'Fucked if I know. Not a bad set of tits for an older bird though!' came the flippant reply. He was more interested in getting his hands on the team's new toy.

'Where's that dog spray Jax?'

276

Once in the back yard, UX646 pulled on protective pads and took out their NATO helmets ready to put on once they got nearer. Where there was the possibility of a dog at the address, they always put the pads on. As for the helmets: apart from the protection they offered from the flying glass of an entry, their appearance added to the shock and awe of an early morning raid. The initial effect was vital if they were to subdue and control occupants, especially those of an unknown quantity.

The enforcer was brought to the front of the carrier so as to be readily to hand and Emma made sure the hydraulic screw on the rabbit was tightened up and ready to go. A brief pump of the handle showed it to be functioning correctly and it too was placed at the front of the carrier along with a hoolie bar. Preparations complete, they piled onto the carrier and Bullseye backed out of the yard.

As they were leaving, Jax saw Angie Brown appear at the back door. Lighting a cigarette, she waited until they had cleared the yard, before leaving through a side gate and walking briskly towards the High Street, a mobile phone clamped to her ear. Jax idly wondered where she was off to, so early in the morning.

No sooner had they got underway, than a hissing sound was heard from the back of the carrier. The noise was followed by the panicked voice of the Cat shouting: 'Shit!' The hissing sound and the Cat's outburst of profanity was quickly followed by an insidious and very noxious smell wafting through the carrier's cabin.

Unable to help himself, the Cat hadn't been able to resist playing with the can of Bite Back. Preparing to use the spray for the first time, he'd wanted to ensure that he was familiar with the safety catch system on the can. Wanting to make sure it would operate once they arrived at the target address, he'd decided to give it a little test spray - just to make sure it worked. Slipping the safety catch to off, he'd given the trigger a little squeeze. The effect of pressing the trigger on a brand new 600ml can of Bite Back in the confines of a locked down carrier, had been both immediate and devastating.

The manufacturers of Bite Back make the following claims about their product:

"Containing a blend of natural oils, Bite Back deters a dog's natural impulse to bite. The effects of the spray both disorientate and distract the dog."

Jax had never witnessed the effect it would have on a dog, but Jesus Christ! It had certainly fucking well disorientated and distracted him and all around him! Coughing and spluttering, Bullseye pulled the carrier over to the side of the road and leapt out in search of fresh air. He was closely followed by the rest of them; piling out of the carrier like pilots parachuting from a stricken aeroplane. Skipper Jarvis said nothing. His customary roll of the eyes and shake of the head as he looked skyward, said it all.

After they'd recovered from the effects of the spray they began to berate the Cat.

'So, if you had a gun, would you squeeze the fuckin' trigger to see whether the safety catch was on?' asked Jax, his head starting to hurt. The Cat looked crestfallen.

'I just wanted to make sure it worked!' he said in a hurt little voice.

'Well' said Jax, his head starting to throb from the effects - 'It fuckin' well does work!'

The carrier eventually clear from the "blend of natural oils" and the execution of their warrant delayed by ten minutes, UX646 jumped back aboard. The smell seemed to have permeated the very fabric of the seats and every now and again, it would waft through the cabin drawing a mixture of curses and muttered threats: all directed at the trigger-happy Cat.

Pulling up short of Roberts Drive, all banter ceased and UX646 went through the pre-raid checks, which by now were second nature. Helmets were pulled on, radios turned down and Emma made one more check of the rabbit tool. Sheepishly, and true to form, the Cat farted, glanced down at the safety catch on his Bite Back spray and pulled on his gauntlets. His stink competed with the lingering smell of the spray. From helmet visors, came the usual muffled and reproachful insults of: "dirty bastard" and "smelly cunt," then Bullseye was driving into the target's road, and silence reigned.

Just around the bend from number 61, Bullseye stopped the carrier. Porridge was the first to leap out, rabbit tool at the ready, followed by Emma, clutching the pry bar in readiness to create a gap for the rabbit's powerful jaws. Behind her, came the Cat - Bite Back at the ready. His primary role was to place the rabbit tool in the gap she was about to create. Next came Jax. Hefting the bright red enforcer onto his shoulder, he prepared himself for the short sprint to the address. It was surprising what eighteen kilos of solid metal could do to your breathing pattern, and halfway into his sprint, with lungs burning, he wished he'd taken up Dynamo's offer of carrying it for him. "Old man's stubborn pride" - that's what the big man had called it - and Jax, though he'd never admit it, couldn't disagree.

Fifteen minutes earlier, the subject of the warrant - Ricky Timms - had been rudely awakened by the opening bars of Rhianna's "Diamonds." It took a few seconds for him to realise that the tinny sound was emanating from his phone on the bedside table next to him. Fumbling for his spectacles, he picked up his mobile. The name Spoons, very quickly caught his attention. He was shit scared of the nasty Jamaican. Suddenly fully awake, he hit the green key. 'Hello?'

Without preamble, the gruff voice at the other end simply growled:

'The feds are on their way. Grab the gear and fuck off out of there.'

His heart in his mouth, Timms leapt out of bed and

ran into the bathroom. Pulling the lid from the toilet cistern, he pulled out a heavily waterproofed packet and rushed back into his bedroom. Hurriedly dressing in whatever was to hand, he stuffed the dripping package containing 500 grammes of heroin down the front of his boxer shorts. Letting Brutus; his Staffordshire bull terrier out of the kitchen, he fled.

Ten minutes later, delayed by the Bite Back incident, Emma reached Timm's house and forced her pry bar in between the door seal and it's frame. The Cat shoved the rabbit's jaws into the gap she'd made, and signaled Porridge to start pumping the handle. In the few seconds that preceded the entry, UX646 held it's collective breath. Then, just as the rabbit started to do it's work, they heard a low growl, followed by furious barking. The Cat gripped his Bite Back spray and waited.

The door creaked and groaned, tight as an archer's bowstring. The gap made by the relentless rabbit tool yawned and Jax, realising that as much flexibility as was possible had been taken up, lifted his enforcer to shoulder height, swung it back, and then punched it's solid mass forward connecting just underneath the door's keyhole.

Two hefty strikes later and the stricken door flew open with a crack like thunder, smashing into the wall behind. Dropping their entry tools, Emma, Porridge and the Cat rushed in yelling: "Police with a warrant!" at the top of their lungs.

This was the danger time, a time when the unknown awaited them. Those involved with drugs lived a dangerous life. At any given time, they could be raided not only by the cops, but also by rivals who would smash their way in to steal their stash. Would there be anybody in, would they be armed, would they stand and fight? Speed, aggression and surprise were key, if the cops were to subdue and dominate those inside.

In the event, Brutus did what most dogs did in this

situation; he initially retreated, before nervously returning and sniffing the invaders. The Cat, who had dogs of his own, put down the Bite Back and offered a gloved hand for Brutus to sniff. The dog accepted the Cat's hand and allowed himself to be stroked. While the others rushed past and thundered up the stairs yelling: "Police!" the Cat took hold of Brutus's collar and led him out through the patio doors and into the back garden. Closing the doors, he went back inside the house to join the others.

Jax, who had been last to enter, ran into the kitchen. It was the only room not to have been checked and while he confirmed it to be unoccupied, he heard the ringing shouts of: "Clear!" as his teammates cleared the upstairs rooms.

Going back into the hallway, he'd been both surprised and impressed by the Cat's dog whispering technique and had just been in the middle of congratulating him, when Brutus padded back into the hallway!

Laughing, but perplexed as to how the dog had managed to make it's way back into the house, the Cat led Brutus back out, this time locking the patio doors. Jax heard the Cat laughing. 'Jax - come and look at this!'

Going through to the back room, Jax saw what had been amusing the Cat. There, on his hind legs, was Brutus, paw curled around the door handle, tongue lolling to one side. The dog actually looked as if he was smiling while pushing the handle down. He was literally trying to open the door to let himself back in. Looking at the claw marks on the handle, it was a trick he had performed more than once! The Cat was pissing himself.

'Clever fucker opened the door and let himself back in Jax - look at his paw: it's just like a hand! I've gotta' get a photo of this!'

'Well, it's just as well he's friendly!' smiled Jax.

Finding no signs of occupation other than Brutus and a still warm bed, the pace of the entry slowed down and UX646 began a systematic search of Timm's house. An hour later and with nothing to show for their efforts, they wound it up, filled out the paperwork and called for the boarding up company to make good the shattered door.

Later, over breakfast at the Hidey Hole, someone remarked about how this was the second so-called dead cert warrant connected to Anderson in a month; to have come up blank.

*

In her office on the third floor of Houndshale nick, Angie Brown was an emotional wreck. This was the second time she'd betrayed her employers for the sake of a moment of madness; for the pleasure of blowing a key player in the borough's underworld, and for being stupid enough to have been filmed snorting lines.

How long would she get away with it? When would that bastard Anderson release her from his clutches? She felt sick, and just like every other victim of blackmail through the ages, she felt like there was no escape, nobody in whom she could confide, and utterly out of her depth.

Since Anderson had sent *that* text, she hadn't slept more than a couple of hours a night, and along with the dark circles under her once pretty green eyes, she was starting to look gaunt through loss of weight. She spent her days behind the closed door of her office, fearing that every time a cop came in to pick up crime stats, it would be to arrest her.

Angie spent most of her lonely nights wide-awake, chewing her nails and nursing a glass of vodka. She was startled by the slightest noise outside her door, thinking it was the preliminary to cops with a search warrant coming crashing through. All thoughts of turning herself in were long since gone; the very first time she'd warned Anderson about a raid, she'd sealed her fate. There was no going back. The trading of confidential information in return for Anderson's silence was the equivalent of Judas Iscariot's thirty silver pieces, and scooping them up, she'd betrayed the job she loved so much. Angie Brown wished she could go to sleep and never wake up. She wished she were dead.

Chapter Twelve

'You'll never get anywhere looking out of the window...'

Taser was finally being rolled out across the Met. For too many years, equipped with nothing more than a small can of CS spray and a puny expandable baton, the cops on the front line had all too often been subjected to serious assaults by those whom they sought to subdue or arrest. On occasion, even those who had appealed for police help; would inexplicably attack them too.

Core team cops were equipped first, followed initially by one person on each of the two BTF teams. Against all odds - and to his eternal joy - Porridge Face had somehow been selected to be the first to carry out the training for UX646.

To say he was over the moon was an understatement. On his first day back at work after completing the Taser training course, Porridge swaggered into the BTF office, with his bright yellow Taser strapped to his hip like a gunslinger.

'A piece of piss that course,' he bragged to anyone unfortunate enough to catch his eye.

'There was only ever going to be one person selected for Taser. The guvnor obviously knew about my weapons experience. Just like riding a bike it was.'

He looked over at Jax. 'The old firearms skills never leave you eh Jacko?'

'Something like that Porridge,' Jax replied as vaguely as he could.

284

Porridge knew about Jax's military background and seized upon what he thought was common ground to engage him in his favourite topic of conversation - guns.

Jax, like most ex-military types, tended to only speak about his army days with people he knew and had shared his experiences. He certainly didn't want to become part of Porridge's imaginary band of brothers; as far as he could tell, Billy Liar hadn't done *any* regular service, and the only time he'd put on camouflage had been as a part time territorial army soldier.

The one subject Jax tried never to bring up was the military; the last thing he wanted was Porridge latching onto him. Thankfully though, Porridge let Jax off the hook and disappeared for a while.

'He's probably in the shithouse practicing his quick draw in front of the mirror,' laughed Bullseye, retrieving his darts from the board.

'Yeah,' chimed Jax, 'you just know, he's gonna' be turning on his laser sight and red dotting any fucker that looks at him the wrong way!'

In the event, and much to Porridge's disgust, skipper Jarvis made him unstrap the Taser from his hip and change into plain clothes. He was to be in the Q car with the Cat, who was equally disgusted to have been chosen to partner Billy Liar for the shift. Once Porridge had returned in plain clothes, a sulky look on his face, Bullseye and Dynamo wrapped up their game of killer on the dartboard and Jax went downstairs to get the carrier ready to go out. With the exception of the Q car, UX646 had been tasked with patrolling Cranston in search of the elusive Asian jewellery thieves.

With Emma in the operator's seat, Jax took a meandering route from Filebridge towards Cranston. They'd only been given a small section of Cranston in which to patrol. Known as a microbeat, it consisted of no more than half a dozen streets, and had been selected by the senior leadership team, due to the frequency with which the local residents had been burgled.

The thought of ten hours driving around those six streets, made Jax drag his heels in getting there. A nice wide detour would hopefully net them something interesting to deal with before they arrived at Cranston.

They hadn't long left the back yard, when on the High Street; Emma spotted a green Renault containing a well-known drug dealer and two young females. The car, which was registered to a female, was well known to CRIMINT and many entries had been made with regard to dealing.

Jax took up a follow and watched as the driver adopted the behaviour typical of someone who realised the Old Bill were behind them. Sticking strictly to the speed limit and meticulously indicating prior to conducting the subtlest of turns - while nervously glancing in the rear view mirror - the Renault driver proved to be no exception.

Waiting until the Renault had turned off the main road so as to conduct a stop away from the bustling High Street, Jax followed it into a side road before putting the blue lights on. There appeared to be some activity in the car with the driver seeming to hand something to the female in the back seat. She in turn, fiddled around with the back of her jeans. To the watching cops, it looked like they were in for a find of some sort.

Once the others had piled out to surround and contain the Renault, Jax drove around it and began to reverse up to it's front to prevent it driving away. The reversing sensors on the battered carrier, hadn't worked for as long as Jax could remember, and although they generated a beeping sound, they no longer signaled the proximity to objects in the way. Keeping an eye on the Renault in his mirrors as he backed up, he was startled to hear and feel, the unmistakable evidence that he'd backed into something pretty substantial!

He was still short of the Renault and hadn't a clue

what he'd hit. Muttering: 'oh shit!' he slammed on the brakes, and not for the first time, cursed his complete lack of spatial awareness. Usually when this happened - which was all too frequent - he remained in the cab for a while, his head in the sand. He was reluctant to face not only his teammates: who would mercilessly take the piss, but more so the occupants of the car he'd just stopped. They would be lapping this up - the Old Bill fucking up.

Eventually, he climbed red-faced from his seat, and trying to act as aloof and unconcerned as he could; without so much as a glance at his amused audience, he inspected the damage.

He'd backed into a telegraph pole - one of a series that lined the entire street. How the hell he'd failed to see them, he really couldn't say.

Looking down, his heart sank as he took in the devastation. The side bumper was hanging off, and the rear step now resembled a giant V where it had ploughed into the unyielding pole.

There was barely a scratch on the pole and the only thing to suggest he'd hit it in the first place, was the fact that the telephone wires attached to the top of it, were dancing like crazed skipping ropes. There was definitely going to be some points going on his driving permit for this one, he thought miserably.

The fact that the telegraph pole was undamaged was of some comfort and meant that no third party would have to become involved. The damage to the carrier, however, was such, that it was beyond using a hammer to unofficially carry out a repair. He was going to have to call it in and throw himself upon the doubtful mercy of whichever traffic garage skipper happened to be on duty.

Returning to his cab, he hit the IDR button, which would activate the carrier's black box system. The black box would enable the garage skipper to download the data, recorded prior to the carrier colliding with the pole.

Generating a CAD, Jax walked sheepishly over to

the others to await the allocation of a garage skipper. All eyes were upon him and he heard the driver of the Renault ask skipper Jarvis whether he, Jax, would get into trouble.

They were all smiling at him, with the exception of Jarvis, who as usual, gave his heavenward look. Jax had hoped that the search of the car and it's occupants, would have taken the heat off him, but by the time he'd gone over to them, the search had been completed without any finds. Jax had no sooner walked over to join the others, when his mobile rang. It was the garage skipper asking for an explanation of his careless encounter with the telegraph pole.

Garage skippers varied in character. Some, who lived and breathed traffic law and spent their days persecuting school run mothers whose windshields weren't fully demisted, liked nothing more than to "stick" police drivers on.

Others, with a personality and still with a vague memory of real policing, tended to be more lenient. This one seemed OK though - he even sounded jovial.

Throwing in a bit of banter, he led Jax to think, he would be one of the decent ones. Asking for a summary of the damage, he asked Jax if he could take a photo of the carrier and MMS it to him.

This usually meant that if the damage were superficial, he'd carry out the procedure over the phone and not have to leave his office.

Jax knew that the minute the skipper saw the carnage he'd caused, all thoughts of a remote solution would be put aside. He'd just have to try and make the carrier look a bit more undamaged than it actually was.

Once the occupants of the Renault had been sent on their way, Jax somehow managed to reattach the side bumper, making the damage look slightly better. Desperately jumping up and down on the step in an attempt to bend the step back down and so make it possible to refit the ripped off plastic trim, he achieved absolutely nothing. The step was unyielding, and in the words of a giggling Dynamo: "well and truly fucked!"

Trying to take a photo from an angle that didn't show too much damage, he sent it off for the garage skipper to have a look at. Within seconds, he called back, and confirmed what Jax had known all along. The damage was too severe to gloss over, and as there was nobody available to come out to him, Jax was going to have to drive the carrier thirty miles to the nearest traffic garage, in southeast London.

'That's one way of getting us out of patrolling our microbeat babes!' laughed Emma.

Jax gave her a rueful grin and tried to ignore the rest of them as they jumped raucously back in. The piss taking was by now relentless, and in full flow.

Calling the Cat in the Q car to let him and Porridge know they would be the only BTF on the grid for a while, skipper Jarvis opted out of the journey to the traffic garage, and got Jax to drop him off at the nick for some paperwork time.

Before they set off, Jarvis looked over Jax's driving permit to make sure the periodical skipper's checks had been carried out. There was nothing a garage skipper liked more than to find a driver's eyesight test was out of date. Jarvis backdated and signed the box that confirmed he'd made his annual check of Jax's civilian driving licence. This procedure ensured Jax hadn't picked up any real world driving convictions, not declared since the last time he'd checked.

Arriving at the traffic garage, Jax parked the carrier and called the skipper to announce his arrival. When the skipper appeared, Jax's heart sank. Clip board in hand with shirt straining over a bulging belly, he swaggered over to the carrier wreathed in self-importance. The name badge stuck proudly to his chest proclaimed that this self-important man was Sergeant Hugh Jardon. His close cut hair gelled into place; he was the exact opposite of the character who'd lulled Jax into a false sense of security over the phone.

Responding to Jax's greeting with little more than a perfunctory nod of the head, he immediately began crawling all over the carrier; thoroughly checking it's roadworthiness. He even enlisted the help of a flunky, who circled the vehicle feeling the tyres and checking the depth of the tread. Looking over his shoulder, he could see Bullseye and the others making "what the fuck?" gestures. Jax shook his head, shrugged, and dutifully followed the skipper around while he carried out his fastidious checks.

After surveying the damage to the step, the skipper turned his attention to the interior of the carrier. Dragging the first aid kit off the shelf, he'd been disappointed to find that it was complete and sealed. His disappointment turned to jubilation however, when his eyes alighted on the vehicle's fire extinguisher. Looking at the dial, it's needle in the red, he triumphantly but unnecessarily exclaimed, that it showed empty.

Plumbed in to a system beneath the carrier and operated from within the cab, the extinguisher was designed to help put out the fires caused by any petrol bombs that may be driven over during a riot. Most of these fire extinguishers on board the carriers in Houndshale's fleet were empty, and had been for as long as Jax had been there.

Checking the extinguisher was part of the pre-driving inspection that police drivers were supposed to carry out, along with lights, engine oil levels, tyres etc. If any faults were found, the vehicles had to be taken off the road until all issues had been rectified. In reality, although lights, tyres and oil levels were generally checked, it just wasn't practical to take an operational vehicle off the road just because the fire extinguisher was empty. It wasn't as if carriers could be driven through a seat of disorder anyway. In Tottenham, there had been so much debris on the streets as to make it impossible to drive anywhere. There, Jax had abandoned his carrier and they'd carried their shields to the front line.

The by-the- book traffic skipper was having none of it.

'Did you DI this vehicle before you drove it?' he barked.

'Yes, sarge.'

'In that case, why didn't you notice that the fire extinguisher was empty?'

Jax tried to explain that the carrier was something of a pool vehicle and available to everyone. The extinguisher had been empty for a long time, and besides, according to the maintenance log, the civilian contractors had replaced the empty extinguisher only two weeks earlier. Bullseye knew something about this and pointed out a small hand held extinguisher, which had been supplied as a replacement and was hidden beneath a pile of paperwork in between the front seats.

Jax, grateful for Bullseye's intervention, showed it to the garage skipper who took one look, held it aloft and said:

'Read what it says on the side - tell me what it says,' he demanded with the air of a superior being.

Jax looked, realised what the skipper was driving at, and like a naughty schoolboy intoned:

'It says powder, sarge.'

'Exactly!' he shouted. 'And now tell me what it says on that one,' he sneered, pointing a stubby finger at the offending empty red cylinder.

Jax knew exactly where this was going, but had to play the game. In a voice flat and devoid of all emotion, he said: 'Foam sarge.'

'So, it's no bloody good in a riot then is it?'

Jax sighed. 'No sarge.'

The skipper, now on a self-righteous roll, began to

lecture Jax as though he was a day one rookie.

'You're responsible for this vehicle!' he bellowed. 'Are you a level two officer?' Jax nodded.

'Well,' he said, sticking out his chest. 'So am I.'

Jax thought this unlikely. Once officers specialised, they tended not to be allowed to be extracted for level two training, and in any case, he very much doubted whether this barrel- bellied sergeant could get his fat arse around the shield run circuit at Gravesend!

'What happens when you suddenly get called out for a riot?' demanded the skipper, by now worked up into a self-induced frenzy.

'The mob are dragging you and your colleagues out of the carrier and trying to chop your heads off and the fire extinguisher is empty!'

Jax failed to see the connection between having his head chopped off and an empty fire extinguisher, but he played the game and let the skipper vent his spleen.

'I know these carriers are old and in shit order and I remember being a PC on borough,' he said sounding conciliatory for the first time. Then connecting his laptop to the carrier's black box, he continued his tirade.

'But, this doesn't mean we can neglect our duties in keeping them roadworthy!'

A few years earlier, Jax might have lost the plot, ripped out fatso's equipment, hurled it onto the floor and told him to fuck off out of his face, but with age came restraint. He knew that in an ideal world where vehicles were perfect and plentiful, he could have refused to take the carrier out with an empty fire extinguisher. He also knew, that whatever he said, the system would ultimately stand by the asshole from traffic - twenty years his junior and totally clueless with regard to Jax's previous experience. While Jardon had been working on getting a fat arse at the school tuck shop, Jax had been riding the streets of riots-torn Northern Ireland in a battered old Land Rover - equipped with nothing more than a tiny hand held extinguisher - much like the one in his present day carrier - and he had survived without getting his head chopped off! But, that was then, and this was now, so he bit his lip and waited for fatso to finish.

The garage skipper wound up his lecture with an explanation about how he was duty bound to award Jax the minimum of one point for the damage to the step. Fair enough, thought Jax, why couldn't he have just said that in the first place? But Jardon wasn't finished just yet.

He announced that failing to correctly inspect a vehicle prior to driving it was punishable by two additional points - 'But,' he added, 'I shall consider the fact that we've had this conversation as sufficient and just give you the one point.'

Jax allowed something of a facetious tone to creep into his voice.

'Thanks *sarge*, I *really* appreciate it.'

Too pumped up with his triumph over a lowly borough PC, the skipper failed to detect Jax's insubordinate tone, and unplugging his laptop, he picked up his clipboard with a flourish and waddled back to his office kingdom.

Jax got back into the carrier followed by the others. Yelling 'CUNT!' at the top of his voice, he felt the anger and frustration of the last forty minutes ebb away. His passengers, not sure whether he had lost it, remained quiet for all of twenty seconds, before dissolving into laughter.

'What was that tosser's name?' asked Bullseye.

'*That*,' replied Jax, 'was sergeant Hugh Jardon.'
'Why?'

'More like huge hard on!' laughed Bullseye.

It took a second for the play on words to sink in, and when the penny dropped Jax roared with laughter.

'I reckon he definitely got a massive hard on when he found that empty extinguisher!'

'With that belly,' said Emma, 'I'd be surprised if he

293

can remember what his cock looks like babes!'

Normal service had been resumed on board the carrier, and as usual, the conversation had rapidly turned to all things sexual. With a broad grin on his face Jax manouvered the carrier through the gates and headed west, towards Houndshale and more familiar territory.

A couple of miles down the road, the guys in the back seats lost themselves in cyber loafing on iphones, or just watching the world go by through the windows. The usual comments were made about any attractive female they drove past, along with cruel asides aimed at the likes of listless young men with their trousers worn halfway down their backsides. Bullseye, gazing out of the window, made one of his random remarks to nobody in particular.

'When I was at school, the teachers used to tell me I wouldn't get anywhere staring out of the window.'

Jax laughed. 'And just look at you now!'

'Yep, they were wrong, I'm staring out of the window right now and - getting somewhere, *and* getting paid to do it!'

'Yeah,' quipped Dynamo - 'But the only place you're getting to is Houndshale!'

They drove in silence for a while, alert to the possibility of spotting some criminal activity, but not really wanting to get involved in something that far from home. After an uneventful journey back to their own borough, they pulled into the back yard at Houndshale and went in search of skipper Jarvis.

*

For the journey to the empire of sergeant Huge Hard On, Jax and the others had temporarily switched their radios from the Houndshale channel, to the local link. This was so that they could listen in to whatever may have been happening in their immediate area and if necessary, react to it. For the duration of their foray into unfamiliar territory, they'd been out of touch with their home borough.

Meanwhile, Porridge Face and the Cat had been trawling the streets of Houndshale looking for trade. Sipping on his obligatory flat white, the Cat had been doing his best to ignore Porridge who was prattling on about some imaginary enemy he'd faced in the jungle.

They were cruising the London Road, paying attention to bookmaker's shops, hoping to find a familiar face dealing cannabis, and after an hour of listening to Porridge's one-way conversation, Cat was desperate for some intervention of whatever kind.

He was relieved when, as they passed a parade of shops on the London Road, he thought he spotted Thomas Riley.

Six months earlier, Riley - a domesticated traveler - had been up in front of the magistrate at Filebridge, where he was due to be remanded in custody pending a crown court hearing for burglary.

A heroin addicted habitual criminal, Riley hadn't fancied being banged up in Wormwood Scrubs awaiting trial; so taking advantage of the lax security at the court, he'd vaulted the dock, shoved an usher out of the way, and punched the elderly security guard before getting clean away.

He was top of Houndshale's list of fugitives and had proved impossible to track down. The nearest he'd got to being recaptured, was when officers acting on a tip off, had attended a caravan site where he was said to be living with a relative. The minute the cops had set foot on the site, dogs had barked, grubby children had appeared seemingly from nowhere and tugged at their clothes; while several adults had subtly, but obviously, barred their way.

Past experience with gypsy sites had taught the cops to approach with caution -and then - only in fairly large numbers. On this occasion, though, Lurch Coverdale and Intel Clarke from the BIU had wanted to act on the info while it was still fresh. They'd drawn a blank with the BTF, who had been away on aid, and the best they'd been able to do, had been to beg a couple of rookie beat cops from the local skipper to go with them.

With dogs, kids and surly adults following them, they'd posted one of the rookies around the back of the caravan in case Riley did one out of the window. Intel knocked on the flimsy door, while Lurch peered through the grimy windows. He had been pretty sure he'd seen movement inside, although nobody came to the door.

Knocking harder, Intel tried the door handle, which to his surprise yielded. The door opened slightly and Intel hesitated while he mentally ran through his legal grounds for entry. He was pretty sure he had power of entry, given that Lurch thought he had seen something move inside.

He was also sure he could enter because the offence for which Riley was wanted; was one which was triable either way - that is to say - it could be tried at both magistrates *and* crown court.

His legal assessment complete: Intel had tentatively pushed open the door, shouting: 'Police!' before moving gingerly inside. Lurch and the other rookie followed him in to the mumbling sounds of protest from their gypsy audience.

They'd no sooner gone into the gloom of the caravan, than they heard a commotion from the back. Rushing outside, they ran around the caravan just in time to see the back of Thomas Riley as he sprinted like a greyhound across an adjoining field. The rookie, they'd left round the back to cut off such an escape, lay where Riley had deposited him - in a patch of stinging nettles - groaning and rubbing multiple stings.

His fellow rookie had gamely shot off after the fugitive, but had only got as far as the second field where, he was lit up by an electric cattle fence.

A young lad from an inner city, it had been his first encounter with what was probably the only electric fence in the whole borough. Yelping, he rolled around in cow shit, rubbing his electrocuted inner thigh. Even Lurch; not exactly known for his sense of humour couldn't help but smile. Riley was now a disappearing dot on the horizon, and he wasn't about to chase after him in his ill-fitting polyester suit.

They'd called up for help over the radio, but by the time the nearest unit had arrived, the elusive Riley had been long gone, and he'd just added assaulting a police constable in the execution of his duty, to his growing list of offences.

The Cat was pretty good with faces and although the guy he'd seen outside the shop was sporting an unruly mop of blonde hair - Riley habitually shaved his head - he had been pretty sure it was Houndshale's most wanted.

Excitedly shouting at Porridge Face to spin the Vauxhall Zafira around, he unbuckled his seatbelt in readiness for a quick decamp. With a screech of tyres, Porridge slewed the car around. Cat laid a hand on his arm.

'Slowly Porridge! Don't spook him!'

'Yeah, yeah, don't teach me to suck eggs!' he grumbled, slowing down nonetheless.

Having turned around, they were now coming up to the shops on the wrong side of the road, but as luck would have it, there'd been a bus stop just short of where the Cat had first spotted his man. It wasn't unusual for a car to park facing traffic while it's driver nipped in for a quick purchase, and as they pulled up, they hadn't seemed to attract any attention from passers by. Porridge had been able to park the Zafira a few yards from the shop from where they could see the suspected fugitive.

Although his shifty eyes constantly darted around, it seemed, he hadn't yet rumbled them as Old Bill.

The Cat, ever fashion conscious, hadn't strapped on his Met vest, or belt kit. He'd reasoned that while out and about in plain clothes, he'd be less conspicuous without the bulk of the armoured vest bulging beneath his clothes. Leaving his CS spray on his belt, he'd opted for jeans and tee shirt and crammed his cuffs and Asp into his jeans pockets. Normally, when he got out to put in a stop, he would hold his radio in his hand, but in this situation, not wanting it to be seen, or even worse, heard by his man, he'd left it on the car seat when he'd got out.

Getting out of the car, the Cat made his way as nonchalantly as he could towards the shop. When he was within fifteen feet of the man outside, his suspicions were confirmed. It *was* Riley.

His heart beating faster, adrenaline flooding his body, the Cat closed the gap. Porridge had also got out of the car, but unlike his partner; he carried CS, cuffs, Asp and radio inside a concealed shoulder harness.

The rig appealed to him and he imagined he was on a secret mission. In his fertile mind, the nylon rig was really a leather shoulder holster and he was packing heat.

Keeping a few yards between him and the Cat, he prepared to cut off any potential escape routes.

The Cat was almost upon Riley, but wanting to appear as though he was going into the shop, he didn't approach him straight away. By now, Riley was watching him intently. His back up against a wall, he had a six-foot wooden fence to his right and the busy London Road to his front. The Cat felt pretty confident that his man was at least contained by the fence, and that Porridge had the road covered. Feeling confident, he changed direction just short of the shop doorway and strode towards Riley.

Riley's animal instinct had kicked in the minute he'd seen the Cat approaching. He couldn't be sure, but he looked familiar, and having a white face, the Cat didn't fit the profile of a local. He decided that he would remain cool and see whether the Cat entered the shop. Glancing to his right he saw Porridge Face. He could tell by the ugly fucker's walk that he was Old Bill.

Just as the Cat changed direction away from the

doorway, Riley turned to the fence and like a commando on an assault course threw himself at it, his finger tips grasping the top. Just as the Cat reached him, he pulled himself up and over the fence as though it had been no more than knee high. The Cat was a split second too slow and had managed to get little more than a feel of Riley's trainers as they followed their wearer over the fence and disappeared from view.

Despite his disadvantage of being a head shorter than Riley, the Cat gamely attacked the fence. Sheer determination, coupled with adrenaline got him up and over the other side. Dropping in a heap on the other side, he looked to his right from where he could hear the sound of splintering wood. Hoisting himself over another fence, he remained there for a second, using the extra height as an observation platform.

Garden fences interspersed with handkerchief-sized gardens, provided obstacles for as far as he could see. Two fences away, he could see Riley vaulting and sprinting across lawns and concrete yards as though he were an Olympic athlete.

Sighing, but not yet ready to admit defeat, he began throwing himself over fences. When he was within one fence of his quarry, he was vaguely aware of the metallic sound of, first his cuffs, and then his Asp, falling from his back pockets and clattering to the ground below.

Desperation to escape a smack-free cell in the Scrubs, gave Riley wings. Although gym fit, the Cat's breathing became ragged, his heart hammered behind his rib cage, and his chest tightened and as he gasped in huge gulps of air. His lungs, starved of oxygen, were starting to burn, his legs and arms ached from fence vaulting and his vision blurred.

There were times to give up on a runner, such as one who may have had little more than a bag of weed on them - but this was different - He would catch Riley if it killed him!

From somewhere behind him, through the roar of blood in his ears, he could hear the crash of splintering fence panels. Assuming it was Porridge Face, he hurdled on. Pausing atop yet another fence, he scanned the ground to his front. Although fences still stretched endlessly in front of him, he could no longer see or hear Riley.

Sucking air into his aching lungs, he resisted the urge to blindly blunder on. He took in his surroundings. Of course, had his radio not been laying idle back on his car seat, he would have been able to call up other units to cut Riley off on the road that ran parallel to London Road. Dogs, helicopters and shit loads of cops would have been a touch of his transmit button away. He could only hope that Porridge had called it in. He could still hear fences being battered down behind him and assumed that his teammate was still forcing his big belly through the fences he'd already vaulted.

His last sighting of Riley had been a garden and a fence away. Since he'd arrived at that last fence, he'd neither heard nor seen him. Reasoning that he couldn't have been more than a garden away, he quietly lowered himself down into the next garden and padded silently across the overgrown lawn. The next fence was at least seven-feet tall and the Cat shook his head and sighed. Pausing at the bottom of the fence, just long enough to listen for any telltale noises, his eyes alighted on an old plastic garden chair.

Carrying it over to the base of the monster fence, he stepped up. The added height from the chair enabled him to see over the fence. Rather than a lawn, the next garden was more of a concrete yard with a shed at the bottom and a patch of dense and tangled undergrowth, which had grown around barely visible rusting lawn mowers and the old abandoned frames of children's bikes. He couldn't hear a dog, but most of the yard was covered in crusty old dog shit and yet more rusting metal. The house itself appeared to be unoccupied.

Pulling himself up and over with the aid of the chair, the Cat lowered himself down and onto the shit strewn concrete on the other side. Now he was there, he could see that the yard was hemmed in on either side by bushy, overgrown Leylandii trees. Growing at a rate of over three feet a year, and now blocking the sun for the bordering houses, the last owners must have been most unpopular with their neighbours.

The Cat took in his surroundings. He hadn't seen or heard Riley for several minutes. Assuming he hadn't been able to push through the impenetrable Leylandii, he must have either gone over the fence at the back of the garden, or still be somewhere nearby. He felt pretty confident that he hadn't gone over the fence; he would surely have seen him from his last vantage point, and even if he had, wouldn't the Cat have heard him?

He listened. Apart from the almost constant whine of passenger jets overhead, and the distant roar of traffic on the London Road, the only thing he could hear was the carnage being caused by Porridge as he bludgeoned his way towards him. The Cat knew that the sensible thing to have done was to wait for back up in the form of Porridge. Together they should be able to contain the garden until reinforcements arrived, then they could carry out a safe and systematic search.

Right at that moment, sense didn't enter into the equation. The Cat had practically burst his lungs chasing the bastard, and - he thought grimly, that if anyone deserved to catch Riley, it was him.

Patting his back pocket, he remembered that his cuffs and Asp were several fences behind him and he made a mental note to never again ditch his belt kit. Just as soon as he could, he'd put an order in for a harness.

Searching for a weapon, he spotted a rusting pickaxe entwined by brambles. Stooping, he tugged it free of the thorny tendrils, and upending it, he banged the abandoned tool onto the concrete, releasing the pick from it's wooden shaft.

Holding the handle above his right shoulder as though it were a level two baton, he approached the rotting shed and shoved the door. It flew open with a protesting groan and smashed against something inside, before dropping from it's hinges and falling to the floor in a cloud of dust and cobwebs. With his hand out, he adopted a textbook officer safety "ready" stance, and shouting: 'Police!' he stepped inside, pick handle at the ready. The shed stank of mould and dog shit and was heaped up with rusting old oilcans, car engine blocks and piss-stained mattresses. Of Riley, there was no sign.

The bastard must be in the house, he thought to himself, and exiting the shed, he made his way back to the front of the garden where the back door to the house hung open on rotten hinges. Close by, he could hear Porridge Face calling his name.

Inexplicably ignoring his teammate, the Cat hefted the pick handle and pushed open the back door to the house. He'd no sooner entered the decaying building and walked into the kitchen, when he was hit from behind.

The length of lead piping, which Riley swung at the cop, mercifully missed the intended target of his head; crashing down instead, off the top of Cat's shoulders, grazing his neck and connecting forcefully with his suprascapular nerve block. Stunned, he dropped the pick handle and almost went down. The blow sent a jolt; akin to an electric shock through the Cat's body and he was momentarily helpless.

Before he could regain his senses, he heard a dull clang as Riley dropped his weapon. Quick as a flash, he threw an arm around Cat's throat, holding him in a choking headlock. With his knee braced up against the small of the cop's back, he reinforced his grip with his other hand and began to crush Cat's windpipe.

The Cat, still reeling from the hammer blow to his

suprascapular, and with painful, stabbing stars dancing before his eyes, scrabbled weakly at Riley's forearm. In desperation, he tried to heel kick Riley's shins, but the rubber soles of his trainers, failed to have the effect that standard issue boots would have, and the more he struggled, the more Riley's grip tightened.

He could feel Riley's hot breath in his ear and smell the foetid smell of stale cigarette smoke and old sweat. Trying to push Riley up against the kitchen wall, achieved no more than a snarl of: 'Oh no you don't you fucker!' before Riley shoved him forward, ramming his head into a rusting fridge freezer.

A faded yellow post it note still stuck to the fridge door swam before the Cat's eyes. He just made out the words: "Don't forget doc's appointment," before blacking out.

Just before he lost consciousness, he heard a blood curdling yell followed by: 'Stitch that you cunt!' and a cracking, yet wet sound; like that of a coconut being smashed open with a hammer.

He didn't know how long he'd been out cold, but when he came to, he looked up from the greasy kitchen floor to see Porridge Face grinning down at him. Sweat plastering the dark curls to his forehead, twigs and fence wood sticking to his clothes; the egg on legs that was Porridge Face, was the sweetest thing that the Cat had ever seen.

Levering himself into a sitting position, he could see Riley slumped like a rag doll in the corner of the kitchen. He was out cold; his blonde hair matted with the thick blood that still ran freely down his face and dripped into his lap.

Wiping his Asp on Riley's shirt, Porridge slammed it onto the floor to retract it, holstered it, winked at the Cat and said: 'Fuckin' pikey cunt! Yaw-wite Adie?'

'Fuck me,' he said weakly. 'Did you kill him?'

'Nah, it's gonna hurt in the morning though!' And

with that, Porridge kicked the motionless Riley in the ribs.

The stricken fugitive stirred, opened his bloodshot eyes and groaned. Before he could come to properly, Porridge grabbed him by the hair and jerked him forwards and onto his front. With one knee on his back, he took out his cuffs and snapped them on. In his best Sweeney voice he said:

'You're fuckin' nicked son!'

'Great,' said the Cat. 'I hunt him down and you nick him!'

Porridge laughed.

'You know me mate, I'm like a pair of Turkish slippers - I always turn up at the end! Anyway, he'd never have got the drop on me, I'd have stalked him like when I was a sniper'

The Cat groaned. 'I need a coffee.'

The wailing rise and fall of sirens heralded the arrival of the cavalry, but all the cops in the derelict house really needed was a van in which to throw Riley.

Dragging him roughly to his feet, they frog marched him out through the garden gate and into the street. Somebody called for an ambulance to check out Cat's injuries.

Porridge Face, enlisting the help of the van driver, chucked Riley into the back of the van, scowled at him and then slammed the cage door before climbing into the passenger seat. The van driver, an unwilling captive audience, spent the journey to the nick listening to Porridge Face spout on about how he'd utilised his SAS skills to save the Cat's life.

Skipper Jarvis was in the canteen. Sitting next to him, were the Cat and Porridge Face both furiously scribbling notes. The Cat had been pronounced fit by the paramedics, and apart from his dishevelled appearance and a graze on the side of his neck; he seemed to have recovered from his ordeal with Riley. Pausing to slurp noisily from his coffee cup, he looked up at the new arrivals.

'Nice of you to join us,' he said with a smile. 'While you lot were swanning around in south London, me and Porridge bagged Thomas Riley!'

'Fuckin' hell Cat, really? Nice one mate!' said Dynamo admiringly.

'Yeah,' chimed Porridge, 'don't forget the bit about him choking you out before I steamed in and laid the cunt out!'

The Cat rubbed his shoulder where Riley had whacked him. 'Yeah, I'll give you that,' he admitted reluctantly,' but who hunted him down eh? Who jumped half a dozen fences to catch him?'

'Listen mate,' retorted Porridge indignantly, 'I'd have been quicker than you over those fences if my leg hadn't been playing up. It's never been the same since I took a bullet in it!'

'Alright, alright boys,' said Jarvis. 'Well done to both of you, now get on with your notes, we've got a job to do.'

'What's that then skip?' asked Dynamo.

'Fast time warrant,' replied Jarvis holding up a sheaf of papers - 'Anderson again. Porridge, you stay here and deal with your prisoner, the rest of you grab a quick bite to eat, then meet me in the yard in fifteen minutes. I'll brief you on the way to the address.'

On the way out, Jarvis held the door open to allow a woman out first. She'd been sat in a corner since they'd arrived, eating a sandwich.

'After you Angie,' he smiled, before following her out of the canteen. He thought that she'd lost a bit of weight, but the thought didn't deter him from eyeing her swaying backside as it disappeared up the stairs to the third floor.

Fifteen minutes later, with the welcome omission of Porridge, UX646 assembled in the back yard. With the carrier taken out of service by Huge Hard On, they'd transferred their entry gear to a minibus; hastily requisitioned from the neighbourhood's team. Still smarting from his encounter with the telegraph pole, Jax had handed over to Bullseye for the rest of the shift. This had led to much piss taking and jibes about what a pussy he was and how he'd let the garage skipper get under his skin. But having backed his own car into a lamppost the day before, he'd wanted to avoid the legendary: "Things come in threes," adage. He'd decided not to tempt fate and had had to put up with the inevitable smart comments: which on his team, went hand in glove with the misfortunes of others.

Once they were underway, Jarvis began his briefing:

'You all know Calvin Anderson, or Spoons, as he's known on the street.'

A nodding of heads confirmed that they did. Jarvis continued. 'The BIU have sworn out a Section 23 warrant for his address. They're convinced he's just taken possession of a large quantity of class A.'

'There'll be nothing there,' said the Cat confidently, 'he never keeps anything at his address.' The others murmured their agreement.

'Well,' rejoined Jarvis, 'you never know; the intel may be right for a change. Anyway - switch on - he's a nasty bastard, and from his balcony, he'll probably be able to see us coming; so no hanging about, and lets get up to his flat sharpish. Jax, you're on the enforcer, Cat, Bullseye and Dynamo, you take the rabbit tool.'

A couple of minutes later, having driven the short distance to Anderson's block, Bullseye parked the minibus out of sight of his balcony. Pulling on pads, gloves and helmets, they lined up on Anderson's blind side, before sprinting around to the front door, hugging the building line for as long as they possibly could.

Inserting a firefighter's emergency key into the notch above the letterboxes, Jarvis twisted it until it released the door's locking mechanism. Shoving the door, he wedged it open with a brick to allow access to any other officers that might be required to back them up should it get messy.

Had they taken the stairs to the sixth floor, by the time they'd lugged the entry kit to Anderson's door, they'd have been fit for nothing, and so they all piled into the lift like sardines. The minute the lift doors closed, the Cat farted and got punched by Dynamo. Holding their breath to escape breathing in Cat's stink, they began to ascend to the sixth floor.

Halfway up, the lift came to a juddering halt. The electronic female voice announced "third floor," and the doors opened to reveal an elderly man. Taken aback by the sight of tooled up, helmeted cops; he stepped back, his mouth opening and closing.

Calling out: 'Sorry!' Jarvis looked heavenward and jabbed the lift's keypad. The doors closed to the sound of muffled giggling, and they continued their ascent.

Spilling out of the lift and into the hallway of the sixth floor, the cops made their way to Anderson's door as stealthily as they could. All hilarity now suppressed, they mentally ran through their entry tasks, each employing their own individual method of pulse rate reduction.

They had executed countless warrants, but each one held potential danger, and the unknown threat always raised adrenaline levels. Once they were in, and had taken control of the occupants, the gnawing stress dissipated as they carried out a practiced routine. With the likes of Anderson, one never knew what to expect. Firearms and knives were always a possibility with people such as him. You just couldn't tell what you'd be faced with upon entry. The one certainty, with Anderson, was that he would be extremely hostile.

As they raced along the corridor, visors misting up, they rounded the corner to Anderson's apartment, only to find the door ajar. The gap framed Anderson, who exuded malevolence from every nasty pore. The cops could see that he'd fastened the door chain.

When he'd got news via his stubby little Nokia, that the feds were on their way, he had been pissed off, but totally unconcerned. When would they realise, that he never got his hands dirty? 'Mugs!' he'd exclaimed to himself before opening his door.

Once he'd got over the surprise of seeing Anderson at his open door, Jarvis said: 'Police with a warrant!' and held up the paperwork for Anderson to see. Sucking his teeth, Spoons snarled: 'You're not coming in, let me see the warrant.'

'Now look,' said Jarvis, 'we can do this the easy way, or the hard way, either way, I'm not bothered, but we *are* coming in!'

Anderson's reaction to Jarvis's ultimatum had been to suck his teeth again and try to push the door shut.

Still keyed up for a forced entry, UX646 weren't having any of his delaying tactics, and shouting: 'Step away from the door!' Dynamo shoved it with such force, that the links of the door chain disintegrated and the door exploded inwards. Momentarily caught off guard, the belligerent Jamaican staggered back a few paces before going down under the combined weight of the entire team. Bundling him to the floor, they flattened him.

Dynamo and Jax twisted his arms behind his back and pulling out her cuffs, Emma snapped them over Anderson's wrists. 'Fuckin pig bitch!' he snarled before Jarvis shoved his face back into the carpet.

Jarvis hissed: 'Calm down, *we're* in charge now!'

Realising that these cops weren't going to be intimidated by him, Anderson decided to play the game. 'Ok, ok, I'm calm, get off me man, I can't breath!'

'Alright, stand him up,' said Jarvis, 'but any screwing around and you'll be back on the deck. Understand?' Anderson nodded.

'Get him up and sit him on the sofa.'

Hauled to his feet and dumped unceremoniously on the couch, Anderson's aggression levels fell away, but the hatred in his eyes still burned bright. Once he was seated, Jarvis showed him the warrant, and to the background sounds of Anderson's teeth sucking and general mutterings, Jarvis's team began their search.

As Emma walked across the hall floor and into the kitchen, she felt a wooden laminate panel wobble slightly underfoot. Borrowing Dynamo's Leatherman multi-tool, she inserted it's screwdriver attachment into a gap and levered up the loose board.

She shone her torch into the under floor space and the beam picked out a package shrink-wrapped in black plastic. Reaching down, her fingertips made contact with the package. Hauling it out, she stood up and took it into the kitchen.

Selecting the razor sharp blade from the multi-tool, she slit the package along it's side and pulling the stretched plastic apart. She gave a low whistle. There, packed tightly, were stacks of banknotes.

Mainly made up of fifties, the lowest denomination in the bundle was a separate stack of twenty-pound notes. Dynamo was searching through the kitchen cupboards. She tugged at his sleeve.

'Look at this babes!' she said incredulously, 'I've not seen, let alone owned a fifty quid note since I don't know when! I'm gonna take another look!'

Returning to the cavity under the floor, she shone her torch into the hole. Flat on her belly, she reached as far into the cavity as she could, and pulled out another black shrink-wrapped package. On opening this one, she was rewarded with more tightly packed bank notes - this time, a mixture of euro and dollar bills. It was Dynamo's turn to whistle.

'Fuck me!' he said, his mouth falling open. 'There must be a couple of hundred grand there!'

'Yeah babes - not bad for someone on

unemployment benefit! I reckon we're in the wrong job!'

Emma took the packages back into the hallway, where - for evidential purposes, she replaced them inside the cavity before photographing them in situ. Taking them back out, she took the cash into the front room, where the skipper was filling out the book 101.

'Found this under the floor skip,' she said handing it to Jarvis who turned the pages of the 101 to the exhibits section. Good practice, when seizing evidence during a search, was to question the owner of the property and record his answers in the book. Jarvis turned to Anderson.

'Is this yours?'

Anderson's mouth twisted into a cruel smile. 'No comment,' he spat.

Unfazed, Jarvis continued his line of questioning:

'What is it?'

'No comment.'

'How much cash is there in these packages?'

'No comment.'

'Is there any reason why this cash would be underneath your floor?'

The Jamaican sucked his teeth, but refused to answer.

'Well, if it doesn't belong to you and you know nothing about it, I guess, it's going to have to come with us and be booked into found property.'

The threat of taking a shit load of cash from him finally loosened his tongue. 'You can't take my money!' he shouted.

'So it is yours?'

'Yes, man, it's my dough.'

Jarvis pressed on: 'Do you work Mr. Anderson?'

'No - that's not your business anyway!'

'Well, I've got to decide whether you are lawfully in possession of this cash. Are you claiming benefits?'

'You know I am!'

'In that case,' continued Jarvis, 'how come you're in possession of so much money when you don't work and claim benefits?'

'Fuck you man! I ain't tellin' you shit!'

Skipper Jarvis looked over at Emma and nodded.

'Mr. Anderson,' she began. 'We *are* seizing this money and I'm arresting you on suspicion of money laundering...'

Anderson got to his feet, his face a mask of fury. 'Fuckin' pig bitch!' he snarled, walking towards her. Jarvis shoved him hard and he fell back onto the sofa. Emma continued:

'You do not have to say anything, but it may harm your defence if you do not mention when questioned, something which you later rely on in court.'

His face like thunder, Anderson glared at the cops, but remained silent. Emma stuffed the cash into evidence bags, marked them up as her exhibits, and Jarvis recorded it in the 101. When Jarvis announced that he would be seizing his computer and the iphone on the table, Anderson looked murderous.

Calling Dynamo and Jax into the room, the skipper asked Emma to leave the room before telling Anderson that he was to be strip-searched. This announcement proved to be the final straw, and getting to his feet once again, the Jamaican tried to push his way past the cops. He abruptly came up against Dynamo's bulk, who along with Jax and the skipper wrestled him to the ground. For the second time that day, the feared Spoons ate carpet.

Pulling him on to his side, Jax hooked Anderson's handcuffed arms over his knee, while Dynamo patted him down. Once this had been repeated on his other side, Anderson was rolled onto his back. Jarvis kept his head still, while Jax pulled down his jeans. Anderson was wriggling and spitting feathers; but there was only going to be one winner and it wasn't going to be him!

As Jax pulled Anderson's jeans down to his ankles, a

stubby little Nokia fell out from his boxer shorts. Jax tossed it to one side, and continued to search him, but found nothing else. Pulling the furious Anderson's trousers back up, the cops stood him up and sat him back down. Jax sealed the Nokia into an evidence bag, and Jarvis added it to the book 101. Anderson made no comment.

As an afterthought, the Cat rummaged around in the kitchen bin. Underneath some greasy takeaway wrappers and soggy tea bags, he unearthed a stained business card. His lips silently formed the words as he read the printed details:

Angie Brown, Crime Analyst, Metropolitan Police, Houndshale.

'Fuck me!' he mouthed, and calling Jarvis to one side, he showed the skipper his find. 'Whaddya reckon skip?'

Jarvis recalled watching Angie's arse swaying up the stairs after he'd held the door open for her earlier. 'Bag it Cat,' he said quietly, before adding: 'But don't record it in the 101 and keep it to yourself for the time being.'

With no other finds of note, the cops gathered up their exhibits and took Anderson out into the corridor, where they bundled him into the lift and into their borrowed minibus for the short drive to the nick.

Once Anderson had been booked in, his phones and computer were booked in with the Borough Intelligence Unit to be interrogated, and UX646 sat down to write their notes. It had been most satisfying to have finally got to nick Houndshale's own "Teflon Don," and if nothing else, they felt pretty sure he'd be leaving the nick without his cash.

It had been a funny old day: what with encountering Huge Hard On, and capturing Houndshale's most wanted. As for Calvin Anderson - that had been the icing on the cake...

Chapter Thirteen

'You do not have to say anything...'

In the BIU office, Lurch hooked up Anderson's Nokia to the computer and activated the software designed to interrogate suspect's mobile phones. All of the calls and texts related to the same number, which when matched up with the only name in the address book, were under the entry: "AB"

Lurch wasn't one to get excited, but when he read the texts from AB, he was flabbergasted. There were seven texts, which although weren't that varied in their content; damned the sender. It became immediately obvious that the sender had been privy to confidential police material and had warned Anderson of impending police raids.

While two of the text messages gave a time, date and address for a raid, another four simply bore the message: "Police on way now!" followed by an address. The seventh text wasn't a warning, but a plea: "*Calvin. I'm begging you to stop making me do this. I can't take much more. If you have any feelings left for me, please leave me alone. A*"

Lurch made a printout of the Nokia's interrogation and took it up to the third floor where he presented his findings to the Detective Chief Inspector who was heading the Anderson case. A simple case of money laundering was normally handled by a Detective Constable from the Financial Investigation Unit, who would interview the subject, and apply to the court for a

313

seizure hearing. In Anderson's case however, the DCI who'd been handed Angie Brown's tea stained business card by skipper Jarvis, had taken over the investigation.

Thanking Lurch, the DCI, grave faced, pushed his chair back from his desk, stood up, and made his way up to the top floor; home to the senior management team. He didn't bother to check the boss's diary with his personal assistant, and striding straight passed the PA's office, he knocked on the borough commander's door. Hearing the Chief Superintendent's cheery 'Come!' he pushed open the door.

'Morning boss,' he said unhappily. 'We've got a problem...'

At around the same time that the DCI was sitting down to his meeting with the borough commander, Angie Brown was in the back yard deeply inhaling smoke from her third cigarette of the morning. When she'd arrived for work, she'd heard on the grapevine, that not only had Anderson been arrested the day before; he was still in custody. Desperately, but as subtly as she could, Angie had made enquiries with the DCs on the third floor, but they'd all denied any knowledge of Anderson.

She had been puzzled by his arrest; although there hadn't been much time to warn him of the raid, she had been sure he'd had enough time to get rid of any incriminating evidence. What on earth could the cops have found to justify arresting him?

As soon as she had signed on to her terminal and the screen had come to life, she'd logged on to CRIMINT in the hope of finding out what had happened. There was an entry relating to Anderson's arrest, but it had flashed red and denied her access. Panicking, and imagining that someone was remotely monitoring her keystrokes, Angie quickly logged out of CRIMINT, her mind a whirl.

She'd contemplated going home sick, but like a rabbit in the headlights, she was paralysed with fear. Her skin felt cold and clammy, but she sweated profusely and developed tunnel vision. Shaking, she felt faint, her heart palpitated and the room swam like it did back in her apartment when she had drunk one too many vodkas - except this wasn't home - this was a place filled with the faces of all those she had betrayed ever since the bastard had walked into her life.

Resting her forehead on her desk, she closed her eyes in an effort to stop the room spinning. Her salty tears rolled down her cheeks and dripped onto her desk, pooling briefly, before forming a rivulet, which halted symbolically, as it came up against the dam made by the leather wallet containing her police identification card.

She didn't hear the door to her office open, and the first time she realised that she wasn't alone, was when she'd felt a gentle hand on her heaving shoulder. She heard the familiar Scottish brogue of her immediate boss, Detective Sergeant George Barnes.

'Look at me Angie,' he said softly. She lifted her head and looked up at Barnes before wiping away tears and smudging her mascara. Sniffing, she accepted the proffered tissue and blew her nose. Barnes cleared his throat and spoke to her again, but his words didn't register; they seemed to be coming from a distant place, like a neighbour's radio. Was she dreaming?

'Angie Brown, I am arresting you on suspicion of conspiring to supply drugs. I'm also arresting you on suspicion of conspiring to launder money, and misconduct in a public office...'

A voice screamed inside her head: *No! Let this be a dream! Wake up Angie Brown! Wake up!* But this was no dream and the next part of Barnes's soliloquy confirmed it:

'You do not have to say anything,' he continued, 'but it may harm your defence, if you do not mention when questioned, something which you later rely on in court...'

The official spiel over, Barnes nodded at the

315

doorway and a uniformed PC came into the office. She recognised him as the jovial Kenyan, Billy Kimathi. He wasn't very jovial today though, and fixing her with a sombre stare, he spoke words that chilled her to the bone:

'I'm going to take you down to custody now Angie,' he said before taking hold of her arm in the way he'd taken hold of countless suspects to prevent their escape. Of course, Billy knew Angie wouldn't try to escape. Holding a suspect's arm was little more than symbolic; but the message it gave was crystal clear. It said: "I am depriving you of your liberty, and for the duration of your incarceration, I'm in charge."

As they were about to leave her office, Billy noticed that Angie had left her handbag under the desk. He pointed to it. 'Is that yours?' Angie nodded miserably. 'Bring it with you,' he said softly and released his grip on her arm.

Once she'd picked up her bag from off the floor, the big Kenyan held out an open hand and indicated the door. He didn't take hold of her arm again, allowing her the dignity of walking down the three flights of stairs to the custody suite under her own steam.

Descending the stairs, they were met and greeted by several people making their way up. Billy flashed his gap toothed smile, but Angie didn't acknowledge them. Keeping her eyes downcast and concentrating on the steps beneath her feet, she had the feeling that she no longer belonged there. She felt like a stranger, a viper in the nest.

Reaching the door to custody, Billy punched the entry code into the keypad. Just like the female half of a couple in the throes of a breakup, who covers her nudity each time her soon to be ex enters the marital bedroom; Angie noticed that Billy shielded the numbers from her sight, just like he did when he took a suspect into custody. In the time it had taken to descend three flights of stairs, Angie Brown had made the transition from trusted crime analyst to suspect...

*

Nadine Cousins sat in the graffiti-scarred bus shelter off Houndshale High Street, waiting for her Latvian minder; Aleksis Viksna, to drive her to her next assignment in Cranston. Sweet Dreams escort agency had been good to her and not only had she been able to afford her daily crack habit, but she'd also had enough left over at the end of the month to buy herself new clothes. It wasn't as if she enjoyed pleasuring smelly, dirty men for cash, but she considered herself a lot better off than when she had worked for Spoons Anderson. The only risk she ran these days, was getting caught with a bit of personal. Even that risk was pretty small, given that Aleksis procured her rocks for her.

Wearing six-inch heels, she was dressed in a skimpy denim mini-skirt and tight fitting low-cut top. She shivered in the night air and smoked to pass the time. She'd already called the client to tell him she was on her way. His accent had west London, but she could detect the Asian undertones of one who had been born in London, but brought up in the closed circle of the local Asian community. He hadn't said much more than to confirm his address - but then, they never did.

Her boss at Sweet Dreams had told her that tonight's assignment sounded like a petene - a pussy - who would probably come before Nadine had finished undressing. She didn't anticipate being in Cranston too long, and if the Latvian's assessment was right; she'd be able to fit in a couple more clients before the night was over.

She'd just been thinking about what her client would be like, when a big black BMW with heavily tinted windows pulled silently alongside the bus shelter; it's twin exhausts emitting plumes of smoke into the cold night.

Standing up, she bent down to peer into the car. The passenger window powered down to reveal the grinning Aleksis, his trademark smouldering cigarette clamped between his thin lips. She could feel the welcome warmth of the car's powerful heater as hot air escaped from the open window and the smell of warm leather filled her nostrils.

Nadine had developed a bit of a soft spot for her minder, and despite his heavily tattooed bulk and shaved head, she always felt safe when he was around. Once he'd dropped her off, he never left until she was safely back in his car. Anything over thirty minutes and she knew he'd come to check on her.

The last time a client had tried to make her stay longer, Aleksis had shoulder barged the front door, dragged the piss taker off her and left him a bloodied mess. She met all manner of weirdos in her line of work - one cheeky bastard had even had the gall to try and steal her mobile! From that day on, she'd taken to hiding it in her underwear until she had been sure the client hadn't been after more than her body.

'Come on darlin,' she said in mock reproach, 'let me in, I'm freezing my tits off out here!'

Aleksis flicked his smoke out of the window before reaching over and opening the passenger door. Climbing in, she settled down into the deep leather seat and enjoyed the warmth. Aleksis leant over and planted a kiss on her cheek. He quite liked the English girl. Sure, she was just another Mauka - a whore - but he'd taken to her and felt protective.

'Where we go Dini?' he asked, using his pet name for her.

She smiled contentedly. 'Cranston Alex - you know Hakim's chicken shop?'

The big Latvian nodded. 'Shit hole,' he replied succinctly, as he threw the big car into drive, lit another smoke and powered away from the bus stop.

As she watched the depressing Houndshale landscape slip by, she wondered dreamily whether one day, she might manage to get away from it all, whether there was a man out there; like Aleksis, who would hold her, love her, and not treat her like the whore she'd become. And then, they were there, outside Hakim's, where the greasy smell of over used oil filtered through the car's ventilation system and assailed her senses. With a sigh, Nadine pushed open the door and glanced up at the grimy windows above the chicken shop. She had a fleeting glimpse of a face at a window, before the filthy net curtains fell back into place. Clambering awkwardly out of the car, she straightened her dress, smoothed her hair, and made her way across the road.

Glancing at his ostentatious gold watch, Aleksis watched Nadine make a phone call before disappearing into the door next to Hakim's. Turning on the car radio, he took out a hip flask from the glove box, took a swig of homemade plum brandy and settled down to wait.

He hadn't been there more than ten minutes, before a set of headlights loomed large in his rear view mirror. Twisting around in his seat, he saw the unmistakable silhouette of a patrol car pulling in behind him. Turning back around, he watched in his wing mirror as two uniformed cops got out and made their way towards him.

One of them, brimming with confidence, was pushing a white cap down over his grey hair, while the other cop - younger, and more uncertain - followed him. All hopes that they were going to Hakim's for their evening meal, dissolved when he heard a tap on his window. Screwing the cap back on the flask, he replaced it in the glove box and swore softly: 'Izdrazt!'

Opening his window, he feigned politeness. 'Can I help you officer?'

The cop's white hat denoted him to be a rat - a traffic cop - and although polite, he was robotic in his approach and spoke in cop jargon.

319

'Good evening sir,' he began, thrusting his face as close to the open window as was possible in order to carry out a "sniff test."

'Did you know that you have a light out?'

'Really? No I didn't know officer,' replied Aleksis, this time feigning surprise. The cop had his hand on the door handle. Pulling it open, he invited Aleksis to accompany him around the back of his car so that he could show him the defective taillight. While he did this, the younger cop took a good look inside the BMW. There weren't any legal grounds to search the car *yet*, but it was early days, and a traffic stop could produce all manner of grounds once it got underway.

The cop pointed to the rear light cluster. 'Yes sir, your nearside tail light is defective.'

Aleksis tried to placate the cop and make a quick getaway. 'Sorry officer, I'll fix it straight away.'

'OK sir no problem. Is the car registered to you?'

'Yes.'

'Do you have any identification on you sir?' asked the rat, edging closer to Aleksis.

Taking out his wallet and extracting his driving licence, he handed it to the cop, whose face had taken on a triumphant look.

'Have you been drinking sir?' he asked rhetorically, 'I can smell intoxicating liquor on your breath.'

'Intoxicating liquor?'

'Yes sir - alcohol.'

Apart from the last nip of plum brandy he'd taken just prior to the cops arriving, Aleksis had put away the first half of the flask back in the office. Nevertheless, he decided to call the cop's bluff. 'No,' he lied.

The cop stepped even closer. 'Well sir,' he began. 'I suspect that you have consumed alcohol and I require you to provide me with a sample of breath for analysis.'

He took hold of Aleksis's arm. Now that he'd given the suspect the requirement to provide a sample, he was now arrestable should he attempt to escape.

'Step on to the pavement please sir. We wouldn't want you to get run over now would we?'

By this time, the younger cop had taken his cue and brought a roadside-testing device over to where his colleague stood with his suspect. He handed over the ESD and casually took up position on the other side of Aleksis. It may have seemed like a casual thing to do, but in time honoured tradition, the younger cop was making sure Aleksis couldn't get away.

Sticking rigidly to the book, the older cop ran through his spiel:

'Have you consumed alcohol during the last twenty minutes?' Aleksis was sullen now and no longer feigned friendliness.

'About fifteen minutes ago,' he mumbled gruffly. The cop explained the procedure.

'I have to wait until twenty minutes has passed since you last consumed alcohol, otherwise this device will read the alcohol in your mouth instead of your body, so we will have to wait another five minutes. Have you smoked in the last five minutes sir?'

'No.'

An awkward five minutes passed with the cops attempting to make small talk to a now very uncommunicative Aleksis. The older cop looked at his watch.

'OK sir,' he said fastening a plastic tube to the ESD, 'I need you to blow into this tube in one continuous breath until I tell you to stop. Form a seal around the end of the tube and blow into it like you would blow up a balloon. I must warn you that if I think you're messing around and aren't blowing properly, you will have failed to provide a sample and you will be liable to arrest. Do you understand sir?'

Aleksis nodded and reached out a hand for the ESD. The cop pulled it away.

'No sir,' he said, 'I keep hold of the device.'

Taking a deep breath, Aleksis began to blow into the tube. The older cop watched the ESD intently while the other one watched over his shoulder.

'That's it sir, keep going, keep going...' The ESD beeped. 'Stop!'

Holding the ESD so that Aleksis could also see it, the cop watched as the amber warning light flicked on, followed, after an agonising few seconds, by a damning bright red light.

If the cop had been triumphant when he had first smelt the plum brandy on Aleksis's breath, he was now cockahoop. It was almost the end of the month, and his drink drive figures were down. He took a deep breath.

'Sir, as the alcohol in your body exceeds the prescribed limit, I am arresting you. You do not have to say anything, but it may harm your defence if you do not mention when questioned, something that you later rely on in court.'

Telling the furious Aleksis to put his hands out to the front, the cop cuffed him into a front stack and ushered him into the car, while the young cop relieved him of his car keys, drove the BMW around the corner and off the double yellows, and locked it up.

Aleksis could hardly tell the cops he was waiting for a hooker to come out so that he could take her to her next client, but as he was driven away in the back of the traffic cop's Volvo estate, he hoped Dini would be ok...

Above Hakim's chicken shop, Balvinder Kapoor waited impatiently for his very own porno bitch to arrive. He'd played out his fantasy a hundred times since his phone call to Sweet Dreams, and any minute now, she was going to knock on his door and bring that fantasy to life. He'd made no effort to clean or tidy his room, and his only concession towards the imminent arrival of the girl, had been to light the biggest burner on his gas cooker to introduce some heat into his pokey bedsitting room.

He hardly ever used the cooker, and deposits of old food were baked onto the once white surface, completely blocking the gas jets. When at first, he hadn't been able to light it; he'd dismantled the burner. Then, using a fork, he dug out the solidified fat and crumbs from the jet. Blowing into the jet pipe, he reassembled the burner, turned on the gas and tried to light it using the igniter button. When this failed, Balvinder lit the escaping gas with a match.

It lit with a *whoomf*, then spat and stuttered, before burning a steady bright blue. Uttering a satisfied grunt, he pulled open the filthy curtain that served to partition the tiny kitchen from his sitting room-cum-bedroom. As he did, he heard the sound of a car door closing in the street below.

Running to the kitchen window, almost opaque with dirt, he tugged at the net curtains and stood on tiptoes, craning his scrawny neck to look out and down into the street. He was just in time to see a high-heeled Nadine tottering away from a big BMW - hips swinging and breasts swaying gently under her low cut top. He felt the beginnings of a hard on.

It wasn't the actual physical sight of the girl that turned him on; more the thought of what he was going to do to the bitch once he got hold of her. She looked up at his window, and guiltily letting go of the curtain, he shrank back inside like a peeping tom caught in the act.

*

Angie Brown followed the broad back of the Kenyan Cowboy into custody. The minute she walked through; a fug of sweaty feet, strong disinfectant, and the pungent stink of skunk cannabis attacked her senses. It was clear that the custody skipper had been expecting her, as the normally busy custody area was all but deserted. The civilian gaolers had been sent away, and apart from the skipper behind the high desk, Billy and her, there was only one other person there - the duty officer - an ex-TSG inspector, who fixed her with a hard glare. The custody skipper was no other than the grey-haired sergeant Blake of narcolepsy fame. Unlike the guvnor at his side, he smiled benignly like some affable Benedictine monk. He began his spiel:

'I am the custody officer. I am independent of the investigation and responsible for your welfare whilst you are at this police station. This officer is going to tell me the reason for your arrest. I will listen to the officer's' account and then decide whether it is necessary to detain you at this police station.' He looked up expectantly at Billy Kimathu.

'Sarge,' he began. 'This is Angela Brown. DS Barnes has arrested her on suspicion of conspiracy to supply class A drugs, money laundering and misconduct in a public office.'

Blake raised his eyebrows in surprise as Billy continued to relay the circumstances of Angie's arrest.

'She has been arrested so that the matter can be promptly investigated, and to prevent loss or damage to evidence.'

'And the arresting officer...?'

'It's DS Barnes sarge,' repeated Billy. He pulled out a crumpled piece of paper from his pocket and read out Barnes's warrant number for Blake to record, before adding: 'He'll be down in half an hour.'

Angie flushed crimson *Angela*? She hadn't been called that since she'd been at school! Blake listened patiently. He could really have done with a quick smoke, but there would be no feeding the chickens while the guvnor stood next to him. He continued his questions:

'Have you been arrested before?'

Quiet as a mouse, head bowed she replied: 'No.'

'Are you dependent on drugs or alcohol?'

324

Angie shook her head.

'Is there anyone at home who depends on you and might be affected by your presence here?' Again: a shake of the head.

Blake pointed to a laminated card stuck to the side of his console.

'Can you look at that list and tell me which best describes your ethnicity?'

Angie thought the answer to be both obvious and irrelevant, but most of Blake's customer's were far from white British. She pointed to W1. Blake smiled his benign smile and nodded.

'Thank you, white British,' and laboriously entered it into his terminal. He looked up at her.

'I'm authorising your detention in order that you may be questioned by way of a tape-recorded interview. After this, I will decide whether you will be charged with the offences or released without any further action.'

Resigned to her fate, Angie declined Blake's offer of the duty solicitor.

Billy radioed for a female officer to attend custody to search Angie, and after a few minutes wait a female DC came down from the third floor to assist. Angie was horrified to find that the newcomer was Sarah Best. She'd struck up a relationship with Sarah - or "Bestie" - as her few friends knew her.

The two women had spent many a time smoking together in the back yard, shivering from the wind and rain while they satisfied their craving for nicotine. They had even gone out drinking together on occasion, and been friends on facebook. Angie had long suspected Sarah to be a lesbian, who without much in the way of friends, had taken to Angie and confided in her. Angie was pretty sure that from this day on, she'd never be able to address her friend as Bestie again, and it saddened her to think about her betrayal.

Sarah was business-like, but Angie could sense some

sympathy.

'Take your hair band out Angie, I need to search your hair.'

Angie couldn't imagine what they thought she could have hidden in her hair, but she wasn't to know that thick hair could hide a junkie's wrap, and it wouldn't have been the first time a cursory search had missed it. She pulled the elasticated band from her hair and not wanting to look a mess, automatically shook her hair free and stretched the band over her wrist. She felt Sarah's fingers as she ran them through her former friend's hair and then saw her hold out her hand for the band.

'I have to take that from you,' she said apologetically. 'It's so that you don't use it to harm yourself when you're in your cell.'

Cell? Oh my God, they're actually going to lock me in a cell! The enormity of her situation came over her in waves, and she felt salty tears pricking at her eyes. Meekly, she slid off the hair band and handed it to Sarah who placed it on the custody counter.

Next, the DC went through her pockets, and to Angie's horror, pulled out a tampon, which along with a disposable lighter and a stick of lip-gloss, she placed on the counter next to Angie's hair band.

Billy and the skipper turned to face away from the women as Sarah got Angie to undo the button of her trousers and slid her fingers into and around the waistband, before running her hands along her legs from crotch to ankle.

'Take your shoes off Angie, I just need to check inside them.'

Angie obeyed, kicking off her ankle boots. Sarah shook her boots and looked inside them before placing them on the floor and continued to instruct her.

'Lean on the counter Angie and show me the soles of your feet.'

Satisfied, the DC gave her back her shoes. 'I need

you to take off your watch and jewellery Angie.'

Miserably, Angie first removed her stud earrings, followed by her wristwatch and thumb ring. Sarah was persistent: 'Take your necklace off too.'

Angie burst into tears and appealed to skipper Blake.

'Please,' she sobbed, 'let me keep it. This necklace belonged to my mum and I haven't taken it off since the day she died!'

The old skipper looked like he was about to cry himself, but said firmly: 'Sorry Angela, I have to take all jewellery from detainees in case they try to use it to harm themselves. You'll get it back before you leave.'

Sobbing, Angie undid the clasp and handed it over. She was briefly encouraged by the skipper's words. *Before you leave*, he'd said.

'So, I won't have to stay here?' she asked tearfully.

Blake realised what he'd said, but didn't want a suicidal female in his cell for the duration and so he told a white lie.

'Well... You'll have to stay to be interviewed and I can't promise you what time that will be, but you won't be staying here.'

Placated, Angie watched while Billy bagged up her property into a self-sealing bag. The only thing left to search was her handbag, and as this didn't require a female, Blake thanked Sarah and told her she could go. Before she walked out of custody, Bestie looked into her former friend's eyes, and giving her a brief squeeze of the arm, whispered 'Good luck Ange...' And then she was gone.

The coded door that Angie would never be on the right side of again, swung shut. When she turned around again, the big Kenyan was going through her bag. He was the first man to have gone through her personal belongings in that way since her abusive husband. He'd done just that whenever he had wanted to check up on her. She felt humiliated, small, and all alone.

Billy piled up her possessions on the counter: cigarettes - which in the no smoking environment of the custody block, she wasn't going to get to smoke anytime soon - makeup bag, keys, purse, and receipts from Tesco. Next, the Kenyan pulled out two mobile phones - her iphone, and the damn stubby little Nokia, she'd grown to loathe. She felt a wave of panic welling up inside her as Billy placed both phones to one side.

'Whaatt, are you going to do with my phones,' she stammered. Blake interjected. 'They are being seized as evidence Angela and will be interrogated by the investigating officer.' He scanned them both to record the IMEI numbers, and handed them back to Billy who bagged them up in a separate evidence bag.

Interrogated! She knew enough about the retrieval of suspect's phone data to know she was in deep trouble. *Yes Angie Brown,* she thought - *you are in deep trouble...*

Once all of her property had been logged and scanned into the custody computer, Blake informed her that as she'd been arrested for a recordable offence, they had the power to take her fingerprints, photo and a sample of her DNA. These samples, he told her, would be compared to those on file and checked against any as yet unidentified suspects of crime.

Handing Billy a custody front sheet containing Angie's details and a DNA form, he told him that his prisoner was now ready to be taken for processing. Billy nodded at the skipper and turned to his suspect. 'OK, follow me please,' he said before leading her down the narrow corridor to the fingerprinting room. On the way, with the casual air of a tour guide, he pointed out the red alarm strips that lined the walls of the corridor, and out of habit told her: 'Make sure you don't touch those, it'll set the alarm off.'

Thinking that setting off an alarm was the least of her problems, she followed him into the pokey little fingerprinting room where Billy sat her down on an uncomfortable wooden seat facing a digital camera. Standing in front of a terminal, Billy laboriously entered her details on the screen, and telling her to sit up and face the camera; he clicked on the green tab. The camera flashed, and seemingly satisfied with the image, Billy grunted, belched noisily, and told her to turn her head first to the right and then to the left while he took side profile pictures.

Pictures taken, Billy beckoned her over to the livescan-fingerprinting machine. The days of taking prints using ink were thankfully long gone. Prints were now taken digitally before being transmitted to the fingerprint bureau, where they would be either linked to known suspects or stored indefinitely. In the case of a suspect who'd given false particulars when arrested, livescan would find them out and transmit by return, the correct identity of the suspect being held. This was particularly useful in the case of gypsy so-called travellers; who habitually, and from a very early age, gave false identity details.

Billy told her to stand up close while he took her fingerprints. As he took hold of her right hand, she felt the callouses on his rough hands and smelt the metallic odour of last night's garlic on his breath.

One at a time, he rolled her fingers across the pad. Magnified, Angie's prints came up on the screen in front of them. Once he was satisfied with the image, Billy stamped down on a foot pedal and committed her prints to file. After he'd repeated the procedure with her left hand, he got her to press her palms onto the pad and clicking on the send tab, he sent them all off into the ether.

By now, Angie had adopted the attitude of the prisoner; who having got over the initial shock of being taken, realises that resistance is futile and obeys every command of their captors. Some did it resentfully and

329

through the sucking of teeth, while others, such as Angie Brown, simply fell in line and meekly did as they were told. Not for her the cop/suspect banter of the habitual criminal; she just wanted the humiliation to be over and to sit in a cell alone with her thoughts.

Billy Kimathu's final involvement with Angie was to take a sample of her DNA. Bidding her to sit back down on the seat, he pulled on a pair of plastic gloves of the kind you might find at a petrol station. Next, he needed to obtain buccal swabs from his suspect. Opening a DNA pack, he extracted two serrated cotton buds on plastic stems.

Telling her to open her mouth, he rubbed the inside of her right cheek with the hard bud. Pressing down on the stem, he separated it from it's bud, popped it into a small plastic collection vial snapped the attached lid shut, and threw away the detached stem. This done, he repeated the procedure, this time collecting a sample from inside her left cheek, before sealing both vials into a self-sealing evidence bag, which he put into a small freezer.

His work done, Billy took her back up to the custody desk to ask the skipper which cell she was to be put in. Typically, while Billy had been processing Angie, Blake had slipped out to feed the chickens.

Going behind the custody skipper's desk, Billy located the clipboard containing Angie's detention log. It was hanging from the hook that indicated she had been allocated cell F2. Opening his calloused hand, he indicated that she should take the right fork of the custody corridor, which led to the female cells.

Following her, Billy waited until she was inside, before pushing the heavy cell door closed. The noise of the door closing and the click of the locks engaging, echoed along the cellblock and to Angie Brown, it sounded like finality personified.

She walked the few steps to the back of the cell, sat

down on the graffiti-covered wooden bench that ran the width of the room, and took in her surroundings. Apart from a very thin mattress covered in blue vinyl, and a matching pillow, propped up against the wall above the bench, her cell was bare. In a corner was a stainless steel toilet bowl without a seat, and with not much more than a low wall to separate it from the rest of the cell. She could see a camera lens that thankfully, didn't appear to cover the toilet. Although she could see a steel knob fixed in a recess on the wall, the flushing mechanism was outside the cell. This was to prevent suspects accessing it and flooding their cells. Some still managed to do this by stuffing toilet paper down the toilet and flushing it until their cell flooded.

Pulling the mattress onto her bench, Angie lay on her back and looked up at the ceiling. There, stencilled in bold black paint was a reminder for inmates to come clean about undetected crimes, and so save themselves from being re-arrested once they'd served their sentence. The world in which she now found herself was as alien to Angie Brown as a lunar landscape, and just when she thought she had ran out of tears, she felt them roll down her cheeks and onto the horrid blue vinyl pillow.

Time ticked painfully away. Nobody came to fetch her for interview, and apart from the half-hourly scrape of the spy hole cover, followed by a face peering in at her: she was left alone. She spent a restless night sliding around on the coverless mattress underneath a scratchy synthetic blue blanket. The ceiling light remained on, but at some point during the night, it was dimmed to the night setting by some well-meaning gaoler.

Every time she tried to sleep, she'd be jerked awake by jangling keys, bantering cops and drunks - both male and female - alternately banging on their cell doors and shouting abuse at the gaoler and each other. During the fitful sleep she did manage to snatch, her dreams were filled with images of the 101 Club, where under the flashing lights of the dance floor, Calvin Anderson leered at her while she snorted cocaine. Bizarrely, her mother and father sat across the club table from her, shaking their heads in disgust and disappointment. When the morning finally freed her from her nightmares and she was dragged back to the land of the living - first by the sound of the Perspex wicket being noisily slid open - and then of keys in her cell door, she felt as though she'd had no sleep at all.

A young female gaoler entered the cell.

'Would you like some breakfast?'

Eating was the last thing on Angie's mind, but she could sure use a coffee. 'Could I have a coffee?' she asked in a small voice.

'Yes of course,' the young girl answered breezily as though she was a waitress in Starbucks.

'Sugar?'

Angie shook her head. 'Do you know when I'll be interviewed?'

The gaoler, used to non-commitedly answering what was a stock question asked by her charges, gave her the stock answer:

'I'll have a word with the custody sergeant and let you know.'

Angie smiled weakly. 'Thanks.'

The girl left, slamming the cell door behind her. Two minutes later, she returned, slid the wicket down and passed Angie a scalding polystyrene cup of barely drinkable coffee. Taking it from the gaoler's outstretched hand, Angie sat back down on the bench that had been her bed for the night. The wicket was pulled back up with a protesting squeal, and she was alone once more.

An hour later, the spy hole cover was lifted and left to swing closed almost immediately. She could hear the by now familiar sound of jangling keys; but whoever was trying to unlock her door, didn't appear to be familiar with the keys, and couldn't figure out which key fitted the lock to her cell. After the sound of several attempts, and much jangling later, the cell door swung open to reveal a middle-aged man, who she'd never seen before.

Tall, handsome and athletically built, the newcomer's jet black brushed back hair, was flecked with silver. He was dressed in a smart suit and wore expensive looking lace up brogues. His manner was business-like, but not outwardly hostile and when he spoke, it was with the lilt that reminded her of happier times. He sounded just like a boy she'd had a fling with many summers ago in Dublin.

When she looked him up and down, Angie spotted a circular red and black tie pin fastened to the man's tie. It depicted turrets and shields and was inscribed with the words: *Bohemian Football Club*. The man, it seemed, *was* from Dublin.

'Good morning Miss Brown,' he began in his soft brogue. 'What do you prefer to be called - is it OK to call you Angela?'

Angie didn't really care what the cops called her, but she didn't want to get on the wrong side of the man in the suit. 'Angela's fine,' she said. The man smiled.

'I'm detective sergeant Jim Dempsey from Ealing CID.'

'Ealing?' she asked uncomprehendingly. DS Dempsey nodded.

'Yes, It's been decided that an outside borough be put in charge of your investigation, Miss... sorry - Angela.'

'Anyway,' he continued, 'I'm to be your interviewing officer, so if you're ready, we can begin. Have you had breakfast?'

'I had a coffee, if that's what you call the stuff here, but I wouldn't mind freshening up and maybe brushing my teeth?

Dempsey smiled empathetically. 'Yeah,' he conceded, 'It's hardly Starbucks, is it? I'll get the gaoler to sort you out with a shower and a toothbrush. Anything else?'

'Well...' Angie began uncertainly, 'When I was booked in, I told the sergeant I didn't want a solicitor, but I think I need to speak to one, if I can...?'

She wouldn't have known it, but upon hearing her request, the DS swore to himself. A solicitor changed everything. It meant having to delay the interview while she sought legal advice and he knew just what the brief would advise her to do. Concealing his disappointment, Dempsey flashed her a charming smile and told her he'd organise a solicitor for her while she showered. He'd thought Houndshale's DCI had been a bit optimistic when he'd told him Brown hadn't requested a solicitor - and that: "*the interview would be a piece of piss.*"

Showered and her teeth brushed, Angie felt almost human and once she'd washed away her night in a cell, she was led up to the custody skipper's desk, where the duty solicitor was waiting on the phone. Introducing herself as Mary Taylor, the brief asked a few questions about her case, before advising her in no uncertain terms that she should make no comment during interview. Should she be charged with any of the offences for which she was accused, Mary assured her that she would be at court to represent her.

Once she'd finished her phone call, Angie was spared the ordeal of being shut back in her cell, being allowed instead, to wait on the bench opposite the skipper's desk until DS Dempsey came back down. She sat there cradling another cup of foul- tasting coffee, and before she had finished it, Dempsey reappeared.

On any other day, Angie thought that she'd have found the Irish detective attractive; but this was no ordinary day and her chat with the duty brief had brought her predicament well and truly to the fore. It didn't help when Dempsey strode over to the custody desk and announced that he was ready to sign her out for interview.

Sign me out? My God, I'm no more than an object to *signed* for - like some kind of UPS parcel! She felt wretched.

The taste of cheap custody coffee lingered on her tongue and furred up her freshly brushed teeth. She'd have given anything to be back in her own home between freshly laundered sheets, where in her fantasy, she would awake to find the whole thing to have been a terrible dream.

The harsh sound of a prisoner buzzing for the gaoler's attention brought her back down to earth. She looked over at Dempsey, who having signed the electronic signature pad, now turned to her, nodded and gestured for her to follow him into an interview room.

Waving her into a chair at the back of the small and airless room, he took a seat opposite her. A table separated them, and apart from a cabinet upon which a tape machine was perched, the room was devoid of furniture. Angie tried to pull her chair a little closer, but it wouldn't budge. Dempsey looked over and smiled apologetically. 'It's bolted to the floor Angela. It's to prevent suspects from hurling furniture around the room. Sorry.'

Angie nodded and the detective continued his battle to free the interview tapes from the cellophane seal that clung so resolutely to the plastic boxes. Finally managing to extract the tapes, he made an attempt at small talk to try and get the woman to relax.

'Sorry all this is taking so long Angela; I've got to prepare a couple of things before we start, and these buggers; 'he said, indicating the tapes: 'are just not designed to be cop friendly.'

'Mind you,' he said, a boyish grin on his face: 'I don't suppose you're feeling too police friendly yourself right now!'

Angie forced a wan smile. 'You could say that,' she said quietly.

Dempsey was now scribbling on the tapes and filling out the label that would be used to seal the master copy of the tape once they'd finished.

'Almost done,' he said cheerily before inserting both tapes into the machine and closing the covers.

'OK, you ready Angela?'

She nodded and he pressed the red record button. The machine clunked into life and began to spool. A buzzing noise filled the room while the tape spooled to the start of it's brown magnetic recording surface, and while it did, Dempsey took one last compulsive look at the laminated prompt notes stuck to the table in front of him.

It wasn't as though he *needed* to look at the list; he'd interviewed hundreds of suspects during his twenty years as a cop, but rookies and old sweats alike, all did it. They all looked at the crib sheet, and for the first few minutes, clung to it like a comfort blanket. Miss one bit out, and you'd be in danger of falling foul of the Police and Criminal Evidence Act 1984. Any solicitor worth their salt - whether present at a client's interview or not - would be given a copy of the tape, and if an omission such as the re-cautioning of a suspect was found, it could - and would - be used to make the Old Bill look foolish and incompetent should the case make it to court.

The buzzing stopped. Dempsey cleared his throat and began. After introducing himself for the sake of the tape, he asked Angie to do the same. He then asked her to confirm her date of birth and whether she agreed that besides the two of them, there was no other person present in the room. He explained that the interview was being tape recorded and that it may be given in evidence should her case be brought to trial.

Angie nodded her understanding. *Trial!*

'So,' she said a tremor in her voice, 'I'll be going to court?'

The detective, quite used to a suspect's interjection

at the mention of the word "trial", looked up from his crib sheet and gave his stock answer:

'Nobody's saying you're going to court Angela, it's just part of what I have to tell you before I ask you questions. OK?'

Angie wasn't convinced, but said: 'OK,' nonetheless. Dempsey continued:

'You have the right to free and independent legal advice. You can speak to a solicitor in private at any time of day or night and this legal advice is free. You can speak to a solicitor in person. If you do not want to speak to a solicitor in person, you can speak on the telephone. The interview may be delayed in order for you to do so.' He looked up to see the same old look of bewilderment that most suspects of previously good character tended to display. Poor bitch wasn't taking a lot of this in, he thought, but continued his spiel.

'I understand you have already spoken to a solicitor on the phone?'

'Yes.' came the shaky reply.

Dempsey cautioned her: 'You do not have to say anything, but it may harm your defence...'

'OK Angela, that concludes the formal part of the interview. From now on, I'm just going to ask you questions about why you are here - why you've been arrested.'

Another nod. Dempsey glanced quickly at the handover pack given to him by the DCI.

'Angela, you were arrested yesterday on suspicion of conspiring to launder money, conspiring to supply class A drugs and misconduct in a public office. What can you tell me about that?'

Just as he'd expected, following her call to Mary Taylor, Angie quietly, but firmly, answered: 'No comment.'

He was used to such tactics, widely recommended by solicitors to ensure that they wrung several more paydays out of a case, but he wasn't duly troubled by her response.

'Can you tell me about your employment with the Metropolitan police Angela?' Such a simple and non-incriminating question, yet, she didn't dare answer for fear of opening the floodgates. She bit her bottom lip.

'No comment.'

'How long have you worked at Houndshale police station?'

Angela, not versed in such situations, had imagined that once she'd made it known she didn't intend to answer the detective's questions, had assumed the Irishman would give up and not ask her any more questions. She didn't know what to do, but all the same, answered: 'No comment.'

Dempsey pressed on: 'Do you know a Calvin Anderson?'

The very mention of the bastard's name brought a flush to her cheeks. Her heartbeat quickened. In a trembling voice she replied: 'No comment.'

Dempsey leaned back in his chair, interlocking his hands behind his head. He looked directly at her face and she looked away, picking at her ragged fingernails.

The only sound in the room was the tape as it squeaked it's way towards it's forty-five-minute limit. After what seemed like an eternity, Dempsey broke the silence:

'Angela, I assume that your solicitor has advised you to give a no comment interview and while, as I said when I cautioned you, that you do not have to say anything, I have to tell you that I believe she has given you bad advice. Should your case go to court, the magistrate will be aware that you were given an opportunity to explain your actions. The magistrate - or a jury - may wonder why you never took such an opportunity to give your side of the story, and they may draw an inference from that.'

Angie kept her head down and worried away at her

nails. Dempsey continued.

'Whether you answer my questions or not, you should know that I will continue to ask them regardless...'

He reached down underneath his chair and when he straightened up, Angie could see that bloody ugly, damning little Nokia sealed inside an evidence bag. He placed it in the middle of the table: in no man's land. She stared at the hateful instrument of her downfall and felt tears pricking at the corners of her bloodshot eyes. Suddenly, Angie wanted to purge herself, to rid herself of the poisonous infestation that was Anderson. She glanced up at the detective.

'Could I have break for a drink of water and a cigarette please?'

Dempsey sensed victory, but didn't show it. 'Of course Angela,' he said magnanimously, 'take all the time you need.'

Then, with his finger hovering over the tape machine's stop button, he intoned:

'Interview suspended at ten thirty-six am for a natural break.' He pressed the button and the machine clunked to a stop.

Smoking had long since been prohibited at police stations, but after a word with the custody skipper, Dempsey led Angie out into the exercise yard. A gaoler appeared a few seconds later with a cup of tepid water in a plastic cup and once she'd left the yard, Dempsey fished out a packet of Marlborough lights and offered Angie one. She took it gratefully and accepted the light, cupped against the wind in the detective's big hand.

He lit one for himself and simultaneously, they exhaled. Angie watched the plume of blue tobacco smoke, as it eddied briefly around the yard before being sucked out through the wire mesh and climbing skywards before disappearing into the leaden sky above. *If only I could escape too...* she thought.

While they smoked, Dempsey made no reference at

all to her case, making small talk instead. Despite her predicament, she found herself joining in with talk of hometowns, family and the weather. The Irishman was a charmer, she thought. Under any other circumstance, she might have actually quite fancied him.

She brought herself back down to earth with a bump. *Men*, she thought. *Nothing but trouble...* and then the moment was over.

Grinding out his cigarette butt on the bare concrete of the yard, Dempsey held out his hand and indicated the door to the exercise yard and said: 'Shall we?'

Meekly, Angie took his lead and they walked back into the foul smelling custody reception area. Dempsey signed her out and led her back into the interview room where he extracted the original tapes and sealed the master copy. Then renewing his battle with the cellophane wrappers of a new set, he hastily scribbled her name and custody number onto them before feeding them into the machine.

'Ready?'

A slight nod of her head indicated that she was. Dempsey hit the record button, the now familiar buzzing noise came to an end and he began:

'I am resuming the interview of Angela Brown...' He glanced at his watch. 'The time by my watch is ten-fifty am on the same day.' He looked up at Angie.

'I'll caution you again - you do not have to say anything, but it may harm your defence...'

God, she thought; I've heard this a few times in the last couple of days! She realised that Dempsey had finished reciting his caution and she'd not even been listening, but when he asked her if she understood, she replied: 'Yes.' She forced herself to concentrate and heard the detective say:

'Do you agree that while we have been out of this room, we haven't discussed your case?'

'Yes.'

He gave her a tight-lipped smile. 'Thank you Angela. I must remind you that you are still entitled to legal advice.' She nodded.

'For the tape please.'

'Oh... yes, I understand.'

'Angela, I asked you earlier to tell me about your arrest and what you think about it.'

Taking a deep breath, Angie spilled her guts. So fast did the whole sordid affair come out of her mouth, that Dempsey - though reluctant - had to get her to slow down while he made notes.

An hour and another tape change later, the detective from Dublin had all the evidence he needed to secure a charge. He wound up the interview.

'I'd like to thank you Angela, for your honesty - Is there anything you wish to add or any point you want to clarify?'

Her answer was barely audible: 'Only that I'm sorry...' and with that, she burst into tears. Dempsey awkwardly passed her a box of tissues; left in the interview room for such occasions.

'Thank you,' she sobbed.

Dempsey concluded the interview, made a note of the time, and then took out the tapes. He picked up the second master and got her to sign all three master tapes before sealing them.

'I'm afraid I'm going to have to pop you back into your cell for a bit while I do some paperwork and make a call to the CPS,' he said in a sympathetic voice that wouldn't have sounded out of place had it come out of a village vicar's mouth when addressing a bereaved parishioner.

He collected up his paperwork, tapes and the horrid little Nokia, and then ushered her out of the interview room. Signing her back in, he got the gaoler to take her back to her cell. Trudging miserably down the dimly lit corridor, Angie was directed back into her cell. The gaoler

341

gave her a sympathetic smile and told her that should she need anything, she was to press the buzzer. She sat down on the bench, and the cell door slammed shut.

At the custody desk, detective sergeant Jim Dempsey allowed himself a little victorious smile. Got the bitch, he thought. Using the cop jargon for the successful outcome of an interview, he addressed the custody skipper.

'Full and frank,' he smiled. 'I'm off to do the paperwork.'

The skipper grinned, sharing the Irishman's victory.

'MG7?' he asked.

'Definitely,' replied Dempsey, and turning heel, he punched in the code to get out of custody. Grabbing a quick smoke in the back yard, he hurried upstairs to compile the MG7 form, requested by the custody skipper. He'd need that to remand the prisoner in his custody until the next day when she'd be sent straight to court. Angie Brown was to spend another night in a police cell...

Chapter Fourteen

"May God make this place a terror to evil-doers"

By the time Balvinder Kapoor heard the long awaited knock at his door, he was so charged with sexual tension that his hands trembled as he unlocked the door and admitted the girl from the Sweet Dreams escort agency. For her part, Nadine Cousins wasn't impressed at all. Taking in the squalor of Kapoor's bedsit, she switched her attention to her client.

Lank, greasy unkempt hair framed a skeletal face, and beady eyes that reminded her of a rat, fixed her in a lascivious stare. She could smell his foetid breath as it hissed through rotten teeth. His not bothering to make an effort with his physical appearance, extended to his clothes.

Dressed in a pair of stained grey jogging bottoms and a filthy white tee shirt, there was absolutely nothing attractive about him. Nadine couldn't help thinking that she'd seen the skinny Asian man before, but couldn't remember where. She swallowed her revulsion and extended a hand.

'Hi, I'm Nadine.'

He hesitated before taking her hand in his. Despite the intense heat of the room, his hand felt cold and clammy. He gave her a disturbing look and grinned. It was at that point that he recognised her; it was none other than the hooker he'd seen at the bus shelter just before the cops came by! He'd liked her then and he liked her

343

even more now; a bit on the skinny side, but she still had enough tits and arse for what he had in mind.

Nadine pulled her hand free from his limp grip. Thank God Aleksis is outside she thought, suppressing a shudder. While on the subject of her minder, she reminded her repulsive client that he had bought no more than thirty minutes of her time. He didn't acknowledge this, but closed the front door, and locking it, said:

'It's better that way, we don't want to be disturbed do we lady?'

"Lady..." where had she heard that before? Never mind, she thought, let's get this over with. She didn't intend to seduce the dirty bastard; by the sound of his laboured breathing, he was more than ready. She took a condom from her handbag.

'Shall I put it on for you, or will you do it yourself,' she asked.

'We're not gonna need that lady, I'm gonna fuck you bareback!'

Nadine suddenly felt afraid. In all her years on the streets, dealing Spoon's drugs and blowing dodgy looking punters, it was the first time she felt properly freaked out. There was something about this one, and client or not, she wanted to get the hell out of there. She walked towards the kitchen window.

'Do you mind if I open the window,' she asked innocently, 'It's boiling hot in here.'

Reaching the window, she opened the net curtains and pushed the widow open intending to signal Aleksis below to come up and get her the hell out of there. A blast of welcome fresh air entered the pokey kitchen.

She looked outside - Fuck! Where was he? Of the big BMW, there was no sign. With Aleksis gone, Nadine was on her own, and she was shitting herself.

She felt his hand on her shoulder.

'Leave the window closed lady, I'm cold.'

He pulled the window closed with a bang and as it

shut, she thought she heard a splutter and then a popping sound somewhere behind her.

She turned to face him. Recoiling from his breath, she forced herself to sound casual.

'Oh, OK babes, what do you want to do then?'

'I wanna' fuck you up the arse you fuckin' whore!'

Nadine backed up against the kitchen wall and tried to bluff her way out.

'I don't do anal babes, It's my piles, just can't do it sorry. Why don't you let me wank you off instead? I'll let you come over my tits.'

She gave him her best sultry look, but his eyes seemed lifeless, like those of the sharks she'd seen on National Geographic back in the escort agency office between clients. Spittle dribbled from the side of his mouth and his breath came in raspy bursts.

Suddenly, without warning, he punched her in the face. Reeling and with blood spurting from her nose, she slid down the wall. As she fell to the floor, her hands covering her face, he aimed a savage kick, hitting her in her stomach. Scrabbling to her feet, Nadine made a bolt for the front door, but quick as a flash, he was on her. With his forearm across her throat, he pulled her towards him, holding her close. She screamed.

'Ssh...' he hissed, stroking her hair with his free hand. She could feel the maniac's hard cock through his filthy jogging bottoms, pressing up against her backside. The fuckin' perverted bastard's getting off on hurting me! she thought desperately, where *was* Aleksis?

Kapoor increased the pressure on the girl's throat and began to drag her back into the room. Reaching his bed, he spun her around and shoved her down onto his semen stained mattress. Landing on her back, Nadine wiped the blood from her face. Her nose had stopped bleeding and she was able to breath through it again. Along with the stench of the mildewed cushion upon which her head rested, she smelt something odd. She couldn't place it, but whatever it was, it was beginning to make her feel lightheaded.

Balvinder strode back to the kitchen. Gripping the partition curtain, he yanked it shut as if to seal her in and prevent her from going back into the kitchen. The room darkened and she heard him stomping back. Risking a peek, she found him to be out of sight. He may have been invisible to her, but the muffled sound of his ragged breathing, betrayed the nightmarish reality that he was still very much in the room.

Balvinder was on his hands and knees rummaging around under the bed. With a grunt, he stood up. Nadine recoiled and screamed in terror.

While underneath the bed, the skinny Asian had donned a latex mask, which covered his whole head: transforming himself into a grotesque Elvis Presley! And that wasn't the worst of it - in one hand, he held a wicked looking kebab carving knife, and in the other, a length of blue nylon rope.

Nadine squirmed and twisted, pulling herself further up the bed to try and distance herself from him. She was more frightened now than when she'd had to go and see Spoons in his apartment to tell him she'd lost his drugs. At least he hadn't been weird - brutal, yes - but not like this fuckin' lunatic.

'Let me go,' she wailed. 'Please, just let me go and I won't tell anyone...'

'Shut the fuck up bitch!' he snarled. I'm in charge now and you're gonna do as you're told - just like all the other stinking whores.'

'Please don't hurt me, I'm begging you!'

Balvinder stooped over her, grabbed her face and held the knife to her throat.

'I said shut the fuck up!' he hissed, spraying her face with spittle through the slit in the mask. Don't you like Elvis lady? 'Turn over and give me your hands.'

Nadine got onto all fours and held out her hands.

346

'OK, OK, just don't hurt me...' At least face down, she was spared the rubberised nightmare image of Elvis brought back to life by a demented pervert.

Looping the rope around her wrists, he jerked on it, pulling her towards the top of the bed. Wrapping the free end of the rope around the wooden headboard, he pulled it tight until there were little more than a few inches between Nadine's face and the headboard. She felt his rough hands on her ankles as he wrenched the shoes from her feet. Sniffing them, he uttered a primeval groan from deep in his throat before tossing them aside. She felt his hands slide roughly beneath her belly; fumbling at the button and zip of her skirt. Triumphantly undoing her button, his hands came back from under her belly and started to tug at the hem of her skirt. She played the only card she had.

'Listen babe,' she said trying to mask the terror and revulsion in her voice, 'It's my time of the month - you know - I've got the decorators in?'

His hands stopped tugging; he slapped the back of her head, hard.

'You dirty fuckin' whore,' he spat. Nadine dared to feel a glimmer of hope.

'I'm sorry babe; I just need five minutes in the bathroom to clean myself up - OK?'

Balvinder seemed to be weighing up what she'd said. She felt his weight shift on the bed. Turning her head, she saw his hands on her rope tether. Freeing her from the headboard, he left her hands tied together.

'You've got two minutes bitch,' he snarled. 'And you better come back clean!' Hauling her to her feet, he shoved her in the direction of his tiny bathroom.

Once inside, Nadine sat down on the toilet seat. His stale piss was all over it and droplets of urine covered the floor. She knew she didn't have long. With her hands still bound, it would have been nigh on impossible to undo her skirt had he not already done so. Thrusting her hands down the front of her knickers, she pulled out her mobile. Gripping it between the palms of her hand, she unlocked the screen.

In such close proximity to the bed, she didn't dare try to call anyone. Instead, she brought up the mobile number for her boss at the agency and sent him a text message: *"Client trying to kill me. Chicken shop. Danger! Call feds now!"*

She heard him shout: 'What are you doin' in there bitch - havin' a shit?'

He laughed coarsely at his own joke.

Calling out: 'Coming babes!' Nadine hid her phone under a pile of dirty clothes and came out of the bathroom. The bastard was sitting on the end of his filthy mattress, his eyes moving like those of a puppet from beneath the otherwise expressionless Elvis mask. "It's now or never" was blasting out from his tinny laptop speakers. She shuddered and hoped to God her boss would call the feds and fast!

The smell she'd smelt earlier, seemed stronger, and coming out of the bathroom, her eyes began to water; she coughed and felt lightheaded, disorientated even. She put it down to the fact that she hadn't scored a rock since that morning. "Elvis" was coughing too...

*

At the Sweet Dreams escort agency, the Latvian boss re-read Nadine's message. What the fuck was going on? She'd only gone to visit one client - the Indian petene - the pussy. He hadn't sounded like he could fight his way out of a wet paper bag - and anyway - where the fuck was Aleksis? He punched in his minder's number. He didn't want to involve the cops if he could help it. Aleksis could sort it out.

Three times, he tried his number and each time, it had gone straight to voicemail. Fuck it! Dini was a tough cookie; if she'd asked for help, she must be in deep shit.

He disabled the "own number sending" function, and hesitated, his stubby fingers hovering over the keys. He really didn't want to do this - but... fuck it! He punched in 999.

*

The London borough of Houndshale was having a quiet policing day. UX646 were trying to liven it up by searching out the local dealers and the burglars who still managed to roam the back alleys and steal Asian gold with apparent impunity. Porridge Face, Emma and Jax were out and about in the carrier and Bullseye, along with the Cat, had taken leave to attend a mutual friend's wedding. That just left skipper Jarvis and Dynamo who were back at the office hunched over Dynamo's long overdue annual performance development review.

Unlike other skippers, who tended to write up generic PDRs, Jarvis demanded that his team at least supply some evidence of their year's good work. From this, he would be able to compile something resembling a praiseworthy end of year report.

When it came to applying for vacancies outside the borough, PDRs had to reflect the fact that officers had been working towards a goal. This could be shown in examples such as detective work - for those interested in a future career in CID - or stop and search figures for those gung ho TSG wannabes.

Dynamo; despite nagging, had characteristically failed to hand in his examples, hoping instead - like some lazy schoolboy - to copy someone else's at the last minute. This was the skipper's version of school detention - something, which to Dynamo, as a schoolboy, had been the norm. Even now, while Jarvis coaxed evidence of good work out of him, the big man couldn't keep still. He stood next to the skipper's computer terminal throwing Bullseye's darts at the board.

Giving his exasperated trademark look to the

heavens, Jarvis said: 'Sometimes Craig; I swear your mother took you off Ritalin too early. Now sit down and let's get this nailed so we can get out on patrol!'

Jax drove the carrier around Houndshale's town centre in ever decreasing circles. Porridge, who to Jax's dismay had jumped into the operator's seat, pointed out random members of the public.

'See him over there? He's a drug dealer. That bird over there - I've shagged her. That bar there - I had a massive fight with a cage fighter in there...' On and on went the bullshit; it was relentless.

Emma, not wanting to get involved in Porridge's nonsense, had chosen the rearmost seat. Jax could hear her on the phone to her boyfriend: it sounded as though they were having a domestic. Jax looked at her in the rear view mirror; it was rare for her to air her dirty laundry at work; in fact, he couldn't recall her ever speaking about her boyfriend. He had never joined them on a team night out, and reading between the lines, he thought that her man resented her spending much of her time with an otherwise all male team.

It was more than a myth that most relationships - male or female - failed to stand the test of time, once one party had joined the job. One thing Jax did know; was that Emma and her boyfriend had been childhood sweethearts. He looked up again, and thought she was crying.

Bored with aimlessly driving around, Jax decided to put Porridge's so called local knowledge to the test. He decided that the next time the ugly fucker pointed out a criminal worthy of stopping, he would play along. He hadn't had to wait long.

'Isn't that Bledar Bajrami?' Porridge asked.

'Dunno,' replied Jax, 'who's he when he's at home?'

'You know, the Albanian dealer from Cranston?'

Jax didn't think the man pointed out by Porridge looked remotely Albanian. If anything, he was Asian.

He'd never seen the man before, but decided to call Porridge's bluff and slowed the carrier.

'Oh, right, you wanna' stop him?'

'Alright then. Don't worry Jax,' he added, puffing out his chest, 'I speak a bit of Albanian from when I was in Bosnia with the UN.'

Jax allowed himself a little private smile and just for sport said:

'The UN Porridge? What's that stand for - Undiagnosed Nutters?'

'No you idiot,' he retorted. 'The United Nations! Thought you were a military man Jax?'

They pulled up alongside the "Albanian drug dealer." Porridge leapt out at the startled man, hand resting on the grip of his Taser. Reluctantly, Jax got out to join him. Emma still on the phone, wiped her eyes and made a "what's going on," gesture. Jax, adopting the skipper's skyward look, waved her off.

The man, who on closer inspection; was clearly an Indian - and a freshie at that - looked bemused as Porridge addressed him as "Bledar."

'Don't mess me around Bledar,' he said thrusting his ugly mug into the bewildered man's face. Then in the slow, loud voice reserved for Englishmen abroad, he jabbed a stubby finger towards him and proceeded to put his knowledge of Albanian to good use:

'Do you-o have any-o druggios on you-o?'

Jax had to turn away; this was pure Porridge - priceless!

After much shrugging and sideways nodding of his head, the unfortunate man succeeded in convincing Porridge that he was neither Albanian nor a drug dealer. Muttering that the man was blatantly an illegal immigrant - the only thing he'd got right about the man - he climbed back aboard the carrier, and for a whole ten minutes, didn't point out another suspect!

To Jax's relief, before Porridge could point out

another victim, their radios crackled into life.

'No units shown free on the RDW; double crewed unit now please to attend Cranston on the "I" India, to a report of threats to kill and possible false imprisonment.'

Jax looked over at Porridge; 'We'll have some of that!' Porridge nodded.

'Fuck all else to do mate.' He got on the radio.

'Show UX646, traveling time from Houndshale town centre. Can you repeat the location UX?'

The operator's voice boomed back through all three radios; now turned right up to be heard over the noise of the blues and twos:

'Location given only as above Hakims's chicken shop.'

'Is the caller still on the line UX?'

'Negative, he wasn't helpful and there were language difficulties.'

Porridge looked across at Jax and raised his eyebrows. 'Brilliant,' he said before keying the mike and acknowledging the operator's update.

'All received UX.'

'Thank you 646.'

The call sounded like a typical domestic scenario; but nobody else had put up for it, and as Porridge had said, there was fuck all else to do. So, with lights flashing and siren wailing, Jax put his foot down and made his way to Cranston.

Back at the BTF office, skipper Jarvis turned up the volume on his radio.

*

In the Cranston bedsit, Balvinder's coughing fit hadn't cooled his ardour. Getting up from the bed, he grabbed hold of Nadine's bound hands and yanked her towards him. Close up, she saw his drooling mouth through the slit in his mask and smelt his foul breath. She recoiled and tried to move away, but he yanked her back up close.

Tugging down her unzipped skirt, he let her step out of it before tearing off her knickers. She flinched as she felt the elastic of her G-string cut into her thighs before they fell away. He cast them aside.

'You better be clean lady!' he said, wagging a finger.

'Now put your arms up bitch,' he rasped.

Balvinder pulled her top up and over her head, revealing her lacy push up bra, which with some difficulty, he wrenched over her head. Her small stretch-marked breasts flopped down. Balvinder growled his disappointment.

'Is that all you've got?' he asked derisively between coughs. With that, he dragged her back onto the bed.

'Get on your belly lady,' he ordered.

Nadine, her throat on fire, and head swimming gave in without a fight and rolled over onto all fours. Balvinder, grunting from behind his latex mask, retied her to the headboard. The Elvis Greatest Hits CD moved on a track and began to belt out "Jailhouse Rock."

Grabbing his muddy training shoe from under the bed, he whacked her hard across her arse. She screamed.

'How'd you like that bitch? You want some more?'

'Please don't hurt me, I'll do whatever you want...'

He laughed callously.

'Oh yes you fuckin' will!' he giggled maniacally, before whacking her again. This served to bring on another coughing fit. He didn't know whether it was the tightness of the mask around his head, or the sexual kick he was getting out of torturing the girl, but he felt giddy and his head throbbed.

Below him, Nadine moaned. Her eyes were streaming not only tears of pain and fright, but also from whatever was in the room; which by now was making her cough uncontrollably.

Pulling down his jogging bottoms, he was pleased to see his cock was stiff as a board, and kneeling before Nadine's upended arse, he grabbed it and spread her cheeks. Spitting on his hands, he wiped them over her anus.

He watched with child-like fascination, as her sphincter puckered open and closed each time she coughed.

'You ready for Balvinder's cock lady?' he asked, giggling like a schoolboy. 'I'm gonna' fuck you in the arse!'

Nadine groaned and hoped to God her boss had called the cops. And then he was in her, sodomising her. She felt pain stabbing deep inside and screamed, but this only drove him deeper and harder. Grabbing a fistful of her hair, he drove his cock faster and faster and while he did, Nadine was punished further as he wailed along to his music, giving an awful rendition of Jailhouse Rock. The spit-laden verse emanated from his mask like a strangled cat:

'If you can't find a partner use a wooden chair...'

She felt his warm spittle dripping onto her arse, and felt close to blacking out.

Shuddering, Balvinder pulled out of her anus, and taking hold of his cock, finished himself off, spraying semen over her back and hair.

Thank God, she thought, it's over.

Balvinder had other ideas though, and dashing her hopes of release and escape, he announced that she was now his to keep and fuck whenever he liked. She wanted to die.

Two streets away from Balvinder's bedsit, Jax killed the siren and blue lights. Turning into the road, he pulled up just short and out of sight of Hakim's chicken shop. Porridge jumped out followed by Emma, who climbed out of the carrier, dragged the red enforcer from it's mounting and with an unladylike grunt, hefted it onto her shoulder.

Jax was last out, and looking up at the window above Hakim's, he announced that he was going to find his way around the back to prevent anybody from making off.

Porridge and Emma crossed the road. Pushing on the red aluminium door to the left of Hakim's, Porridge found it to be open. As quietly as they could, the cops climbed the narrow staircase. As soon as they reached the top, Emma's eyes began to smart.

'What the hell is up here Porridge? It smells... weird.'

He shrugged and made his way onto a small landing. There was nothing to his left save for a rusty old bike. Looking right, he could see three doors. The first, with bars across the entrance, appeared to be some kind of storeroom - probably belonging to the shop downstairs. He put his ear to the second and listened. Hearing nothing and already suspecting the call to be what the cops called LOB and stood for: "Load of bollocks," he moved on to the last door in the corridor and pressed his ear to it. Emma, feeling the weight of the enforcer, put it down for a rest while they figured out what was going on.

He could hear coughing - it sounded like two people - a male and a female. His ear still pressed to the door, he also heard the sound of a female sobbing. It was only faint, but it seemed to confirm that they had the right room. He knocked loudly, yelling: 'Police! Open the door!'

He heard shuffling from the other side of the door followed by a muffled voice:

'Go away officer, everything's fine here. We don't need you!'

Porridge had heard it all before and he wasn't going to be put off that easily. 'Open the fuckin' door NOW!' he screamed, emphasizing his request with a hefty boot to the door.

Silence. Then the sound of a female voice, pleading from behind the locked door: 'Help! Please help me officer! He's got a knife!'

The cry for help was followed by the sound of flesh on flesh as Balvinder viciously slapped Nadine across the face.

'Fuck this,' shouted Porridge; the word "knife" was all that he needed to hear, and unholstering his X26 Taser, he stood back from the door.

'Right Emma: when I tell you, put the door in. Standby...'

Emma picked up the enforcer and waited.

'OK babes,' she said, 'ready when you are.'

Whatever had made Emma's eyes stream on the stairs, seemed to be coming from the room they needed to enter. She couldn't quite identify the smell, but it was familiar, reminding her of her childhood. Forcing herself to concentrate, she waited for Porridge to prepare his X26. *He's loving this*, she thought with a smile.

Porridge's Taser was already fitted with a cartridge, with a spare clipped to the butt. Pressing the illumination selector button on the top of his X26, he watched as the flashlight came on. Pressing it a second time, he activated the laser sight, ready to "red dot" the knifeman inside.

Aiming it experimentally at the wall, he grunted his satisfaction when a red dot appeared. Slipping the safety lever to *fire*, he pressed the red button on top of his Motorola radio. From now on, his mic would be open and every word, every sound, would be broadcast to every radio on the UX link.

He nodded at Emma. 'Ready!' he yelled.

Emma swung the enforcer with all her might, smashing into the flimsy wood just above the lock. The door burst open, slamming against the wall and then they were in. A wave of something noxious hit them, making their eyes run and their throats burn. What the fuck was that stuff?

Coughing, Emma stepped aside and she let Porridge take the lead. Shuffling forward, the bright yellow Taser gripped in his outstretched hands, he took in the scene.

To his right and slumped on a filthy mattress on all fours, he saw a naked female; her hands bound and tied to the headboard. Stooped over her was a nightmarish version of Elvis reincarnated. And... he was fuckin' naked too!

Clasped in his right hand, Porridge could see a kebab knife - not much use as a stabbing weapon, but it looked as though it had a razor-sharp edge.

That cunt Elvis was getting nowhere near him as long as he had his beloved X26!

Elvis stood up, swayed on his feet as though drunk, and faced the cop. Porridge brought the Taser up to bear. The red dot danced on his sunken chest...

Porridge's next words burst out from skipper Jarvis's radio and reverberated around the BTF office.

'Drop the fuckin' blade numb nuts - NOW!'

Jarvis and Dynamo uttered a collective: "Fuck!" and scrambled for their kit belts. As they took the stairs two at a time, they heard Porridge scream:

'Taser! Taser! Taser!'

Porridge had his finger on the trigger now, taking up first pressure. He was a millisecond away from turning Elvis from soft locomotive flesh to something resembling an immobile wooden log. He began to squeeze the trigger...

Like a bolt from the blue, Emma suddenly knew what the smell in the room was. *Of course!* On winter's nights, when she'd been a kid, her father always struggled to light the ancient gas fire in their front room. The igniter hadn't worked for years and her dad had taken to lighting the fire with a piece of tapered newspaper. Even with the gas switched on, it had always taken an age to light, and when it did, the surplus ignited with a *whoomf!*

By the time the cloud of built-up gas burst into yellowy-blue flame; enough gas had seeped into the room to fill it with eye watering fumes.

SHIT! She opened her mouth to scream: 'GAS!' at the exact same time that Porridge discharged his Taser.

The two blast doors at the front of the cartridge

357

jettisoned with a loud pop. A blast of compressed nitrogen launched two barbed darts; each connected to nine metres of whisper- thin wires. The thirty-eight millimeter darts, carrying fifty thousand volts, rocketed towards Elvis's chest at fifty-five metres per second. The first dart struck him in the stomach; it's barb burrowing under his skin. The second missed, sparking off the metal bed frame.

The very instant the Taser dart made contact with Elvis; there was a blinding flash of light followed by a dull *crump*. Balvinder disintegrated in a misty cloud of pink vapour as the kitchen window blew out and the wall nearest the bed was converted to flying brick. Chunks of supporting steel girder formed deadly shrapnel, which sang as it zinged around the wreckage of the room.

Under the weight of the collapsed wall, buried in masonry, dust and steel, Nadine's life ebbed away as she suffocated beneath the debris.

Porridge was blown off his feet and slammed like a rag doll, into what was left of the doorframe. He slid slowly down the wall and onto the floor. His arms and ribs were smashed by the impact, and bright red ribbons of blood ran from both nostrils. Emma, a jagged chunk of steel protruding from her forehead, lay motionless on the rubble-strewn floor.

The sound of wailing sirens filled the air as every available cop on the borough responded to the open carrier of Porridge's radio. The last they heard of the task force cop had been his yelled transmission of: "Taser! Taser! Taser!" followed by deathly silence.

Upon hearing Porridge's transmission, Jax had raced down the dog shit-strewn alley, which a few minutes earlier, had led him around the back of Hakim's. He'd just put his hand on the front door handle to the side of the chicken shop, when Balvinder's room had disintegrated. Almost blown off his feet, he narrowly missed being decapitated by the flying shards of glass from Hakim's storefront window.

Pushing open the door, he entered the hallway, where he took the stairs two at a time, before sprinting along the landing. Picking his way through the carnage that had been Balvinder's bedsit, he came to Porridge.

His teammate was motionless, his arms twisted at an unnatural angle, and blood pooling in his lap. With his own pulse racing, he tried to find some sign of life. He stooped down, and turning his head to one side, he felt for exhaled breath on his own cheek. There was none.

Turning around, he saw Emma. Apart from the blood already starting to congeal around the shrapnel in her head, she looked uninjured. Repeating the procedure he'd used on Porridge, he again failed to detect any sign of life.

He knew what he had to do, but he couldn't administer CPR to both of them; he was going to need help - lots of help. He got on the radio; giving his exact location, followed by a situation report. He asked for an ambulance, the fire brigade and a supervisor.

Looking around the room, he saw a pale hand sticking out from under a fallen wall. Body parts belonging to the late Balvinder Kapoor - Elvis fan and Houndshale's most wanted flasher - were strewn around the remains of the kitchen like a macabre jigsaw. Lengths of his bloody intestine festooned the mangled remains of a stove: looking for all the world, like satanic pink party string.

'*Jesus Christ!*'

Hitting his transmit button, Jax made another request: 'Make that as many ambulances as possible. I've got multiple casualties...'

By the time he'd finished transmitting, skipper Jarvis and Dynamo ran into what was left of the room. Jax, who had had a chance to get over his initial shock, began to organise them:

'Skip - see to Emma - Dynamo - give me a hand

359

with Porridge.'

The three men went about their grisly work in silence. Each of them knew exactly what to do: they'd done it before on more than one occasion - compressed lifeless chests and blown into the mouths of strangers. This time, though, the bloodied, lifeless forms at their feet weren't strangers.

They kept blowing, and with fingers linked, they tirelessly used the heels of their palms to keep vital blood pumping through the hearts and arteries of their friends. They never once stopped or gave up on them, and when the paramedics arrived, kind, but firm hands were needed to pull them away before gently leading them out of the hell that had been Balvinder's bedsit...

*

Cell F2's Perspex wicket clattered down, waking Angie Brown with a start. Automatically, she glanced at her left wrist, before remembering that her wristwatch was sealed into a plastic evidence bag somewhere behind the custody desk. She had no idea of the time or how long she'd been asleep. The gaoler's face appeared at the wicket and her befuddled brain registered a man's voice offering her a meal. Through eyes swollen from crying, she peered back at the gaoler.

'What time is it?' she asked.

The gaoler, whose watch wasn't inside an evidence bag, replied: 'Just gone half five; would you like something to eat?'

Despite the upset of the last few hours, Angie's stomach rumbled. 'Erm, what have you got?'

The gaoler went through a list of microwave meals, which were so intensely processed, they had consume-by dates long into the future. She settled for chili con carne and asked for a drink of water. Calling a cheery: OK! Through the wicket, the gaoler slid it closed again and went off down the corridor, keys jangling on his belt.

Ten minutes later, a rattling of keys announced the gaoler's return. Opening up her cell door, he passed her a plastic TV dinner style container containing a volcanically hot portion of grey mush. Apart from the odd red kidney bean, there had been nothing to identify the mess as chili con carne. Handing her a plastic implement, which was a spoon and fork combined, he placed a polystyrene cup of tepid water on the bench next to her, and with a jangle, was gone. The cell door slammed behind him and she was alone once more.

As she tackled the red-hot goo, she wondered how much longer she would have to be there. Surely the Irish detective must have finished his paperwork and CPS consultation by now?

Two hours later, as she lay on her bench looking up at the Crimestoppers stencil on the ceiling, her question was answered. She heard the metallic sound of the spy hole cover being moved to the side, and then saw an eye briefly observing her. This inspection was followed by the fumbling of several keys being tried in the lock and was accompanied by soft swearing. Finally finding the right key, detective sergeant Jim Dempsey appeared in her cell. He was apologetic:

'Sorry, it's taken so long Angela; you won't believe the amount of paperwork I've had to do!'

Thank God, she thought. *I'm finally going to get out of this place!*

Dempsey's next words hit her like a punch to the stomach.

'CPS have reviewed the evidence Angela and you are to be charged.'

Angie's heart pounded. *Charged!* How could this all be happening so soon? What happened to being bailed for a few months pending a decision?

'What are the charges?' she asked weakly.

'I'll let the custody sergeant explain,' he answered, 'if you'd like to follow me Angela, he's ready for you now.'

361

Angie felt numb. Getting up, she meekly followed the detective out of her cell and along the dark corridor. The custody sergeant, dominating from behind his high counter, was waiting.

'Angela,' he began grimly, 'you are to be charged with two offences today. Listen carefully while I read out the charges...'

Angie went weak at the knees. Oh my God, she thought; it's really happening - I'm actually being charged!

She looked up at the skipper on his dais. He regarded her sternly before launching into legalese...

'Between June and December of this year, at Houndshale, you conspired together with Calvin Anderson and others, to supply an unknown quantity of crack cocaine, a controlled drug of class A. This is contrary to section one (1) of the Criminal Law Act 1977'

Angie felt beads of sweat forming on her brow, but despite this, she felt cold and clammy. Thinking that she was about to fall over, she clung to the counter. The sergeant continued with the second charge.

'Between June and December of this year at Houndshale, while acting as a public officer, namely a crime analyst within the CID department at Houndshale police station, you misconducted yourself by disclosing information of a confidential nature for the criminal use of others. This is contrary to Common Law.'

The sergeant looked up from his computer screen. For the next part of what he had to say to the shocked woman before him, he needed no prompts from his screen.

'In relation to these charges: you do not have to say anything, but it may harm your defence if you do not mention now, something which you later rely on in court - anything you do say, may be given in evidence.'

He glanced over at DS Dempsey. 'No reply, at 1945 hours.'

Dempsey nodded and recorded the fact that she had

362

made no comment in his notebook. Passing it over to Angie, he pointed to a space and asked her to sign to that effect. The skipper also had her sign his electronic signature pad.

She felt numb. At least, she thought, I'll be able to get out of this place now and go home for a nice warm soak in the bath. She assumed that she'd have at least a week, if not longer before she'd be summoned to court, by which time, she hoped to have pulled herself together. She was just fantasising about this, when the skipper spoke to her again. His words shook her to the core.

'Angela, DS Dempsey has made representations to me to the effect that you be remanded in police custody. The reason for this - and I'm in agreement - is that you are vulnerable and should be in a place of safety. For your own protection, you will be remanded here overnight and put before the next court, which will be tomorrow morning at Filebridge magistrates.'

Remanded? Court *tomorrow!*

Feeling helpless and very small, she looked at Dempsey. 'Please don't make me stay here,' she croaked hoarsely. 'Let me go home, I'll be fine, and in any case, I need to shower and change my clothes.'

The DS had the good grace to look sorry for her, but that was about as far as her plea had got her.

'I'm sorry Angela,' he said softly, 'if you like, we can send an officer to pick up some clean clothing from your home?'

She looked from Dempsey to the stern-looking sergeant. She could tell that they had made up their minds. Dempsey had wrung a confession from her, and her guilt had dripped from her like dirty water from a dishcloth. They no longer had any interest in keeping her sweet. She was fucked, and acquiesced - not that she had a choice...

She looked at the floor. 'Yes please,' she said, all the fight gone from her. The sergeant handed her a copy of

363

the charges and nodded to the gaoler. Obediently, like a lamb to the slaughter, Angie kept her head bowed and allowed herself to be led back to her cell - it would be at least twelve hours until she made her appearance at court. Twelve more sleepless hours of grime, smell, and noise loomed ahead of her. As she lay under her scratchy blue blanket, the tears no longer came. Numb, and in a state of mental exhaustion, she closed her eyes.

Nine hours later, she was surprised to find that she'd slept through a night of key jangling, drunken yells from across the corridor, and the stink of incarcerated bodies seeping insidiously under her cell door.

Accepting only a cup of coffee, she sat on her bench and waited for what would happen next. She hadn't had to wait long and when the keys jangled in the lock for the last time, it was to let her out and into the custody area, where two escorts from the security firm SERCO were waiting for her. While her partner filled out transfer forms, the dumpy female escort patted her down before attaching her to the open end of the handcuffs, hanging from her leather wrist strap. The escort's voice was gruff, but not unkind. Angie was the first of many prisoners yet to be handcuffed to her that day and she was in a hurry.

'C'mon then love,' she said. 'Let's get you to court.'

And with that, she was led out through the custody cage and helped up the steps into a prison van where she was put into a cubicle for the drive to Filebridge. Shut in her sweatbox, the tears began to flow again. After a short journey, Angie heard the beep, beep of the van's reversing sensor, and once it had backed into the custody bay at court, she was led out of her cubicle and into yet another custody area.

Once booked in, she was taken to a cell to await her hearing. Other than the fact that Mary Taylor had assured her she would be at court to meet her, Angie had no idea what would happen next.

A couple of hours later, she met Mary, who

explained that she would be brought before the magistrates who would hear her plea and directions for trial. Mary was visibly disappointed to hear of her client's confession, but told her not to worry. She promised that she would do her best to get her bail.

Bail? She thought, what did the woman mean *bail!* Surely, she wasn't going to end up back at Houndshale nick!

'What do you mean Mary,' she asked. 'I've already spent two days in a cell, I thought you said this was a plea and direction hearing?' The brief looked sheepish.

'Well...' she began as if addressing a child, 'the offences for which you've been charged wouldn't normally be tried by a magistrate. They only tend to deal with the initial hearing, and in most cases, send you for trial at crown court at a later date.'

Jesus! Crown court? Angie swallowed hard. This was serious!

Mary continued with the bad news. 'The police have recommended that the magistrate further remand you until your trial. At this point in the proceedings, it's my job to try and make sure you get bail.'

'*Try*,' she gasped, 'you mean I could get locked up back at the police station until my case comes to trial?'

The brief put a hand on Angie's shoulder. 'Not the police station Angela,' she said softly. 'A prison.'

Prison! The word jolted through her body like an electric shock. She cried out in anguish and tears rolled down her cheeks. The brief handed her a Kleenex and continued with the bad news.

'I'm going to try Angela, but to be honest; things are stacked against us today. Your case is due to be heard in court three, and whereas Filebridge normally hosts lay magistrates - that is to say people like you and me - today, court three is presided over by a stipendiary magistrate.'

Angie knew a little about lay magistrates. They tended to be well meaning but clueless men and women who in their ignorance of the law, were guided by the court clerk. Stipends, on the other hand, were professional magistrates who failed to be swayed by defence solicitors. They knew the law and were keen to dispense the full weight of it. She felt Mary's hand on her shoulder again.

'So yes, I'm afraid that I'm not hopeful of getting him to grant you bail...'

Angie was no longer listening. She'd gone catatonic.

The next hour passed her by in a haze of legal jargon and headmaster-like speeches by his Worship Algate, who loftily dismissed Mary Taylor's attempts at getting bail for her client. At the end of it all, she was led back to the court cells to await transportation to prison. Her case, set for some time in the distant future, was to be held, as Mary had predicted, at Crown court, and later that afternoon, along with several others, she was loaded back onto a SERCO prison van for her journey. Her destination, was to be HMP Holloway; a women's prison in Islington, North London.

Let out of her sweatbox, Angie found herself in yet another prisoner processing area; only this time, it was the real thing. Standing before a prison guard, her handcuffs were removed and she endured yet another body search.

Holloway no longer requires female inmates to be strip searched, but having handed over all of her personal belongings, she was sent off to have her mug shot and fingerprints taken for the second time that week.

Holding lifers with nothing to lose, a recent inspection report had concluded that the prison was a place of violence and constant bullying. Holloway houses violent drug addicts, prostitutes and petty villains: It wouldn't take more than a perceived disrespectful look for a newcomer to be beaten up.

Her process complete, A. Brown, prison number C478654; clutching coarse bed linen and a towel, was led away to her cell. Along the way, she was hit by a cacophony of catcalls, abusive shouts from inmates, and the deafening sound of shrieking, but unseen women.

Locked in her cell, the awful reality of prison life began to sink in. Echoes, footsteps, the banging of cell doors, the rattling of keys, sobbing and hysterical laughter, lights out...

This, and the uncertainty of how long the nightmare would last, was the new world, which Angie now inhabited. Not for the first time, she'd come to grief at the hands of a cruel and manipulative man.

The original Victorian motto for Holloway prison, when it was built back in 1852 had proclaimed: *"May God make this place a terror to evil-doers"* Angie Brown hadn't set out to be evil; she'd just wanted to feel wanted - even cherished - for the first time in her life.

She'd honestly believed that in Anderson, she'd found something special, but as with all her relationships, the dream had crumbled into dust. If this really was a place for "evil doers," why the hell was *she* there instead of the bastard who had seduced her, screwed her, and fucked up her life?

Epilogue

Calvin Anderson smirked as he reclaimed the cash seized during the search of his apartment. Having been to court to explain why an unemployed man of limited means had been in possession of such a large amount of cash, he'd successfully argued that it was the proceeds of a previous business gone wrong.

In contrast to Angie Brown's appearance before the stipendiary magistrate six weeks before, he'd come up against a lay magistrate who, after agonising over his first case of money laundering, had accepted Anderson's explanation. He'd ordered that the police hand back the money and had added no more than to order him to contact the treasury with regard to any unpaid tax.

With regard to the accusation of conspiracy to supply drugs, he'd had his bail date changed yet again. This was to enable the hard-pressed detectives of the Houndshale CID department to put a strong enough case to the CPS. They had to be convinced that it could be won without sending them over their budget. With a total lack of witnesses prepared to offer evidence against the Jamaican enforcer however, this seemed more and more unlikely. One detective remarked that to try and gather enough evidence with which to convict Calvin Anderson was akin to attempting to plait fog.

*

All Saints Church, Carshalton, was built so long ago as to

be mentioned in the Doomsday Book of 1086. Within it's flint and red brick walls, the congregation gathered for a funeral. The plain pine casket, borne upon the shoulders of the surviving members of uniform-x-ray 646, made it's way slowly and solemnly down the aisle. The casket passed rows of benches filled with a mixture of police officers dressed in ceremonial tunics, sombre men in dark suits and women in mourning hats. As it passed, women wept openly, men sniffed and bowed their heads and children stopped fidgeting.

The only member of UX646 not bearing the pine box sat on the front bench. As the casket containing his former comrade reached him, he gripped his crutches and struggled gamely to his feet. With his face partially bandaged and a plaster cast restricting his movements, Porridge Face turned to face the funeral procession and saluted.

Once the bearers had reached the end of the aisle and halted before the marble altar, they lowered the body of Police Constable Emma "Babes" Cash onto the waiting trestle. Her father: himself a retired police inspector, stepped forward and placed her hat onto the casket. Standing there for a minute with head bowed, he remembered his pride as he'd watched his daughter; the fresh-faced recruit, march past the saluting dais during her passing out parade on that crisp autumnal day at Hendon training centre. Wiping away a tear, and stifling an agonised sob, he retook his place at the front of the church.

Following the funeral service and a moving sermon given by the same vicar who'd baptised Emma twenty-six years before, Holy water was sprinkled on the casket, Emma's hat was picked up by her father, and her earthly remains were lifted from the trestles and hoisted back onto the shoulders of UX646.

To the peel of All Saints twelfth century bells, Emma "Babes" Cash was lowered into the ground. After the congregation had thrown dirt onto her casket, her family, along with UX646, made their way next door to the Greyhound Hotel.

Once a dignified period of respect had elapsed, the Cat sneaked off to his car and came back with an ipod dock - which after consultation with the management - he rigged up behind the bar.

Suddenly, the subdued chatter among the mourners was interrupted by the sound of a forty-eight year old tune. At first startled by the musical interruption, the mourners slowly broke into smiles and joined in with the chorus of Sonny and Cher's "I got you babe." Among the cops of UX646, normal service had been resumed...

*

Later, on the same afternoon that UX646 bade farewell to Emma, another funeral service took place. The dreary and industrial looking crematorium that hosted the crushed body of Nadine Cousins, was poles apart from the pretty church at Carshalton. Apart from two burly Latvians, a hard-faced young woman from the Sweet Dreams agency, and a clutch of nosey old ladies, there was nobody to witness her final departure.

Nadine had never thought about her funeral. There had been plenty of awful times when she'd scrabbled around on the floor mistaking lint for crack - there had been numerous occasions when as a prostitute, she'd wanted to scrub down her abused body with bleach - and as a child; when she'd lost her mum and dad, her world had crashed down around her.

Yes, there had been many a time when Nadine Cousins had contemplated suicide, but she'd never thought about her actual funeral.

Had she thought about it - had she planned the service - she certainly wouldn't have had her coffin disappear behind a curtain and into the furnace, to the mournful default sound of: "Abide with me."

Had she ever thought about it, she would probably have chosen her favourite Robbie Williams track: "Angels." But she hadn't; and so her coffin now inched towards the flames of the crematorium's oven to a hymn - the words of which neither Latvian knew - and to a hymn that the hard faced-girl refused to sing. The reedy voices of the nosey old ladies competing with the tinny loud speakers, echoed falteringly around the near-empty hall, and then Nadine was gone...

After her flesh had been burned and her bones pulverised by the crematorium's grinder, her ashes; poured into a plastic container, were collected by Aleksis. He'd been the closest thing to a friend that Nadine had had in the last days of her life, and although he hadn't a clue what Dini would have liked done with her ashes, he'd felt duty bound to take possession of them.

Walking back to the big BMW, plastic container in his meaty hands, Aleksis got into the passenger seat. Four weeks after the explosion above Hakim's chicken shop, he'd been to court and stood before the magistrate charged with drink driving. He'd not been that far over the limit and so he'd had the right to request that the police doctor take a sample of his blood.

He'd always been told that if he were ever to be arrested for drink driving, he should request the taking of blood. That way, he'd been assured, by the time a doctor could be found, his alcohol levels would have dropped sufficiently to scrape a pass. In the event, though, the police doctor had only been in the neighbouring borough, and so had come within half an hour.

So yes, nowadays, Aleksis rode in the passenger seat. He still had eleven months and two weeks of his driving ban left to serve, and if he hadn't been a blood relative of the boss at Sweet Dreams, he'd have been out on his arse.

Later, when the Latvians got back to the office, Aleksis put Dini's ashes on top of a filing cabinet.

One day, he thought, I'll scatter them somewhere

371

nice...

*

The instructor from CO19 stood in the gym at the Territorial Army training centre in White City. With a supercilious look on his face and hands on hips, he was welcoming the day one trainees for the X26 Taser course. After his welcome speech, he led them into a classroom where they would be told about the technical aspects of the X26.

The day ones would have to endure the tedium of the classroom and watch endless slides on legislation, before they would be able to get their hands on the coveted bright yellow weapon.

Such classroom sessions wouldn't have been complete without the obligatory horror stories, resulting from the inappropriate use of Taser since it's addition to the police armoury. This was the part that the instructors loved and there were two anecdotes in particular, that today's instructor never tired of relating to his day one trainees.

One concerned the use of Taser on a man who'd doused himself with petrol and who upon being Tasered, spontaneously combusted. The instructor had a short video clip of said combustion, with which to horrify his audience.

The second real life example - and the instructor's favourite - had been the tragic case of a gung ho cop at Houndshale, who'd blasted his X26 at a knife-wielding man in a gas-filled room. There hadn't been a video clip of this, but upon being shown the still photographs of a rubble-filled room, the students usually fell silent. Some even left the room.

The bright pink ribbons of intestine festooning a gas stove, the unmarked face of a woman crushed to death; and the female police officer with a chunk of shrapnel buried deep in her forehead - *always* shocked the day one trainees...

Postscript

Op Withern is the name given to the operation assembled to track down and convict those involved in the violence and burglary committed during the riots of August 2011. It is to the credit of those officers involved with the investigation and their tireless tenacity, that so many of the criminals - among them, the yobs that Jax faced on the Tottenham High Road - have been brought to book.

At the time of writing, 5000 suspects have been arrested with an impressive conviction rate of 87%. More than 9000 items of evidence have been meticulously exhibited. Withern will draw to a close at the end of 2013, although there are still those who have so far evaded capture by fleeing to their countries of origin. This is ironic, since some of those concerned had claimed asylum in the UK claiming to be persecuted back at home.

In the face of a toothless police federation, from whom the bobbies on the beat get nothing more than a diary once a year in exchange for costly subscriptions; the Home Secretary has butchered the police service like never before. Embarrassed by the federation during conference; heckled and booed by it's members, she has had her revenge. A three-year pay freeze, followed by a massive pay cut for anyone foolish enough to join, has sunk morale to an all time low.

An increase in pension contributions, abolition of allowances and overtime payments slashed - in some cases replaced by compulsory working rest days - has meant that more and more cops no longer answer the phone for fear of being called in on a hard earned rest day, with nothing more than a promise of a day back - at the system's convenience.

There are those who, in accordance with new money saving rules; having reached the last eleven years of their service, and having planned for retirement, must now serve an extra five. And there are those who are soon to start their career on a wage less than that of a junior manager supervising the flipping of burgers.

Officers: I salute you all, and hope that as is usually the case, these things will come full circle and you will once again be afforded the recognition and respect you deserve - though I fear this may take some time - and good officers will be lost along the way.

In my criticisms; both above and throughout Front Stack, I have been deliberately vague. I have no wish to harm any particular branch of the service, and have only alluded to that, which is common knowledge. My intentions are not to damage the morale of the service to which I owe some of the best years of my life.

VM Frost
London, October 2013

A note on the author

VM (Jack) Frost was born in Stamford, Lincolnshire. Moving with his Air Force parents to the Mediterranean island of Malta in the 1960's, he remained there until 1976, when he returned to the UK to complete his education.

Leaving school with negligible qualifications, he joined the British army where, after completing several operational tours, he left as a senior non-commissioned officer. Since then, he has undertaken such diverse work as: grill chef, baker, mechanic, and builder.

After a period working as a residential social worker with troubled adolescents, he became a police officer; firstly with Thames Valley Police, and then later the Metropolitan Police, where for the remainder of his 15 years service, he served on the front line, carrying out both investigatory work and public order duties, including the quelling of the Tottenham riots; for which he was commended for bravery. Front Stack is his fourth book.

Read on for a taste of
Double Locked

By VM Frost
Available soon...

UX646 were on a late shift. Adjourning to the office for their evening meal, they set about microwaving ready meals, dissecting hot chicken - and in the case of the hungry caterpillar that was Dynamo - tucking into his fourth meal of the day. Bullseye threw darts at the board while he waited his turn at the food-encrusted office microwave, and Porridge Face - who was now out of plaster and bandages; sought to engage whoever would listen to his bullshit stories.

It had been a slow shift so far, and skipper Jarvis was just about to begin a trawl through the "Emerald" wanted persons database, when his phone warbled it's Paul Weller ring tone. It was Lurch.

The BIU man had visited the on call magistrate and sworn out an out of hours search warrant. The target of the Section 23 Misuse of Drugs Act warrant, he said; was to be the George and Dragon public house in Shanworth.

Given that it was a pub, Lurch had successfully requested three serials from the TSG Commissioner's reserve. These were level one trained officers who took turns to provide a reserve contingent Met-wide. He told Jarvis, that they were on their way from a TSG base in the north of the capital, and in the absence of any other tasking, they were available to raid the pub.

Even with blue lights and sirens, the TSG officers were unlikely to arrive at Houndshale for another twenty minutes and once there, they would still have to be comprehensively briefed. Lurch's problem, was that he needed some fast time intelligence with regard to Skinny Man's location - assuming he was there - and an idea of the numbers drinking in the pub.

Jarvis knew all about Jax's failed attempt to join the surveillance teams earlier in the year. He'd heard the story of how Jax had fallen foul of the prim and proper human resources woman on the interview board, but he was also aware that Jax had resolved to have another crack at it some day.

'Whaddya reckon Jax - fancy a go at a bit of surveillance,' he asked with a smile.

Before he could answer, Porridge Face butted in. 'What's that skip? surveillance you say?'

Jarvis shot the ugly man a look that said: shut the fuck up Porridge, but with skin as thick as a rhino, Porridge ploughed on.

'Did I tell you about the time I was on covert operations with the SAS in Northern Ireland skip? I spent six weeks dug in outside an IRA boss's house. Shit in plastic bags and ate cold food for the whole time I did...'

Jarvis put a hand up to silence what would have inevitably become a lengthy soliloquy about Porridge's fantastical ramblings. There wasn't time, and in any case, he didn't trust Porridge to go to the shithouse unaccompanied; let alone, to a hostile public house. He let him down gently:

'Tam,' he smiled, 'Jax wants another crack at the surveillance game, so I'd like him to have the chance of doing this one mate. OK?'

The skipper's diplomacy won the day and Porridge spread his hands in surrender.

'OK skip,' he said, adding enigmatically: 'but don't forget, I have skills...'

Jarvis looked to the heavens and took Jax aside for a briefing. All he had to do, it seemed, was to get into his jeans and tee shirt and get dropped off just short of the pub by Bullseye in the unmarked Vauxhall Zafira.

Known as the Q car, the Zafira was long past it's sell by date and most of the villains on the borough knew it. They'd even posted it's details on Facebook! It was due for replacement any day, but until then, Bullseye would drop Jax a couple of blocks away and remain in the area should he get blown out at the George.

Stopping on the way, Jax picked up a copy of Motorcycle News. A biker himself, he reckoned that he could use the paper as cover. If questioned by hostile locals, he intended to say he had agreed to meet someone in the pub who had advertised a bike for sale. Beyond that, he didn't really have a plan. He'd just have to play it by ear. The one advantage he did have - which in a multicultural borough like Houndshale was unusual - was the fact that Shanworth's residents were predominantly white. The tattoos, that ran the length of both arms: a legacy from his army days; would help too.

Bullseye pulled into a quiet cul-de-sac a couple of hundred yards away from the George. Unbuckling his utility belt, Jax dropped it in the passenger seat foot well. Tugging his police radio from his back pocket, he added it to the pile of handcuffs, Asp baton, and CS spray. Finally, he extracted his warrant card from his other pocket and handed it to Bullseye.

With the final vestiges of his cop persona relinquished, he opened the door, and to a: 'good luck mate,' from Bullseye, he left his teammate. With the knot of apprehension deep in his gut, he made his way to the pub.

With a confidence that belied his raised pulse rate, Jax pushed open the door to the George and Dragon. He'd not had the pleasure of having been inside before - the George was a pub, which sorted out it's own problems without involving the cops.

The gloomy interior was sparsely furnished. Most of the furniture had at some time been trashed and was now held together with black tape and ill matched wooden splints.

Over at the bar, with the draught beer taps long since turned off in favour of cheap bootleg booze, the landlord hovered nervously. It was immediately apparent, that he was no more than a figurehead. He'd adopted the role of a man, who despite having his name over the door as licensee was now not much more than a whipped dog, which did as his nasty drug-dealing patrons told him. Jax could almost taste the atmosphere of fear and distrust.

There was only one person at what was left of the bar; an old boy in his late 50's, and by the look of him - his greasy head resting on the bar top and a wet patch at his crotch - he'd probably been drinking all day.

In front of the bar, where the landlord ineffectually mopped the filthy bar top, there were two bench style seats set around a dilapidated table. Another old guy occupied one of the benches, nursing a pint of flat lager.

In a room just to the left of the bar, a group of raucous young men shot pool balls around a threadbare table. As one, they looked up from their game and eyed Jax suspiciously.

Ordering a beer, Jax made small talk with the nervous landlord, who seemed glad to have someone new to speak to. Swigging a couple of mouthfuls from his bottle, Jax made his way over to the bench and sat himself down with his back to the wall, and a view of the pool players. Unrolling his Motorcycle News, he made a pretence of scanning the small ads - and without his glasses - it really was a pretence!

Looking over his paper, he did a head count of the pool players. He didn't know Skinny Man; but the spindly, pock-faced youth about to pot the black ball, certainly fitted the bill, and if he wasn't Lurch's man, then Jax didn't know who was.

As casually as he could, Jax took out his phone and punched in Lurch's number. After what seemed like an eternity, he heard the doleful Yorkshire man's voice.

'Hel-lo, Simon Coverdale.'

'Lurch,' replied Jax, smiling and trying hard to maintain the air of someone who had just been called by an old friend. 'It's Jax mate. Can't really talk, but just ask me the relevant questions and I'll answer.'

Skinny Man and his pool-playing friends were staring at Jax. You could cut the atmosphere with a knife, but Jax was determined to pass on whatever information he could before he was unmasked. He bobbed his knee up and down in frustration as Lurch lumbered through his response.

'Ah, Jax', he said. 'Where are you?'

Suppressing a retort of "where the fuck do you think I am you cunt!' Jax took a deep breath.

'Lurch,' he said with a casual laugh. 'You know where I am, just ask me what you need to know!'

'Is that Vinny Jackson from the BTF,' he asked ponderously.

Jax bit back his anger. Here he was at the request of the BIU man, and the twat didn't even know why he was calling him for fuck's sake!

'Simon,' he said, through gritted teeth, 'Is sergeant Jarvis there?'

A short breathy silence was followed by an impossibly slow drawl of: 'sergeant Jarvis? Ah... yes, hold on, I'll put him on the line.'

Put him on the line! Fuck me Lurch, get with the 21st century for God's sake!

'Yes please Simon, put him on.'

A glance over at Skinny Man was enough for Jax to know that he had more than piqued the interest of the George and Dragon's resident coke dealer, and Jax watched as he went into a huddle with his cohorts.

The welcome voice of skipper Jarvis came on the line. 'What's up Jax?'

'Skip, everything's fine, just wanted an update. Can't

say too much, but basically, the target is at the address and numbers are no more than ten. Are TSG on the way yet?'

Jarvis, cool as ever was reassuring. 'Hang in there mate, TSG have just finished their briefing and should be leaving in the next couple of minutes. Are you sure you're OK?'

Jax looked over at the pool players, who by now were paying a lot more attention to him, than to their game.

'I'm OK skip, see you in a bit.'

'Ok mate,' replied Jarvis, adding: 'Don't put yourself on offer Jax, if you think they've sussed you, get out of there.'

For the benefit of Skinny Man and his mates, Jax forced a laugh and acted as though an old friend had just told him a joke.

'Ok skip, see you soon...'

Draining his bottle, Jax put down his paper, and with as much confidence as he could muster, he stood up and walked over to the bar to order another beer. The landlord went off to a back room to open another box of bootleg Becks. From the corner of his eye, he could see Skinny Man making his way over to the bar, pool cue still in his hand.

The landlord reappeared and with a shaking hand, set the green bottle of lager down on the grimy bar. As Jax reached for it, Skinny Man sidled up to him.

'Yawight,' he asked with a hint of a sneer.

'Yeah, all good mate,' replied Jax taking hold of his beer. Skinny Man persisted:

'You from round here?' he asked adding, 'never seen you before.'

Here we go, thought Jax, where the fuck is the cavalry!

Taking a swig from his bottle, he said:

'No mate, I'm from Richmond, but I'm supposed to
382

meet a bloke who's selling his bike.' Indicating his rolled up copy of Motorcycle news, he added: 'Fuck knows where the cunt is though!'

Skinny Man's eyes looked as though he'd been dipping into his stash and his flash to bang time appeared slow. It seemed as though he hadn't been expecting the kind of answer, the stranger had supplied him with. He clearly found Jax's response taxing and his cannabis-befuddled brain was working overtime.

His fellow pool players; all clutching their cues, began to edge there way over to the bar in a macho display of support for Skinny Man.

Jax had seen it all before. The same atmosphere he'd experienced when in rival squaddie bars all over the world, had been as universally threatening as that in the George and Dragon tonight. The snarling dogs were beginning to circle, and it was only a matter of time before alone and isolated, his window of escape would slam shut.

Every fibre of Jax's body screamed for him to get the hell out of there, and then, just as the pool players of the George and Dragon made their move, the door to the pub flew open and crashed into the adjacent wall sending chunks of plaster skating across the bare wooden floor. The air was rent with the welcome shouts of:

'POLICE WITH A WARRANT!'

Skinny Man's first reaction was to try and vault the bar and escape through the back door, but with help finally on hand, Jax beat him to the mark. Grabbing him by the scruff of the neck, he slammed his face into the bar top.

Skinny Man lifted his head and shook mucus and blood from his face. Spitting broken teeth from behind his split lips, he swayed on his heels, eyes swivelling in an attempt to regain his vision.

From nowhere, a black-clad giant of a TSG man twisted the drug dealer's hands behind his back and snapped the bracelets on. The rest of Skinny Man's gang, shocked by the TSG's speed aggression and surprise, gave up without a fight and threw themselves to the sticky floor.

Leaving the BTF to deal with the detainees, the Commissioner's reserves swept through the pub checking every nook and cranny for suspects. They found the landlord cowering in the washroom and led him out into the bar where he was processed by the BTF.

The piss-stained man at the end of the bar awoke, opened one eye, and taking in the fury that was the TSG, he staggered for the door. He didn't make it, and tripping over the prone forms of Skinny Man's gang, he fell headlong among them.